Praise for Tracy Groot

"Groot has done good historical homework. She has also created memorable characters both major and minor. . . . The pacing is page-turning."

PUBLISHERS WEEKLY, starred review

"A beautifully written retelling of an age-old story. . . . Tracy Groot is a first-rate storyteller."

ROBERT HICKS, *New York Times* bestselling author of *The Widow of the South*

"Groot . . . does good historical work with details and subtle psychological work with her characters. . . . WWII–era novels are popular; this is a superior, page-turning entry in that niche."

PUBLISHERS WEEKLY on *Flame of Resistance*

"This well-researched novel is filled with intrigue and captivating characters that should please fans of World War II fiction."

CBA RETAILERS+RESOURCES on *Flame of Resistance*

"Scrupulously researched and lovingly written, *Flame of Resistance* plunges the reader into an exhilarating story of courage, grace, and one endearing woman's leap of faith."

THE BANNER

"Groot ensnares readers with accurate historical detail and gripping prose. With complex characters, authentically reflecting good and evil . . . , [*Flame of Resistance*] overflows with intrigue, passion, sacrifice, and humanity."

RELZ REVIEWZ

"Tracy Groot adds fine research on [D-Day] and [the] World War II environment, both of which make *Flame of Resistance* a powerful saga that . . . retells the story of Rahab."

"The suspense is great, the characters excellent, the romance held in check, and the spiritual elements are extremely encouraging. For those who enjoy historical fiction, but don't care for a strong romantic storyline, *Flame of Resistance* is an excellent choice."

"Gritty and moving, *Flame of Resistance* . . . raises challenging questions about redemption, perceptions, and the cost of doing the right thing in an evil world. I highly recommend it."

"[A] well-paced, beautifully written historical novel. . . . Entertaining and compelling."

"Groot cleverly combines historical research, Scripture, and thrilling imagination to create an ingenious story built around the Gerasene demoniac. It's one of the best fictional adaptations of a biblical event I've had the pleasure to read."

"Groot's well-drawn characters . . . embody mercy in this subtle tale that cleverly avoids retelling New Testament stories, instead forming a sort of commentary by telling parallel stories."

"[*The Brother's Keeper* is a] lyrical and affecting first novel."

THE
SENTINELS
OF
ANDERSONVILLE

CHRISTY AWARD–WINNING AUTHOR

Tracy Groot

Tyndale House Publishers, Inc.
Carol Stream, Illinois

Visit Tyndale online at www.tyndale.com.

Visit Tracy Groot online at www.tracygroot.com.

TYNDALE and Tyndale's quill logo are registered trademarks of Tyndale House Publishers, Inc.

The Sentinels of Andersonville

Designed by Ron Kaufmann

Edited by Kathryn S. Olson

Published in association with Creative Trust Literary Group, 5141 Virginia Way, Suite 320, Brentwood, Tennessee 37027. www.creativetrust.com.

Scripture quotations are taken from the *Holy Bible*, King James Version.

The Sentinels of Andersonville is a work of fiction. Where real people, events, establishments, organizations, or locales appear, they are used fictitiously. All other elements of the novel are drawn from the author's imagination.

For information about special discounts for bulk purchases, please contact Tyndale House Publishers at csresponse@tyndale.com or call 800-323-9400.

Library of Congress Cataloging-in-Publication Data

Groot, Tracy, date.
    The sentinels of Andersonville / Tracy Groot.
        pages cm
    ISBN 978-1-4143-5948-9 (hc)
1. United States—History—Civil War, 1861-1865—Prisoners and prisons—Fiction. 2. Andersonville Prison—Fiction. 3. Prisoners of war—Georgia—Fiction. 4. Prisoner-of-war escapes—Fiction. I. Title.
    PS3557.R5655S48 2014
    813'.54—dc23   2013031516

ISBN 978-1-4964-2255-2 (sc)

Printed in the United States of America

23 22 21 20 19 18 17
 7   6   5   4   3   2   1

For Jack

"Business!" cried the Ghost, wringing its hands again.
"Mankind was my business. . . ."
CHARLES DICKENS, *A Christmas Carol*

Note to the Reader

DURING THE LAST FOURTEEN MONTHS of the Civil War, Andersonville Prison in Sumter County, Georgia, was a place of unimaginable suffering. In fourteen months, 45,000 men passed through the gates. Of those, 13,000 died, primarily from starvation and exposure.

Portions of this book contain disturbing descriptions of prison life and conditions. In the matter of historicity, novelists often wrestle with the question of how much to put in, how much to leave out—too little detail risks giving an incomplete picture; too much risks becoming gratuitous. Since detail is necessary to tell the truth of Andersonville Prison, I chose to err on the side of truth; and even so, a few facts refused to flow from my pen.

All descriptions are taken from source materials including diaries, memoirs, letters, and archival documents such as the transcript of the trial of Henry Wirz, courtesy of the Library of Congress. The descriptions came from those who lived it.

—*T. G.*

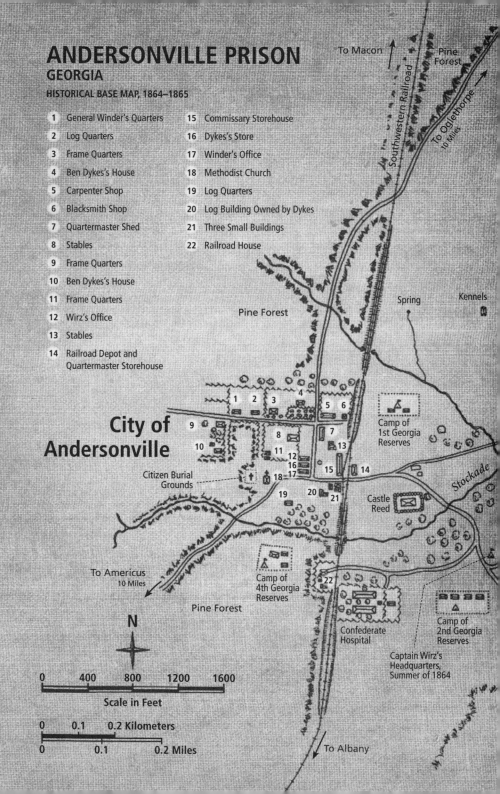

ANDERSONVILLE PRISON
GEORGIA

HISTORICAL BASE MAP, 1864–1865

1 General Winder's Quarters
2 Log Quarters
3 Frame Quarters
4 Ben Dykes's House
5 Carpenter Shop
6 Blacksmith Shop
7 Quartermaster Shed
8 Stables
9 Frame Quarters
10 Ben Dykes's House
11 Frame Quarters
12 Wirz's Office
13 Stables
14 Railroad Depot and Quartermaster Storehouse
15 Commissary Storehouse
16 Dykes's Store
17 Winder's Office
18 Methodist Church
19 Log Quarters
20 Log Building Owned by Dykes
21 Three Small Buildings
22 Railroad House

To Macon

Pine Forest

Southwestern Railroad

To Oglethorpe
10 Miles

Spring

Kennels

Pine Forest

City of Andersonville

Camp of 1st Georgia Reserves

Stockade

Citizen Burial Grounds

Castle Reed

To Americus
10 Miles

Camp of 4th Georgia Reserves

Confederate Hospital

Camp of 2nd Georgia Reserves

Captain Wirz's Headquarters, Summer of 1864

Pine Forest

N

0 400 800 1200 1600
Scale in Feet

0 0.1 0.2 Kilometers

0 0.1 0.2 Miles

To Albany

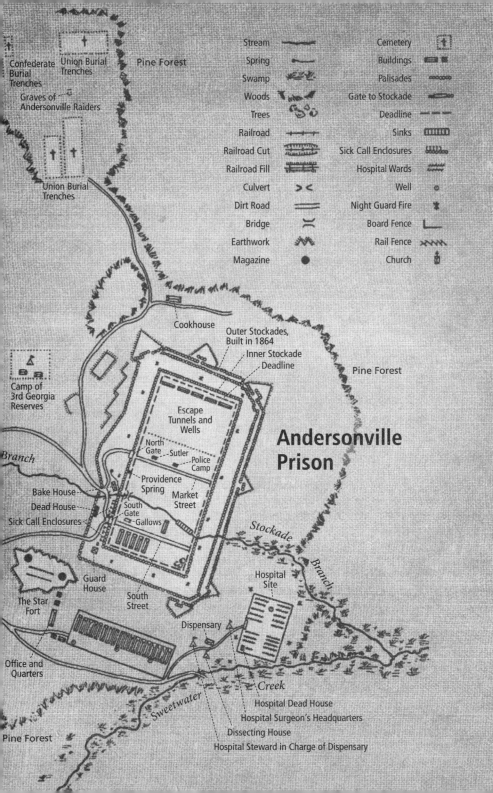

Legend

Stream		Cemetery	
Spring		Buildings	
Swamp		Palisades	
Woods		Gate to Stockade	
Trees		Deadline	
Railroad		Sinks	
Railroad Cut		Sick Call Enclosures	
Railroad Fill		Hospital Wards	
Culvert	><	Well	o
Dirt Road		Night Guard Fire	
Bridge		Board Fence	
Earthwork		Rail Fence	
Magazine	●	Church	

Confederate Burial Trenches

Union Burial Trenches

Graves of Andersonville Raiders

Pine Forest

Union Burial Trenches

Camp of 3rd Georgia Reserves

Branch

Cookhouse

Outer Stockades, Built in 1864

Inner Stockade

Deadline

Pine Forest

Escape Tunnels and Wells

North Gate

Sutler

Police Camp

Providence Spring

Market Street

Bake House

Dead House

Sick Call Enclosures

South Gate

Gallows

Andersonville Prison

Stockade

Branch

Guard House

South Street

Hospital Site

The Star Fort

Office and Quarters

Dispensary

Creek

Sweetwater

Hospital Dead House

Hospital Surgeon's Headquarters

Dissecting House

Hospital Steward in Charge of Dispensary

Pine Forest

GEORGIA

N

Dalton

Lake
Sidney Lanier

Hartwell
Lake

Rome

Russell
Lake

Gainesville

Weiss
Lake

Kennesaw
Mountain

Marietta

Athens

Smyrna

J. Strom Thurmond
Reservoir

Atlanta

East Point

Augusta

Oconee

Savannah

West Point
Lake

Ocmulgee

Forsyth

Milledgeville

Ogeechee

Flint River

Macon

River

Columbus

Fort Valley

River

River

Perry

Andersonville

Americus

Savannah

Cordele

Dawson

Altamaha

Walter F. George
Lake

Albany

River

Chattahoochee

St. Andrew
Sound

Lake
Seminole

Valdosta

Okefenokee
Swamp

Prologue

"Ya killed yet, blue belly?"

He woke to the taste of gunpowder on his lips.

Lew was holding his last shot. The other hand was full of rifle. He'd fallen asleep in the middle of loading, and some paper from a cartridge was stuck to his lip. He spit it away.

"Why don't you come and see?" he hollered back. Didn't come out as a holler. Came out as a dry croak.

"Got water for ya."

"Don't need it. I'm drinkin' the blood of my comrades."

"Well, ain't you a regular Davy Crockett."

The voice came from the woods at the perimeter of the battlefield— if you could call it a field. A clearing, more like, not bigger than Carrie's kitchen garden. Only Carrie's garden had vegetables in it, not piles of dead men.

"You have brought up an interesting point on our collective

history," Lew said. He waited for spit to speak again, and realized things were quiet. "Where's the rest of your boys?"

No answer.

Lew grinned. "Why, you are all alone, Johnny Reb. They moved on and charged you with the task to collect me. You know I'm a good aim."

"Haven't seen better," the Reb called generously.

"How many did I get, last go-around?"

"Two."

"You sore about that?"

Silence, and Lew's grin eased. "Hope I didn't tag a friend."

Finally, "Aw. Not takin' it personal. Woulda done the same in your spot."

"Let's discuss prisoner exchange: I'll catch up with my boys, you catch up with yours, and we'll call it even. Tell 'em you waited me out, and I died of my wound."

"What wound?"

A year ago at Gettysburg, Lew had taken a ball in the shoulder and figured that would put paid on all future ills. But early this morning, after a hot and heavy skirmish and orders to move out, he got up to follow Robert, and to his surprise, his leg did not comply.

When Lew didn't answer, the Reb said, "What's the interesting point on our collective history?"

"It's this: Which side can claim Crockett for his own?"

"Why, the South, of course. He was a Tennessee man."

"Oh, you're missin' the point entire." Lew grasped his last shot, and let his hand fall. "I'm tired of this, Johnny. You clear out. Clear out!"

"You're gettin' irritable."

Lew and this unseen Reb had exchanged jeers until conversation became amiable. He'd heard other Johnnies yell at this Reb to end it, something easily done with an organized assault. Lew was in the middle of a clearing on a bluff, dug in behind the piled-up bodies of his men. A sheer drop behind left only a two-thirds radius for which to be vigilant, but the fellow must have been of some minor rank, or maybe the boys respected him, because no assault had come.

Lew waited for spit. "I aim to catch up with my regiment. I recommend you get yourself scarce before I come out, for I am determined."

He let his head fall back on Robert. He closed his eyes and was just about seeing Carrie again. Robert had died hours earlier. He came back when Lew didn't follow, and got it in the neck.

"Where ya wounded, blue belly? Sure isn't your mouth."

"My name is Lew." He just wanted to sleep and could do it right against a dead man. He was fearsome tired, due in some measure to his wound.

"I know it. Gill told me. Didn't think it was polite to use 'til you gave it."

Lew's eyes came open. "Harris Gill? Is he all right?"

"He's walkin'. Got a message for you. Said, 'Tell Lew to drop his gun and come along.' Said if he's gotta wait the war out, he wants to wait it out with you."

"Not likely. He said, 'I hope Lew guts ya head to toe,' and probably added some impolite observations about your parentage."

A pause. Then, "That's about right. Cussin'est man I ever met. Ever' time you laid in a good shot, he rang out a vile sort of hallelujah. But back to your 'point entire' which you said I am missin'. What point entire?"

The voice was closer. It was the closest anyone from the perimeter had dared to come yet. Lew couldn't see him. The stand of woods was thick and dim and Rebs always took good cover.

"Why, the sadness of it all, Johnny. What would our foredaddies say about this fighting? Don't you feel a bit queer over the fact that George Washington is *my* foredaddy as well as yours? This is not a normal war, for we are kin. If my grandkids carried on this way, it'd break my heart."

"I have thought on it. Weren't we hellfire and brimstone for a fight, couple years back? Wish the politicians've had it like we have."

"Stick 'em out here, the war would be done in a day."

"That's our thinkin', too. Listen: You lay down that rifle and come along. Your men wish for you to accompany them to their temporary accommodations, courtesy of Jefferson Davis."

"I must respectfully decline your hospitable offer." He waited for spit again. He hadn't had any water since early morning. It was heading past thirst into torment. "A man isn't made for confinement. I'd rather buy my passage on a battlefield than be bored to death in a stockade any day."

"I reckon your Carrie would see it different."

"Oh . . . doggone it." Lew felt the fight go right out of him.

What was boredom compared to seeing her face just one more time? One more time, God willing, and he'd die a man redeemed.

A twig snapped on his right. He groaned. "Don't make me shoot you."

"No terms except an unconditional and immediate surrender can be accepted," came the cheerful reply.

Lew grinned, and it rolled into a laugh. Ulysses S. Grant's very words to Fort Donelson, apparently famous enough to make the rounds in Rebel lines. Grant's victory at Fort Donelson had been a disaster for the South. It opened up Tennessee for a Northern advance. Lew tossed the last shot aside. He couldn't shoot him now. He couldn't shoot him a long time ago.

By now Lew knew the fellow came from Alabama, had a twist of tobacco if Lew had coffee, couldn't pick between Rosaline and Irene, and was currently reading number 5 or 6 of *Nicholas Nickleby*—his reading had improved considerable since being in the Confederate army, and he felt his station in life would certainly improve. Might even get himself a job at the new telegraph office in Huntsville. In turn, the Reb had learned that Lew and Carrie had a small fruit farm in Ezra, north and west of Gettysburg, where he grew apples, cherries, peaches, walnuts, and blueberries. He had four children, and didn't know the name of the last. And at thirty-two, he was the oldest private in his regiment. Some called him Pap.

Another rustle. Lew sighed. "I am not gonna shoot you and you know it. Just get on, and we'll—"

"Why, das right nice o' you, Yank."

Lew looked left, and there on a rock stood a big greasy man with a tobacco-stained beard and a mossy green leer.

He was not at all what Lew expected. One look told what sort of man this was—a forager, a bummer, a skulker, and the worst sort. It wasn't the stuffed haversacks slung over his shoulders. It wasn't the knapsack stenciled with the 12th Pennsylvania. It wasn't the Union pistols in his hands, and it wasn't the filthy blouse stretched tight over a gut that had no cause to bulge if he lived the hard life of a decent soldier. It was Colonel Ford's brass-buttoned coat. It had a new hole ripped into the side, jagged, darkened, wet.

The man looked down at the coat. "He wudden even daid yet. Look at dem buttons. Two rows!" He cackled. "Cain't believe my luck."

Colonel Ford had once halted an entire column to gaze on a quiet meadow carpeted in wildflowers. *Let it stouten your hearts, boys,* he'd hollered with joy. *There is beauty yet in this world.*

"Had to keel 'nuther Yank runt half-daid hisself, cuz he wudden gone lemme git 'im. Lil squawkin' pisspot. I made *him* squawk . . ."

Charley Reed, the regiment's drummer boy. Colonel Ford's honorary aide. He was thirteen.

"I didn't take you for a baby killer, you bottom-feeding carp."

The skulker stilled. Then the pistols came up, but before he got off a shot, an explosion, and the man fell. He tried to get up—another shot, and he lay still.

A man came moving smooth out of the thicket, crouched, rifle leveled.

This Reb was younger, cleaner, leaner, with long yellow hair flowing out from his brown slouch hat. He wore red-and-white-checked homespun, tucked into brown trousers. He lowered his rifle when he saw the other was dead.

Lew croaked, "Now *you* resemble your voice. How come you killed one of your own?"

"He had bad grammar. We don't put up with that down here." He picked his way over bodies to Lew's corpse-built breastworks. He propped his rifle against the stack of dead men, unslung his canteen, and tossed it to Lew. Then he settled at once to a long, considering look at Lew, as if recalling their entire faceless conversation and fastening every word to this particular corporeal being.

Lew in turn did a study of his own, and the blond man ten years younger soon became the one who spoke of Rosaline and Irene, and reading considerable better.

But the Reb took longer to scout out the terrain of Lewis Gann. He had an earnest face with interested blue eyes that would be done when they were done, and not a trace of self-consciousness attended his inspection. In fact it was such a thorough winnowing that Lew couldn't help smiling, and he did so simply because he liked the man.

A smile soon answered, and the perusal was done. "Hello, blue belly. I am Emery Jones, and you are shot up some."

"Yep."

"Reckon you can move?"

"With help."

"Let's get on, then, to your temporary accommodations."

"Where we headed?"

"Place called Andersonville, and I am your escort. It is a spell from Kennesaw, but once there you get to wait out the war. I just about envy you."

"We've heard of Andersonville. I'm not sure I envy me."

"Don't believe everything you hear. *I* heard you Yanks were fearsome ignorant, but early on in our conversation you used the word *perpetuity*."

"I did, didn't I?"

"'I will sit here and shoot you in perpetuity.' Boy, you've got some Grant in you. I knew then I had to save your life."

"I could've taken that bad grammar man," Lew said indignantly.

Emery shook his head. "Saved it 'fore then."

"How so?"

"Well, I would tell you, but you look as though . . ."

And he was off and dreaming of Carrie again.

PART ONE

Q: From your observation of the condition and surroundings of our prisoners—their food, their drink, their exposure by day and by night, and all the circumstances you have described— state your professional opinion as to what proportion of deaths occurring there were the result of the circumstances and surroundings which you have narrated.

A: I feel myself safe in saying that seventy-five per cent of those who died might have been saved, had those unfortunate men been properly cared for as to food, clothing, bedding, &c.

—TESTIMONY OF DR. JOHN C. BATES, FROM THE TRIAL OF HENRY WIRZ

1

JULY 1864
ANDERSONVILLE PRISON

Two men stood sheltered from the blazing sun in a sentry box at the top of the stockade wall. One thought of his rheumatic knee, and one thought of Violet Stiles.

Violet Stiles had large blue eyes and other features Dance Pickett could never remember, subjugated as they were by the eyes. So, wanting still to conjure her face, he allowed aspects of her nature to form the forgotten features: She was naïve, patriotic, self-righteous, kind (he allowed her that), and merry (he couldn't be unfair, she had laughed heartily at the antics of the younger sisters at the Stiles dinner table last Sunday); but naïve, patriotic, and self-righteous were the overriding elements of her nature, and they fashioned a caricature image of a dark-haired girl with gigantic blue eyes and tiny everything else, including figure and feet. It was like looking through field glasses at the wrong end to find great, startling eyes, with all else crabbed and distant.

Violet Stiles represented all that Dance despised in Southern womenry. He didn't despise women as a general rule, but he hated what the war brought out of them. Violet was like all the rest, a fire-breathing patriot determined to do her duty by any hapless Confederate soldier who had the misfortune to cross her path. Did she suppose men actually *wanted* to be fussed over and praised and—worst of all—*encouraged* for the Cause? She was so *meaning* and *feeling* and *earnest*—the most ignorant, galling, entertaining creature he'd ever met.

The guard next to him shifted, and Dance stopped laughing.

No wonder they didn't like him. At least they left him alone. He touched the shoulder strap of his leather scrip. In there was a bit of his favorite Shakespeare, and he decided to indulge the fellow.

"Burr, hear me out, and I'll confer on you something fine: The poet's eye, in a fine frenzy rolling, doth glance from heaven to earth, from earth to heaven; and as imagination bodies forth the form of things unknown, the poet's pen—" Dance paused for dramatic effect, allowing, hopefully, his listener to form a pen in his mind—"turns them to shapes, and gives to airy nothing a local habitation and a name."

"Pickett, I don't know as I should hit you or treat you kindly," said Burr. "If you was my boy, I'd beat you half to death and let the good Lord take care of the rest."

The leather pouch had been a Christmas gift from his mother when he was a boy, carried in the Revolution, she said, by her grandfather. Dance had examined it for signs of Revolution. The nick on the flap, surely from a musket ball. Stains were surely blood. Mother seemed to know just what her son would do with it: make it into a sanctuary.

Early on he took particular care with the papers he put into the scrip. They were quotes and isms, poetry and prose, declarations and decrees and bits of airy nothing, and nothing could go in there indiscriminately.

The result was such that his scrip powered him through his first two years at the University of Georgia. It powered him through the patriotism of his father and the death of his mother. But it had no power here. He had not opened his scrip since the day he was posted to the garrison at Andersonville Prison, for the stockade was a different sort of sanctuary, and two sanctuaries could not exist in the same place. It was a law of religion or physics.

"Here they come," Burr grunted.

Dance took his eyes from the men in the stockade to the men approaching the stockade, coming through the stand of pines from the Andersonville depot, a quarter mile distant. They came in long shambling columns, Captain Wirz riding his old gray mare alongside.

"Run, you fools," Dance muttered.

They were two hundred or so, held in check by Wirz's commands and curses and occasionally brandished pistol, as well as thirty or so armed members of the Georgia militia and any escorting regulars. Dance looked away.

He shifted his weight to the other leg, glanced from habit to his ancient musket propped at his side, and fell once more to the interesting ponderation of Miss Violet Stiles. Dance selected an early Stiles Sunday dinner and rolled it out on his mind's stage.

Stiles Sunday Dinner. Volume Two.

Characters: The entire Stiles household, the mayor of Americus and his wife, Dance Pickett, and another member of the Georgia militia, an uncouth geezer on burial duty named Linney.

Act One: Dance must endure the patronizing efforts of Miss Stiles to engage Linney in conversation.

"I understand you are posted at the prison, Mr. Linney," Violet said, her voice cultured enough to jelly eels. "How do you find the work?"

Linney stopped midchew, surprised and not altogether happy to find attention on him. They might, after all, see him slip biscuits

THE SENTINELS OF ANDERSONVILLE

into his dirty vest. Linney gulped some wine and sent a look to Dr. Stiles, who was busy cutting meat for one of the younger girls and admonishing her to chew carefully.

"Reckon I find it all right. 'Cept I cain't talk about it or I'll git in trouble."

"Your discretion does you credit. Security is very important, for Yankee spies abound. I understand General Winder has called down detectives from Richmond. Goodness, what an important job you have. You are certainly our protector." She gave a little shudder, and Dance gripped his cutlery. She recovered from her theatrical musings, and asked brightly, "Where are you from, Mr. Linney?"

"Skull Gully. More of dem peas, ma'am. Some of dem biscuits."

"Please," Dance prompted.

"Please," said Linney.

"Certainly, Mr. Linney," said Violet with a frosty glance at Dance. "Tell me, Mr. Linney, where is Skull Gully?" said she, all melodic politeness once more.

"South."

"It must be a very nice town."

"It's a swamp. More o' dat wine, ma'am. Please."

"But it isn't polite," protested the youngest Stiles girl. "You've already had three glassfuls. Mercy me."

Dance choked on a biscuit. Violet's gaze rained down violence on the girl.

"Why, certainly, Mr. Linney." Violet reached for the wine.

"I won't tolerate it," the little girl said, and snatched the decanter. "He is being rude and we do not tolerate rudeness at this table."

"Posey Stiles," Violet breathed, eyes glowing red.

This time Dance couldn't hide the laughter.

It caught the attention of the oft-distracted Mrs. Stiles, who smiled with bemused approval at her laughing guest and returned to remonstrate with the other girls while keeping conversation with the mayor's wife.

"Such a lovely brooch, Esme. It's only a little gristle, Daisy, eat it. You should wear it more often, I've not seen it since the pink taffeta last Christmas. Rosie, wipe your mouth. I declare."

"Say your name again to me," Dance asked of the little girl with the decanter safely between her knees, "for you are my favorite Stiles, and I wish to remember it always."

She smiled up at him, glorious in her defense of the family wine, triumphant that someone admired it.

"I am Posey Eden Stiles, called so because my sisters are Violet, Lily, Rose, and Daisy, and when I came along Papa said I made a posy. So though I am *officially* Pansy, I am *called* Posey and I like it right fine."

"You like it very much," Violet corrected severely.

"Mr. Linney said *right fine* a minute ago, and I liked it."

"I like Posey right fine, too," said Dance. "And you were entirely correct to waylay this man from drinking all your wine. Such rudeness should be corrected, and hastily." He looked at Linney, who was slipping a spoon into his vest. "Linney, guardian and protector of genteel Southern womenry, I request that you apologize for your rudeness, and return to the table your recent acquisitions."

That had been the first time he saw Violet mad. But Volume Eight was the memorable best. Dance had gloried to see that a methodical chipping away had at last revealed the true Violet. On that infamous evening he had seen in full what had only peeked from behind a well-bred cloak—a tempestuous nature nigh unto feral, not at all civilly Southern as he was sure she had supposed. He didn't trot out Volume Eight very often. He saved it for when things were especially bad. Today was tolerable. He couldn't remember Volume Nine. It did trouble him some.

Violet Wrassey Stiles desperately needed guidance at this critical juncture in her young life. *Someone* needed to devote delicate method to make it clear that Volume Eight Violet was the one to be admired, not fought and subdued in favor of the other person he didn't much like at all. Clearly Dr. and Mrs. Stiles had a handful with that one, and would not mind the kind intervention of a concerned distant cousin—

"Strike me dumb," said Burr. "Look over there."

What Dance saw first made him squint, then made him lunge to the rail. A girl came out of the pines, following at some distance the columns of prisoners. He gripped the rail.

"That a *woman?*" Burr said.

"It's Violet Stiles," Dance breathed.

"Uh-oh." He had heard of the Sunday dinners. "What's *she* doin' here?"

"She can't see this." He broke and ran for the ladder.

"Where you goin', Pickett? Pickett! Oh, let her see, I say! Don't no one ever see. Fancy-pants what never put themselves in the way of mizry will find naught but mizry at the end."

Burr suspected he had said something wise, thought it should be wrote down, set himself to memorize it on account he couldn't write, then caught sight of a Yankee too close to the deadline and grabbed his musket. "I see you, Old Abe," he bellowed down into the stockade. "Do not try me today, for I am in a foul temper'ment."

2

AMERICUS, GEORGIA, in 1864 was a town proper with its post office, three churches, three newspapers, three general mercantiles, a couple of mills, a blacksmithy, two inns, a courthouse, and a few notable lawyers and statesmen; but Americus triumphed over other small communities in Georgia in that it boasted not only a train depot, when the Southwestern Railroad came through in '54, but a telegraph office: that bustling junction of grave importance where mysterious electrical impulses rode along frightening snake-black wires to land upon official telegraph paper in portents of good or evil—usually evil. Just such a paper was waved at Violet Stiles as she was passing the little office located outside the depot.

"Miss Stiles!" cried the telegrapher from within. "Oh, Miss Stiles!" He didn't wait for her to come in, but hurried around the counter and out into the street.

Violet was surprised the young man knew who she was; she'd seen him, but they had never exchanged more than a polite nod. He was one of the many new faces in Americus, likely connected to military matters. And these days most matters were military.

"Reckon your package has come, Miss Stiles, but I reckon it got put off with some of your father's stores at the Andersonville depot. Two boxes, two Stiles—reckon it's an easy mistake."

Violet took the paper, the first time in her life a telegram had been addressed to her, and read as much as the young man had spoken.

She'd waited for the parcel of seashells like Christmas, the entire Stiles household had. The seashells were soon to be buttons, a scheme long planned and anticipated. A month earlier she'd told the family of her idea, and, apparently charmed and grateful for the diversion, Papa had written directly to his cousin in coastal Savannah.

The same blockade that caused a dearth of buttons had caused a dearth of thread, but Violet tirelessly collected thread from various ingenuities. She unraveled a barley sack, and rewound it over cards made of cut-up fans. She raided the ribbon box, and colorful silk-wrapped cards soon joined the burlap. She picked lengths of thread out of old quilting scraps, and painstakingly tied them together.

She arranged the threaded cards in a basket and brought them out for visitors to admire. She'd soon receive a parcel from Savannah filled with *uniform* shells, she told them, and the shells would be tightly wrapped with this good thread and sold very soon at the Americus Mercantile.

Violet's zeal provoked good-hearted generosity, and neighbors dropped by with ragbag scraps for her to unravel. She received each item with great enthusiasm, and showered upon the giver praise to equal a gift of silver.

Her seashells—so close! Ten miles close! What vex*ation*! She barely refrained from crumpling the paper into a ball. The temptation brought protocol to mind and she asked with a shade of reluctance, "Do I owe anything for this?"

"Payment is on the sending end, not the receiving end, unless the receiving end is manned by an immoral character." The young man drew himself tall, as if to assure her no such immoral character was in her vicinity. "You want I should send a reply with your instructions?"

As payment was on the sending end, she shook her head.

"Well, I reckon none is needed as they will surely have the doctor take your parcel home this evening." He pulled off his hat, and his face reddened. "Say, Miss Stiles . . ." And he launched into a speech Violet did not hear.

It was *impossible* to wait until Papa came home. He came home *late* on Thursdays. She could not *endure* the thought of her shells *languishing* in—

". . . the dance next Saturday at the Millards'. I would be honored if—"

She seized his arm. "When does the train leave for Andersonville?"

"I—what? Oh—maybe five minutes, maybe ten. I would be honored—"

"Freight or passenger?"

"Passenger. But—no, wait! Come back, Miss Stiles! It's the one-fifteen and there's no return today! You'd have to wait 'til your father comes back from the . . . Oh, doggone it."

She ran down to the end of the depot, up the stairs, and past the depot office to the platform, where Silas Runcorn was pasting a label on a crate.

"Mr. Runcorn! I need a lift to Andersonville. I cannot pay, but the train is going there anyway."

"Miss Stiles, that kind of reasoning will bankrupt the Southwestern line." Mr. Runcorn replaced the brush in the glue bottle and straightened. "So you got a telegram. Could have told you myself. Wasted paper is an outrage these days. Silas Junior wrote to us on wallpaper. Yankee wallpaper, Mrs. Runcorn informs me, for it was ugly."

"I see it this way," Violet said. "The railroad has cost me a fearful inconvenience, and likely profit, as by now I would be making my buttons and they would be for sale far earlier. Among my multiple early orders, your own wife has ordered a set of green silk buttons which I had planned to augment with an *extra* black thread at *no additional charge* to ensure a lovely contrast with Mrs. Runcorn's green brocade; but I grieve to say that this delay will cost your dear wife some early happiness. As we all know, happiness these days is a commodity—"

"Make hers first and I'll find you a seat."

Violet beamed. Then she quickly looked about for a young personage she could send home with a message, and found it in little Jupe, the Negro belonging to one of the absentee station owners.

"Can I borrow your boy, Mr. Runcorn?"

"Make it quick, Jupe. No dallying."

Clearly glad for the diversion, Jupe set his broom outside the office and came running. He likely knew that any errand for the Stiles family ended in something good.

Violet bent to him. "Shall you be rescued from this work fit for only women and girls?"

The child nodded.

"Shall I entrust to you a man-sized errand from which I am not at all sure you will return? For I tremble at what sort of reception my message will have."

She held up the telegram. Her voice lowered. "When Mrs. Stiles reads this and discovers that I have, in fact, gone to Andersonville without prior consultation as to her wishes, why, child . . ." and she shook her head slowly, the child soon doing the same. "Have you ever seen Mrs. Stiles in a temper?"

He continued to shake his head in mute awe.

"It may be worth the journey entire. You may lose your life.

Perhaps only a leg. I am sure a lemon tart, which Ellen is currently baking with some leavening gotten from an unscrupulous blockader, surely a shady deal to send us to prison and endure agonies unknown, may be of *some* comfort should you live to eat it; but—! Should you find yourself on your deathbed at the hand of Mrs. Stiles, be consoled in the singular knowledge that *you*—" she poked his chest— "are one of the celebrated few to have witnessed—"

"Miss Stiles, you will not hold up my train," called Mr. Runcorn from the platform.

Violet straightened. "Thank you kindly, Jupe. You go see Ellen. She'll fix you up right fine."

Solemn little Jupe took the telegram, broke loose the sweetest smile sure to get two tarts from Ellen, and dashed away.

———

Camp Sumter was the official name of the prison for Federal soldiers, though no one called it that. They called it by the name of the nearest town. Trains did not stop at Andersonville in the early part of the war. It was only a whistle stop then, barely a town, with only a few scattered farmers. Now, with the construction of the prison early this year, it had military buildings near the depot, connected with business at the prison stockade a quarter-mile march past the depot through the pines. Some of the buildings were commissary warehouses, some were offices and accommodations for the officers assigned to the prison. A dry goods store lay not far from the depot, the only private business in Andersonville.

When Andersonville had been selected as the site of a Federal prison camp, a hue and cry went up in Americus not seen since the passage of conscription. No one wanted a stockade full of murdering Yankees only ten miles off. Who could sleep at night? One little prison break and they were dead in their beds—and likely to *get* that way through vile ordeals unimagined. Despite a ruckus much publicized and editorialized by the papers in Americus, plans went through, and the prison opened to receive its first group of five hundred prisoners in February.

The train carrying Violet Stiles thundered into a crowded depot. As Violet had spent the journey vision-dazzled with cards of buttons replacing cards of thread, she'd only been vaguely aware of occasional gusts of fetid odor, as if the train had gone over a foul swamp. The smell persisted, however, and finally made its way into Violet's notice, for as the iron horse reared to a stop in a spray of cinders and soot, it was as if the train had come *in*to the smell. As she stepped down to the small platform, she dug into her pocket for a handkerchief and pressed it to her nose.

She had never been to Andersonville alone. She had never been anywhere alone, not by rail, and though the town was only ten miles northeast, it occurred to her what a fine, daring thing she had done. She fastened her bonnet strings and set her chin as if she knew exactly what she was doing and where she was going and stepped into the crowd.

The fine feeling soon began to crumble, and not because she couldn't decide which building was the parcel warehouse in the thronging confusion of men on the platform and all about the depot; not because of the pervasive odor she tried to keep at bay with a press of thin linen; not because it finally came upon her that she would have to spend the entire day here, without food, until Papa came for the horse and carriage provided by the benevolent Maxwells, which took him home every Thursday to Americus. It was because she was suddenly aware that she was the only woman in the biggest collection of men she had ever seen, and because most of those men, she realized with a thrill of horror and shock, were Yankees.

———

"Not much longer, Lew. You get to reunite with your men and put up your heels while the rest of us poor devils see this thing through."

Lew Gann did not answer. He studied the landscape rolling by at all the speed the train could muster, maybe six or eight miles an hour. The terrain, endless stands of pine trees and corn, was a different sight from northern Georgia, where the mountains reminded him of home. The view was interesting to a farmer in love with the land, but interesting too because Lew had never been so far south; before the war he'd never been farther south than Maryland, and then he'd only stepped over the line to say he had been out of state.

"I could do for a rest m'self," Emery Jones commented in that easy, pleasing way of Alabamian speech: soft *r*'s, extra syllables, and no hurry to go anywhere. "No rest for the weary. Or is it the wicked? I mix that up."

The train shuddered over a length of track warped out of alignment, and righted itself before too much brain rattling had occurred. From the Battle of Kennesaw, as they were now calling it, it had been a long, weary journey on rolling stock because the so-called axle grease, a fly-specked concoction which smelled like rendered hog, had to be applied ten times as often as proper grease. The Confederate army had commandeered all the grade-one grease for the hotter spots of the war to keep supply lines intact; and just how did this make sense, Lew wondered, this close to Atlanta? They didn't consider *this* area hot? Well, they didn't know old Billy T. then, did they. Maybe Sherman hadn't done so well at Kennesaw, but a few flanking moves and before you could say Jefferson Finis Davis he'd be on Atlanta's front porch sipping lemonade.

Lew decided to keep that last thought to himself, and found it easy; the farther south they went, the less he talked. Yes, Lew had heard of Andersonville, and so had Emery, but grim as it sounded it didn't mean much to Lew right now. All he knew after three years of fighting was the cold reality of war, and cold reality said he'd never see Emery Jones again. It hit him as hard as losing a man from his company.

"You once said you have two boys and two girls. Yet you do not know the name of the last. How can you know if it is boy or girl, yet not know the name? I have thought on this for a month."

A whole month they had been together, where Lew almost died, and then he lived, and then they started their journey south on a series of miserable train trips: Kennesaw to Atlanta, Atlanta to Forsyth, Forsyth to Macon, and Macon just about to Andersonville. All that time, they talked.

They talked religion and politics, army life and women, peace-time and war, and they let each other in on the curious ways of the North and of the South. They argued and debated the reasons for the War of Northern Aggression—as Emery put it—a usual thing for soldiers around a campfire but far less usual if campfiring with the enemy. They talked even when Lew was delirious with fever in a Negro cabin near Atlanta, and then, Emery told him, conversation was interesting indeed.

It was an uncommon friendship, and both knew it.

"I lost some of Carrie's letters in a battle," Lew finally said, after regaining his balance from a particularly hard jolt. "She'd told me the baby's name, but I couldn't remember it. I was too ashamed to own it to her, so I took to calling him Little Mite. 'How's Little Mite?' I'd say in a letter, and here's the funny part: she'd answer, 'Little Mite's just fine.' Never said his name again like I hoped, because the nickname stuck. What is more, I've received letters from my mother, and guess what she calls him? Little Mite. It is a hard thing, Emery, to not know the name of your own child. He's almost a year old."

"That is rough," Emery said.

Landscape rolled by, corn and pine and pine and corn. Not much else out there. Some rice, looked like, and beans. Peas, they called them down here. He wondered what they called actual peas. He went to ask Emery, but asked him something else.

"You never did explain that very curious inspection you gave when we first met, face-to-face. As we are about to part, I'd like to know what it meant. 'Cause it was more than fixing words to my face."

"Well, Lew, I was trying to discover if you were worth the oath I gave."

"*Oath?* What oath?"

Emery took off his hat and put his finger through a hole. "The first man you killed in that standoff was a childhood friend of Captain Graves, and Graves wanted you dead. Offered fifty Federal greenbacks to the man who killed you, and made it clear it should be done even if we took you prisoner. Your Harris Gill gave a decorated opinion that that would be murder, not fair war, and so he ended up with a split mouth, courtesy of Captain Graves.

"By this time I'd taken a shine to you, 'cause of the word *perpetuity*, and the other boys did not hold it against you that you were fighting so hard to live. They admired your courage, with a more fearful admiration of your marksmanship, and even found some amusement in that smart mouth of yours. We counted the loss of Graves's friend toward war, nothing more.

"Captain Graves, howsoever, was not of our mind. Never was. It was his daddy who got up the regiment, and stuck him in charge by right of wealth alone. Well. Some money spends well, and some don't. We came up short in Graves. He wanted your Yankee head on a pike, but as the men were, in your particular case, reluctant to despoil Federal property—" Emery shrugged—"I made a proposal, and Graves accepted."

"What on earth did you propose?"

"Well, part of that configuration entailed seeing you and Harris Gill to Andersonville. When you took sick, I sent Gill on with Corporal—"

"I know that part," Lew said impatiently. "Get to the oath part."

"Well, I ain't gonna tell you."

"What do you mean you're not gonna tell me?" Lew demanded.

Emery replaced his hat. "Tell you what. You take care of yourself in the pen, keep yourself healthy and don't make anybody mad, and I promise you this: I'll meet up with you in Ezra when this war is done and I'll tell you then. And you better be satisfied with that, 'cause this is the last oath I am makin' on your behalf."

"You're taking the job."

"You ain't rid of me yet. I aim to fruit-farm. You can teach me."

"I am glad to hear it. But Emery? What *is* that stench?"

"Well, I was tryin' not to notice 'cause of our earnest conversation. I thought it was you."

"I will not own such a pestilential stink as that. Smells like the sinks of the entire camped Army of the Potomac."

The rest of the men in the boxcar noticed it, too, and the train finally pulled into the Andersonville depot.

3

VIOLET FIRST WENT to the small platform depot, less than half the size of the Americus depot, on the east side of the tracks. There she was informed she'd have to check with the commissary agent at the large building on the west side of the tracks, because the clerk could not find a box for Miss Violet Wrassey Stiles; it was likely thrown in with the box for Dr. Stiles, and any boxes on military business went to the commissary building.

Violet crossed over the tracks on a path of wooden planking, only too aware of the stares from the men milling about her. It was her first time to encounter Yankees—other than a distant view of a few escapees from Andersonville, rounded up by farmers on the outskirts of Americus. Though she was madly curious, she could not observe them when this closely observed herself. At least the July heat answered for the flush in her cheeks.

Yankees and Rebels alike followed her progress to the commissary building. Confederate soldiers touched their hats and offered pleasantries she barely acknowledged, while the Yanks were staring but silent; they knew enough not to address a Southern woman without risk of recrimination from the nearest Confederate. She ducked into the long wooden building with some relief.

"I am here to pick up *twelve* barrels of whiskey, Corporal, not seven." A man in his forties shoved a paper under the nose of a boy in his teens. "See that signature? This is for the hospital. Do *you* wish to tell him how five barrels have gone missing between here and Macon?" He snatched the paper back. "This is all the pain-killer them poor boys have, even for amputations. How anyone can justify stealin' from dyin' men is beyond my education. Yankees or not."

"This is all they rolled off the train, mister. I ain't sayin' they weren't stole, but—"

"Who rolled 'em off the train?"

"The railroad agent."

"Yeah? And who'd he roll them to?"

The boy nervously scratched his neck. "Well . . . I saw Mr. Duncan with him. . . ."

The man's face hardened. He nodded in disgust, as if things made sense. "You been to that Federal hospital, son?"

"No, sir."

"You take a walk in them wards, boy, and you will wish for whiskey just for the look. Now I ain't gonna sign for this until I have *twelve*, not *seven*, so I propose you either look up Duncan or you search the guard tents—"

"Hello, ma'am," the young man said, eager for the diversion. "You Miss Stiles?"

Violet nodded.

"Got a box right in the back for ya. Lemme get the paper and you can sign for it." He hurried off.

Violet looked at the barrels labeled XX WHISKEY XX, and

thought of Dance Pickett and his uncharacteristic behavior last Sunday, the first time he'd missed dinner in two months.

"Is your father Dr. Stiles?" A noticeable softening had come to the man's face. "Works at the Yankee hospital?"

"Yes, sir. Every Thursday."

He seemed to want to say more, but a train whistle blew, and a black locomotive rumbled into the station.

Violet looked around the building. It was dark in here, compared to the blazing July sun outside. Close by were several sacks of meal piled against the right wall, while several barrels marked MOLASSES and VINEGAR lined the left. Beyond these were other sacks and boxes and barrels and crates in various states of order and disorder. It was a busy place. Men came and went through the wide entrance facing the train tracks, bringing things in or hauling them out. Outside, Violet could see dozens of men pouring out of the train that had just come in. This, however, was not a passenger train. It was a freight train, and men came out of cattle cars, more blue-clad, dirty, disheveled Yankees, hesitating on the platform, not sure where to go, looking about with wary, sun-squinting interest until a guard ordered them along.

"Tell your father he needs to be more careful."

Startled, Violet found the man had come closer, and had bent to examine the heel of his boot.

"I beg your pardon?" she said.

"Here you are, Miss Stiles. Sign here."

Violet turned to receive the much-anticipated box—and stared at it.

"It's been opened."

"Yes, ma'am. We have to search everything."

"How do I know I am receiving exactly what was sent?" The boy didn't answer. Frowning, she took the pen he had dipped and signed where he pointed. "I declare. Postmaster Haines wouldn't put up with this."

He shrugged. "Orders of General Winder."

"General Winder or no General Winder," Violet muttered.

"Perhaps *he* knows of the missing barrels." The man straightened to take up with the clerk once more. Violet took her box from the counter, and after a glance at the man, went outside.

She looked for a shaded place to sit away from the crowds of men, but found nothing near the commissary building. Hefting the box, which was only the size of a hatbox but was rather heavy, she threaded her way through groups of men on the expanse of grass behind the commissary, hoping her fixed gaze and lifted chin would ward off any inappropriate comments. There was a well at the edge of the commissary grounds, and across the street from the well, three small buildings. The center building seemed to be some sort of dry goods store, about the only place a woman could be respectably found in Andersonville at the moment, so she made straight for it.

But the storefront was quite thick with men, so she kept walking and passed between the store and the small building on the right, where a placard on the door said CAPTAIN H. WIRZ. She came out to the back of the buildings.

It would be a long time until Papa came from the prison, maybe four or five hours, so she took her time selecting a decent place to wait. A stable and corral lay behind the office of Captain Wirz, but the backyard of the dry goods store was free of both man and beast. Gratefully, she took the box to a shaded corner of the store and set it down. It wouldn't do to sit on the box, as she planned to immediately explore the contents, so she looked about until she spied a very large woodpile beneath several shade trees.

Some of the wood was stacked as tall as a man, some only knee high, and that would answer perfectly for a stool. It was farther away from the buildings, so even better. She picked up the box and was soon pleasantly situated. It was secluded and much cooler, and from here she could see the Maxwells' horse in the corral, so she would know when Papa came.

At last she put her attention on the box from Savannah, tempted to unravel her bonnet strings for thread and . . . and last Sunday, Dance Pickett had drunk whiskey meant for the hospital.

"Look there, Violet!" Lily had said. "Isn't that Dance? Why is he walking funny?"

Papa had gone with Mother to assist a midwife with a difficult birth and Ellen was putting the youngest girls to bed. Lily and Violet were sitting on the porch when Dance came strolling up, none too steadily.

"Yes, it is I, Miss Lily. As to my ungainliness: It may be due to the fact that my sensibilities at present are somewhat . . . bacchanalian in nature."

"You're sick?" said Lily.

"Lily, go help Ellen," said Violet.

"We missed you for supper!" Lily complained. "It's dreadfully dull without you. I have a new picture of P. G. T. Beauregard."

"Lily, go inside," Violet said.

"Hello, Miss Stiles." Dance nodded genteelly. "I am drunk."

"I can see that."

"I will say things I am certain to regret, but, happily, will not remember."

"Lily, go *inside*."

"I will certainly not!"

"Instantly, or Mother will hear of it."

Lily gave a small, exasperated shriek, then flounced out of her chair and went inside.

"What is that you're carrying?" Violet said, disgusted. "Is your whiskey in there?"

"This? Heavens, no. This is a sanctuary. Nothing has gone in there since my posting, and nothing has come out, for two sanctuaries cannot exist in the same place. It is a law, don't you see? Heaven and hell cannot coabide. The whiskey is in *this* pocket. It is an experiment, this whiskey. That's what Linney told me."

"Linney? That disgusting, vile—"

"Miss Stiles! How unchristian! Do go on."

"An experiment in what?"

"I wanted to see if he was right."

"About what?"

Dance stopped at the bottom of the porch steps and looked up at her. Slanting rays from the lowering sun came through the magnolia alongside the walk, and showed the expressive brown eyes stained red. He studied the porch steps.

"Oh dear. I will not attempt those stairs. There are two sets and both are moving. It is unsportsmanlike. Is anyone using this tree?" He took hold of an overhanging limb from the magnolia and steadied himself.

"What is Mr. Linney right about?"

"What? Oh, that." A cagey grin came. "No, you'll not trick me. We are not to speak to you of it. To you, Miss Stiles, especially you! You must remain a bastion of glorious ignorance, and thus remain for us, a bastion of . . . something . . ." He frowned, thinking. "I forget what. Something very important. The gist of it is you will continue to be the only thing in our lives that shall remain unsullied. We need you to stay who you are, for if you saw it, we would lose you. I would—" He stopped short, and then said, "Oh, I *am* drunk."

"I think you are unhappy, Mr. Pickett, and have been for a very long time."

"Yes!" He pointed at her. "Clever girl." He drew himself up with as much stately dignity as he could manage. "You have found me out."

"Why are you unhappy, Dance?"

"Say again?" He cupped his ear. "No 'Mr. Pickett'? Our relationship has advanced. You must define: Was that a brotherly Dance, or was it something altogether more interesting?"

"Dance?" said Papa, coming up the walk. "Violet? Is everything all right?"

"Ah, Dr. Stiles! Look to her—the lovely goddess of the porch! Not to worry." He made a motion to button his lips. "A bastion of ignorance she remains."

"Papa, he is drunk. It's that Linney."

"No! I'll not hide behind the skirts of any Linney. I am fully cognishent it is *I* who . . ." He paused. "Cognish . . . ? I am sensible it is *my* doing. It was an experiment, Dr. Stiles. It didn't work."

"Come with me, son," Papa said gently.

"Wait! I may yet have something to say which I will regret. Ah, there it is—my father wouldn't put up with this! 'They are only Yankees, Dance, and God hates Yankees. You will not shame the name of Pickett. You've shamed it quite well, right up to the steps of the governor's mansion. I was Joe Brown's confidant, you know! His personal friend, his intimate acquaintance. Why, he consulted me on matters of state and you . . . have ruined everything.'"

He fell silent. "I don't know what to do, Dr. Stiles. One day you and I must have a frank talk, for—" his breath caught—"I don't know how to help them. And I don't know how to stand and watch anymore."

Dance released the magnolia limb and stood in the slanting rays. His clothing was disheveled; his usually tidy hair, uncombed.

Dance Weld Pickett was a university man. He was very clever, and proud of his cleverness. Cynical of everything, and proud of that, too. For his wit and charm and courtesy, and especially for his teasing, he was the favorite Sunday dinner guest of the entire Stiles household. This was a Dance she'd never seen.

He lifted stained eyes to her. Violet took an involuntary step forward.

"Come along, son," Papa said, putting an arm about his shoulders. "Easy does it."

"It was just an experiment."

"Of course it was," Papa said soothingly.

"It didn't work."

"I'd expect not." He led Dance away.

—

Sometimes in their travels Emery made a show of Lew being his prisoner. He'd give him a little prod with the rifle butt, or speak to him rough. When any interest in the two men subsided, so did Emery's vigilance, and they settled down to companionship once more. Here at the Andersonville station, vigilance could not be laid down. There were too many Confederate officers and soldiers about, regular army or reserves.

Dozens of prisoners arrived at the depot all afternoon until they numbered in the hundreds, and they fell out in groups all about the tiny town, waiting for the arrival of Captain Henry Wirz, commandant of the interior of Andersonville Prison. Some prisoners slept; others played cards or smoked pipes or traded with Rebel guards. Some inquired about rations, of which, they were told, there were none. Negroes moved about with buckets of water, and that was all the ration they'd get this day, as the warehouses at Andersonville were behind on shipments from the commissary stores in Macon and Albany. So the Federals at the Andersonville station would go hungry today, but they were soldiers and settled down to it with no more than a few sullen grumbles. Some had hardtack or dried meat or fruit to fall back on, some looked wistfully at the sutler's stand set up a small distance from the depot, but many of the prisoners had no money, and if they did, would likely find a Rebel sutler's price to be just as sky-high as a Yankee's.

After reporting to the assistant provost marshal, Emery was informed that Wirz was at the stockade and would be along soon. He was ordered to fall out with his prisoner until Wirz arrived, then wait until the prisoners were sorted into divisions and escort them to the stockade with the other guards. After that he was to report to Wirz, by signed order of Captain Graves.

"Let's try behind the warehouse, blue belly," Emery said, shouldering his musket and nodding where Lew should walk. They went behind the building, but the expanse behind it, all the way to the well on the edge of the property, was full of men.

They threaded through the men to the three buildings opposite the well, but it wasn't much better there. The name GENERAL JOHN WINDER was tacked to the door on the first building. The second looked like a dry goods place, from what they could see between milling men. They went around the first building and came out to a nearly empty area. A corral lay far on their right, and the good horsey smell was much better than the persistent stink near the depot. Emery motioned to some trees on the left of a large woodpile.

Lew eased down, resting his back against a tree, stretching out his healing leg. Emery tossed down the haversacks between them and gratefully took a tree himself. The planked seats in the boxcar had no backs.

"I am thinking this," said Emery quietly, his voice set only for Lew to hear. A squad of six or seven prisoners had followed them, under guard of two Confederate soldiers, and threw down their things behind the dry goods store, some ten yards away. "I got some tobacco left, and some dried meat."

"Dried mule. I'd rather eat horse. Mule is grainy. I wonder if it

27

is because it cannot reproduce. Perhaps that also explains the odd flavor."

"Shut up and listen: I want you to take it. You'll have something to trade with in the pen."

"Not doing so. You'll have nothing left."

"I intend to marry your sister if she is as pretty as you say, and I will not have my betrothed accuse me of not taking care of her brother."

"I've told you, she's engaged."

"You keep saying that and I keep trying to find its relevance. Besides, if her intended is in the war, he'll likely die in battle."

"If you are her unintended intended, do unintendeds *not* die?"

"My argument is she'll forget all about him once she sees me. I have an effect on women you have not yet learned. Lew—is it *a*ffect or *e*ffect, with an *e*?"

"Well . . . I'm not sure."

"The word stumps me. Also, *diarrhea*. I spell that different every time."

"That you would have multiple occasions to spell it at all amazes me. But I am *not*—"

"Shut up and listen. Once I have delivered you safe to the pen, I have orders from Captain Graves to report to Captain Wirz who will, God willing, send me back to my regiment as Graves specifies, and that'll be somewhere near Atlanta where I will personally lick Sherman. God *not* willing, Wirz will conscript my services for his own garrison, as commandants are wont to do if they are low on men, at *which* point I will certainly relieve you of my provender. I will hunt you down for it, in perpetuity. No terms except an unconditional—"

"One of these days I want you to come out and say you admire Grant."

"Lew. My kinsmen are right over there."

"Well, I admire Bobby Lee."

"What is not to admire? But you'd not say that if we were in the North and I was *your* prisoner with *your* kinsmen nearby. I do regret to inform you he's gonna lick Grant at Petersburg."

"Have you learned nothing from Vicksburg?"

"Well, now—he wasn't fighting Bobby Lee, was he?" Emery beamed a wide, comical grin, and Lew chuckled. Emery took his knapsack and began to rummage. "Lew, we don't have much time left. Does anything remain unsaid?"

"Your oath to that Captain Graves."

"Remains unsaid. 'Til I meet your sister."

"An oath made on my behalf is something I feel I have a right to."

"How do you feature? *I* made it, it's *my* business, and there's the end of it."

Lew drew up his leg and unpinned the flap to examine his wound. The Negro woman in Atlanta had given him a pin to close the ragged gap made by the bullet. From what Emery could tell, the wound was healing well. She used a greasy concoction that seemed to speed it up.

Lew refastened the flap. "There is one subject we haven't spoke on. I didn't want to court your ire. But it bothers me some, and when this is said, all is said. It is on the subject of slavery."

Emery sighed. "Wish we could leave that alone. We've done all right without it. Well, let's have it then."

Lew adjusted himself to fit the tree better. "Well, Em, here it is: we had an escaped Negro following our camp. We had to saw a neck iron off him. Tricky work. As we did so, we observed his condition, and it was bad. Had a cut-off ear. Had a brand on his thigh, made by a hot iron. And his back . . ." Lew shook his head. "You are the South to me, and I know you don't have it in you to treat a man like that. So I want to know why you fight for those who do."

While Lew was talking, Emery had pulled off his hat and made a game of winging it at a sapling stump a few feet off. After retrieving it twice, he dug in his knapsack for a fishhook and string, and attached it to the hat. He winged it at the stump and ringered it, then with some satisfaction, pulled in the hat with the string. Lew knew it was Emery's way of listening.

"Don't know how a nation can treat folks like that."

"Well, Lew, the whole South ain't that way, and a man can be against slavery without being Union. He can just love his home, and love his people, and fight because you are down here and we're afraid of what you might do. You mustn't believe the whole South would do for that man as was done—it ain't right, and decent folks know it."

"I *have* been ashamed at how some of our boys have treated the Negroes. We're not all of us emancipationists. Some of our boys are ignorant and cruel."

Emery reeled in his hat. "Decent folk, both sides; folk suitable for tar and feathers, both sides. That is the war in a percussion cap. On slavery itself, well . . . sometimes you go down a road a spell before you find it's not the one you want to be on. At which time, a course correction is called for, only we kept on. This particular course correction came from the North. I hope you all don't get uppity about it." He winged the hat and ringered the stump again. He tried to reel it in, but it snagged. "Is all off your chest?"

"As I feel mostly relieved, I guess we can be quit of that topic. Yet there is one thing more."

"Go on," said Emery, patiently tugging the line.

"On June 28, I was due to muster out—the day after Kennesaw." Emery stopped pulling the line.

Lew forced a smile. "There's a kick in the teeth, hey? Did my three years, all set to go home, and now this. Colonel Ford didn't even tempt me with a reenlistment bounty. He was a Penn boy, too.

He knew I did my part." He picked up a twig and dug at the ground. "I miss my children, Emery. Miss my farm, my dogs. And I miss Carrie like . . ." He fell silent. He broke the twig into little pieces. "I'm a farmer. I'm not a warrior. I never figured on fighting a war in my lifetime. Never thought I'd miss three years of my children's growing up. And that is all, Emery. That is everything."

After some time, Emery pulled the hat line again. "You'll get home, Lew. This war won't last forever. And what about prisoner exchange? Always chance for exchange. You hang on to that."

Lew scattered the broken twig pieces and sat back against the tree. He looked up at the leaves.

The day was sulfurous hot, but under this tree, next to this wood-pile, it was nearly pleasant. It felt good to rest after one miserable conveyance on the rails after another.

"I have to tell you that Northern Negroes are different from Southern Negroes," Lew said. "I found this out a few months ago when on campaign in Tennessee. It's the singing. A group of 'em were following camp. One of 'em led off in song, then the rest joined in chorus, and I tell you, though I couldn't understand half the words, yet I was drawn into that song and felt of it. Felt where it came from, and where it was going. All of us quieted down to hear it, and when it ended, felt like the sun went down and left the sky a thing of beauty. All was sad and quiet and good. Sure wish I could hear that again. I think the Northern Negroes would learn something from the Southern, when this is all done."

Emery held up his hand.

"Is that a religious affirmation?" Lew asked. But Emery put a finger to his lips, and motioned to the squad of men behind the dry goods store. All of them were looking at something on the other side of the woodpile. Something dangerous, by their stares. Emery slowly stood and crept over to the woodpile. He raised himself up, and peered over.

THE SENTINELS OF ANDERSONVILLE

It was a girl.

She had not yet noticed the squad of men staring at her, nor did she see Emery looking down. It was evident she was listening intently to the conversation on the other side of the woodpile, and soon it was evident that she wondered if she had been caught; then her eyes widened as she caught sight of the staring men across the way, and a blush leapt to her cheeks; and then she realized where some of them were looking, and slowly looked up.

A face full of blue eyes framed by dark hair and bonnet gazed up into Emery's. His first thought was to bless her out for eaves-dropping, but no one could take up with a face like that. Lovely cheeks, lovely lips, and eyes gone slightly wild with what Emery took to be fear, and fear in a woman got his gourd. The entire effect melted his perturbation like butter in the sun.

"How do," he nodded.

She nodded back.

He touched his forehead since he'd not reeled in his hat. "Corporal Emery Jones, 22nd Alabama Volunteers, Company C. Appreciate it if you keep quiet on anything you may have heard, ma'am."

She nodded.

"Rather not have things go hard for me from simple mis-understandin'."

"Of—" She cleared her throat delicately. She rose, and discreetly dusted off her backside. "Of course not," she said, mighty dignified. "Besides . . . well, I do believe my thinking of Yankees may stand to be adjusted somewhat. Once I have time to consider it. It is a very new idea. You have startled me, right in the middle of this consider-ation, and I have not come to any conclusion."

She lowered her eyes, and a blush pinkened her cheeks. Emery smiled.

"Attention!" called a man who came around the corner. "You boys gather up your charges and meet Captain Wirz on the east side of the depot. He'll count 'em off into nineties, and we'll walk 'em to the pen. Any of you headin' back to Macon, check in with the provost marshal and get your passes. The rest, report to Sergeant Keppel at the stockade for reassignment to the garrison. Get going, now. Wirz don't like dalliers."

———

It was an ever-widening world for Violet Wrassey Stiles.

She sat very still at the woodpile, sorting through many heady impressions, two foremost in her mind.

First, the Rebel talked to the Yankee *wholeheartedly*, as if he were *not* a pillager, murderer, and defiler of Southern women, while the *Yankee himself* talked as if he were not. To consider a Yankee as something other than a hateful aggressor bound to brutally dominate the South was a terribly new and difficult thought. While it was perfectly acceptable to say out loud that at this point, the outcome of the war did not look good, and that General Cobb or Governor Brown might've done better than Jefferson Davis, it was another thing altogether to even *think* that the Yankees may have been a *tiny bit* (and the words *tiny bit* could not be more severe) misjudged, that the South had been *perhaps* misinformed as to the character of them *all*.

She could not bring these dizzying ideas to any sort of conclusion, so discomfortingly did they feel of treason. Yankees had done murder, and this was an indisputable truth. Many boys from Americus lay in far-off graves, and to think well of a Yankee was like killing them all over again.

The second impression was that the Confederate soldier was handsome. He'd certainly had an effect on her. Or was it *affect* . . . ?

Oddly, Dance Pickett came to mind.

And then came a different thought altogether, ousting both boys, and she looked to where the Federal men had filed away.

Papa worked at the Federal hospital at the prison. He'd forbidden her and the entire household from going near the prison, which was an easy thing to do since it was ten miles from Americus. He said it was not fitting for women to be around so many men. He said there were camp diseases.

She held very still, as if listening for something distant. Things about Papa and his volunteerism tried hard to make sense right now. *Tell your father he needs to be more careful.*

The glorious Cause, which some hateful newspapers were now calling "lost," had always seemed a little independent of Papa, which had bothered Violet—he was not as patriotic as she wished him to be, content to remain in a vexing state of even-keeled benignity. But Papa had changed in the last few months. He was quieter. His smile was quick and gone. He'd even cut off his beautiful beard, and the family had never known him without it. Lily had cried for two days.

Just before he cut it, Violet and Papa sat on the porch on a Thursday evening after he came home from the hospital. He was very tired and had closed his eyes, resting a spell before Ellen called them to supper. Violet took the chance to study him when he couldn't see her concern. How pale he was. How puffy his eyes. How—and something *moved* on his beard.

It was a single, creeping, gray-colored *vermin*. She saw another.

Horrified, she tried to flick them away without disturbing Papa, but the hideous little things stuck fast. She looked about, then went to the magnolia tree and pulled off a leaf. She crept back up the stairs, and tried to scrape one off with the leaf without rousing Papa. He did rouse, saw Violet, and followed her eyes to the vermin. He calmly pinched it from his beard and flicked it away. She pointed to the other. He took care of that one, too.

"What *are* they, Papa?" she asked, nose wrinkled.

"Why, the first was Miss Mary, and the second was her beau, come courtin'." He smiled tiredly, and patted her arm. "Not to worry." And she wondered what she should be worried about.

The next day, Papa cut off his beard.

Tell your father he needs to be more careful.

Was Papa in trouble? What trouble could come from volunteering his medical services?

She picked up the box of seashells and brought it over to the corral, where the smart black Maxwell brougham waited outside the stable to be harnessed to the smart black Maxwell horse. She put the box inside the carriage, then closed the door, tied her bonnet strings, and headed for the east side of the Andersonville depot.

4

A DIRT ROAD cut through a stand of pines and led east from the sandy bank of the depot. Two hundred and twelve weary men moved slowly through double lines of guards. Most were captured in the hard fighting northeast of Atlanta, where Sherman ground his way south, inch by bloody inch; some were transferred from other prisons close to the fighting, where Confederate authorities feared to be overrun by wild, vengeful Yankees come to set their captives free.

The men were from all over the Union. Most were native-born Americans; others were immigrants—German, Irish, Italian, French, Polish. There were a few Indians, one from a tribe in Minnesota and one from Kansas, and two black men from the 54th Massachusetts Colored Division. There were hapless sailing men from the Dutch Indies who had taken their chances supplying blockaders and gotten caught in the cross fire, arrested because they might be Union spies. There were a few Marines, some sailors. Most were army regulars, and most of those were veteran volunteers. Some were pressed, and some were bounty scags, men who would sign up in one county to collect an enlistment dole, then head for another county and do the same. The men represented every character and position in society, except those in the echelons of the rich; that sort could hire substitutes to do their fighting for them.

They were mostly farmers. They were blacksmiths and shoemakers, hatters and coopers, shopkeepers, sheriffs, and barbers. They were teachers, lawyers, printers, and daguerreotypists; groomsmen, carpenters, barkeeps. Most were young, and of those, the average age was twenty-one. The oldest in this group was forty-seven, a brawny blacksmith from Iowa.

A man of smallish build rode alongside the men on a gray mare. He wore a gray cap and a short gray coat. His hair, beard, and eyes were black. He was from Switzerland, and had immigrated in 1849. His name was Captain Henry Wirz.

"Pye Gott, if you tam Yankees don't tay in dem ranks—no rations!" He swung his revolver about in a menacing fashion. "Tay in dem ranks, you no good . . ." and off he went in a flourish of profanity.

A few looks of mild surprise went his way, and a few veteran campaigners shook their heads; they were quick to sum up different sorts of leadership, and this ranting captain who had nothing to rant about—who would fall out of rank while sandwiched between armed guards?—would likely shake down to be the punitive, nit-piddly sort, the kind to set you on edge for future or imagined offenses just because he could. Some men could lead with few words, and others couldn't lead with many.

Lew Gann had seen his type on both sides of the line. A man like that in a position of power was unpleasant at best, and dangerous at worst.

"You dere!" Wirz roared, and spurred the gray mare ahead.

"Welcome to Andersonville," Emery quipped. He walked

alongside Lew in a line of guards. "I'd stay on that fellow's good side, if I were you."

"He don't have a good side," the guard ahead of Emery said over his shoulder.

"Who, Wirz?" snorted the guard behind. "I'll see his good side on a cool day in hell. Which, sad to say, is where you boys is headed."

"Don't drink the water," the guard in front advised. "Not from the stream. Only as a last resort, and only on the west side where it flows into the stockade."

"He's comin' back, Drover."

"Head for high ground—it's better there. Do *not* go for the water under the deadline. Ain't worth the risk. Stay out of the—"

"Drover."

"God be with ya, boys."

Lew and Emery exchanged a glance.

"What is that smell?" a man next to Lew asked. "Judas! Smells like an open sewer in New York City."

The guards were silent. Wirz trotted up.

———

Violet waited until most of the men had gone through the pines and then followed. She was careful to keep a good distance between herself and the end of the line. No one noticed her.

Where was the hospital located? Was it inside the stockade?

"Hello, Papa! Why, I happened to be in Andersonville, picking up my seashells, and . . . and you will kill me where I stand." Maybe she could tell the truth. "The truth is, I wanted to see where you work. You said we couldn't go near the prison, but you didn't say anything about the hospital—and you will still kill me dead."

Papa, I want to know why you look the way you do. I want to know why you and Mother have hushed conversations that end with

Mother angry or crying. I want to know why the guards aren't supposed to talk to us about their jobs. I want to know why the light has gone out of your eyes.

I'm not a child anymore. I lost a fiancé in this horrible war, and that earns me something. I want you to talk to me, and not like the other girls. I want to know why you should be more careful, why that man was afraid for you, and why I am now, too.

The last Yankee prisoner walking in the tramped-up dust of two hundred men glanced over his shoulder, then looked again at Violet. She smiled and gave a little wave. He did not wave back.

She frowned. Perhaps he didn't deserve the smile and wave. So much for her attempt to be kind on behalf of the one good Yankee named Lew. She'd tried to spy the good one in line, but she had only seen his back when he and Emery Jones left to be counted into groups; other than a limp, she wasn't sure she'd know him.

"You tay in dem ranks, you no-good dirty . . ." and from this far back Violet heard such a violent outpour of cursing, her steps slowed in shock. Half those words she'd never heard. Half she had, but never in this profusion.

It was that Captain Wirz. She had stood around the corner of the commissary building when the men were counted into groups of ninety. He then selected a sergeant out of each group to take charge of that group for roll call and rations—and all the while, through the counting, the instructions, the choosing of the sergeants, came a constant flow of vitriolic words. Even the Yankees, who were likely well acquainted with and perhaps even the inventors of such profanity, seemed surprised.

On behalf of the hosting nation, she was piqued with Wirz. He ought to show a better example of Southern graciousness than that. These aggressors needed to know what sort of decent folk they had trespassed upon. Once they found out, they might repent and go back home. What a thought! And then things could go back to when they were lovely and normal.

The one good Yankee she had seen gave her hope. It was the first real hope she'd felt in a long time, and wasn't it strange to come from such an unexpected source. She realized at this moment how downtrodden her spirits had been. When Papa was unhappy, she was unhappy.

She put her hand to her nose. What an *awful* stench! Was it like this every day? And Dance had to put up with it?

———

Dance jumped down from the ladder and lost sight of Violet. He couldn't see past the slowly moving group of men. They were now crossing the footbridge over Stockade Branch, and when the dirt road came to a T, the group would swing to their left.

Many people came and went around the stockade. Violet would not get much notice unless she came right up to the north gate. It was heavily guarded with double doors, and she'd not get in. From there the prisoners entered a holding pen, and once they were all inside, the north gate door would lock and the final entrance to the stockade would open. It wasn't the north gate that worried him.

On her right, when the road came to the T, she'd see the dead house, with the dead being loaded even now, and past it she'd see the sick, waiting in groups outside the south gate for an opening at the hospital. The dead and the sick were two things Violet Stiles must not see, for then she would see Andersonville, and Dance would lose her.

He started for the oncoming men with long strides. He couldn't run, he couldn't risk the attention.

Violet, why? Why now?

Volume Eight came before his eyes, and he knew it was his fault.

"You remain a mystery to me, Mr. Pickett," Violet had said at the dinner table. "A man of your education, your family? You could have gotten an early post to any regiment you chose, especially if your father is friends with the governor. Everyone knows Joe Brown is loyal to his friends. Yet you are content to serve guard duty when I know you have it in you for something more. You have no desire to distinguish yourself for the Cause. I find it selfish."

"I am far more than selfish, Miss Stiles: I am an infidel. I don't believe in the Cause."

"Oh, I suppose that puts you in fashion. Is that a university sentiment?"

"It is a Dance Weld Pickett sentiment."

"What good is all that learning if you don't have a patriotic bone in your body? Are you not a Southerner? Are you not a Georgian?"

"I'll tell you what I do believe: This war has rescued you and your kind from boredom."

"Me and my kind. What is your meaning, Mr. Pickett?"

"You'd be lost without your little knitting brigades. Your letter-writing campaigns. All for the Cause. All for our boys. You and your kind sicken me."

"*You* sicken *me*!"

"Why, Miss Stiles. Such lovely color in those cheeks. Temper does you proud."

"Why do you—? All I want to do is help! All I want to do is my duty!"

"I've seen your sort of duty."

And this is when Dance should have stopped. But he kept on, because he was angry, because Violet was so willfully blind just like everyone else. He could not bear the thought that maybe she really was just like everyone else.

"I saw women just like you visit their 'duty' upon wounded

soldiers in Richmond." His tone went mocking and girlish. "'Gracious, Mary, look at this disgusting wound—oh, the horrid smell!' 'Oh, look at that one, Emma! He'll lose his leg for sure! Who will marry him then?' And that boy had to lie there and take what was visited upon him—determined charity from genteel women who wouldn't *touch* him with gloves on! They did nothing real! Nothing that mattered! They went just so they could say to their friends, 'I did my duty. I visited the sick, like visiting Jesus himself. Pin me a badge, right here!' Yes, you sicken me with your 'duty.' All of Americus sickens me. Such a fine sermon that preacher gave this morning, don't you think? On the Good Samaritan? Everyone amening the man? What a joke. The Good Samaritan. Of all things he should choose to preach on. Never saw such a collection of hypocrites in my life. Americus is one great *cesspool* of hypocrisy!" He banged the table. "*Maybe* I'd change my mind if even *one* of them—"

He saw Posey's face first. He saw Mrs. Stiles next, whose eyes were lowered. Dr. Stiles, whose face had gone stiff. The entire table had gone silent.

He noticed the empty decanter. It had only musty sediment left at the bottom.

"Mercy. Why . . . I've gone and had three glassfuls."

"Four," Posey said, her voice small.

Next to Mrs. Stiles sat the preacher's wife. And on the other side of Dr. Stiles was the preacher. He never dreamed anyone would hear the conversation at the other end of the table, not above cutlery and chatter and children.

He didn't care about the preacher or his wife. He didn't care about anyone in that room more than he cared about Dr. Stiles. Not a trace of reproach in that face. Just heaviness.

A flush of shame swept over him.

"Sir . . ."

"What is wrong with Americus, Dance?" Posey asked, stricken.

"Nothing, Posey. Sir, I'm—"

"I like Americus right fine. Don't you?"

He couldn't lie to Posey, not looking in her eyes.

"No, little girl. Mostly I don't. Most of it is uglier than . . . the worst things I've seen. But this part of Americus, right here where I'm at—this is the best part. Do you know how much I love coming here? Do you know I wait for it all week long, and start waiting the minute I leave that door? It is the best place on earth, Posey girl. Best place I've ever been."

Posey slid off her chair and crept into Dance's lap.

She wrapped her arms around his neck, and rested her chin on his shoulder. He froze.

"Have you had a bad week, Dance?" she asked softly.

All the air went out of him.

The faces came before him. They were before him every waking moment, and never left his dreams.

He prayed to God not to do something exceedingly stupid.

He whispered, "Pretty bad, Posey girl," then gently lifted her off his lap and into Violet's, folded his napkin, and left.

The next time he showed up at the Stiles house for Sunday dinner, it was long over, and he was stone drunk.

She was here because of him. He had provoked her. He had dropped hints all along because he wanted her to know. He wanted her to see. What was in him that wanted her to see and to know *this*? How perverse! How cruel and mean and past the worst thing he'd done because the truth was, he was getting back at her. Getting back at all of Americus. He wanted her to come and see so she would be as helpless as he, so she would meet her match and be brought down, and he had wanted to see her face when it happened.

Dr. Stiles would not have fought so hard to protect her unless he was right about her, and Dance was wrong.

He had to get to her before she saw. He couldn't run. He ran.

———

The dead house was made of pine boughs, and gave dead men more shelter outside the stockade than the living had inside.

Every morning, anyone detailed for dead duty carried out corpses by stretcher from the stockade or from the hospital and took them to the dead house. They piled the bodies into the pine-bough structure until there was no more room, and then they piled them outside. There the bodies would wait until the wagon came to move them out, sometimes not until the next morning. When the wagon came, the dead-duty men loaded it up, and when it was full, a full load being twenty or so, off it went to be met by the boys on burial detail in the graveyard for Federal prisoners, a good spell north of the stockade.

A major had ordered six ounces of whiskey every evening to anyone on dead duty. Most men had seen dead bodies before they came to Andersonville. But none had seen them like this.

"I think this is Mosquito Joe," said one of the stretcher bearers, blotting sweat from his face with his sleeve. "Remember him? Used to sit by the letter box all day."

"Don't look like him," said the other, after a squint.

"None of us look like us," the first muttered.

"Here comes more of our boys. Wonder if Sherman's taken Atlanta yet."

———

Rolling smoke came from one of the buildings on the hill on Lew's right. The Star Fort, a guard called it. It had some cannon trained on the stockade, while others faced out. Wirz's headquarters was up there.

Past the fort was a collection of tents, likely the quarters of Johnny Reb guards. A Rebel flag flew at the Star Fort. It struck Lew how few times he'd actually seen the Rebel flag since being in the South. He missed the Stars and Stripes like he missed a home-cooked meal.

The closer they came to the stockade, what sounded like a distant drone of bees rose to the sound of the common habitation of thousands. For a man who liked the habitation of trees and land, it was not pleasant. He had never been locked up before. Confined places put a sweat on his neck.

Nerve yourself, Gann, Lew told himself. What's a little incarceration to seeing her face again?

Later, Lew wondered why he'd had no premonition. It vexed him some that his powers of discernment were asleep that day, unless the things outside the stockade were premonition enough.

Two men loaded a wagon with fence rails, near a woodhouse draped in pine boughs. Some of the rails came apart before they were loaded, and the men bent and picked up the pieces and tossed them into the wagon. Dry rot, likely. This climate played merry hob on wood. Past the woodhouse, he could see a collection of at least a hundred men. Some rested against the palisade wall near the gate, some lay down flat. Even from here, some fifty yards away, he could see the men were very sick. A few others, presumably doctors, moved among them, assessing conditions, directing orderlies.

Poor devils. It wasn't bad enough they had to be incarcerated, they had to endure—

"Emery," Lew breathed. "Those aren't fence rails."

"What am I seeing?" a soldier said in horrified disbelief. "Are those—men? Are those our boys?"

"What in the name . . . ?"

"It's all true," someone whispered. "All we heard was true. God save us."

"Keep up your courage, boys," Drover said.

"What kind of place is this?" Lew whispered, and fear ran down his muscles like water poured. "Emery?"

But Emery didn't answer. Lew figured he had come to the same conclusion. They were not fence rails. They were, in different stages of mortification, corpses.

The soldiers had seen bodies after battle, but those bodies were clothed, and filled out the clothing. They had seen bodies laid out in lines for burial, long, heartbreaking lines, but the burial that awaited these blighted forms must be as ignominious as their deaths and their current handling.

Most of these bodies dried up of life were skeletal, some appendages grossly disfigured by bloating—if the appendages were there at all; many of the corpses lacked arms or legs, sometimes both, and some bodies came apart while being transferred to the wagon. Ghastly, staring faces had wide-open mouths, where souls had finally escaped, revealing blackened gums grotesquely swollen, studded with few teeth. Flies swarmed the dead, and in many bodies, maggots showed white in eyes and noses and mouths, in amputation wounds, in multitudinous sores.

There were not a few of these corpses in and about the pine-bough structure. There were over a hundred, all of them in various forms of the same condition. Every one of them a Union boy. Every one a beloved son, or brother, or husband, or father.

"I don't wanna die like that," a man quavered. "Someone shoot me first!"

"You'll have your chance for that, Billy Yank," one of the guards taunted. "It's called the deadline. You jist give 'er a try."

"Close your mouth," Drover snapped.

"Simon, if I go like that," a young man earnestly entreated his friend, "don't tell my mama."

The lines of the marching men slowly bent left at the T, every man among them staring at the grim sight as they passed.

"You tam Yankees! Tay in rank! Close up, dere—back in line!"

A Confederate guard rushed past, likely on his way to the privy. Likely gone a little mad, too, for Lew heard him say, "Violet! Violet, where are you?"

———

The innocent world of Violet Stiles came to a close.

She had seen the men gathered at the south gate, saw from a distance they were sick, knew her father might be among them, and headed there directly instead of following the prisoners.

If not there, Papa would be in the hospital. The hospital must be on the other side of the great, long fortress. She saw only a few buildings on the hill, with a few cannons pointed at the stockade. She frowned. That wasn't a very friendly way to treat their guests, and guests, however Yankee they were, is *what* they were, just temporary visitors. She determined *this* was how she'd think of the prisoners, on behalf of the one good Yankee. It wasn't a particularly new thought; Hettie Dixon, Mother's oldest and fiercest friend, had "got hold" of the Scripture that spoke of prisoners, and sought to memorize it upon the Knitting Brigade. While Violet had felt it was a trifle over-righteous because they were Yankees and the Scripture did not seem to apply to Yankees, she now decided—

Violet stopped. She didn't know what she was seeing.

She was close to them now, those at the gate, but did not know what she was seeing. Her mind could not close upon anything familiar, could not affix the sights to comprehension.

Her eyes fell at last upon a long gray pile of sticks some ten feet away, and she determined to stay with these sticks until they made sense. The sticks were moving somehow, moving while still, and bit by bit it crept into her consciousness that vermin covered the sticks so completely they were like an animated garment. Bit by bit it crept into her consciousness that the sticks were a man, and the man was living. Bit by bit, she comprehended dull blue eyes in a shrunken face.

The eyes were glazed with misery. Violet saw down into a soul where the man lay at bottom, caught fast in suffering. He was there, he was trapped, and he was alone.

She could not move.

He saw her. Something in the blue eyes responded. Something answered at the bottom of the well. A light came. He tried to open his mouth, like a dying fish on a riverbank. He tried to speak with gray, cracked lips. He tried to lift his head, scattering flies in the attempt, but it proved too much. His fingers twitched, and he moved his hand toward her.

Violet put out her hand and started for him.

"Violet, no!"

Someone pulled her back. She pushed him away, and continued for the man, hand outstretched.

"Violet, you can't be here!"

The man waited for human touch. It was all he needed, more than food or medicines, for he was long past that. All he needed was for someone to know he was there. More forcefully, she shoved away whatever kept her back.

"Oh, Violet! Violet!"

Someone picked her up.

"No, no . . ." Frantic, she fought to get back to him, but she was caught in a tide that bore her away. She twisted and caught a last glimpse into the blue-eyed well.

The hand dropped, the light extinguished, and the dull glaze returned.

———

Foreboding filled Emery. What he had witnessed was not the outcome of war. Something far more insidious was at work. Those poor wretches had died not of decent battle wounds, but of starvation. Most had signs of fearsome disease. Many were naked, and any clothing was in shreds.

They had whittled away to nothing.

How could this be?

And if those were the dead, what did the living look like?

Heavy gates swung open on iron hinges. The prisoners began to file into the holding pen.

Emery held Lew back long enough to unsling his haversack and shove it into Lew's hands. He took it without protest. Emery tried to say good-bye, but words failed.

"Stop looking like that," Lew snapped. "Whatever is on the other side of that gate is not you, and therefore is not the South. And . . . well, I'm not laying down for anything, but if you make it up to Ezra and I am not there, do me a favor. Learn the name of Little Mite. Then one of us will know."

"Get moving!" a guard shouted at Lew.

"I don't want to shake hands lest things go badly for you. Take care of yourself, Emery Jones." A quick smile, and Lew was gone.

The heavy gates closed, and a guard turned the iron key. He signaled to the man in the sentry box, who signaled to someone in the holding pen.

Emery stood motionless, staring at the massive wooden doors.

Then he raced to the ladder of the nearest sentry box and went up as fast as he could. He came out to a platform and hurried to the rail overlooking the pen.

The sight took his breath, and he grasped the rail for the momentary vertigo.

A milling gray mass of thousands upon thousands opened to his eyes. In some places they stood so close that not an armspan separated them. There were a few tents spotted throughout, but no barracks. At the bottom of two slightly inclined opposing banks, a brown, slowly moving stream stretched across the stockade from east to west. It was less populated near this stream; surely from this area rose the putrid smell that was now past description.

The men were filthy, ragged, and thin, many nearly skeletal, many so diseased and broken down that even some fifty feet away from the nearest soul, Emery could tell it was not long before they would join their comrades outside in the sick group—or in the dead. Many walked slowly, like old men, and so they appeared, yet the average age could not be above twenty-five.

He couldn't even conjure an oath. It was past crying out with his mouth.

Movement down left caught his eye. Men began to pour out of the holding pen.

There seemed to be an invisible line between the new prisoners and the longtime inhabitants of Andersonville. They sized each other up until someone broke the momentary lull with a joke or a greeting. Soon the new-timers began to move forward, and were surrounded by the old-timers who called for news of the war, or asked for goods to trade, or offered to show them around and tell them the way of things.

"Lew!"

Lew looked up, put his hand against the sun, but couldn't locate Emery. Maybe he was unsure his name had been called at all.

Emery leaned to bellow once more, but a grizzled middle-aged guard laid a hand on his shoulder. "You don't wanna make his countrymen wonder if he's a traitor."

"He's no traitor. He's my friend." Emery's throat all but closed.

"Sorry to hear it, son."

He watched until Lew stepped off into the milling gray mass and disappeared.

5

HER FACE WAS WET. Her hair was damp with tears. He couldn't leave
her. If he moved, she clutched his sleeve.

"Violet," Dance whispered. "I need to get your father. You stay
right here. You'll be all right."

They were a short distance from the stockade under some pine
trees.

"I have to get back to my post." He didn't care about his post. He
didn't care what they did to him.

His arm was tightly about her, and she huddled close. If he loosened his grip, she clutched closer. They sat next to each other on the
pine-needle ground, and it was getting uncomfortable. But he didn't
care. He could hold her all day, shielding her from the sight of those
walls.

"Violet, I'm sorry," he whispered. He tenderly smoothed dark
mussed hair, tried awkwardly to tuck it under her bonnet and
straighten things. "Sorry you had to see such things. The man you
saw will be gone soon. I've gotten so I can just about time it. Won't
be long, Violet. He's not gonna suffer anymore."

"What's wrong with her, Pickett?"

Dance looked up. It was Sergeant Keppel. He peered down at Violet, concern mingled with dissatisfaction. He didn't like surprises, and a girl alone on the grounds was a surprise.

"She took a turn."

"Must be the heat. Who is she? What's she doing here?"

"She's a—cousin. Daughter of Dr. Stiles. He works in the—"

"I know who he is. Does she have a pass?"

"No, sir."

"Then get her out of here."

"Yes, sir." He tried to stand, but Violet clung fiercely.

The sergeant bent to inspect her flushed face. "She don't look so good." He looked about. "You there! Yes, you—come over here. What's your name, son?"

"Emery Jones, sir. Corporal, 22nd Alabama."

"What are you doing, wandering around?"

"Just got here. Delivered a prisoner."

"Headin' back to Macon?"

"No, sir." The corporal looked back at the stockade. "No, I am not."

"I'm Keppel. You're to report to me. This girl's taken with the heat. Help that boy get her home."

"I should let her father know—" Dance began.

"I'll inform the doctor. You don't bother him. He's got a horse and buggy in town. Have Swedberg hitch 'em up and get her on home. Stop at the depot and get her some water."

"Yes, sir."

"I'll get someone to take your place. Get along, boys. Get her that water, first thing. Jones, report back to me this evening, I'll get you assigned." He looked once more into Violet's face. "You just take good care of her. That there's the daughter of Dr. Stiles." His voice had the tone of someone who had taken off his hat.

———

They were halfway to Americus, an hour on the road, before it occurred to Dance to introduce himself to the corporal from Alabama. Neither had spoken much, and Violet had not spoken at all. The blond fellow drove, perched in the seat in front. He seemed as moodily preoccupied as Dance. It was a good thing Keppel had sent him along. Dance could not have managed both Violet and the horse.

All the way to the train station for water, and then to the corral for the buggy, Violet clung to Dance as if letting go meant falling off a cliff. Her shoulder just fit under his arm, and both arms circled his waist. It made for awkward walking. Once situated in the back of the carriage, she clutched his arm.

He knew what this clinging was; all had come apart at the seams, and she ran for safety like a deer from a forest fire, found it in the only familiar place around.

You are always certain of a dark motive in others, she had once accused him, and she was right. All this time he'd thought she knew how bad things were and had been playing a game of pretty ignorance. How wrong he'd been. The day he made Violet mad, he thought he had gotten to her core; now he knew he had not seen it until this day.

Sitting beside Violet, even in her disheveled, staring state, he knew things were right for the first time in a very long time. Right for her and right for him. For Violet was genuine. And if the ways and means committee that constituted a genuine Violet was too drum-banging and earnest for his taste, it didn't matter. The anvil on his chest was gone, because she knew the truth of the prison, and he knew the truth of her.

"I'm Dance Pickett," he said to the man with the reins. "And no, I am not."

"You're not what?"

55

"Related to George." People were forever wondering, if not asking outright, whether he was related to the general who had led the ill-fated Pickett's Charge at the Battle of Gettysburg.

"Emery Jones, 22nd Alabama Volunteers."

"Georgia militia. Feel free to despise me." The army regulars hated the militia, especially the volunteers. Joe Brown's pets, they called militiamen. If that was the case, being the son of J. W. Pickett made Dance his lapdog.

"I don't despise you," Emery said absently. "I don't know you yet."

He checked Violet, because her grip had loosened. The carriage, an expensive affair which had splendid suspension, swayed gently on the road. That and the rhythmic clop of the horse's hooves and the darkened interior had put her almost to sleep.

"What happened there?" Emery asked, his voice hollow. "That ain't us."

"It's some of us."

"The fellow I was escorting, I told him it wasn't true, all the rumors about Andersonville. It made a liar out of me."

"You weren't even in the pen. That'll make Beelzebub out of you."

Emery wore a red-checked shirt tucked into brown trousers. His slouch hat sat back on his head. Blond hair nearly tipped his shoulders. His feet rested on the board, and his boots were worn through in places. All of him stood in need of laundering, like any soldier. He was maybe Dance's age, maybe younger. What set him apart from other soldiers was the thoughtfulness on his face.

"How long you been there?" Emery said.

"Mid-March."

"What happened to that place? Moreover, how do you stand it?"

"Listen, Alabama: I don't want to talk about it because you really don't care. All you regulars do is see how fast you can get reassigned, and that is your singlemost distinct and enviable advantage over militia. So don't ask me how I can stand it, because you won't be around long enough to see."

Emery didn't answer, and Dance grimaced. He could already see this man wasn't like the others. The worst would say the Yankees were getting what they deserved. The best said nothing at all. Along comes this fellow, who asks questions. Who did that? No one.

Dance toyed with the end of Violet's bonnet string.

"The three *W*'s. War, Winder, and Wirz. That's what happened to Andersonville."

"Spread that on the table for me."

Dance studied him. "What sort of regular are you?"

"An irregular one."

"You a Yankee spy?"

"Nope."

"All right then. Here is what happened to Andersonville. First, war. This one has dragged on too long and at this point our resources are played out. We are hard-pressed to feed our own troops, much less our prisoners. Second, Winder. Some idiot made him a general and put him in charge of Andersonville. Third, General Winder appointed Captain Wirz. While Wirz is not a particularly cruel man, he is not a good one either. And Andersonville did not need a good man. It needed a great one."

"You've had time to think on this."

"No one has asked me this. I have saved up for just such an occasion. I will now present my summation. Andersonville is the way it is because of people like Wirz and me, people faced with problems they do not know how to fix. People turned back at every try because of a stupefying governmental bureaucracy as filthy as the inside of that stockade. Lastly, and this drives it home: Andersonville is the way it is because of the town we are heading for: Americus. They are indifferent. Men die, and Americus sleeps."

"Reckon someone better wake 'em up, and that right quick."

"You wanna stir up the devil, have at it."

"The devil ain't in Americus. He's back at that pen."

"An emphatic 'No, he isn't' to that. He's in that town, root and tree, and they spread themselves beneath his bounteous shade."

Emery's lip rose in disgust. "You owning their inaction to the devil?"

"Emphatically not."

"Good. 'Cause I've heard that tack, and them as do are cowards."

"I am merely pointing out that his crowning achievement is a blindfold. Only the devil could blind good people to such evil."

Emery considered it, and shook his head. "I'd say it's trickin' them into thinkin' they can't take it off."

Dance fell back on the luxurious leather seat. He stared at the quilted ceiling. "This is the first decent conversation I have had since my posting."

"Glad to accommodate. You have a philosophic bent, just like the man I turned in. Wish with all my heart I hadn't done that. Wish I'd turned him loose."

"You were just doing your duty."

"How many men have died, people just doing their duty?"

Dance's breath caught. "Thousands."

Emery looked at him. He turned back to the road, face grim. "I was bound by oath to deliver him. What is better? Keep an oath, or save a life?"

"I can't answer that."

"Neither can I."

"I can't answer anything these days."

They drove for some time.

"Well, I'm gonna get him out."

He said it as easy as "Pass the peas."

"Is that so. Two guards were arrested last month for trying the same."

"I expect they were militia."

"Another time, I'd laugh. What happened to keeping your oath?"

"Kept the first. That's done with. Made another, back when we passed under that water oak. Hickory Shearer says that's the best time to make one."

"Suit yourself. It's your lily-white neck, not mine. One of those guards was hanged." Dance closed his eyes. "And in case you think to, don't ask me for information about the prison." He settled to a doze. Violet's hand had slipped from his arm; he put it back and held it there.

———

It was a comfortable house with a comfortable porch, clapboards painted gray, all else trimmed in white. Dr. Stiles had put up an iron rail next to the steps for Grandma Wrassey, who passed in '61. His wife sometimes hung herbs to dry from the rail when other places were taken. Little bundles hung there now, tied by colorful scraps of yarn.

The sun was beginning to set. It came through the magnolia and set some of the gray clapboards to green-gold. A bird lighted on an herb bundle, pecked first at the yarn, pecked at the drying herbs, eyed the four people on the porch, and flew away.

Violet's account of how she came to be at Andersonville ended with the very encounter Dr. Stiles had fought to prevent.

She picked up a handful of seashells and let them drain into her lap. "Now I know why you smell of turpentine when you come home."

When the prison had first opened and hospital supplies had not yet arrived from Richmond, Dr. Stiles collected what he could from home, and his family helped. They tore old sheets into strips and rolled bandages. They scraped lint from old linen, for packing wounds. But time went on, and supply never met the need. When scurvy began to present in late April, they collected and dried herbs as pathetic substitutes for proper antiscorbutics. But there was no abatement of prisoners daily pouring into the stockade, and the worse the conditions became with the unthinkable concentration of men, the more Dr. Stiles withdrew his family from the tentacled need of Andersonville.

He did it in a calculated fashion. He began to collect less, speak of it less, and then collected nothing, and spoke not at all. The family was so occupied in other war efforts, this one dropped off and was all but forgotten.

"Turpentine is all we have for some wounds."

"You said it was for varnishing the hospital barracks."

"I let you believe so. There are no barracks." He wearily rubbed his forehead. "Where is your mother? Where is everyone?"

"Grandpa Wrassey's. Liberty calved today."

"Violet, it wasn't as bad in the beginning."

"There was a beginning to that—? Such a place could only have its origin in hell."

And Dr. Stiles saw the first good sign since he arrived: a flush of color replaced the white.

She finally looked up from the seashells. "The guards, Papa . . ."

"They are informed before they come for dinner to never speak of the stockade."

"By you, or by that awful Captain Wirz?"

"By me."

She nodded with the air of bitter understanding coming to one long deceived. He took her hand from the seashells and held it in both of his.

He had a ten-mile carriage ride to leave behind all he saw, and bring none of its infamy to his doorstep. Any guest guard was forewarned that if he spoke a word of his vocation, he would never dine with the Stiles family again. Not upon his family, not on his bevy of precious innocents, would he allow a single word to conjure a single image. His family knew things were bad there, the whole town of Americus did; but unless they saw it, unless anyone saw it, they knew nothing.

She slipped her hand away.

"A man said you were in trouble, Papa."

"What man?"

"At the depot. A big . . . warehouse. He said for you to be more careful. What could he mean?"

"Why did you defy me, child?" Dr. Stiles said softly. "I left as soon as Captain Wirz sent for me. He was kind enough to—"

"You would have me . . . occupied in . . . *seashells*." Her breath came quicker. "In *buttons*." She snatched a handful of seashells and flung it away. Some pinged off the iron rail, some set the bundles to swaying. "What a coward you must think me."

"There is nothing of the coward about you. And there is nothing you can do, Violet."

"But you do it!" She jumped to her feet, scattering seashells to the gray clapboards.

"Indeed I have never felt more worthless, and I am a doctor. But I can't do much without medicine and bandages and good food."

"We could hold another benefit! We could—"

"My darling, this town is benefited out. And what is more, it won't have it. Not for them."

A cry of impotent rage, and she pressed her fists against her eyes.

"Come sit with me, my darling. Tell me what you saw," Dr. Stiles said, knowing it was better to draw out infection than leave it be.

"I saw a man," she said behind the fists. "He was lying on the ground. He held out his hand, and I did not go to him. Worst thing I've ever done."

Dance raised his head at this. He looked as if he would say something, but said nothing.

"Tell me what you saw," Dr. Stiles said gently.

"Some had their arms and legs drawn up, as if they were in a frozen fit," Violet said behind the fists.

"A manifestation of scurvy," Dr. Stiles said.

"Some crawled on hands and knees, their legs were so swollen."

"Edema, from scurvy."

"Some of their faces were black."

"That's from the pine smoke, early on when they were issued wood rations," said Dance, his voice low and gentle to accommodate the mood on the porch. Violet lowered her fists to look at him. "Those are the men who have been around longest."

Such a many-sided boy, this Dance Pickett, son of his wife's cousin. He could command a table sober or inebriated. He could make Violet fume one moment and laugh the next. Though his classes were on hold because of the war, Dance was enrolled at the University of Georgia to study patent law; yet over the past few months they had known him, he had displayed an acumen of the times that Dr. Stiles had seldom seen in his contemporaries. Dr. Stiles wondered if this boy could not hold his own in Congress one day.

It was no wonder that Andersonville affected him the way that it did, those occasions of drunkenness and temper—Dance saw it entirely. He saw it every day.

"Why don't they clean the black off?" Violet asked. She slipped back into her chair.

"No soap. No clean water. Some use the sand to scrub, but even that is filthy. If it doesn't have excrement in it, it has fleas or lice or maggots. They try to keep clean, but some have just given up."

Violet looked at her hands in her lap. "Is it a hog sty in there, Papa?"

"It's not fit for hogs," Dance murmured.

"My pass extends only to the Federal hospital. I've not yet seen into it."

"Papa, they have sores. Terrible sores. They were . . ."

Likely filled with maggots. Dr. Stiles rubbed his forehead. "Gangrene," he said heavily. "It is prevalent."

She raised her eyes to her father's, and his heart missed a beat. Did he know this girl? This was a new expression. He'd not seen it when she lost her fiancé, or when her beloved Grandma Wrassey died.

"Have I lost you?" Dr. Stiles wondered, a catch in his voice. Was this his little girl? Had these beautiful eyes truly looked upon such wretchedness? "I never wanted you to see. In that day I thought I'd die."

"Oh, Papa." Violet took his hand.

Keep it together, Stiles, he told himself. "Parents have a hard time, letting their children see. It is an awful world, Violet girl."

"Children have a hard time, too, letting their parents." She kissed his fingers, and held them tight. She gave a small smile. "But you are here yet, and I am too. What will we do to help them, Papa?"

"Violet—" he began, shaking his head.

"What is the town doing to help those boys?" said Emery Jones, the new guard. Dr. Stiles had learned no more than his name.

"Nothing, Alabama," Dance said, as if thrice repeating himself.

"Very little," Dr. Stiles admitted.

"Why not?" Emery said, looking from one to the other.

Dr. Stiles sighed. "Mr. Jones, that is a difficult question to answer. It will take more than a porch conversation, and my family is coming back soon. You will have had to live here to understand the way of things."

"*I* live here, and I don't understand," Violet declared.

"Men are dyin'—right in this town's backyard!" said Emery.

"Son, many do not know—"

"They know, all right," Dance muttered.

"I didn't know," Violet said quietly.

"I saw a passel of civilians at the Andersonville depot," said Emery. "They were sellin' vegetables and such to anyone gettin' off the train. I bought some pecans and says to one of them, 'You from around here?' She says, 'What, this jumped-up town? Heavens no, I'm from Americus.' So how can you say, sir, this town don't know about those men?"

"Well, Alabama, there's your problem," Dance said, slapping his knee. "They are *not* men, according to General Winder. They are a species called 'Yankee,' and woe to the one who thinks he sees in them a form like unto humanity."

Emery took off his hat and rolled it between his palms. He put his finger through a hole, then clapped it back on his head. He got up and went to the rail. He leaned on it and flicked a dried bundle with his finger. It tick-tocked back and forth.

"I put a good man in there today." He gave another flick. "Lewis Gann, 12th Pennsylvania. He is a fruit farmer. Thirty-two years old. Wife named Carrie, four children."

"I liked him," Violet said. To Dance and Dr. Stiles, she said, "I overheard them at the woodpile before he went in. What was the oath you gave, Mr. Jones?"

He set the bundle to swinging again. "You are a first-rate listener."

"Now that I think of it," said Dance, interested, "why should it take an oath to escort a prisoner?"

"That's between me and him."

"But you never told him," Violet said.

"I will, one day. We're gonna meet up in Ezra. He's gonna teach me how to fruit-farm."

"If he lives, that is," said Dance. "Violet, you just save that look for Posey. I am tired of stepping around truth." He didn't quite look at Dr. Stiles. Then he softened somewhat. "I am sorry for your friend, Emery. But once he goes in there, you may as well know they only come out sick or dead. And very few of the sick survive that hellish hospital. Some have escaped by tunneling out, but most of those have been caught. Their only hope is exchange, and so far that's a ship that won't come. Until then it's just plain survival until the war ends."

"They ain't gonna have a chance for survival if they ain't properly fed. Why is that so? Never saw the like, and I've seen other prisons. They were skinnier'n apple peels."

"The South is getting worn out with need," said Dr. Stiles. "Sometimes there isn't enough to stock the commissary, sometimes it's fouled-up transportation that's the problem. . . . You are a soldier, you know about supply lines. You've known hunger."

"Not that kind of hunger. I looked on them boys and felt such shame. There's something deeply wrong there. How *many* are in there?"

"Last count I heard was about twenty-two thousand. But that was a few weeks back, and more keep coming every day."

"There's some twenty-eight thousand now," Dance said quietly.

Emery stared. "In twenty-some acres of ground?"

"Twenty-six," said Dance. "Used to be sixteen and a half. They enlarged it last month."

"Twenty-eight thousand men in twenty-six acres," Emery said in awe. "More than a thousand men to an acre. I'd not believe it lest I seen it."

"Take out the swamp around the creek, and the space between

THE SENTINELS OF ANDERSONVILLE

the deadline and the stockade wall, you've got about seven or eight feet of living space per man. At the rate they keep coming in, that will drop to six pretty quick." He hesitated, then said, "And August is the hottest month."

"I can't imagine what conditions will be like then, or how many dead," said Dr. Stiles.

"I can," said Dance.

Emery was silent. He settled to flick the herb bundle again.

"Papa," Violet said, "Mother will be here soon, and everyone else, and I have to know before I leave this porch what we will do to help them."

"Nothing *can* be done. The scope is too big. The problems of administration . . . too vast."

"Maybe for us, but not for a town. They have a right to know what's going on up there."

And Dr. Stiles felt the final push toward a confrontation he had long feared. It stood before the moldering evil that encompassed Andersonville and Americus, an evil that could not be defined. When Dr. Stiles had a difficult time explaining anything, he knew it was because something rotten entangled the details. Things should be able to be plainly discussed. There was nothing plain about Andersonville. There was something wicked in its enterprise.

Wicked? Truly, wicked?

What else could answer?

"They don't want to know," said Dr. Stiles at last. Many of those who did not want to know were his friends.

"But they do, Papa!" Her lips trembled, but she seemed resolved to take herself in hand. She drew a steadying breath. "*I* would have wanted to know. There *must* be others like me."

"Your father is right," Dance said with resignation. "You don't believe it, but it's true—they don't care. They don't want to care."

"You're wrong!" She rose and went to the rail, opposite Emery.

The Stiles home was situated at the end of Lamar Street. A quarter mile down the road was the town square. Dr. Stiles looked down that road. Some of the bitterest truth to bear about the Andersonville Prison was that Dance was right about Americus. They didn't care. They didn't want to care. And he knew his daughter. She would not believe anyone could be indifferent to suffering, because she was not.

But Dr. Stiles understood this town, and what he understood that these young people did not was losing a child. George was three when he died of pneumonia. How many Americus boys had been buried since the war began? Less than half of their bodies made it home for burial. How many funerals had they attended? Silas Runcorn's oldest boy. Judge Clayton's son, Thaddeus. The beekeeper's son.

"If we gave them a chance," said Emery, eyes on the town. He straightened. "If we got up a . . . committee. Folks in Huntsville are keen on committees."

"A society," Violet said quickly. "A society to help the Andersonville prisoners."

"We could hold ourselves an indignation meeting," Emery said, looking at each in turn. "We'll make it known that men are starving to death ten miles away."

"There are good people in this town, Papa," Violet said earnestly. "They need to be educated. Let's do that, and give them a chance to help!"

"Tell you what—all they gotta do is stand where Dance stands," said Emery. "That'll cure 'em. First they'll wanna choke whoever let the place get that way, but after that, they'll pitch in. Let 'em see for themselves, and there'll be no stoppin' 'em."

"Friends of Andersonville Prison!" Violet said. "The F.A.P.! We can hold meetings right here! We can organize! What do you think, Papa?" She began to pace. "We could put up handbills all over town.

We could put them up at the Andersonville depot! Colonel Hancock can write an editorial for the newspaper. We can send one to the *Macon Telegraph*!"

"Tell you what—you get a bunch of folks together, they'll come up with ways to get them boys food."

"Massive amounts!" Violet rejoiced. "More than *we* could ever do! Remember the biscuits Ellen and Mother used to make for the ones in the hospital? Multiply that by *thousands*, Papa!"

The light in her eyes. Would he dim it?

Only Dance understood. There he sat, silent and sullen, with folded arms and hooded eyes.

Was he wrong, laying the injunction upon this boy to never speak of the prison conditions? To bottle it up? To leave infection be?

"Most important, we gotta get people down there," said Emery. "Dance can show them."

"On Mondays, people could get into the habit of making extra biscuits," Violet said, touching one forefinger to the other. "Tuesdays, extra corn bread." She touched her middle finger. "On Wednesdays, we could go out to the farms and—"

Dance stood abruptly, shoving the chair back. He said to Emery, "We best get back." He nodded good-bye at Dr. Stiles, with a quicker nod and touch of his hat to Violet.

He was down the stairs and a few steps past when Violet cried, "Dance Pickett, you come back here!" She pounded the rail. "You *come* back here!"

He froze, standing hunched and fisted, and finally turned upon them a very dark and belligerent countenance.

"I will not get involved in this. Not even for you, Miss Stiles." A look of open hostility went to Dr. Stiles himself. "Not for anyone."

"All those figures you gave, sounds like you already are," Violet snapped.

"Those the calculations of a man who does not care?" Emery added.

"Scientific observation. You can ask your father about that. They sent some doctors to study gangrene in the Federal hospital because of the reports of such uncommon amounts. Such is the fame of Andersonville. Boiled down to a study of misery." He looked at Emery. "I never said I didn't care. But I will not host a raree-show."

"I am not *leaving* here until I know we can help! No one is leaving! Let us have some resolution!" She came to Dr. Stiles in his chair and knelt. "I will *die*, Papa, if I cannot help those wretched men. Will you not give your blessing? Is it not Christian to feed our enemies?"

"To feed these enemies is to forgive them," said Dr. Stiles. "That, my girl, this town will not do."

Dance came up the stairs two at a time. His face had cleared completely of its pugnacity. "Yes, that's it exactly! That's the truth, Violet, *that's* the answer—*don't* get this town involved! But if *you* want to help, then—"

Violet rose quickly and backed away from them. She looked from Dance to her father.

"You kept me in the dark. What *sin*!" she hissed, clutching her skirts. "And yes, I will name it so!" She pointed toward the town. "I will not have them as blind as I was! I will sin against God and those men he created if I do!" She dashed angrily at tears. "Can you not see what great wickedness it is to keep us blind? To *keep* us from helping them?"

Dance looked at Emery, and Dance's shoulders finally came down. "A blindfold is a great wickedness."

"It is time to take it off," Emery said, coming away from the rail to stand next to Violet. "We can do that. The F.A.P.—that sounds pretty good."

"Papa, I don't want to make buttons. I want to take hold the hand of a dying man. I want to let him know someone is here, on the outside of his—" she wavered, but took hold of herself—"dreadful misery. That's all he wanted to know—is someone there, and do they care?"

Dr. Stiles regarded the three. Violet and Emery looked as if one word would set them to a flurry of activity. Dance had no eagerness about him. If he had articulated his dread with nothing more than *I will not get involved*, Dr. Stiles knew why. He looked toward the town.

They would feed each other, and clothe each other, and comfort each other well. They loved their own, and loved them well. They were a fiercely loyal lot who had gone through much adversity. They came alongside loved ones and liked ones and even unliked ones to share their grief and shake fists at the North and at the sky because they loved their own. Blow after blow had rained upon the South, and now Sherman stood at Atlanta's door. Americus had suffered, and feared what it would suffer yet. But they would hold fast together, no matter what the North sought to visit upon the noble South. To them, this enemy was surely different than the enemy Jesus talked about in the Gospels, for to feed this enemy was to not love their neighbor. It was, in fact, to hate him.

Should he throw these young people to the ravenous wolves of love? For on behalf of every boy lost in Americus, the town would see these three torn apart.

And then in the middle of this dark despair, a thought came sterling clear: it wasn't up to him.

His daughter was twenty-one. He thought he could shield her from the wickedness of attrition. He found that he could not, and knew he was wrong to try. This Emery had to be her age or older. Dance was twenty-three.

"Papa? Will we help those men?"

Let them find out about this town on their own. They would raise a hand to help the enemy and would learn what Dr. Stiles had learned. Let the learning be their own, not his.

"We will help them," Dr. Stiles said heavily, and bleakness settled in.

Dance turned away.

Violet seized her father in a fierce hug, then grabbed Emery's arm and pulled him aside, talking a mile a minute.

Dr. Stiles rose and went to Dance's side at the iron rail.

"I don't know what you are about, sir."

Dr. Stiles smiled against the dread lodged deep in his heart. "I have come to love that forthrightness."

"When she sees this town for what it is, she will lose faith in humanity. What then, Dr. Stiles?"

"I don't know. But I was wrong to keep Andersonville from her. I have to let her go, Dance. It is a hard truth when you are a father."

"What will happen when she finds out they think her father is a Yankee spy?"

"Has it come to that, then?" Dr. Stiles said. He lifted his eyebrows. "It is a remarkable thing to find myself disreputable. I have so long enjoyed a good reputation. I did not know it until now."

"Has your practice dropped off?"

"It has."

"Have you lost friends?"

"I have."

"Some think you a saint, and others a traitor." He hesitated. "Those are the ones who worry me, sir."

"Me, too," said Dr. Stiles.

"I'm trying to say, you have made enemies. And now . . ." He didn't quite look at Violet.

"Dance, a few minutes ago a thought came. 'It isn't up to you,' said that thought. And while it relieves some of my burden, and calls me to take my hands away, it leaves behind a question: Have I raised her right? Have I done my best by her? I'm not sure I have. I'm not sure any parent can give a full yes to that. So I will pray that my deficiencies will be filled in by God's grace, and I will let her go. And if she . . ." He paused. "If she falls, and if she's hurt, I hope she will not be turned back."

"Mother will want to join," Violet complained, joining them at the rail. "There will be no stopping her. She will want to run things. That is why Emery and I have made you president, Dance, and just spare us your protestations—Mother respects you, and she does not respect Papa or me. You are the only way we can have her involved so that she won't take over."

"I best go in and tidy up before she comes," said Dr. Stiles. "And I expect you'll be wanted back at the garrison. Boys—thank you for taking care of my girl. I am deeply grateful." He shook their hands. "Mr. Jones, I am sure Mrs. Stiles will want to thank you herself; do come for dinner this Sunday if you can. If we have no other guests that day, it might be a good time to begin discussion of this, well, new enterprise." He kissed the top of Violet's head, and took his leave.

The three were left in a curious silence.

Dance thought about his father and Dr. Stiles. They were very different men, and the chief difference was that he could have a conversation with Dr. Stiles and not want to kill either him or himself when they were through. Father's answer to everything was to run roughshod over everyone; Dr. Stiles meant to make a man understand things. And what were those words that came out of his mouth? *I was wrong to keep Andersonville from her.* . . . ? I was *wrong*? Dance chuckled. Those words had never once passed his father's lips.

"Miss Stiles, you have shamed your gender," Dance said, leaning on the rail. "Making me president because of your mother. Such mealy manipulation."

"Dance, please, please." She put her elbows on the rail and rubbed her temples.

"Did you tell her your plan, Alabama?"

"No, I haven't. Because I have a better one." He pulled a dried stalk from an herb bundle and stuck it in his mouth. A slow and wily smile came.

"Do tell," said Dance.

"Hickory Shearer says don't use your wheelbarrow for a single stick. If you're going to the woodpile, fill it up."

"Hickory Shearer should say it plainly."

"If bustin' one Yank out of that prison should hang me . . . what'll they do if I bust 'em all?" He grinned. "Hangin' won't be good enough. They will appoint unto me such fearsome tortures as have not yet advanced upon the mind of man."

"Now this is the first interesting thing you have said since we arrived. I all but despaired you were the same man I met in that brougham."

"What is going on?" Violet said, looking up from her temple rub.

"And you, Miss Wonderful Stiles, have set up the perfect cloak for the progression of my scheme," said Emery. "The F.A.P.: Friends of Andersonville Prison. Will anyone truly ken the depths of that name?"

"Hold on a minute," Dance said slowly. "You truly intend this."

"I keep my oaths."

"I see no water oak around here."

"That magnolia answered." Emery took the straw out of his mouth, and peered at Violet and Dance. "We are Rebels, are we not? Then let us rebel against what is not us. Because that ain't us, and it never was, and only by bustin' out as many men as we can will we erase some of the shame on our heads."

His words found such resonance in Dance's heart that for a second time in a month, he feared he might do something exceedingly stupid.

Violet's mouth was open for a long time before she said, "Can we feed them on the side?"

And Dance did something exceedingly stupid.

He pulled her close, but didn't know what to do when she was there. He couldn't kiss her in front of Emery, and she might not want him to anyway, so they looked at each other for a long moment until Dance finally let go.

Violet stood on tiptoe and kissed him on the cheek.

"On Sunday we shall plan the demise of Andersonville Prison. Let us do so in such a way that all its suffering will be eradicated in totality. Good afternoon, gentlemen. Until Sunday." She curtsied and went into the house.

PART TWO

Just as the Creek Indians had considered the area their granary, Sumter and surrounding counties were known during the Civil War as "Little Egypt" or the "Egypt of the Confederacy" because of their huge harvests. How, then, could hunger at Andersonville be so severe that thousands of men died of malnutrition and related causes?

Uriah B. Harrold, a commissary for the Confederate government, reported that in the month of August he shipped to Andersonville the following supplies:

113,000 lbs. Bacon
90,000 bushels Meal
1,000 sacks Flour
10,000 lbs. Rice
131 barrels Sirup
20 barrels Whisky

These supplies alone could have alleviated the desperate need within the post and prison, and Harrold was but one of fifty commissaries supplying them. The warehouses at Albany, forty miles from Andersonville and far larger than the one at Americus, were said to be taxed by the huge stores assembled there.

—*Americus through the Years: The Story of a Georgia Town and Its People, 1832–1975* BY WILLIAM BAILEY WILLIFORD

6

WHEN THE BULLET took Lew at Gettysburg, he didn't know where he was hit, or, for a time, that he was hit. It spun him around and he fell, not of his own free will. He was aware that something bad had happened, but for a moment, didn't know what. And that is how he felt when the gate closed behind him at Andersonville.

For a few moments the incoming men hesitated at joining the prison population. They were not assigned barracks. They were supposed to stick to their detachment of ninety, and what that meant, no one was sure; the Federal sergeants assigned to the detachments seemed as unsure of immediate direction as their charges. It was strange to be cut loose after days or weeks of Rebs telling them where to go and what to do. The men at the front of the incoming group began to spread out, and Lew went forward with the rest for his first size-up of the prison and its captives.

Lew tried to get some bearings, but bearings wouldn't be had. A massive congregation of faces stared back as if he were a preacher on a pulpit and had come with something to say, faces and faces in myriad shades of dust and gray and grime and sunburn, most of those faces blank with mild interest, a few with smiles of welcome and bitterly wry commiseration.

He didn't know where to go, but he wanted out of this pulpit. He thought he heard his name and turned around to see, but sun and sound and faces confused him; so he squared himself and stepped into the crowd, doing his best to keep to its edge.

"What news, boys? Sherman taken Atlanta, yet?"

"Any o' you with the 19th Michigan Infantry? How'd old Thomas do on Hood? Lick him at Peachtree?"

"You boys step on over—you ain't gonna find a better place to trade than at Fetchner's stand. Right this way."

"Anyone with the 19th Michigan?"

"Fair trades, and double return on greenbacks. Right this way."

"Don't listen to him, boys, you steer clear of Fetchner's—bunch of sharpers and swindlers!"

"Pay no attention to that man!"

"19th Michigan?"

"That is a fine way to treat a 12th Pennsylvanian."

Lew stopped, but he didn't seem to know the fellow who stood grinning at him. When he did, it was past time to cover for his shock. "Well, you are not Harris Gill."

"It is he. Reduced."

Had he served with this man for three years to barely know him now?

Had he come to such a state in only a month?

"Thought I was rid of you, boy-o," Harris said, coming forward with his hand out. Lew took it, and Harris gripped tight. "Been lookin' for you every day, hopin' I'd never see you."

"You been here since Kennesaw?"

"Aye. Where you been?"

"Sick." He looked down at the bullet flap, a relief from Harris's distressing appearance. "Took a bullet and took some infection, but she's pretty well cleared up."

"That's good. You don't want to come in here with any weakness. It'll attack there first."

"What will?"

"Andersonville."

Harris Gill was Irish. He came as a boy with his family to America on the heels of the potato famine. He worked with his brothers at an ironmongery in Pittsburgh. His last name was McGillicuddy, but in a farsighted move he had mustered in as Gill to make roll call easier, as most of the men calling roll tended to chew names whole.

He made corporal soon after mustering in with Lew and the rest, but he soon owed the regiment fund seventeen dollars for cussing, one dollar per word. As privates were not fined, he committed an infraction to send him back to ranks (a cordial invitation to a major to kiss his backside), thus saving his paycheck in another farsighted move.

Harris Gill once saved the unit's colors, and for it received a medal for honor. He had traded it for some pickles and a stack of dime novels at a camp store near Gettysburg.

"You've lost some weight," Lew said lightly, in the biggest understatement of his verbal history.

"The South seeks to cure me of gluttony."

"Is there a place we can . . . ?" He looked about.

"Aye. You're in it." Men in front, men behind, men on both sides, jostling, pushing past. "There's no gettin' out of it, Lew. There's only gettin' used to it. Come—I'll take you to Hotel Ford. You can mess with us, as one of our members was paroled last night."

"Paroled?" Lew began hopefully, but Harris shook his head.

"He's dead. Come, I'll give you the lay of the land."

—

"Don't take it in all to once," Harris advised as they threaded through the crowd. "You must take time to accustom."

A man stumbled into Lew and moved on. Lew noticed a few vermin on his sleeve from the encounter and quickly brushed them off. "I am not sure I wish to."

"First day is bad, next are worse, but after that you fashion tactics. Don't try first thing to see the place as a whole. You'll set a course for despair. I've seen it happen to men I thought possessed of strong inward constitution. You got to make friends early with an old-timer; he'll steer you right. For now, you be as a stone skippin' off water, boy-o, and don't sink in just yet. Get them blinders up a spell."

"Where are the barracks? Where are the tents?"

He spread his arm. "You're lookin' at 'em. Take it as is. Speculate later."

Any "tents" Lew saw were low-slung affairs of sun-bleached pieces of calico or burlap, shirts or coats, strung together and pitched on sticks. A quick guess said maybe one of every ten men had shelter. The "tents" were scattered about, no rhyme nor reason in their placement. It was nothing like a camp or bivouac. There were no orderly rows with tents laid out in lines and men walking along paths or avenues. The impression clung, and it troubled him almost more than the men he passed who showed clear signs of starvation. There was no order. Everywhere he looked was thick disarray, and it made Lew's mind see not individual men, but a spikey brown mass of confusion.

A skipping stone, he told himself quickly. He averted his eyes.

"Some of the guards are good men, especially army regulars. But it's mostly militia now, and they're not worth half a plug. They're mostly old fellas or young fellas, trigger-happy and green."

"Trigger-happy . . ."

"Aye. I have to talk to you about the deadline."

He steered Lew to the outer edge of the crowd. A thin split-rail fence held up by posts ran all along the perimeter, twenty feet from the stockade wall.

Harris pointed to one of the sheltered sentinel posts, small booths spaced at intervals along the top of the stockade, all the way around. "See them boys? Mark 'em. They have orders to shoot if you go under that rail, and they'll do it. I make it my duty to tell newcomers about it; if a lad hadn't told me, I'd be dead. I was at the creek and he fetched me back just as I was dipping for cleaner water on the other side of the line. He pointed, and I look up and see a boy young as Charley Reed with a gun trained on me. He had an idiot grin I would've given a French leave to wipe off."

"I don't expect they give French leaves around here."

"I haven't seen a woman in a month," Harris sighed.

They began to thread their way north along the deadline path. Other than the "street" that opened into the stockade from the north gate, this path seemed to be the only sort of order.

They came to a man lying in the path along the deadline. Lew knelt to check him. "Harris—I think he's . . ."

"Just keep walkin', Lew," Harris said softly. "They'll collect him. Sometimes I just about envy 'em."

They walked on.

"What about exchange?"

"Oh, and exchange is a precarious topic. It's all we talk about, and it's our only hope. Yet I have seen no evidence of it. Some old-timers say there hasn't been a man exchanged yet. I don't know if it's true or not. One thing you'll learn about the pen—rumors are the great entertainment. You don't know what to believe. I've learned to confine belief to what I see."

As they progressed, Lew tried to keep his blinders up as Harris had advised. He did all right with the great brown mass, but wondered how exactly he was supposed to avoid noticing the wretched man they had stepped over or the appalling smell, now so bad that Lew tasted it. Hardest of all was to avoid noticing Harris himself.

Harris and Lew met when mustering in at Philadelphia, had served in the same regiment, same company for three years—they were messmates; and Lew had walked right past him, so changed were his form and face. Last Lew had seen him, Harris probably weighed 170 pounds—he must have lost 30 of those. How was that possible in one month? His cheekbones stood out, his jaw cut a profile it never had before. It was unnatural. To see it in men he did not know was one thing, but to see it alter a man he knew brought it home. Harris's face, with the fair complexion of the Irish, had taken a sun beating like nothing Lew had ever seen. The sun had burned and blistered and reburned the blisters, leaving a red corrugated ridge on his forehead and cheeks. But the sunburn wasn't the worst.

He started out with, "Where's your hat, Harris?"

"Traded it for some sweet potatoes. Wish I had it back."

"And what happened to your lip?"

"Weakest part got attacked. Before I came I had a bust lip."

"Get in a fight again?"

"Something like that. Once here, it took infection."

"Why don't you have a doctor take a look at that?"

"Oh, I tried. It's not bad enough."

"They're refusing you treatment?"

"No, but other boys are in far worse straits. I felt ashamed, waiting in the sick call line, so I quit it."

The swollen, oozing lower lip worried Lew. A black spot within a ring of white infection was either dried blood or something worse. "That would get you out of the ironmongery for a week." Lew stopped walking. "Harris—what happened here?"

TRACY GROOT

"Come on, brother."

"What happened to you? Why have you lost so much weight? Why is your lip like that, with no one to look after it? What kind of place is this?"

Harris pulled him back into step. "I *told* you, lad—today, you don't speculate. Plenty of time for that. Hotel Ford is not far, now. Though I suspect the colonel would find it a dubious honor that we've named it for him. Glad they siphon off the brass for elsewhere. Don't expect most would make it here. 'Cept Colonel Ford. He'd make it, all right."

"Hold up a minute," Lew said slowly. "Don't you know about Ford?" By his look, he didn't. "Harris, Ford's dead. Charley Reed, too."

Harris stared, then looked away.

"We took a beating on Kennesaw, didn't we," he said thinly. "Seems we are blown off the earth, the 12th."

Lew dreaded asking about the other five men in their mess. Messes became like little families. Only one in theirs had died early on, and Robert had plugged that hole. "Robert's gone, too, Harris. He came back for me, and got it in the neck."

"That I saw."

"What about Dunn?"

"Killed. He was right next to me, and then he was gone."

"Brewer?"

Harris hesitated, and then said, "Dead."

"How'd he get it?"

Harris was about to answer, and then his face brightened. "Artie Van Slett's alive. He's a lodger at Hotel Ford. His leg is some bad, but I tell him every day I won't let him die 'cause he owes me seven dollars." He grinned, pushing up the burned red ridges of his face. "Same old Artie. His complaints will outlast his ailments. I'll worry

83

when he shuts up. Well, I guess that leaves only Jasper." He looked hopefully at Lew, but Lew shook his head.

"I was hoping you'd know. Can't remember the last time I saw him."

Harris took it stoically, then gave a bright and false grin. "Well, if any of us made it, Jasper did. If he finds out we're here you can bet he'll come break us out. Or tell Sherman how to do it." The false smile vanished, and he said mostly to himself, "Charley Reed, too? Oh, that is hard."

"He died defending Ford from a Reb skulker."

"Did he, now?" The bright false smile came back. "Well, and he was a corker, that lad."

"The skulker got his own."

It was the only news to get Harris's true attention. "Did he, now? I hope you paid those honors."

"Nope. I'd thrown away my last shot. He'd drawn on me with two pistols, Colonel Ford's own, and I had time only to think what a sour arrangement to be killed by my own colonel's guns. Then all of a sudden out of the woods comes a Johnny Reb just a-blazing. Blasted him right off his perch, and when he tried to get up, blasted him again."

But Harris was not surprised. "Aye—must've been him who struck the deal with that dirty Captain Graves, the lowdown piece of . . ." and Harris performed one of his legendary feats of profanity, cussing the Rebel captain up one slope and down the other. "You saved your own life with your banter, lad. You and that young Reb were going at it when you said something that got his fancy. He laughed and laughed. Kept repeating what you said. I can't remember what it was. It was not a common word."

"Perpetuity," Lew said absently.

"That was it."

"Harris . . . what deal did he strike?"

"Didn't he tell you?"

"Flat-out refused."

"Well, isn't that somethin'. A Johnny Reb with courage and grace."

"We always knew they had courage."

"Not this kind. You'd killed the friend of that captain, and he proposed that anyone who killed you should get himself fifty Federal greenbacks. I didn't have real difficulty with that, until he said, 'Get him to surrender. Once you take him prisoner, shoot him.' Well, I humbly offered a contrasting view on this proposal, but the piece of—" more legendary profanity—"was obstinate. He even shocked the other Johnnies with this cowardly tack. Then the one with the yellow hair says, 'Captain Graves, you let me collect this blue belly. Do him no harm, and I will reenlist.'"

"Reenlist . . . ," Lew said uncertainly, an awful feeling coming to his gut.

"Well, this Johnny was due to muster out, and Captain Graves had a hard time getting the boys in his company to reenlist 'cause no one liked him—this I learned later from a Reb who escorted me and Artie here. Well, this captain seemed keen on the soldiering qualities of that particular Johnny, so he agreed readily. Made him sign a paper. And I've been lookin' for you ever since."

"That *stupid*—"

"I think it was uncommon nice."

"He traded three more years of his life for—?" Lew couldn't think straight. "What's reenlistment in the Confederate army? Is it three years, same as us?"

"Three years."

"That—" He could only make a fist.

Harris slapped him on the back. "Someday I hope to buy the lad a drink."

"You think that will happen?" Lew snapped. "He survived this miserable war for three years, same as you and me—you think he'll manage it twice?" Lew looked around at the jostling press of humanity. "You think my children will see their father again? You think Carrie—?"

"Pack 'em away, Lew," Harris said. "They don't belong here. Our war has changed. We'll get a plan for survival, we'll stick to it, and we'll stick to each other. That's what the old-timers say." A man pushed into Harris, Harris pushed him back. "Some try and do it on their own. Look at them, look at their faces. They are alone in this great festering wound. Some survive that way, but not many."

His tone grew soft. "Pack 'em away, Lew, the living and the dead. Your family. Robert, Dunn. Brewer and Ford. And that bonny Charley Reed. We'll put all we have into outlasting this place. We'll unpack 'em, one day, in a place fit for it."

7

THE NEXT DAY, Violet returned to Andersonville.

She knew enough to steer clear of the prison, especially since she had Lily along; they were going only to put up and distribute the handbills they had made, inviting the town to an Indignation Meeting on Tuesday Night on the Pleasantly Situated Lawn at the Home of Doctor Norton Stiles and Family, inaugurating a New Society called The Friends of Andersonville Prison.

Violet thought it especially important that the military officials in Andersonville be apprised of the meeting. She had derived a grim sort of pleasure at the thought of their reading the handbill. If she worded the document in such a way that culpability seemed to be laid directly upon local officials for the Appalling Conditions of Starvation and Neglect of Human Beings incarcerated in the Andersonville Prison, well, as Hettie Dixon said, Truth hurts.

"P. G. T. Beauregard wouldn't put up with it," Lily had firmly avowed. A family meeting last night brought all, including Ellen, into the truth of Andersonville. The idea of organizing a committee to come to the aid of the starving wretches, Yankee though they be, had found such a welcome that Violet broke down into tears. It prompted an immediate reaction from the twins, Rosie and Daisy, who offered to go without okra if it could help them out, and from Posey, who declared that she *loved* the poor starving Yankees even if it sent her to hell.

Mother, after she had dried her eyes, predictably took charge. "We will have the first meeting Tuesday night. You must write on the handbill for folks to bring their own blankets to spread on the lawn, for I fear we do not have enough. I do worry about refreshment; there isn't enough loaf sugar for decent cakes. We will have to resort to the sorghum syrup. I wish I could prophesy as to how many will attend; gingersnaps, then, for if we bake too many they will keep, though I am sorely tired of gingersnaps."

Because yesterday's trials had exhausted her and had produced a queasy stomach and a headache, Violet retired early and did not consult her father on the wording of the handbill. She rose late, and he was already gone to Macon with the other doctors of Americus for a forum about the conditions of government impressment for the civilian medical profession.

She had asked Mother to listen to what she composed for the handbill, and Mother had warmly approved, noting how admirably Violet managed to say things, and felt sure that it would find a sympathetic audience.

Violet, Lily, and Mother copied the sentences on pages carefully torn from Papa's old medical journals, as no paper suitable for handbills was to be had in all of Americus. If she felt a twinge of doubt that perhaps some of the verbiage was going too far, she consigned it to the pit from whence it came, and assured herself that the conditions of the prison proved no one had gone far enough.

Lily and Violet put up five bills in the town square of Americus, four on the corner water oaks, and one on the podium where the Americus Brass Band played. They put one on the bulletin board outside the depot, and one in the depot itself. Silas Runcorn had read the bill and kept his counsel. Violet was disappointed. And if she had hoped to get a few free fares to Andersonville since the train was going there anyway, not to mention the fact that her father owned shares of stock in the Southwestern Railroad, she was disappointed in this as well.

"I've never been to Andersonville alone," Lily said, excited.

"You aren't alone," Violet pointed out.

"Same as," Lily said, leaning over Violet to look out of the window as the train came into the Andersonville depot. "Mother's not here."

"We must stick together," Violet said, taking Lily's arm as they stepped down to the platform. "There are nothing but soldiers here, most of them Yankees bound for captivity, and you must remember that however they have been maltreated at the prison, they remain our enemy and must be afforded all the caution given a sleeping bull. The good men of the Confederate army would never allow anything to happen to us, but we must not give them undue reason to defend us."

"Oh, he's handsome," Lily whispered. "The one by the barrel."

Lily was fifteen, and would find the barrel handsome.

"Think of it," Violet said as they made their way to the commissary building. "If our brother had lived he would be here, perhaps escorting these men—" *to their doom,* she nearly said.

"Decidedly not," Lily said. "He would have served with Jeb Stuart and saved his life from that hateful bullet. Perhaps he would have saved Ben." She glanced at Violet. "Does it pain you to hear his name?" It was a rare moment of the consideration of feelings other than her own, and Violet was pleased for her sister's progress.

"Not as much," Violet said.

Ben Robinson, Violet's fiancé, had gone to war in one of the first units organized in Americus, the Sumter Flying Artillery. The Americus Brass Band had led the procession to the depot, and off the Sumter County boys went in a wake of waving handkerchiefs and tears. No one had doubted they would all come home as they left, handsome and whole. Ben was killed with five others from his unit on December 20, 1861, at Dranesville, Fairfax County, Virginia. A caisson had blown up and took Ben with it. He was buried in Virginia, where exactly, Violet did not care to know. They'd grown up together. They were betrothed. He was gone, and that was that.

"Do you remember George?" Lily said wistfully. "I wish I did."

"I remember." Violet was six, a year younger than Posey, when little George died. It was the first and the last time she had seen Papa cry. Such a terrible wrenching in Violet's chest it had produced. She had never seen a man cry. She never thought they could.

They made it through the gauntlet of staring men, both North and South, and came into the welcome dimness of the commissary building. Lily pulled back her bonnet and looked about with interest. Violet went to the counter behind which the same clerk stood.

"Good day, Miss Stiles," he said pleasantly.

"Good day. I have a bill here I would like to post. Is there a public area where it will be seen?"

"Well, ah . . ." He looked around, and then pointed. "I reckon you can tack it to that square pillar as you come in."

Violet looked. It was a thick load-bearing square post, and the tan of the paper would stand out noticeably from the whitewash. "Thank you, that'll answer just fine." She held one out. "Would you like to read it? I encourage you to come. It's to help those poor boys in the prison."

The young man took the bill. "You mean the hospital?"

"That, too."

He read the bill, and Violet watched his growing dismay with growing dismay. He looked at her. "The *prison*? I thought you was talking about the Confederate hospital, just up the tracks."

"*That* one is sufficiently cared for," Violet said icily. "Relief societies to the moon and back for that one." She should know, she had run a benefit just last month.

He began to shake his head. "Oh, I don't think you can put this up. Not as written. General Winder won't like it."

"General Winder won't like it?" Violet snatched the bill back. "How do you think those boys like starving? Do you think they *like* scurvy? Have you seen the effect?"

"Why, Corporal Womack. What have you done to court the displeasure of this lovely young lady?"

A tall man with black hair and very pale eyes smiled down at Violet. He lifted his brown derby and must have thought his pale eyes to be quite something, for they stayed on Violet's face as if expecting a blush. He was handsome, she supposed, but his lips were spare; when his face made to be pleasant, they disappeared, leaving behind a smile she did not trust.

He looked at Corporal Womack, then at the bill in her hands.

"May I?"

Reluctantly, she gave it to him.

He was all in brown, the derby, the vest, the jacket, the trousers, the leather shoes. He was probably broiling, and the style was not at all Southern. She wondered if he were one of those detectives General Winder had brought down from Richmond.

He read the handbill. Something in his face changed, and Violet did not like it.

He turned the pale eyes, which he supposed of devastating effect, upon her. She matched the stare and plucked the bill from his hands.

"Are you from Richmond?" she asked.

"Baltimore. You are Miss Stiles?" His accent was decidedly Northern. "The one who took a turn yesterday?"

Now the blush came, and she busied herself with counting the handbills. "Yes. I'm better now, thank you."

"I can see that." He looked her over with a frankness bordering on impertinence. "Captain Wirz was quite concerned."

"Was he? I would rather he concern himself with those poor men in that stockade."

"I wouldn't put up those handbills if I were you."

Violet's heart picked up pace. She didn't know what to say.

"She can put 'em up if she wants to," said Corporal Womack, his voice high and strident. The young man's eyes were a little wide. "Gimme that thing, Miss Stiles."

She handed him a bill, and he rummaged beneath the counter for a hammer and nails. He marched to the square post and tacked it up in the center. Then he came back to the counter swinging the hammer in a rakish way. "There you are, Miss Stiles."

"Thank you, Mr. Womack," Violet said archly.

"A pleasure de-vine," he said, eyes fastened on the Baltimore dandy as he tossed the hammer to the shelf.

"Miss Stiles, my name is Joseph T. Howard." He lifted the derby again. "I wish to acquaint you with it, for I will surely be at that meeting. Your sort of meeting is just my sort of business."

"And what business is that?"

The lip disappeared into a garish smile. "Why, the investigation of treasonous activities."

"Treason? I expect you'll have to take up with the authorities on that—for their treason against *mankind*."

The pale eyes flickered. He walked away.

"Northern trash," Corporal Womack muttered. Then he said,

"Bully for you, Miss Stiles. 'Bout time someone put those uppity—" Then he saw Lily. She gazed at him with such open admiration that he blushed crimson. He swallowed, squared himself, and said, "Do you know, I just might come to that meetin'. To keep the peace and all. But Miss Stiles—I wouldn't put any more of those up. You can bet someone'll tear that one down before the end of the day. You don't want—" He glanced at Lily.

"I don't want what?"

He hesitated, and then said earnestly, "You don't want to make things harder for your daddy. I don't know what he's thinking." He looked at the handbills. "You best bail him out by not postin' these at all. Them are dangerous words."

"They aren't his words, they're mine," Violet said quickly.

"Don't matter, I suppose."

She looked doubtfully at the papers. Then Lily was at her side. She slipped her hand around Violet's arm and gave it a squeeze. She said to Corporal Womack, "Can we borrow your hammer and some nails?"

———

"Treason!" Violet said. "I declare! The idea of a foundational pillar of Americus embroiled in *treason*! A charter member of the First Methodist!"

"Where did you say General Winder's office is?" Lily asked.

Violet shook the handbills. "Are these so inflammatory? What is treasonous about feeding starving people? I *de*clare!"

"Right on his front door," Lily said grimly. "That's where it will go. Just like Martin Luther did. Then one for Captain Wirz's front door, one for the dry goods store, one for the stable, one for the mill . . . I do wish we had made more. Oh, Violet, my blood is taken up! I have never felt this way. I hope it lasts forever."

———

"Pickett! Pickett, you gotta see this."

Drover ran up the rungs, a paper held high.

"This was tacked up at the depot." Drover gave him the paper, then leaned on his knees to catch his breath. "I've never seen so bold!"

Dance spread the paper on the rail.

AMERICUS, AMERICUS

Is it Possible that You are not Aware of the Appalling Conditions of Starvation and Neglect of the Human Beings incarcerated in the Andersonville Prison? Is it Possible that a mere Ten Miles separates Heaven from Hell?

Come to be Informed at an Indignation Meeting this Tuesday Night on the Pleasantly Situated Lawn at the home of Doctor Norton Stiles and Family, at the east terminus of Lamar Street, inaugurating a New Society called . . .

The Friends of Andersonville Prison.

Let the People of Americus rise up in Indignation at the Hellacious Unjust Treatment our Enemy receives at the hand of our Very Own Government! In the spirit of Southern Loyalty to Humanity, let us Secede from the Awful Indifference of a Government that should Doom men to such Misery. This isn't Us, and it never Was.

Refreshments will be served. We respectfully ask each family or individual to bring his own spreading blanket.

"You ever seen so bold?"

Dance laid his hand on the paper.

"Dr. Stiles is my man 'til I die," said Drover.

"May I keep this?"

"You bet—I just as soon get it off my person. Don't let Wirz find it on you. He and Winder are in a state."

"I'll bet they are."

"You goin' to that meetin'? Don't know if I dare."

"Well, I had better." Dance felt lightness in his head. "I happen to be the president of the F.A.P."

Drover breathed a respectful curse. "You know what, Pickett? I figured you had something like this in you." He looked out over the stockade, scanning the acres of men. "I haven't felt this hopeful for them in . . . never." He went to the ladder. "I gotta go tell James. Do you know he wrote a letter to Jefferson Davis about this place?" He disappeared down the ladder.

Burr squinted at the handbill. "What's that say?"

Dance read it to him.

Burr whistled. "Good night Irene. The doc's gone and laid down a line o' thunder."

Dance went to the corner and picked up his leather scrip. He never thought the day would come that he would open his sanctuary here in this profane place.

He unwound the string.

He read the bill one more time, then slipped it into the scrip, closed the flap, and rewound the string.

"Pickett, what you got in there, anyway?"

Dance came and rested his elbows on the rail. He felt lighter than air. *Americus, Americus.* She said it as if she were the one standing right here. And she said it for the world to see.

"I have a sanctuary in there, Burr. One day I will open it up upon this place."

"What will happen then?"

"Why, I will send the words out over the men, and they will

reach up and take hold. They will be lifted away, and thus borne home."

"One word per man?"

"One word."

"Why them is powerful words, then," Burr said kindly.

"Yes, sir."

"You best take care of them words, for that would be a sight." Then Burr said, "Take care of yourself, too, Pickett, and some for Dr. Stiles. That handbill is throwed down and there is no fetchin' it back. Wish I'd throwed it, 'cept I got a family."

"So does he."

———

Papa sat at the table with his head in his hands. The original handbill lay on the table before him.

"Papa, please say something."

The buffet clock ticked.

"You were gone, and—"

"I wish you had consulted me before you put this up. With all my heart I do."

"I'm sorry, Papa."

"You meant well," he said, lifting his head. He patted her arm.

"Norton, I do not understand," said Mother. She picked up the bill. "What is so bad about this?" Her eyes narrowed, and went to Papa. "You have never been shy about saying it like it is. This is as it is. Am I correct?"

"You are. But things are . . . different. They are as they never were."

"How so? Tell me this instant, how so?"

"Wise as serpents is our prescribed tack, and I missed it. I wish I had more serpent in me."

"There was a man at the warehouse in Andersonville, Papa," said Lily. "His name is Howard. He said this all looked like treason. What could he mean by that?"

"Treason?" Mother laughed. "Your father?"

But Papa did not laugh.

"Norton Avery Stiles. You tell me this *instant* what you have done."

"Multiple things. Multiple small things."

"What things?"

"I have written letters. To the war department, to Howell Cobb. Joe Brown, Jefferson Davis. Abraham Lincoln."

"Lincoln!"

"I have—"

"Norton Stiles." Mother's hand flew to her throat. "You are not a *spy*. Are you a *spy*?"

"Polly, please."

"Say from your mouth you are not a spy."

"I am not a spy, my dear."

"Goodness gracious!" Mother laughed nervously. "Of course you are not!"

"But I am a traitor." He folded his hands. "I take food to the sick patients at the Federal hospital when it is forbidden to do so. I smuggle small things. A sweet potato in each trouser pocket. A packet of gingersnaps in my vest. I drop them on the ground where they can find them. I let them fall through my trousers."

The picture of a sweet potato falling through Papa's trousers finally undid Mother, and she laid a hand on her cheek.

"How vulgar! They eat them from the *ground*?"

Surprisingly, Papa chuckled. He took Mother's hand and kissed it, smiling at his wife with affection. Then he picked up the bill and read the first line. "Americus, Americus . . . ," he murmured.

"I was thinking of 'O Jerusalem, Jerusalem,'" Violet said, who now wished with all her miserable heart she'd never taken up a pen. "'Thou that killest the prophets, and stonest them which are sent unto thee, how often would I have gathered thy children together, even as a hen gathereth her chickens under her wings, and ye would not!'"

Then it seemed as though only Violet and Papa were in the room. He turned upon her such a direct gaze it made her swimmy.

Papa was a mild man, courteous and kind, possessed of even thinking, slow to make decisions but steadfast in sticking to them, a lighthouse on a rock, a calm beacon in storms. But for a flash, a storm broke wild and bright on his face.

He rose from the table, and with his voice curiously thick, said down to her, "I am fearfully proud of you."

He took the paper and left the dining room.

8

VIOLET COULD NOT CLOSE her eyes, for when she did she saw a dropped hand. She saw a light go out at the bottom of a well. She did not go to him, did not go, and felt upon her heart hot lines as if laid by a poker.

She stayed home from church this morning because Mother said she looked poorly. Violet did not mind as she couldn't bear the thought of being cordial, and had no worship in her.

Church service would soon be over. Reverend Gillette would shake hands with his flock and bless them to their week. Did she not go to church because she did not want to face what her family must have?

Violet walked around the table, laying the spoons. Dance and Emery would be here soon. Today was the planning day for the Friends of Andersonville Prison. But Violet knew none of the anticipation that should have attended this day. She was about to embark upon the greatest venture that ever met her heart, and she felt lame out of the gate.

Ellen made Papa's favorite dishes to let it be known she was upset with Violet for upsetting Papa. She went early to the colored chapel, a building built behind the Methodist church, and before chapel, made two kinds of bread to go with three jellies—quince, guava, and pawpaw; from the stove now came a leg of mutton with mint sauce, buttered purple hull peas, creamed corn, and field mushrooms stewed in butter with pepper and pounded mace.

She shook up the fire to brown the meringue, and took down the jar with Papa's tea. The blockade made the cost of Papa's favorite tea prohibitive—five dollars a pound before the war, now *forty* dollars—but Ellen had fashioned her own brew from wild herbs and leaves from fruit-bearing plants, and he declared that it tasted better than Phoenix Tea.

The mace for the mushrooms likely came from the Trades Pile, as they called it, the corner of Dr. Stiles's office which held all the things people traded for Papa's services. It was a measure of the times that they finally resorted to the pile, for most of what people traded wasn't worth much. Now, with the practice of wartime economies, the Trades Pile was consulted with sobering frequency. Mother once remonstrated with Lily for melting the soles of her slippers on the fender. Rosie went off unnoticed to the pile, and to the astonishment of all, produced a pair of worn but serviceable pink silk slippers.

Rosie and Daisy were custodians of the pile, and at any given moment could tell you if soap or sugar or potatoes or mildly weevily flour were available. Lately dry goods were scarce, and the pile consisted mostly of the same old molasses, cornmeal, and dried peas.

Most of the week the family dined from things from the Trades Pile, but Sunday was different. On Sundays, the family dined as if there were no war.

Violet laid the knives. Ellen was cordial if cool, and arranged the jellies near Papa's place setting with a little more fuss than necessary.

When Violet did not ask about her silence, she said, "Been some time since I seen da docta go down so low in da mouf. Been since little George."

Violet did not answer. She laid the forks.

"I wunda how it went in da white church. I knows how it went in mine."

"And how did it go?" Violet asked wearily.

"We spent da whole time prayin' for da docta."

"I don't know if that cheers me up."

"It wudden meant to."

Violet tossed down a fork. It plinked on the plate.

"You mind dat china. Dat be Miss Polly's weddin' gif' from Judge—"

"Templeton."

"You mind dat tone."

"Ellen, if it means anything at all, I'd give the last button in Americus to have that handbill back."

Ellen paused beside Violet on her way to the kitchen. "Dat is good enough for me, chile," she said, considerably mollified. "Sin 'fessed is sin fo'given." She was humming by the time she opened the oven to remove the pie.

Violet went to the kitchen. "Exactly what is sinful about what I wrote?"

"Nuthin'. Elda Clem read dose words in da chapel and we praise de Lawd. He ain't read nuthin' like dat since Mista Lincoln's 'Mancipation paper. Dem po' Yankees be treated somethin' shameful. Elda Clem say it a calumny 'pon dis town."

"Then why do you make me feel lower than a footprint?"

"'Cause you ain't got no sense, chile."

Violet went back to the dining room.

All plans for the redemption of the prison had abandoned her, and right now she didn't care about discussing things with Emery Jones, that spirited boy with ambition to surpass her own— *If bustin' one Yank out of that prison should hang me . . . what'll they do if I bust 'em all?*

She thought of only two things: How had people treated her family over that hateful handbill, and how angry did the bill make Dance?

———

Dance loved it here, everything about it, the home and those who peopled it. He loved the collection of daguerreotypes in the parlor. He loved the corner of the parlor sacred to the manifold projects of the Stiles women—baskets of yarn for the Knitting Brigade that met every Monday, piles of paper from the collection box at church for the Letters to Our Soldiers campaign, and a place dedicated to the collection of packaging materials to send foodstuffs and sundries from home. Packaging materials were easier to collect these days than foodstuffs and sundries.

He loved this dining room, the neat line of covered dishes on the sideboard, and the colorful rag rugs he could see from here on the kitchen floor. He liked the stain on the wallpaper near the ceiling, which he had not noticed until Mrs. Stiles pointed it out and said with dignity that it represented a Post-War project. Such triflings as stained wallpaper and worn clothing would not trouble *them* for the time being, as they had *pressing needs* to take *their* concern. Stained wallpaper was certainly not a *pressing need*. It was a verse in Titus.

He liked it best when no other visitors came on Sunday, when it was just the Stiles family and he, and that was rare. But today he didn't mind that Emery came, for he seemed to belong as much as Dance. Emery suited comfortably.

Dance sat in his usual place, on Violet's right. Posey sat on her left, with Emery between Posey and Lily. They sat to the table a little later than usual, as Ellen declared upon first sight of Emery that he would not sit to the table as is. "When was da las' time dat shirt was boiled?"

Emery looked down. "Well, ma'am, it has been too long. I forget about my appearance in civil society. Been on campaign for some time."

"We haven't had any *real* soldiers yet," Rosie said, and Dance had to make a sour smile behave. "I look forward to dinner conversation. I wish to hear of battles."

"Take dat off. I'll git you an old shirt of da docta. Gimme dem trousers, too, and your draws."

"Ellen, I do not think it polite to say *drawers* in front of company," Mrs. Stiles said. "What is more, it is the Sabbath."

"Da Lawd say it fine to do a good turn on da Sabbath, and as I ain't nevah done anyone's draws 'cept family, I is about to win m'self a place to de Lawd's right hand. Come wif me, young mista."

Emery obeyed. He presently returned with a scrubbed face and damp hair, rigged out in old clothes a size too large. The pants were cuffed, the sleeves turned back, and suspenders held everything together. The children laughed at the sight, and Emery turned in place to display himself. "Why, I have a sudden compellin' to practice med'cine. Anyone feelin' poorly?"

All laughed except for Violet. It looked to Dance as though she hadn't slept in days. She had barely spoken a word since they arrived, and she seemed to be avoiding Dance altogether.

Dr. Stiles said grace. Dishes were passed, plates were filled, and first bites had been taken when Posey opened discussion with "Papa? Can I be a traitor and a Christian at the same time?"

The table stilled.

"Mrs. Robinson says we are traitors, and I said what does this mean, and Tessie thought it meant we were headin' to hell. I said I am so going to heaven and they'll let me in quicker than you."

Dr. Stiles finished chewing, wiped his mouth with his napkin, took a sip of water, and confirmed with soothing finality, "You are going to heaven."

"I don't like saying *hell*. It feels like I have cussed. Even though I *haven't*." A quick glance at Mrs. Stiles. "And I will tell Tessie I don't think they'll let me in quicker. I will clear the air."

Violet put down her fork, which, Dance noticed, hadn't done more than prod a mushroom. "Well, on that encouraging note . . . how did it go?"

Dance noticed that Emery listened as intently as he; ordinarily, Dr. and Mrs. Stiles liked it when the guards went to church with them, but Emery had overslept. The trains ran only three times on the Sabbath from Albany to Macon, and he managed to find Emery only minutes before the eleven-fifteen.

"We're not supposed to tell you," said Rosie.

"Out of kindness," Daisy added kindly.

"I am a Traitor Christian," Posey said with satisfaction, spooning large amounts of jam on a slice of bread. "You can call me T. C."

"Enough jam," Mrs. Stiles said sharply. "Violet, dear . . ."

"Where are the Runcorns?" Two place settings lacked diners.

Mrs. Stiles lowered her eyes. "Ravinia had a headache."

"Did everyone have a headache?" Violet asked.

When Dr. and Mrs. Stiles said nothing, Lily said quietly, "There are more against us than for us, Violet."

"But *some* are for us," said Daisy.

Violet placed her hands in her lap. "Do you think anyone will come?"

"This is the bad part," Posey said, laying down her bread.

"Brace yourself," Rosie advised.

Dr. Stiles raised his eyes to Violet's. "The Millards moved the dance to Tuesday night. Reverend Gillette announced it from the pulpit."

"Oh," Violet said in a very small voice.

County dances in southwest Georgia were as famously attended as those in Augusta and Savannah—and an established date was never moved. This Millard social had been planned for over a month. Dance had long seen the announcement on the board at the depot. He gripped his cutlery.

"Did you see their faces?" Lily demanded. "They all looked as if they had pulled off something fine."

"Not our Hettie Dixon," Rosie said. "She said out loud the Millards ought to be ashamed."

"She didn't say the Millards. She said *someone* ought to be ashamed," Lily said. "I think she meant Reverend Gillette."

"I think she meant everyone," said Mrs. Stiles. "Reverend Gillette did not seem very happy."

"It is a hateful turn of events," Rosie said stoutly.

"I wish for revenge," Posey said.

"We will miss the dance out of love for you," Daisy said. At Rosie's nudge, she added, "And 'cause of starving Yanks."

Because he sat at her side, Dance could see that Violet had clutched the fabric of her dress into her fists. "Did they not understand the handbill?" she said, a slight waver in her tone. "Was I not clear?"

"You were perfectly clear," Dance half growled.

He wished he had been at the church this morning. He realized he'd bent his fork in half and went to work straightening it.

"I suppose you feel mighty justified," Violet retorted, half glancing at him. "This town is—"

"That's not what I meant. Well—it is. But that bill—"

"He means nothin' whatsoever has changed, Miss Stiles," said Emery Jones placidly. "Come Tuesday, we will hold the meetin' as planned, and get on fine with whomever the good Lord sends. Don't you worry. You wrote a fair piece, and it'll speak to them as has ears to hear." It was as if he'd blown a soothing wind over the table. He buttered his bread. "Miss Posey, can I trouble you for that jam? Or should I call you Traitor Christian?"

Those smooth words served up on a plank of blue-eyed Alabama charm didn't fool Dance. One by one the family resumed eating, and when all were fully occupied Emery slid him a look. Oh, he had something up his sleeve, all right. Dance could hardly wait to find out.

Violet looked at her plate. After a moment, she took her fork.

Mrs. Stiles, grateful, looked at Emery and cast about for something to say. "Huntsville, Dr. Stiles says. I don't know anyone from Huntsville. What is it like, Mr. Jones?"

"Same as here, ma'am." He wiped his mouth with his napkin. "Good people, good place. I was raised by my uncle and aunt on a small sugar farm, just outside Huntsville."

"What happened to your folks?" Posey asked.

"Well, Miss Posey, my mama took sick and died when I was just a baby, and my daddy took sick in his heart. One day he got on a ship and just sailed off. Never heard from him again."

"That is tragic." Posey stopped eating. "How come he didn't take you with him?"

"I expect he didn't know how to take care of a little one. Maybe he was too sick in his heart to try. But I'll tell you what. I reckon I had no better fetchin' up than with my aunt and uncle. They are quality down to the ground."

"I am glad to hear it," Posey said earnestly.

"The *mule*, now . . . he wasn't quality. I cannot say in polite company what *he* was."

"What mule?" she asked.

"Well, my uncle owns a sugar mill. Do you know what I was forced to do at your age?" He shook his head. "I can scarcely tell it for shame."

"What?" Posey asked breathlessly.

"Well, we had this mule to power the mill. We'd harness that old thing up and he'd walk round and round and round and so grind up the cane. Now that mule, who lives to this day from sheer hate, refused to budge *one inch* unless *yours truly* was sitting on him. Out of all the kids on the farm, that mule picked *me* for a childhood of misery. Starting when I was four—" he held up four fingers—"until I was eight—" he added four more—"I had to ride that thing for hours on end or he *would not budge*."

"The devil," Posey breathed.

"How do you think I felt when friends would come fetch me to fish, and there I was, trapped on that pitiless crank 'cause he would go for no one else?"

"Your childhood was stolen."

"It could rain like peas, and I had to lay on that wide stinkin' back and turn round and round or there would *be* no sugar, and my family would *starve*."

"I hardly know what to say. You've had it rough."

"Well, I've come through. It had to be borne."

"It had to be borne."

"There's nothin' we won't do for our families. Am I tellin' the truth?"

"Nothin'."

Dance wished he could think of something clever to say. Posey was his, not Emery's.

"Did you ever get in trouble for things?" Posey asked.

"Some things ain't fittin' for mamas to hear," Emery said out of the side of his mouth, with a little move of his head toward Mrs. Stiles.

"I wish to hear of battles," said Rosie, putting down her milk.

Emery Jones was a natural raconteur. Off he went in stories of camp life and soldiering, beguiling the whole family except for Violet. Dance would feel a measure of satisfaction in this, except that her unbeguilement was linked to the thing that never left Dance alone. She poked at purple hull peas with her fork.

"So I says, 'But that chicken was a Yankee spy! I *had* to take it into custody.' Tasted good, even if it was a traitor."

The family laughed, and Dance said very softly, "Violet, that bill was—"

"Did I not lay out the case?" she whispered. "Should I have been more descriptive? I *did* mention starvation, did I not? My heart is so heavy I don't remember *what* I wrote."

"Violet, you need a revelation. Not everything that interests you will interest others, no matter how shining good it is. That is the truth, but you do not believe it."

"I don't know what pains me more, their suffering or the fact that it *appears* this town won't do anything about it. I close my eyes and I see . . ." She touched the edge of her plate. "It's not as if they die from *battle*, but still they die from the hand of us *Southerners*, in a separate war, one with no nobility."

"I see it daily."

Violet looked at him. "I'd break in half."

"Part of me has gone away. Else I'd break, too."

"I wish you didn't have to see it, Dance."

"Better me than—" He looked away. He picked up his fork and idly stabbed his food. "As to your handbill, Miss Stiles—"

"Oh, I know what you think of that, same as everyone else. You think I'm foolish."

"That time I got off easy," Emery was saying. "I had to stand on a barrel and recite the Articles of War." The family laughed. "I made a few things up to interest the boys."

"For a tiny while you gave me hope for this town," Dance said. "I let myself wander about with it, for I haven't felt it in so long, and if I had it only for a time, it did me good."

"Do you think anyone will show?"

"No. Oh, I don't know. Maybe a few. But I think the town has shown itself."

"So do I."

Violet slipped out of her chair and left the room. And the brave efforts of diversion were revealed as just that, for the table went silent.

———

Emery admired his fresh clothing. "I haven't felt this clean since I left home, and that was three years ago. My aunt would want to thank you. It's right kind of you, ma'am." He nodded at Ellen, and she nodded back. She had brought a tray to Dance, Emery, and Dr. Stiles with cold tea and lemon meringue pie. She turned to go into the house, but paused in the porch doorway.

"We was wonderin'—can coloreds be Friends, too?"

At Emery's blank expression, Dr. Stiles said, "She means the Friends of Andersonville Prison."

"Elda Clem read dat bill and say we is bound to help, since dey down here fightin' for us. I ain't no spy, no more'n you, Docta, but us coloreds built dat prison. We didn't knows we built it for mizry. Elda Clem say you need us, we stand by."

"Sure you could be a Friend," Emery said. "I reckon you could come to the meeting on Tuesday. Your whole church could come. What do you say, Mr. President?" He looked at Dance, but Ellen shook her head, incredulous.

"You ain't got no sense, neither. I is the only one left. Lawd, have mercy, someone hold up dese arms. Dis battle gonna be *long.*" She turned into the house.

Dr. Stiles remembered the day the children realized that Ellen was not a family member. In January of '63, he had read the Emancipation Proclamation to the family, because however the war turned out, it was an historic document that would sooner or later change lives. It did not seem to mean much until Rosie said suddenly, "Is Ellen a slave? I didn't know we *had* slaves."

"Does that paper say she will *leave* us?" Daisy said.

"Ellen, are you a slave?" Rosie called to the kitchen, alarmed.

Dr. and Mrs. Stiles had exchanged anxious looks. They didn't know what would happen when things came to this; on the crumbling institution of slavery, no one seemed to know the rules. Ellen had been Polly's maid since she was a child, and had come to Americus with Polly when she married and moved from Augusta.

The three younger children had jumped from their chairs and run to the kitchen, while Lily and Violet hurried to the kitchen doorway to look on.

Rosie threw her arms around Ellen's middle. "Are you a slave, dear Ellen?"

Daisy burst into tears. "Don't leave us!"

"Don't leave us!" Posey wailed.

"Jesus saves!" Ellen cried. "What is all dis fuss?"

"That *hateful* paper says you will leave!"

"Are you going to *leave?*"

Ellen gathered them in. "Mista Lincoln say I free, chile." Black wrinkled hands smoothed flossy blonde braids. "So dat mean I free to stay. Where old Ellen go, if her fam'ly be right here?"

The three younger ones wailed louder for relief. Violet and Lily threw their arms around each other. Dr. and Mrs. Stiles sat at the table, holding tightly gripped hands.

"Why shouldn't they come?" Emery said.

"Same reason Violet should not have posted that bill," Dr. Stiles said. "All is tenuous. Come on, boys. Finish your pie. Then we'll talk."

———

Late in the afternoon Emery and Dance said good-bye to the rest of the family and left for a stroll with Dr. Stiles to the train depot. The last train for Andersonville left in an hour. They did not go through the town, but took the fields until they came to the train tracks, then walked along the tracks.

"Last night I had a visitor, boys," said Dr. Stiles. "It was not a friendly call. Man by the name of Howard, works for General Winder. He warned me against having the meeting on Tuesday. Said there was time to put up a retraction."

"Retraction?" Dance repeated.

"What did you tell him?" said Emery.

"I thanked him for his interest. He said, with a rather unpleasant smile, that it might be difficult to hold a meeting if no one showed up."

Emery and Dance looked at each other.

"You think he's behind changing the Millard date?" Dance said.

"Undoubtedly."

"Does Violet know about this?"

"She does not."

"Why would the Millards allow the date to be changed in the first place?" Dance said.

"I understand they welcomed it. They were in full agreement, to prevent the F.A.P. meeting."

"What is *wrong* with this town?" Emery exploded. "Is this my country?"

"It is your country, son, winding down from a long and terrible war. There has been great loss, and unless Lincoln loses the election, the South is finished. Everyone knows it but Jeff Davis, and he will not be convinced. Americus has lost many sons, and we grapple with a broken dream of independence. We grapple with dwindling morale, patriotic lethargy. We are played out, and Governor Joe is tossed between sending more men and preserving them. What an unenviable position he is in. He only wants to save lives."

"How does that justify Andersonville?" Emery said.

"I do not seek to justify. I wish for you to understand that you deal with a town that is weary of war, and filled with grief. Violet's fiancé was one of the first to die. The Runcorns lost their firstborn. Judge Tate lost two nephews. And the Millard family—they lost their youngest. To put thoughts of charity to men who in their minds murdered their boys . . . it asks much of a beaten-down community."

Emery stopped walking.

"You say all that, and all I see in my mind is a man eaten with maggots. I see another so starving he—it won't come out of my mouth what I seen him eat. If the Cause is lost, so be it, but at *this* price?"

"I understand this town, son. I grieve for their losses, as much as I grieve their loss of sight."

"Sir . . . what is this all about?" Dance said.

"The things Violet said about the government in that handbill, while truthful, came at a very tricky time for me. Dance, I'd like to ask that should anything happen, would you look after my family? I am not sure the town will remember who they are. They may forget that I am one of them, and they are me."

"What are you saying, sir?"

Dr. Stiles resumed walking, and the other two fell into step.

"I've worked at the Federal hospital every Thursday since the end of March. I have a pass from General Winder. It must be occasionally renewed, and a few weeks ago, for the first time, he was reluctant. He displayed open distrust of me, and I finally saw the same paranoia others have. He is convinced of Yankee spies behind every bush. This same conviction attended him at Richmond."

"My father said they ran him out of town," said Dance.

"So they did. He had extreme distrust of the civilian population. Who knows but that this repeats in Americus. In Richmond, everyone had to have a pass, coming or going from the city. He had hired detectives from Baltimore to ferret out Yankee sympathizers—and the detectives themselves had an unfavorable reputation. Winder generally made himself a nuisance. Well, the city clamored for his removal, and he was relieved of duty. Sent to the field in North Carolina. He appealed to Jefferson Davis, and some weeks later, to the woe of all concerned, was appointed the post at Andersonville."

Dr. Stiles paused to pull up a foxtail weed. He put it in his mouth, slid his hands into his vest pockets.

"General Winder looks upon any intended kindness as intended treachery. He is unreasonably distrustful. His temperament is changeable. He is not steadfast—except in suspicion."

"Is the quartermaster related to him?" Emery asked. "Same last name."

"Nephew, I believe."

"Things are adding up," Dance said grimly.

"Is the quartermaster rotten?" Emery asked.

"I don't know as he is 'rotten,' but he seems to suffer from a common malady called Don't Do Enough, as afflicts anyone in the orbit of Andersonville," said Dr. Stiles. "Don't care enough to do enough. Don't have the canniness to do enough. It starts at General Winder, and flows down like oil from Aaron's beard. He has profound fear of a prison break. Yet should he look into the stockade, which he actually prides himself on never doing, he would see no basis for his fears. How can such emaciated men rise up? For all of the challenges visited upon Andersonville, it needed a special commander. And that commander was not found."

"You tell me of those challenges," Emery said hotly. "For I wish to understand why those men are starving. Look around you! I see a cornfield right there, at my front and my back! Pinewoods abound, yet I do not see wood given to the men so they can cook their rations. How is it half the time they are issued *raw* cornmeal? And such cornmeal it is—peppered with flies! I've sifted through it and do you know what I have found? Ground-up cob!"

"You think we don't know?" Dance scorned.

"I been here less than a week, Dr. Stiles—I can lay out solutions to those *challenges* before breakfast. What ties the hands? What prevents? That stinkin' cesspool those men bathe, drink, and *defecate* in is a crime on humanity. Why ain't it drained? Why ain't there barracks? Why ain't tents been issued? I asked the same of that quartermaster, and you know what he did? He shrugs." Emery imitated him. "Just shrugs. Said things were mighty complex and no one understood how hard things were for him. Then he says he's got to be someplace, and off he goes, to *no* place—for I followed him."

Dr. Stiles had listened with concentration, letting him talk it out.

"Lord have mercy, the smell alone is thick as paste," Emery muttered after a time, subdued. "I don't know how y'all have stood it thus far. I got a friend in there, Dr. Stiles. I can't have him be as those they carry out every mornin'. I counted sixty-seven yesterday."

"Where are you posted, son?"

"Dead duty."

Dr. Stiles looked at him, surprised. "They don't usually assign newcomers to dead duty. And it's usually Union boys."

"I requested it of Sergeant Keppel. I'm assigned a squad. Gets me inside, where I can keep an eye on my friend."

"You've seen him?"

"Didn't, until yesterday."

"I'm surprised you found him at all. How does he fare?"

"Well. He's only been there since Thursday. But I am glad he has a durable constitution."

"That is good. It will serve him."

"He is worried about his friend—man from his unit, got here a month before we did. Says he's got a fearsome infection in his lip. Can you do anything for him? Lew says he won't go to the hospital, and I think his chances better for that. I haven't seen anyone come out of them wards yet but on a stretcher to the dead pile." Emery shoved his hands hard in his pockets. His voice lowered. "I didn't know the human frame could take so much."

"The Federal hospital stores are played out. I dare not pilfer any more from the Confederate hospital." Dr. Stiles sighed. "I've been concocting my own supplies, with Ellen's help. I'll see what I have. For the time being, have him keep it clean as best as he can. Have him find some clean sand and scrub it daily."

"Ain't no clean sand in there." His voice was tight, and Dance and Dr. Stiles glanced at him.

He stopped walking and put his face against his arm. "I'm ashamed. I'm ashamed," he murmured, blotting his face. He pulled down his hat and put his fists in his pockets.

Dance bent to pick up a rock. "Brand-new to Andersonville, on dead duty, and you are ashamed?" He sidearmed the rock and hit a tree. "You ought to be ashamed for being ashamed."

The three fell into step.

After a time, Emery said, "How are you in trouble, sir?"

"As to that." Dr. Stiles took the foxtail weed out of his mouth.

"The Confederate government has appropriated funds to the Andersonville Federal Hospital for its provisioning. A colleague recently brought to my attention grave discrepancies in the hospital records book. A lot of money's gone missing from the fund, money that was earmarked for food and medicine and bandages for the sick prisoners. I didn't believe it at first. I couldn't believe it. I stared at those figures and thought they'd fix themselves before my eyes. They did not. I am unaccustomed to this sort of corruption." He put the weed back in his mouth. "I am not a quarrelsome man. Generally, I can see both sides of an equation. But when the equation does not balance, in this case quite literally, one sees clearly to try and correct the sum."

"What did you do?"

"We went to the head of the ward and, as it turns out, keeper of the hospital fund." He smiled ruefully.

"*He's* the one who—"

"I am not saying he is, and I am not saying he isn't," said Dr. Stiles carefully.

"Well, what happened? What did he do?"

"Said it wasn't any of our business and put the book under lock and key. So we went to the head of the hospital, and he said he would check into it. That is Andersonville-speak for 'a whole lot of goin' nowhere.' We then took the matter to Captain Wirz, who referred us to General Winder. We took the opportunity not only to point out the discrepancies in the hospital fund, but to put forth our concern over the conditions of the wards and the general state of the men, which is a direct result of starvation, exposure, and a filthy environment. Here is the perverse paradox: as a result of our inquiry, we are accused of having Northern sympathies, and our duties were suspended on the spot, pending investigation."

A curse burst from Emery.

"Indeed," said Dr. Stiles. "What is more . . . all of this transpired on Thursday—the day my daughter came to Andersonville."

The doctor waited for the full import to fall upon the young men. It came to Dance first.

"And the next day . . . *Americus, Americus*. The handbill puts it all on the government."

"Mmm-hmm."

"Winder thinks that bill is retaliation." Dance looked at Dr. Stiles. "From you."

"You see it rightly."

"But you was just tryin' to point out *stealin'*!" Emery said. "What does that have to do with . . . ? It has no *logic*!"

"Well, Corporal Jones, this is Andersonville. Lay down your logic at the gate. It has no welcome here."

———

Emery and Dance watched the doctor walk away.

"What are you thinking, Alabama?"

"I like that family."

"What's the other of your thinking?"

Emery slipped his hands into the band of his trousers. "Changin' the Millard dance to Tuesday. That make you mad as me? I saw you bend that fork."

"Should've been a neck."

"How many friends you got in that garrison?"

"I mostly keep to myself because it is my nature, but I have a few."

"You got any friends in high places?"

"Well, my father is friends with Governor Joe Brown, and on any given occasion he will make it known that he taught at Yale Law School the same year Brown attended. That high enough for you?"

"Won't suit my current purposes, but I will keep it in the attic. What about that Sergeant Keppel?"

"I don't know as we are friends, but we are not enemies. He likes Dr. Stiles."

"Would he do for him?"

"I don't take your meaning."

"Would he *take pains* to put himself *out* to secure a good *turn* for him? Am I speakin' English?"

"You are speaking Alabamian. I think he would. What's on your mind?"

Emery turned on him a gaze so compelling it didn't matter what this boy was about to propose, it would get done: "Where's that Reverend Gillette live?"

"Uh-oh. Well, I do not know. I'm sure it's easy to find out." Dance scratched his jaw. "I insulted him a few weeks back. It troubles me some, as I don't remember exactly *how*. That was good wine. Blackberry."

"Is he a rotten man?"

"In truth, he strikes me as a good one. A chief joy of mine is to point out hypocrisy, particularly in clergy, but I've not seen much in him. I've liked his preaching, though he is a Methodist. I am Episcopalian." He said uneasily, "I think the insultation had to do with his Good Samaritan sermon."

"Why, I feel heaven's stamp already."

And Emery unfolded a plan so outrageous that Dance laughed until the train came, and that night, laughed until sleep came. And that night, Emery Jones did not sleep.

———

At the Americus depot, while Dance laughed himself sideways on a bench, Emery asked the station agent if he knew where Reverend Gillette lived, as he had a matter of conscience to discuss. The agent, who fought in the Mexican War, knew soldiers had much to confess, gambling and drinking and all manner of promiscuity at the head of the list. He patted the penitent on the back and said he was a good fellow, then gave directions to the Gillette home, a tidy little clapboard affair right next to the Methodist church.

———

At dawn, when Reverend William Gillette emerged from the privy at the back of the house, a sack came down on his head. He was carried through the corn, dropped once from his struggles, and bundled into the back of a wagon.

Persecution for preaching the gospel had surely come upon him, and he prepared to die for Jesus.

9

VIOLET AND MOTHER PREPARED the parlor for the Knitting Brigade. The Americus Ladies' Knitting Brigade met every Monday afternoon. In the first year of the war they had thirty-some members, and the parlor was packed. The ladies of Americus were like those in any other Southern city. Indefatigable energy filled parlors with socks and blankets, patch kits and soap, jars of jelly, jam, and butters, and all manner of packaging materials to send forth these tokens of home, sure to sustain the homesick and strengthen the weary.

The war ground on, and most parlors became less concerned with necessities for the troops and more concerned with necessities for their own households. Knitting Brigade attendance began to flag. Now, ten women was a good turnout.

Violet picked a protruding feather from a davenport bolster. "How many do you think will come today?"

"Do not take that tone, my dear. It is depressive. I like what Mr. Jones said, for it heartened me: the good Lord will send those as have ears to hear."

"That is regarding the Friends of Andersonville Prison meeting tomorrow night."

"Apply it to today's Brigade as well. It is a precursor."

"I can't argue with that. My stomach is in fits." She examined the feather she'd plucked. "I hope they leave the tar at home."

Mother stopped in the center of the parlor and put her hands on her hips. She looked down at Rosie, Daisy, and Posey. Posey was marking black dots on wooden cubes. "Posey pie, what are you doing?"

"Making dice to sell to the troops."

"Making *what*?"

Rosie looked up. "There is profit to be had, Mother."

Daisy shrugged. "They're going to gamble anyway. Might as well have fine dice."

"While *we* make a profit."

Posey held up two of the dice. "See? They're a little big, but they should suit right fine."

"They should suit *very well* and you three stop it this instant! I *de*clare! Gambling!" She called to the kitchen, "Ellen, is that basket for Widow Hatcher ready? I have three young miscreants in need of decent occupation." To the miscreants, she said, "You clear this up and throw those in the wood box. Ellen needs more kindling."

"Mother, this is our *stock*!" Daisy protested.

"All our profits . . ." Rosie groaned.

"It must be borne," Posey said stoically. She began to gather the blocks into her apron.

"Posey, mind that ink . . . ," said Mother.

"Widow Hatcher doesn't need a basket," Daisy said. "She is plenty fat."

"She is ornery, to boot."

"Last time we were there, she hardly took the basket for pride."

Mother looked at Daisy. "I told you to leave it on her porch."

"We wanted to see her thanks," Posey said from the kitchen, where she was emptying her apron into Ellen's wood box.

"She wasn't thankful," Rosie said.

Mother's eyes went wide. She said dangerously slow, "Leave it on her porch this time."

"Yes, ma'am," all three chimed, subdued.

Lily was sorting through the latest collection in the Pressing Needs box. "Look. Someone gave a very nice pencil." She held it up.

Posey came back from the kitchen, the basket for Widow Hatcher on her hip. She paused next to Lily. "Well, that is tempting."

"Is it *your* pressing need?" Lily asked, an eyebrow raised.

"No. But I cannot deny it is tempting." She put down the basket, and peeked under the dish towel. "Well, this is tempting, too. I wondered why it was so heavy."

The twins came close. "What's in there?"

"A whole roast chicken. A jar of Papa's guava jelly."

"Some of the madeleines for the Brigade," Rosie accused. "Will there be enough for us?"

"Listen to me." Mother's hands went to her hips, a common pose when addressing the three. "This war has touched us all. *We* have no men to send, but others have sent theirs. We must stand by them. How do you think she makes money when her husband is dead and her only son gone to war?"

"She makes those ugly chair cushions," Daisy said.

"They don't sell much," Rosie, the ringleader, said thoughtfully. "She has not much skill. People buy them from pity. Mama bought eight and we do not use them." She looked at the other two. "Let us try and be kind." Rosie picked up the basket, and the other two followed her out the front door.

"Has she any word yet?" Lily asked.

"I haven't heard," Mother said softly.

Widow Hatcher's son had been gravely wounded in battle at a place called Peachtree Creek. It was not far away, north only by a few hundred miles.

"It is time to follow the news again," Violet said. "The war comes to us."

When Ben had gone off, she led the family in keeping track of troop movements by scouring four newspapers. She loitered near the telegraph office, inspected the bulletin board in front of the depot to read daily postings that newspapers couldn't keep up with—and to read the lists of the glorious dead. After Ben's name appeared on that list, Violet's patriotic fervor dried up and she never went back to the boards.

She came alongside her mother, who had devoted herself to helping the Confederate soldier, and instead of troop movements Violet's world became Americus once more. The unpeopling of Americus had become a grief the entire community bore together. No one wanted to read the news anymore; they did, but not for the Cause. They did it for the boys of Americus still fighting, boys they all knew. Boys she'd gone to grammar school with, or Sunday school. Boys she'd danced with at parties; boys who had once plowed the home fields, now buried in distant ones. Husbands, sons, fathers—lost. Widows' weeds replaced party dresses. Black crepe was everywhere, and now Yankees were on Georgia soil. Would they breach Atlanta? How long before they did?

"*Will* there be enough madeleines?" Lily asked.

Violet shook from her thoughts. "I cannot imagine more than half a dozen showing up."

"Hettie will be here," Mother said firmly. Hettie Dixon, a widow so long that most took her for an old maid, was Mother's fiercest friend. "And Constance Greer. The two Louises and the two Marys."

"The *one* Mary, I should think," said Violet. After all, Mary Robinson, Ben's mother, had told her daughter the Stileses were traitors.

"Perhaps so. But stay on what Emery said, Violet dear." Mother paused in her tidying up to give Violet's face a quick caress. Just as quickly, her attention was diverted. "Lily, why is that candle and picture still there? It looks like a shrine. Are we Catholics?"

"I find it a fitting way of remembrance," Lily said of the rippled candle stub in a pewter holder. Next to it was a picture of Jeb Stuart, the dashing cavalry officer killed in May. Lily had clipped the picture, weeping, from an illustrated newspaper.

"The poor boy," Mother murmured, laying a hand on her cheek. "And so handsome." Then she said briskly, "Take it to your bedroom. We must mind our p's and q's today. We can't have them thinking we've gone Yankee *and* Catholic all at the same time."

"Dey all think de 'Pocalypse be on 'em." Ellen offered half a madeleine to Mother.

Mother chewed and concentrated. She nodded. "They're perfect."

"You notice anythin' diff'rent?" Ellen said slyly.

Mother shook her head, and Ellen broke into a wide smile. "Dis time I makes 'em wid *no* yeast powda. Ain't *got* no mo', so I jes beat up dem eggs extry high with dat Dover, and Lawd have mercy if dese ain't betta."

"They are supreme," Mother pronounced. "You should make them like this always."

The door banged open and Posey charged in, straight for Mother. She threw her arms around Mother's middle and buried her face.

"Mercy!" Mother gasped. "What's happened?"

Rosie and Daisy came in. Daisy, her face stricken, started for Ellen until she realized Rosie had not, and remained in place. She looked down.

THE SENTINELS OF ANDERSONVILLE

Rosie said slowly, "Widow Hatcher was *kind*, Mama. It was unsettling."

"She was crying," Posey said, muffled.

"Oh no! Is it Frank?" Mother said.

"No." Rosie put her hands behind her back and leaned against the wall. "She was hungry is all."

"She shall have my dessert," Posey wept into Mother's apron. "Even if it is custard pie."

"Mine as well," Daisy said.

"She was eating the madeleines and crying at the same time. It is not Christian of me, but I am angry at those Yankees," Rosie said. Tears rose in her eyes. She glanced at Violet. "Maybe even starving Yanks. She was *that* hungry." Rosie wiped her nose. "Mama, she asked us to go down to the bulletin boards with her. She is afraid to go alone. May we?"

Mother nodded.

"Come on, Daise." Rosie held out her hand. Daisy took it and the two left.

Posey was shaking her head in Mother's apron. "I don't have the heart."

Mother held her close. "It's all right, child. Besides, I need your help. Tessie Robinson will likely come, will she not?"

Posey sniffed. "To eat madeleines is all."

"The two of you can serve today."

Posey looked up. She brushed tear-damp hair from her face. "Can we use the silver tray?"

"If you make sure it is suitable. No tarnish."

Posey dashed off.

"Ellen, move Widow Hatcher from the monthly list to the weekly."

"I'se already done it in m'head." She headed for the kitchen.

"Don't you take down dat tray, Posey. You gonna topple dat tower. Wait fo' me."

"Mother? Violet?" Lily said at the porch door.

Mother and Violet hurried over.

"Goodness gracious." Mother's hand went to her throat. "Look at them."

"Hettie, Constance—*both* Marys! Louise, Grandma Percy—is that *Sallie*?"

"Sallie," Violet said, lip curled.

"Ann Hodgson! Oh, it's good to see her! Look, she brought baby James—the girls will be thrilled. There's Big Sue—"

"Don't call her that," said Mother automatically.

"Mae Belle Dreyer, the other Louise—Mother, is this a good thing or a bad thing?"

"I hardly know. They look a mob. One thing is sure—we do *not* have enough madeleines. Stall them, girls! Show them the new trellis. I will help Ellen make more. We must not look as if we expected few!" They rarely saw Mother run, but she grabbed her skirts and ran.

"What can it mean?" Violet wondered. "They do look like a mob."

Lily must have wondered, too. She grabbed Violet's hand and squeezed.

———

Colonel Hettie Dixon called the Americus Ladies' Knitting Brigade to order, General Polly Stiles presiding and momentarily occupied. Old Business: Sell 100 pairs of Socks at the Millard Dance for the Americus War Widows and Orphans Fund. New Business: the Millard Dance, now Fraught with Ominous Portents. And Hebrews 13:3.

Twenty-one, not including children, Violet counted. They had to pull in chairs from the dining room and porch. The children sat in the middle, on the carpet. What did this turnout mean? It looked like the first several months of the war when they packed the place out every week. And sure enough . . . an unnatural silence reigned. Some had socks in their laps, but any attempt at knitting seemed pretense. This was not about socks for the Millard dance.

Hettie picked up the Pressing Needs box and shook it. "Dig deep, ladies," she said cheerily. She slowly drew an edged handkerchief from her pocket and placed it in the box. She had got hold of Matthew 5:16 months ago, and memorized it upon the group: Let your good works shine and spur others to the same. Slow made them shine and spur.

She started to pass the box, then noticed the pencil. "Now look at this." She took it out and held it aloft, as if brandishing the standard of a regiment. "Is this not Christian kindness?" She put it in the box and passed it to Grandma Percy. Grandma Percy rummaged through it, examining items with interest—especially a folded square of calico, which she was reluctant to replace—and passed it on without contribution.

Americus tried to behave as though not much had changed, in keeping with fashionable, dismissive defiance of the North, but calico at twenty-five dollars a yard when it went for eighty cents in '61 was not easily ignored. Pencils could not be had at any price. Shortages of paper, pencils, and ink made Letters for Our Soldiers more difficult to produce, and envelopes had to be fashioned from old forms and receipts donated from local businesses.

Penciled on the side of the box in Lily's neat hand was Titus 3:14, copied under the dictation of Hettie Dixon.

"This is our Pressing Needs box," she had informed the ladies at the Brigade's inaugural meeting in June of '61. "Blockade or no blockade, we will station it at our various churches *every* Sunday for collection, for the verse does not say, 'Give to pressing needs *only* if there is no blockade.' You will notice the change of words in the scriptural text from 'necessary uses' to 'pressing needs.' Do not be alarmed. It is an illumination regarding *direct doctrinal application*, courtesy of Dr. Amos Wiley. Do not fret yourselves, ladies—it is a *legal usage* of Scripture. I have not incurred a plague."

The ladies were in no apparent danger of alarm.

Not much had changed in three years.

"I got hold of Hebrews 13:3," Colonel Hettie now said. "About the prisoners." She quoted the verse, inviting not a mote of interest in direct doctrinal application.

"I heard the same announcement was made at your church as ours," Constance Greer, a Baptist, said to Violet. Constance wore the same corkscrew ringlets she had when she was a girl. They framed a puffy, aging face. "The Millards' dance is *tomorrow* night. Not Saturday. *Tomorrow.* There is a great deal of consternation over this. At *our* church, at any rate."

Twenty-one ladies seized upon the unprecedence, and off they went, a lighted match thrown down on turpentine-soaked cotton.

Hettie reached for the metronome. When prodigious chitchat produced fewer socks, she employed the metronome. It set the knitting pace and production increased. She once told Mother if they would not listen to Scripture, they *would* produce socks.

"Has anyone ever *heard* of changing a dance date?" asked Mae Belle Dreyer, an Episcopalian. Episcopalians were practically Catholic, but not quite, so Mae Belle was treated normally and not with overpoliteness.

"What provoked it?" said Louise Spencer.

"What, indeed," said Mary Robinson darkly, needles clicking.

"It *is* inconvenient." Constance, a spinster fraught with good works, winced. "I had planned to knit and knit on Thursday's trip to Albany. I have two pairs to go and *would've* had them done by Saturday. It will not be my fault, yet I will not feel as if I've done my duty."

"I made four pairs extra," Hettie said soothingly. "Two can count toward yours. Come, my lovely ladies, let your needles fly. Nothing has changed. Nothing has changed. Widows and orphans, widows and orphans." She said it in time with the metronome.

"I *wish* I could make the meeting tomorrow night, Violet dear," Constance said, corkscrew curls shaking in sympathy. "But I had pledged my help to Josie Millard for preparations."

"Perhaps you should postpone it," said Sallie Peyton, across from Violet. "Who would show up?"

Sallie Peyton had come only twice to Knitting Brigade. She and Violet had been classmates at the Furlow Masonic Female College at the far west end of Lamar Street. While Violet and Lily disliked Sallie discreetly, the younger Stiles girls disliked her with open relish. She was rich and pretty to a fault. Far worse, she had come with her parents for Sunday dinner a few months back and flirted shamelessly with Dance. Posey had stepped on her foot.

Before Violet could answer, Hettie announced, "It shall carry on as planned. Tomorrow night I will be *right* here, *in* this place, *with* all my heart, for the sake of Hebrews 13:3. Dorsa Walker will be in charge of selling the socks at the Millards'. It is all arranged."

"Will you postpone it?" Sallie asked Violet.

"Starving men don't have time for us to postpone," said Violet.

"I fear you won't have much of a turnout," said Sallie.

"Neither will the dance," Lily declared.

Hettie sighed and clicked off the metronome.

"Too bad *Dance* won't be there for you to *dance* with," Posey commented. The extra madeleines were not yet ready to serve. She sat on the floor with Tessie Robinson, winding a hank of wool into a ball. "Emery Jones neither. I plan to marry him one day. I kindly appreciate you all steer clear of him."

"Why, Violet," Sallie said, "do you intend to steal the few eligible dancing partners we have?"

"I don't have any dance in me, Sallie. I've seen the prisoners."

"Who would want to dance with a Yank?" Sallie laughed, sure others would laugh along. No one did.

"Violet's right," said Ann Hodgson. She was the only one without the pretense of knitting in her lap. "You know she is, Sallie Peyton. You were at the same picnic as I. You saw down into that fort. I saw you throw them your crusts."

"Yes, it was a pitiful sight."

"You made sport of them."

"I did not!"

"You threw down your crusts and laughed while they scrambled about."

"That is ugly," said Posey, lowering the yarn.

"You can bet *that* guard wouldn't dance with you," Ann told her.

"Which guard?" asked Violet.

Ann looked at Violet. "There was a boy around our age in one of those lofts. You have to climb a ladder to get to it. The lofts look down into the stockade. Well, Sallie and Florence and I went over because Sallie said she wanted to see Yanks up close. We went up the ladder, and . . ." Ann looked at the rest of the Knitting Brigade. "I've never seen anything like it. Such a tremendous amount of men. They were filthy, and terribly thin. They were starving. I have never seen starvation. It was . . . overwhelming."

Ann Hodgson did not often come on Mondays. She lived closer to Andersonville. She was a year or two older than Violet, and Violet had always admired her. She had a plain, confident face and a plain, confident manner, much like Hettie Dixon. Her husband of three years was in the war. John came home once on furlough, and later came baby James. He was seven months old. As Lily had predicted, Rosie and Daisy had received him with delight and took him over to see Widow Hatcher.

131

"Was this the picnic Papa spoke of?" Lily said slowly. "The one where you ate on a hillside right in front of the men? And the garrison staged a mock battle for your entertainment?"

"It was fun." Sallie shrugged.

"It was shameful," said Ann. "I didn't know where we were going to eat. I didn't know what they were going to do."

"What about the guard?" Violet asked.

"That Dance Pickett thinks he's some peacock just because of his father," Sallie said.

"What did he do?" Violet asked Ann.

"Took her wrist and said if she threw any more crusts, he'd throw her. The other guard laughed and laughed."

"He ought not have *touched* me!"

"That's the best thing I've heard all day," said Posey.

"How you ever thought you'd amuse anyone with that behavior," Ann said. "No one thought it funny." She looked at Violet. "I'm not here to knit. I don't have time these days. I'm here to tell you how I felt when I saw that bill posted at the Andersonville depot."

"Here it comes," said Grandma Percy.

"I want to tell you what you are up against."

"I'm getting a feeling."

"No," Ann said, shaking her head. "Listen. After that picnic, I took a wagon with Isaiah and we went out collecting food, round where I live. Most were willing to help. That wagon bed was full. We drove up to the big gate and I went to the office of Captain Wirz, who is the commander of the prison. I told him we had collected food, and would he please pass it out at the normal time for rations. Well, he was agitated. He said I would have to get written permission from General Winder. I said, 'Whatever for? It is simply food for starving men.' He said it had to be done, and so I left Isaiah with the food and James and I went to town. Captain Wirz went with me.

General Winder was in his office with two other men. I stated the case and asked if he would give me a writ." She fell silent.

"Go on," said Hettie.

She looked at the ladies. "You will hardly guess. He said he wondered just how far my Yankee sympathies went. He said James likely had *Northern* blood in him . . . if you take my meaning."

A collective gasp.

"That cannot be true," Mary Robinson said. "General Winder is a gentleman. He paid his respects to Henry and Josie Millard when they lost Toby."

"Captain Wirz suggested I set up a house of ill repute near the stockade."

Another gasp.

"Only he didn't call it that. He called it far worse. And they all laughed."

"I will not sit and listen to these falsehoods." Mary Robinson put her knitting back in her bag. "It is wicked."

"It is true." It came from Sallie Peyton, whose voice had changed.

All eyes upon her, she murmured, "Mama and I were at the dry goods store. General Winder's door was open. I didn't hear what the general said, but I did hear Captain Wirz. He said it to be heard. They did laugh. Ann cried."

"I didn't cry at that. I cried when General Winder told me to take back the food from where it came. I said, 'But sir, men are starving.' He said, 'That is neither here nor there.' I said, 'It is mercy—it is a matter of humanity.' He said there was no humanity about it; that my act was intended as a slur upon the Confederate government and covert attack upon him. I said, 'Sir, I do not take your meaning; this has nothing to do with you.' He said, 'Get out, and take your food with you.' And that is when I cried.

"Captain Wirz escorted me back to the wagon, and when it was

THE SENTINELS OF ANDERSONVILLE

just us, he seemed different, as if he were sorry. That could be my imagination—I was crying so, I didn't hardly notice him. I got in the wagon and we started to drive off. Then I heard someone yelling. It was the guard, the young one. He came running up, and said, 'Thank you, thank you!'" Tears came, and she blinked them back. "I was in such a state I could hardly understand him. I said, 'But I didn't do anything,' and cried even harder. He said, 'Oh, but you did.' Captain Wirz came, and he yelled and cursed at the guard to get back to his post. But that boy just stood and stared him down. He made a fist and I thought he was going to hit him. I said, 'Don't.' Isaiah got nervous, and we drove off."

"That's my Dance," Posey said.

"How do you think Josie Millard felt about that handbill?" said Mary Robinson, whose closest friend was Josie. She looked them round. "What about Judge Tate? He lost his nephew Thomas and just lost Brett at Peachtree. What about the Runcorns? Do you see Ravinia here? She hasn't missed a meeting—why do you think she'd miss this one? What about Clara Hatcher? What about loyalty to our *own* people, to these poor souls who have given all? Charity begins at *home*."

"If we do not denounce the Yankees, we are sympathizers. And if we endeavor to feed them, we are traitors." Ann lifted her hands and dropped them. "My husband fights for the South. As to the Cause, I am Southern, born and bred. Our only hope is for Lincoln to lose. Get him out of office, perhaps the tides will turn. Maybe even the border states will turn. But starvation has nothing to do with politics. Mrs. Robinson, if you could just see them."

Constance rocked in place and fanned herself, corkscrew curls trembling. "I'm all aflutter. I see both sides. I want to feed them. But poor Josie Millard . . ."

"I cannot feed a man who killed my best friend's boy." Tears came to Mary's eyes. She fiddled with the half-finished sock in her lap.

The room grew very quiet. The ladies exchanged glances, and then pitying looks went to Mary, and some went to Violet.

"That is love, too," Mary said. "She is the kindest woman I know, and her heart is—" She took a moment to collect herself. "Her heart is broken. He was like a son to me. I nursed him when Josie was sick. I half raised him. I cannot feed a Yankee. It would be false of me. False to Toby, and to—"

The room held its breath.

Mary raised her eyes to Violet.

"I still have the pearl beads for your dress," she said softly. "We got them from Augusta. Remember the lovely shop?"

The collective gasp was no louder than rustling silk.

"Some think I am hard-hearted, because I did not cry at his service. Well, a dead woman can't cry, and I wish I had stayed dead." Tears freely fell. She couldn't talk above a whisper. "You are such a good girl, Violet Stiles. You are spirited, and strong, and how my boy loved you. How I looked forward to being your mother-in-law."

Hettie took the handkerchief out of the Pressing Needs box and slipped it onto her lap. Tessie went to her mother and cupped her hands around her face. "Don't cry, Mama."

"We held out hope for Toby because if he made it, some of Ben would too. They grew up side by side. They were brothers." She pressed the handkerchief to her eyes. "They murdered my boy. I cannot feed them, Violet. What I can't understand is how can you?"

How Violet had dreaded this moment.

There was nothing to do but step into it. "Most times I couldn't cry either, Mrs. Robinson," she said softly, feeling peculiar, as if someone else were speaking. "Some thought me cold. Isn't it strange? The two who loved him most? How alike we are. I've always thought it."

Mrs. Robinson had set the course of conduct for bereavement, and Violet had followed her example readily. Her parents did not know what to do. They once called in Hettie, who was always on hand for any Stiles crisis, but all Hettie did was sit with Violet on the porch and hand her an occasional homemade peppermint. That day, Hettie became more than a family friend. She became Violet's friend.

She felt the accustomed emptiness when she reached for Ben, and yet something was different. For the first time in a very long time, it didn't hurt as badly.

"I was at the prison and I saw a man. He was a step away from death. And a light came to me, then. In that moment, he was not North and I was not South. He was just a man, suffering dreadfully. It was as if he lay all alone at the bottom of a very dark well. If my Ben were in that well, I would have wanted someone to come and let him know he was not alone."

"Remember the prisoners," Hettie Dixon whispered.

"I saw those men that day, and all I could think of was my John," said Ann Hodgson, eyes brimming. "What if he were in a Northern prison, suffering so? I learned I cannot help by going straight up to the gate. Violet, that handbill is straight up to the gate. Maybe it will work if you get this town on your side. But if not—don't you give up, Violet Stiles. I found other ways. You can too. When I saw that handbill, I was no longer alone. I knew, then, how the guard who thanked me felt."

"Cast down," Hettie whispered, "but not destroyed."

"I'm here to say thank you, Violet."

"Madeleines?" Mother stood in the entryway holding a silver tray, a flood of tears streaming down her face.

"News!" someone shrieked outside. "There is news!"

For a moment shock took the parlor and no one moved, then all hurried as one for the porch.

It was Hanna Percy, daughter-in-law of Grandma Percy.

"What do you think?" she gasped, waving her hands in the air. "Oh, oh, what do you think?"

"Tell it," ordered Grandma Percy.

Hanna took a second to catch her breath, and then screamed, "Reverend Gillette has been *kidnapped*!"

———

It was a pleasant day, not as hot, and Emery and Dance enjoyed the drive.

"What are you fixin' to do after the war's over?" Emery asked.

"I'm studying to be a patent lawyer, University of Georgia. But do you know, I think I'll do a bit of traveling before I go back, once this war is done. I'd like to go west. It doesn't seem as frightening. Lawless men, Indians on the warpath . . . all just Sunday school, next to Andersonville. How about you?"

"Pennsylvania. That's in my cards. I might take a look around before I do. See New York. All them little states. I'd like to see places where the Revolution was fought. My great-granddaddy fought at Kings Mountain."

"Mine fought, too. Wish I knew where."

"I will die for Jesus," said the man under the hood in the back of the cart. "But if you touch my family, I will kill you."

Dance grinned at Emery. He was starting to like this preacher.

"Your family's in no harm," Emery chuckled.

"What do you plan to do to me?"

"First, we will get you to recant your religion. Aw, I'm just teasin'. I like religion. The good kind. The truth is you need to see something, Rev'rend. We have arranged a tour for you."

Dance nodded. "I'd say they could use the services of more clergy. So few go in. None from Americus."

"I'm happy to serve whoever needs me, but is this necessary? Where are you taking me?"

"Belly of the whale, for you would not go to Nineveh."

"I see. Does this make you God?"

"No," said Emery. "I'm just mad."

"What are you mad at?"

"Your Millard message," said Dance.

"What message?"

"Did you or did you not advocate the change of date for the Millard dance?"

"I certainly did!"

"For the sole purpose of defeating the F.A.P. meeting?"

"Of course! I did my duty!"

Emery shook his head. "I despair."

"What else should I have done? General Winder said it's a front for a Yankee spy operation. Sent someone to talk to me personally. He said they have moved into Americus and are fomenting discord, a whole band of 'em. They are the forerunners of— What is that smell?"

"You best get acquainted with it."

"Smells like an overflowing privy. Where was I? Forerunners. Will you take this bag off my head? It's itchy and humiliating. I see a bug. I think it is a weevil. It's heading straight for—oh, there it goes. Wonderful. It's in my beard. It will nest and breed."

"Why were you reluctant to make that announcement?"

"Because my board is not in accord. It makes me unhappy."

"Why is it not in accord?"

The burlap sack went silent. Then, "Some said that meeting is for humanitarian purposes."

"You didn't believe them?"

"I didn't know what to believe. I've got a general in the army telling me one thing, other folks telling me the opposite . . . so I went privately to Henry and Josie to know their mind on the affair. They were the ones who convinced me, not General Winder and his men. The dance is to raise money for the war widows and orphans in Americus. This couple lost their beloved boy, but have taken pains to look to the distress of others. Pure religion is to take care of widows and orphans. I made my choice over a suspect and unproven organization, and I stand by it. Will you please take off this sack?"

Dance looked at Emery, who nodded.

"Much better. Thank you. Hello, Mr. Pickett. Thought it was you." He looked at Emery. "Who is your friend?"

"Corporal Emery Jones, 22nd Alabama Volunteers."

"How do."

"How do."

"You boys fixing to take me to that prison?"

"Yes, sir."

"See for myself, I suppose? Hope I have an epiphany?"

Emery chuckled. "Yes, sir."

"Well, why didn't you just ask me?"

"Didn't think you would come."

"I might not have." He looked at Dance. "But he made a fair case, a few weeks back. I have thought about stopping into the provost marshal's office for a visiting pass."

"That is exactly how nothing gets done," Emery said. "Too much thinking, not enough doing. You are about to have a chance to rectify. We didn't just get you a pass. We got you an identity. What's the name, Dance?"

"Private Hinton A. Dayton, 7th Pennsylvania Artillery."

"He died yesterday. I have spoken with Atwater, and he will hold off on recording his name for a day or so."

"I'm not sure I understand," the reverend said slowly.

"Oh, I think you do. Private Dayton."

—

It wasn't often a single prisoner entered the stockade. The pass-through door closed and locked behind Reverend Gillette, and a great wall of men stood before him, hundreds, thousands deep. All Yankees. All staring at him.

"19th Michigan?"

10

"Any word on Rev'rend Gillette?"

"Nothin'. They're havin' a prayer vigil at the Methodist church, and one at the Baptist, which is right ecumenical of 'em. There's folks all over the telegraph office. They called in the militia, they telegrammed Gov'ner Brown. They believe it has to do with the Millard dance."

"They never did!"

"Yup. They're sayin' it's that faction called Friends. General Winder's sent down a fellow from Andersonville. One of them detectives. He'll smoke it out. He has a resolute cast."

"I hear Dr. Stiles is in a fix."

"Oh, he stepped in it this time."

"I thought he was a good man. What a shame. Any ransom note on Gillette?"

"There was a note stuck up on the bulletin board at the depot!"

"There never was! Is it still there?"

"Nope. The detective took it."

"What'd it say?"

"Oh, I worked it in so's I could tell Bets. 'Dear Americus. We have confiscated your reverend. We will return him hopefully unharmed. Don't know exactly when. Yours in perpetuity, The Kidnappers.'"

"Perpetuity!"

"Ain't it a handle?"

"I never heard it."

"It means it goes on and on and on. Silas Runcorn told me. Told how to say it, too. I had to work it over to get it right."

"They arrest Dr. Stiles?"

"No, but they run him down to the provost marshal for questionin'. Judge Tate had a fit on that, and ordered him released."

"What's gonna happen to him?"

"Don't know. But one thing's sure: if I look into the meanin' of that note, the kidnappin's ain't done. *Perpetuity*, and all. Yours in *perpetuity*. Think on that and let it chill your innards."

"What is this country comin' to? Never took the doctor for a turncoat."

———

He wasn't as old as Lew expected. The man turned into the prison could not be above forty.

Lew had orders just like this reverend, who was to make a circuit of the entire prison, and then wait for Lew when he got back to the north gate. Lew, unknown to the reverend, was to follow behind and make sure no harm came to him. He was to have him back by ration time, when it would be easier to get him out. The hope was for this man to see enough that he should make an impression on a meeting tomorrow night at the home of some influential doctor in Americus, the town closest to Andersonville. The meeting had to do with raising help for the boys in here. Lew needed no convincing to do his part.

When he first saw Emery Jones on dead watch, Lew landed a

TRACY GROOT

punch so solid that both went down, Emery from impact and Lew from follow-through.

"You stupid—!"

"Do you know," Emery had said, sitting in a dusty heap, "I had to do some talkin' to get this detail?"

"You reenlisted!" Lew grabbed a handful of dust and threw it.

"I needed an address."

"You—what?"

Lew had stared at him dumbly from where he sat. Some men stopped, transfixed, to see if anything would come of this shocking squabble between a Confederate guard and an inmate, while others kept moving. They had to look through a line of shuffling legs to see each other.

"Your sister's address. I forgot to ask for it. She live in Ezra too?"

"You stupid, crazy Reb."

"I'll tell you what gets me about her. You said she was in a fire to sign up after Fort Sumter." Emery wiped his nose and checked to see if there was blood. "She made a fuss that here she was, a better shot than most men, but her job came down to the home front." He waited for a denser line of men to pass so he could see Lew better. "You said she was so hollerin' mad you could put lead in her mouth and she'd spit out bullets."

Lew shrugged. "She took to the home front. Organized a league. Went and volunteered at Cooper's."

"*That's* what I liked! Not just the mad but what she done with it. That is a quality girl."

"Well, she doesn't live in Ezra. Lives with my folks by Marsh Creek, in Adams. North and west of Gettysburg."

"Much obliged." He got up and dusted off his seat. He slipped his hands in the band of his trousers. "See you around, blue belly." He walked off some, then came back and put out his hand.

143

THE SENTINELS OF ANDERSONVILLE

The preacher had so far fended off men from Fetchner's sutlery pretty well, and when it was apparent that he had no news, others left him alone. That left only folks determined to do a good turn for new-comers, and folks determined to do bad ones. As he had no tempting haversack or bulges, these mostly fell off too. It came down to just the man and one pesky individual who followed him south along the deadline until they came to the footbridge over the foul creek. Then the pesky man took his leave and attached himself to someone else.

Lew could almost pity the preacher. He had stopped a few times as if to vomit, but each time he got hold of himself pretty well until he came to the creek. He started for the footbridge, paused to empty his stomach, and started again, hand over his nose and mouth.

"I didn't know what I was deliverin' you up to," Emery had said on their own tour. Emery had 'conscripted' Lew and they walked about on the hunt for dead bodies.

"No one could."

"I wouldn't have, had I known."

"I know it, Em."

"And you were all set to muster out."

"Well, so were you."

They walked for a time.

"You meet up with any of your boys?"

"Artie Van Slett and Harris Gill. Artie's not doing so good. Harris's got a bad infection in his lip. He's getting feverish. Won't go to the hospital."

"I keep tryin' to figure out how this hellhole came about."

"You and us all. Before the war, I'd heard of battles where ditches ran with blood but didn't believe such a thing as actual until Gettysburg, where you'd take a step and the ground would squish. We heard worrying things of Andersonville, but nothing short of being here can make you believe it. I wish Sherman knew."

"They say he does."

"That is not possible. He'd bust us out. He'd exchange. I don't know why it seems exchange has shut down. You hear anything on it?"

Emery glanced about, then said quietly, "I'm working on a plan to get you out."

Lew made sure Emery was looking in his eyes. "I heard they hanged a few who'd done that, back in June. You've done enough on my behalf. You do any more, I won't forgive you."

The preacher's orders were to walk the circumference of the prison. He was not to stop until he made it all the way around. If the stockade was empty, such a walk would take an hour. With almost thirty thousand men, it would take the better part of the day. Longer, if the preacher kept stopping as he did. A man lay on the south bank of the creek next to the footbridge. The preacher helped him sit up. Not ten steps later, he helped another man carry his comrade to the sick call at the south gate. There, the preacher stayed for an hour. He first seemed overwhelmed at the sight of sick men numbering in the thousands, all lined up to see if they could gain admittance to the hospital. Then he went to a man lying near the gate, who apparently had called to him. He talked with him some, then sat beside him.

"You sit tight, Lew. I'm working out a plan," Emery had assured him.

"I keep reaching for the name of Little Mite, but it has not found its way south," Lew had said. "I should've bit my pride and asked Carrie when I could."

"Can't you write letters?"

"There's a letter box at the south gate. One of the old-timers says don't bother. He's written home a dozen times since March, hasn't heard back. Some do hear back, some don't. A Negro from a colored troop told me his friend was taken as a slave to one of the head doctors.

From a warrior to a slave, can you beat that? I can't even think of it, makes me so mad. Well, this man says lots of letters come in, but that head doctor's wife and someone else goes through them. They take money and valuables and then burn the letters. Some get through, but not half as should. I will not have Carrie's letter ransacked."

"She can send it to me. I'll get it to you."

"That's just one more thing to put attention on you. Emery, you vex me. I am in enemy territory but you are not. Do not make yourself an enemy among your own people."

"They have me in with the 3rd Georgia Reserves. Half of 'em are boys, other half are grandpaps. They don't notice nothing."

The preacher was listening intently to the man he sat next to. He said some words and then bowed his head and prayed with the man.

A Catholic priest came in every day, Lew was told. He stayed somewhere on the grounds outside the stockade. He heard that this priest crawled into filthy hovels to minister to them of his kind first, them not of his kind next. Didn't matter your insights, religious or not, this priest was on hand for you. Lew was told he ate whatever rations the men ate.

It did something to watch a man care for another.

———

Reverend William Gillette thought he had nothing left in his stomach, but even what was not there threatened to make a show. He wasn't sure what was worse, crossing that filthy creek or coming upon this particular concentration of men.

The creek and its banks, a spongy area more marsh than solid land, was a living mass of putrefaction and filth. The assault on his senses was more than just smell; it seemed the whole of it would crawl down his throat. He saw a man covered in large gangrenous sores filled with flies and maggots, lying half in the water and half out. He thought the man was a tree stump. He saw another man scoop a handful of the brown creek liquid, sort through the handful, and pluck something from it to eat.

"You try and stand up 'til you got to lay down. That's how it works."

The man he sat next to repeated this over and over until Reverend Gillette finally realized he was either sun touched or had gone past endurance in every way, mental and physical. The man had hailed him, and it was the first thing he said when Gillette bent to listen. It took some doing not to recoil from the fetid breath.

"You try and stand up 'til you got to lay down."

"Why is that?" he asked politely.

"Bugs." The man's eyes tried to focus. "You try and stand up 'til you got to lay down. They eat you up at night."

"Where you from, son?"

"Maine." He thought a moment. "Presque Isle."

The young man lay curled on his side, huddled against the earth as if poured upon it, as if afraid someone would move him. He was better clothed than some Gillette had seen, but was thinner than others. Except for his legs. From the knees down, his legs and feet were so swollen it was no wonder he didn't stand. The legs of his trousers from the knees down had been split to accommodate.

"It's not as bad as I thought it'd be," he whispered.

"What is not?"

"Layin' down. You can't stand up all the time. You try and stand up 'til you got to lay down. That's how it works."

The boy's face was blackened with smoke or grime. His light-brown eyes stood a sharp contrast. "Can you take off my shoes? I want Mickelson to have 'em."

"Son . . . you don't have any shoes on."

"Oh."

Gillette sat beside him, trying to contain what threatened to overflow. This boy was one of thousands gathered at this gate. Some were in far worse condition. Some had gums so hideously swollen they couldn't close their mouths. Some had filthy bandages wrapped around wounds from past battles, uncleaned and unchanged, weeks or months old. Some were so thin the mind had a difficult time assigning such thinness to a human being. It was not natural, and the mind didn't want it to be.

"Are you waiting to get in the hospital?" Gillette asked the boy.

"There ain't room. We got to wait for others to die. My friends brought me. I used to do the bringing."

"You got a girl in Presque Isle?"

He smiled a little, turning his face shyly toward the ground.

Gillette smiled. "You do have a girl? What's her name?" Whoever she was, she'd not see this boy again, not this side of heaven. "What's her name, son?"

"Angelina," he whispered against the ground.

"Is she—" Gillette swallowed hard. "Is she pretty?"

But the boy did not answer.

Gillette laid a hand on the boy's shoulder and hung his head.

———

Lew met up with Harris Gill on the east side of the stockade.

"How's our preacher doing, boy-o?"

"Taking his time. He doesn't seem to be in a hurry."

"Aye. He's only halfway around. It'll be way past rations when he makes it back. That him?"

"That's him."

"Why, he looks like Colonel Ford."

"I've thought the same."

"Remember the snowball fight? He jumped off his horse and pitched right in."

Lew smiled. "Took cover behind it."

Harris laughed. "He knew we'd never hit that horse."

They watched the preacher.

"There goes his vest," Lew observed.

"Och, the silly man. He'll have no clothes left when he gets to the other side."

"He gave his shoes to that man always sitting at the deadline by the sinks. What do they call him?"

"Prairie John."

"Prairie John. He an Indian?"

"I think so. Artie may have consigned all Rebs to hell, but you know what, Lew? I'd like him to meet that one." Harris's face went blank. "The laddie's not well today."

"You don't look so well yourself," Lew said, finally noticing Harris's flushed face.

"I'll be fine. But that Artie. All the times I've told him to shut up, I'd give something pretty to hear him again."

———

Dance started to look in earnest for Reverend Gillette.

What if something happened to the preacher? What if he ran afoul of one of the more militant Regulators? Six Union men called Raiders were hanged a few weeks back for the plunder and murder of their own men. Law and order was mostly restored through a policing crew called the Regulators. But some of these men used their power as unscrupulously as the Raiders.

What if they figured out the reverend was a Confederate? What if someone knew him from Americus?

"Pickett, you are in a state of agitatement," Burr observed. "I don't know as I prefer this or the other."

Suddenly the plan didn't seem like such a good one. If something happened to the preacher . . .

"Someone's callin' for you."

Dance started, looking this way and that over the men, but Burr was looking at the ladder. Dance went over, and Emery Jones was at the bottom. He was clearly about to ask after the preacher when Burr stuck his head over the hole to peer down. Dance shook his head and Emery turned away.

Dance went to the rail. After months of allowing this mass to become one blurred entity, he now sought out single faces. To his surprise, many of those faces were familiar.

"What you up to, Pickett?" Burr said, squinting.

Perhaps the mass wasn't as blurred as he thought.

———

Harris Gill performed another neat trick of profanity to fashion from cusswords an intricate wrought-iron majesty. But Lew had no time to admire the edifice, for two known rabble-rousers, Raider-gang remnants, were heading straight for Reverend Gillette.

"That preacher made me nervous the minute I saw him," Lew said through his teeth as he and Harris pushed their way through. "Emery Jones, I will kill you."

"We just wanna see what's in your pockets," the tall one was saying. "You gave away them fancy shoes, you must got somethin' else."

"Gentlemen, I assure you, my pockets are as empty as my stomach." The preacher turned them inside out. "Oh. Well, I do have a few of my daughter's jacks. You are welcome to them."

"What is that accent? You a *Reb*?"

"You some kind of spy?" The shorter one grabbed the preacher by the collar. "They send you in to ferret out tunnels?"

"You know what we do to spies?"

"Of course he's a spy, boy-os." Harris came beside the preacher and whacked him on the back. "But he's *our* spy, ya great peawits."

"Don't you recognize him?" said Lew. "That's Little Mite Badger. That's his spy name, anyway. You should know him from *Frank's Illustrated*. My wife's in love with him."

"*All* Pennsylvania women be in love with him," Harris said sadly.

"I ain't seen a *Frank's Illustrated* in months," said the tall one.

"Well, I'm just in from Kennesaw. He came with me. They got him round about . . . where'd they pick you up, Mr. Badger?"

"Oh. Ah—near the Chattahoochee," the preacher said. "After a . . . struggle." He put up his fists.

"Lew brought me over to shake your hand." Harris stuck out his hand and the preacher shook it. "Heard you got some vital information to Sherman. Too bad it cost your freedom."

"Yes, well . . . Stars and Stripes forever," the preacher said.

The two thugs nodded. "Stars and Stripes forever," the tall one said. "Did you meet Sherman?"

"I did. He is . . . very committed. I was impressed."

"What's he look like in real life?"

"Ah, he's not as tall as I thought he would be."

"Boy, I sure woulda liked to meet him."

"That woulda been first rate." The tall one nodded. "Sorry you've come to these straits, mister. It's a real shame."

"Well, our lot is common," the preacher said.

"Listen, anyone gives you trouble, we're by where Mosby used to be. You ask for us by name—Elliott and Stern."

"I am obliged, gentlemen." The preacher gave a little bow.

The two started off, but Lew said, "Say—don't let out he's here, him being famous and all. You know how people are." Lew winked. "We'll let the fellow have some peace for a bit."

The tall one nodded grimly, as if to say the prison would deal with him before it dealt with the spy. The two left.

"Little Mite Badger," said the preacher, watching them go.

"It was all I could manage in short time," said Lew.

"Is there such a man? A Union spy?"

"No." Lew looked him over. "I'm Lew Gann. This is Harris Gill."

"William Gillette."

"Listen, Preacher, I need to have you at the north gate by ration time. That's not far off. You were supposed to just walk and observe."

"I am observing." They shared a long look.

"You want to observe more?" Harris asked. "We'll take you to Hotel Ford. It's where we sleep at night."

"Harris, that'll take too long," Lew protested.

"You should get someone to look at that," Gillette said, glancing at Harris's swollen lip.

"Artie's worse off. He's our messmate. We've been together for three years. If you can manage any help for him, why—I'd convert. To the everlastin' despair of my mother and all the saints."

"Catholic . . . Protestant . . . Does it really matter here?" the preacher said. He stared into the crowd of men.

"Say, now," said Harris. "Don't you despair, Father. You be as a skippin' stone. Don't sink in; just—"

"What's the matter with you?" Lew gave Harris a little push. "Let him sink. That's what he's here for. He's here to take in the whole of it, and bring it out there."

"They won't believe me."

"They might."

"I don't know if I would have believed me." He looked at Harris. "Where's Hotel Ford?"

11

THE RATION WAGON CAME AND WENT.

"What worries you, Pickett? I see you, Old Abe!" Burr hollered down. He shook his musket.

"I am here to be seen," the Yank hollered back.

"You keep toein' that line, you gonna lose some. Do not try me."

"For you are in a foul temper'ment," the other mocked with a Southern accent.

Burr grinned and lowered the musket. He looked at Dance, and the grin soured. "Pickett, you got me nervous."

Dance leaned on the rail. He studied Old Abe.

Ann Hodgson, Emery Jones, Violet Stiles. A wagon full of food, a kidnapping, a handbill. What had Dance done? He applauded.

"What is that man's real name?" Dance said.

"Tucker P. O'Riley, 12th Iowa."

"How did I know you'd know it? Burr, I believe I have cast off the two most important things to safeguard my sanity in this place. It is a paradox."

153

"What are them two things?"

"The ability to see and the ability to feel. Maybe to see and to feel is to act."

Burr spit. "I 'spect so."

"You missed me," Old Abe called.

"Oh, I wasn't aimin' for you, you old pisspot. You'd know if I was." He reached into his pocket. He sent out a furtive glance, then dropped a sweet potato over the rail. Old Abe made for it even as it fell, but it took a bounce and landed in the dead zone, two feet short of the deadline. He stopped short and stared up at Burr. Burr looked at the nearest sentry booth, but the fellows there were chitchatting. He gave a quick jerk of his head. Old Abe quickly reached over the line, snatched the sweet potato, and withdrew into the crowd.

"Do you know who my father is?"

"James Weld Pickett. Friend of Governor Joe Brown. Taught at Yale Law School same year Brown was there. Campaigned to get him into office. Y'all have dined together on multitudinous occasions."

Dance stared. "I've told you about him?"

"Lots of times."

"I don't remember."

"That ain't a surprise. Half the time you just listen to the wind in the pines."

"Well, I've shamed him, Burr."

"How'd y'all shame him?"

"My brother Beau's in the navy. He sails with the CSS *Florida*. He's very proud of Beau. I am, too. But early on I didn't make an effort to fight in this war, not like Beau did. I was trying to see how I felt about it. I didn't want to bleed and die for something I didn't believe in. If I believed, I could do that. I could."

"Go on."

"I was confused, and I was angry, and all I wanted to do was study and get on with my life and the war was nothing but an interruption. I took too long figuring it out." He chuckled bitterly. "I was the last one left in my classes because everyone else had gone to war, including the professors. The registrar finally told me not to show up. Do you know, anyone in the beginning who said they were against the war was a social exile? And now it is in fashion to do so? I hate what is in fashion. I have a contrary nature."

"Boy, I have seen *that*."

"Here is the truth: I was too afraid to let my father know how I felt about the war because I did, in fact, know my mind right from the start. But I didn't want to hear him say I was wrong."

"'Cause you loved him?"

Dance opened his mouth to spit out an answer, but a different one came out. "Well—yes. I hated to disappoint him."

"That's how it goes all over with fathers and sons, Pickett, high or low. Folks as wear broadcloth, such as yourself, or folks as wear homespun, such as me."

"He'd like you, Burr. You should meet him one day. He can fill a room."

"Well, I'd believe that. Now what're you trussed up about? I ain't seen you like this since that girl."

"The one I insulted?"

"Nope. Though I like tellin' that. The other one, Miss Stiles."

"She doesn't truss me up," Dance said, a curl to his lip. "Talk to Emery Jones about her. She'd follow him out on thin ice."

"Who'd follow me on thin ice?"

Emery came up the ladder.

"Violet Stiles."

At the rail, Emery edged out Burr, who pulled away to study the other two. One anxiously looked along the deadline north, while the other anxiously looked south.

"What you boys up to?" he asked. "You and Sergeant Keppel and the turnkey . . . you all is up to something."

"Any sign?" Emery asked.

"No."

Emery pushed his hat back. "I wonder now if this wasn't my best idea. There may be things I hadn't thought of."

"Well . . . I wasn't going to say anything. You seemed to have everything in hand, and I didn't want to dampen the momentum."

"What you two done?"

"What are the consequences of kidnapping, lawyer boy?" Emery said, scanning the stockade under his hand. "How bad an offense is that?"

"Aside from personal affront?"

"In the eyes of the law."

"I wouldn't think as much about what will happen to us as what is happening to him."

"I'm not worried about him. Lew will take care of him. What worries me is not being around to take care of Lew if I am off being hung."

"Hanged. Don't worry about that. We'll put it on Burr."

"What you gonna put on me?"

"We kidnapped a man," said Emery. "A preacher. We turned him into the pen to get a fill of it before the Millard dance tomorrow night, in hopes to set him preaching rightly once more."

"I thought his lectern would be a nice touch," Dance mused. "Set it up by the fiddlers."

"But we've lost him," said Emery.

"Where does Lew abide?" Dance stared under his hand into the thousands.

"I don't know."

"Where does he sleep at night?"

156

"I took your meaning the first time, and said I don't know."

"Boys, I'd laugh myself right out o' the county if I wudden petrified. That is some cockamamie number you have pulled. Y'all have stepped in it for sure."

"We know it."

Dance lowered his hand. "Whiskey, kidnapping . . . nothing works for me."

"What are we going to do, Dance?"

"I don't know."

"I'll tell you a thing I do know."

"What's that?"

"I am not the one Violet would follow."

———

Hotel Ford was a five-foot-square claim over a place half burrowed into the ground. The first occupant who did the burrowing had died, deeding the place to Bart and Andy Rogers, brothers from the 2nd Delaware. Bart and Andy made room for Harris and Artie. Bart died, making room for Lew.

Hotel Ford was smack in the middle of the northeast quadrant of the pen, where it took five minutes to make fifty paces. Just south of the hotel was a well, dug and maintained by a group of men. They charged for the water, but at a fairer price than most, and if the boy with the bullet-creased cheek was on guard, it was always free.

"We're coming to the new part," Harris said as they continued north along the deadline on the east side. "They expanded this place about a month ago."

"I know they pressed some of Howell Cobb's slaves to do it," said Reverend Gillette.

"Why didn't they press them to build barracks?" Lew asked.

"I don't have an answer for that."

"Is Cobb a big to-do? I don't have a handle on who he is. I know he's a general, and from this area."

"Well, he's a big to-do around here," said the preacher. "Very wealthy. Owns over a thousand slaves."

"Why hasn't he done something about this place?"

"I don't have an answer."

"Listen, Father, do you have any news on exchange?" Harris asked.

"I'm afraid I can't help you there either. I don't pay much attention to the newspapers anymore."

"The whole system is shut down, and we don't know why," Harris said. "One thing is sure—if Lincoln or Sherman had a boy in here, you bet it'd start up quick again."

They picked their way through, stepping over or around men.

"We're coming into our neighborhood," Harris said. "How's the arm, Indiana?" he asked of a man lying half in and half out of a tent—such as it was. It looked like a threadbare curtain stitched to an equally threadbare set of trousers, held up by two sticks.

"Not so good," said the man.

Harris squatted and took a peek under a filthy bandage. He examined the wound, picked a few things out of it, and resettled the bandage. He patted him on the back and said, "Don't strike your colors, lad."

They moved along, until a boy not more than fifteen came up to Harris. "Jim's taken to his bed again. Says he'll go over the deadline and stand until they shoot him. Says he's given up." The boy hung his head. "I can't have him give up."

Harris's face changed. It balled up like a fist, and with the shiny, gruesome infection that swelled his lower lip and chin, the effect was frightening indeed. He took his time rolling up one sleeve and then the other. He followed the boy.

"Preacher, you're gonna wanna cover your ears," Lew said uneasily. "In fact—you don't want to see this. It's not fitting for a guest."

The preacher had every intention of seeing it. Everyone in earshot did, and the party picked up interested persons along the way. Harris Gill had a reputation for breaking up monotony.

The boy stepped aside and Harris fell upon the tent like a thunderclap. "Come outta there, you no-good—" he hollered, finishing with an admirable wrought-iron feat of profanity. He seized a protruding foot and yanked a man out, along with the tent itself, leaving behind another man surprised from a nap.

Harris untangled the tent from Jim and hauled him eye-to-eye. "Get up, you great coward! Don't let me see you like that again!"

"Aw, Gill, it ain't gonna work this time," the man groaned, trying to push from Harris's grasp. "I got no spirit left. I'm too hungry. I'm dyin' of it."

"Don't strike your colors! You fight, boy-o, or by the saints and all their trappin's I'll beat the shillelagh out o' you! Your own mother won't know ya!"

"She won't know me now!" Jim cried, and went slack in Harris's grip, uncaring when Harris shook him like a rag doll.

"Stop it!" cried the preacher, but Lew pulled him back and said, "Just watch," in his ear.

Harris threw the man to the ground and followed him there, dropping flat to his stomach. They were forehead-to-forehead, as if they were about to arm wrestle. Instead, Harris grabbed the man's hair and pressed his face in the dirt. "There ya go! A little taste o' Southern hospitality!"

The man tried to squirm away, but Harris held him fast. The preacher lunged, but Lew dragged him back.

"You wanna be buried in it?" Harris shouted.

"No," came the muffled response.

"Come again?"

"No!"

Harris let him go. He stood up, brushing off dust. "Any more talk like that, boy-o, I'll drag you to the line myself. Now get your arse up."

Jim rolled to his back. He coughed and lay breathing hard, face coated in grime, nose bloodied. He stared at the sky for a moment and then belched. He murmured, "Excuse me." Onlookers chuckled, and Jim protested, "I didn't do that 'cause I swallowed dirt. I do that when my stomach grumbles. It is my personal constitution." He sat up and took stock. He looked up at Harris. "I had a weak moment."

"You're not allowed a weak moment, lad. We are an army. Our surroundin's don't change that, and our current battle is to survive this hell. Now I outrank you, you sorry piece of—" mild profanity. "This neighborhood is my detachment; you follow my orders. Don't let me catch you weak again."

Jim wiped his nose. "I keep thinkin' of my wife and baby."

"That's a sin here. Pack 'em away and say a hundred Hail Marys."

"Don't know Hail Marys. I ain't Catholic."

"Well, I won't hold it against you. Talk to the preacher, here. He'll fill your suitcase with some good stout religion, and if it ain't Catholic we won't hold it against him." He eyed onlookers. "Anyone who does will answer to me."

Jim looked up through dust-coated lashes at the preacher. He sighed. "I know the Twenty-Third Psalm. I could say that."

"That will do nicely," said Reverend Gillette, and he helped the man to his feet.

———

"I collected your rations," said Andy Rogers, as Harris, Lew, and the preacher crawled into the tent. Artie lay in the same position Lew had left him in this morning. His ration, a three-inch square of corn bread with a handful of beans on top, lay on the ground next to him.

There was room enough for the men to sit Indian style. The tent itself was far better than others. It was Emery's blanket. Lew had found it in the haversack Emery pushed into his hands when he first came in.

When was that? Mere days ago? Felt like a month.

Emery's sack contained wonders the others had not seen in a long time. Strips of dried mule, some crackers, a few small apples. Lew had shared all of it out the first day. Yesterday they traded the sack itself for water for Artie.

Andy looked warily at the preacher, until Harris said, "He's just visitin', lad. From the other side."

"Oh. Well, that's okay. You get your rations yet?"

The preacher didn't know what to say.

"You can have Artie's. He ain't eatin'." Andy took Artie's food and placed it on Gillette's palm. The preacher looked at it dubiously. He glanced at the others.

"This is all you get for supper?"

Andy laughed. "Are you new?"

Harris said, "That isn't supper, Father. That's breakfast, lunch, *and* supper. That's a day's worth."

"A few peas and a bit of corn bread with raisins." He looked at it disbelievingly. "This cannot be. I must speak to General Winder." He lifted it to his nose and sniffed. He recoiled.

"You have raisins in yours?" Andy said, leaning to see. Then he stared at Gillette. "You *are* new. Those aren't raisins."

Gillette put the bread and peas in a slant of light through a gap in the tent and examined it. His face stiffened. "Gentlemen, I cannot eat this. You are welcome to it."

"Actually, this is a good day," Lew said, inspecting his portion.

"It is baked. You should see what they call 'bacon.' I didn't know it came in colors."

"You'll get used to it," Andy assured. "Don't give it away. Put it in your pocket for later." He glanced at Artie. "He won't mind. I'm sorry, boys, but I don't think he's gonna last until morning. He looks like Bart did at the end." He eyed Harris. "Gill, you ain't lookin' so good."

Harris crawled over to Artie.

Artie lay as if sleeping. It was easier to see him this way, instead of thrashing about in pain and delirium.

"He ain't gone yet, Gill," said Andy. "I checked a minute ago. He's just sleeping. He'll have a peaceful time of it."

Harris stretched out beside him.

"Don't it seem like he's already in that good place?" Andy said gently. "Seeing things we wish to see? Why, look at him. He is already at rest. He ain't mindful of this place no more, Gill, and that is a good way to go."

Reverend Gillette crawled over. He lifted the pair of trousers that Artie had used for a coverlet and stared in horror at the wound in Artie's thigh. He re-covered it. "Why wasn't this man taken to the hospital?"

"He was," said Lew. "There wasn't room."

"I am glad he is here," whispered Harris. "With us."

Reverend Gillette laid his hand on Artie's leg and prayed for him silently, and then did the same for Harris after he had fallen asleep.

12

TALK IN THE SENTINELS' BOOTH had taken a philosophical turn, as things often did when answers could not be had. Instead of speculating on the missing Reverend Gillette, the three men packed snug at the rail spoke of the war and of Andersonville.

"We all thought Jeff Davis was our man," said Emery.

"Yep," said Burr. "Him or Cobb."

"You can't shake the feeling that something went terribly wrong at the breaking of the nation," said Dance.

"No matter what reasons we had for leaving, we should've stayed. That's what my uncle says. The rending ought not've come. But it did. We got a divorce."

"All became different and difficult and wrong and hasn't stopped being that way," said Dance. "And now, this. Anomalies like Andersonville sprang from the breaking of the nation."

"We strayed into territory unknown, and we are not yet quit of it," Burr murmured. Dance glanced at him, and Burr spit. "You gonna put that in your scrip?"

Dance smiled faintly. "I might." He remembered when the slopes before him were empty and green. Now, not a blade of vegetation remained in twenty-six acres. It was either trampled or eaten. He had better shelter than they, this open-air affair that kept off sun and rain.

"I wish I could explain this place for the meeting," Emery said.

"I have visited every word I know," Dance said. "Nothing pins it down. I've brought it to this, that if hell is a province or a state or a country, Andersonville is a town in it."

"Pickett, I been thinkin' on somethin'," said Burr. "Why don't you get your daddy out here? Then maybe he could get Joe Brown to come on down. I don't think old J. B. would put up with this if he saw it."

"He doesn't have as much sway with Joe Brown as he believes. And he won't come. I have written four times asking him to, and four times I have received a similar reply: 'I will not shed a tear for a Yank. You are too soft, Son. If it's bad as you say, and you are given to embellishment, what have *you* done to change things?'— his hale and hearty answer for all." His voice lowered. "He'd deny this place even as he looked on it, for he'd never believe it of our fair Confederacy and never understand the bureaucracy that got it this way. Much as I hate that bluff and bluster, the thought of extinguishing it is . . . Andersonville would crush the old man. That, I cannot bear."

The three thought on this.

"Well, the sun is about to set, and I never thought the day would end like this. I pictured triumph." Emery pushed away from the rail.

Dance turned. "What are you going to do?"

He paused. "You know what? For the first time in my life, I do not know." He went down the ladder.

"He's getting worse." Andy put his hand on Harris's forehead. "He's awful feverish, and that ain't the heat. I ain't seen him eat, Lew. Have you?"

"No."

"Have you seen him drink?"

"No."

"We should get him to the lines."

"They'll do as much for him as they did for Artie," Lew said. "Is there anything you can do, Preacher? Artie's past help, but not Harris."

The preacher looked up from where he had lapsed into a quiet, faraway state. "I don't know," he said. "I will try."

Andy looked uncertainly at Lew, then at the preacher. "Who are you?"

"Son, I have asked myself that since I came. My name is William Gillette. I am a Methodist minister from Americus. It's a town not far from here."

"I thought you was Southern. You said 'war' a little while ago, but said 'whoa-ah.' This awful whoa-ah, you said. I like to hear you people talk."

"How long have you been here?"

"Since May. My brother and I. He died last week of—well, it's not manly to say, but it was diarrhea. Mississippi Quickstep, we call it. He got it from the food and water, though he was healthier than me when we came in. The healthy ones seem to fall off fastest. You people gonna help us? Is that why you're here?"

The preacher studied Andy. Then he looked at Lew. "Yes, it is. And yes, we are."

"I wish it had come sooner," Lew said coldly.

"So do I."

After a moment, Lew looked away. "I'm afraid you're gonna have to spend the night, Preacher. I was supposed to have you to the gate hours ago. I don't know what'll happen now. I hope they don't get in trouble. If Captain Wirz finds out—"

"I will tell him it was my doing," said the preacher. "Don't worry about your friends."

Lew snorted. "I will worry about him 'til he's dead. He is unpredictable. Reminds me of my little sister."

"How do you know him?"

"He took me prisoner on Kennesaw. I got sick on the way here, and he took care of me. We got to be friends. Listen. Here's what we're going to do. Tomorrow morning I will go to where I first saw him a few days ago, on dead duty."

"Dead duty . . ."

"He's in charge of a squad of Union boys who bring bodies to the south gate. I'll see if I can find him where I did last. If I can't, we'll be at the north gate for ration time. The wagon comes around four, but men gather a few hours earlier. If I can't find him on dead duty, my bet is he'll meet us at ration time again."

"Perhaps he knew it would take a long time, my tour of the stockade."

Lew shook his head. "He never planned for you to spend a night. Nights are worse than the day."

"Maybe he did plan for it," the preacher said dryly.

———

Night closed on Andersonville.

"We should go right now and tell his wife," Emery said, head in his hands. "This is the worst thing I have ever done."

Dance and Emery sat outside Emery's tent, in the camp of the 3rd

Georgia Reserves. Things were usually quieter at night, but General
Winder had increased the patrols around the stockade and the picket
lines, a few miles out; a Union rescue attempt by a general named
Stoneman, while foiled up near Macon a few days earlier, had put
the entire camp on high alert. For once, Winder's extreme paranoia
showed validity. Some of the same cavalrymen who sought to liberate
Andersonville were now its prisoners.

The three-gun redoubt thrown up east of the 3rd Reserves camp
now had six guns, half of those trained on the prison itself. The guard
at both gates had doubled. From here, Dance could hear a sentinel
in his perch sing out, "Eleven o'clock, and all is well!"

"She's gonna have a long night of it," said Emery miserably.

"So is he. Maybe good will come of it."

"There are so few things I regret. I can't think of one except this.
What's gonna happen if we can't find him? Thousands of men in
there, Union men, the enemy, and I turn loose a *Confederate* to them.
Not all of 'em are like Lew. Prob'ly most aren't. What if they kill him?
What was I thinkin'? All my life that's all I heard out of my uncle.
What were you thinkin' . . ."

———

"One ten, and all is well!"

Lew timed the calls. Every half hour or so the guard in the nearest perch called out. Seemed it should be quicker than that, if they
did it without letup. Tomorrow he would measure the exact distance
between perches, and figure out exactly how long the call did take
to round the stockade. Such was Andersonville. You had time for
things like that.

Lew couldn't sleep for the strangeness of sharing the tent with a
Confederate. The Confederate couldn't sleep either.

The men lay the only way they could fit, on their sides in

single file. When one got unbearably uncomfortable, he would say, "About-face!" and the crew would turn to their other side. Except for Artie. He lay on his back and did not move. Harris and Andy finally drifted off.

"I will endeavor to obtain some sort of treatment for your friend," said the preacher. "My wife is a fair hand with herbs. She can prepare a poultice."

"Now I know how bad he is," Lew said. "Nothing brings out his skill with adjectives more than vermin, and they're the worst at night. First night I haven't heard a peep. When did you give your socks away?" The preacher's bare feet shone in the dark.

"I don't remember. Sometime before the altercation with the man who wanted to go to the deadline. Do they really shoot anyone who steps over the line?"

"Most times. The ones who have no sense. I don't like a youngster with a rifle. A fellow fell into the deadline just the other day, just fell, he didn't aim to. He was joshing with another. Lucky for him the youngster had poor aim—not so lucky for the fellow he shot instead." Lew hesitated; he wanted to tell what he had learned about Brewer, but didn't like what it suggested of Brewer's character.

Was he ashamed of Brewer? How could he judge anyone who lived here? Was he not living it now? Did he not know? Brewer was a good man.

"Before I came, one of our mess was killed at the deadline. He was sick, and he saw what this place did to others, and the last thing he said to Harris was, 'I'm not going out that way.' Before Harris could stop him, he stepped over the line, and he was gone."

Silence. Then, "I am truly sorry to hear it, Mr. Gann."

"I don't want you to think badly of him. He was a brave man. It was his choice, and it was a bad one, and he was sick when he made it. On deadlines in general, well, to me that seems to fall in line with a more natural aspect of war, for the sake of prison security. But for everything else, for the starvation and the exposure and the miserable hospital conditions, I want to know one thing: Why hasn't your town risen in rage at this treatment by your government?"

No answer. Then, "I do not believe they truly know. Not like I do."

"Listen to those boys out there." He allowed the groans of the suffering to fill the space. During the day it wasn't noticed as much. This was what made nighttime the worst time, more than vermin. "All this suffering, and I am astounded they do not raid the office of General Winder and demand justice."

"Well, you say the word *justice*, and that has all to do with it. To them, you are the invader. The killers of their sons."

"But this place—"

"You killed their boys, Mr. Gann. To them, you killed their boys."

"But you aim to go back and tell them to help us. Us 'boy killers.'"

"I do."

"Then you are more compassionate than they. Why is—?"

"No, I'm not," said the preacher, and Lew heard an emphatic ring. "There is no difference between Americus and me. A few weeks back, my sermon was about the Good Samaritan. To draw a correlation, I used Federal soldiers as they who ambushed the man on the road."

"You made us the robbers."

"I did. You are still a robber to me. A brutal invader, he who would . . ."

At the word *invader*, Lew remembered the conversation with Emery and felt again a wave of understanding. When the South set foot on Pennsylvania soil for Gettysburg, fear and alarm and fury leapt in the breasts of all.

". . . and when you say justice, an old thing boils in my blood. Do not set yourself up as innocent. Do not set the North up as such.

Do you know how many funerals I have officiated? Boys blown up so badly there was nothing to collect to send home?"

"That is war."

"That is war, yes, I know. But I have held the hands of the mothers and the fathers. Did anyone know what we were getting into? Either side?"

Lew was silent for a moment. Then he said, "Harris told me he's seen Americus come to gawk at us, Preacher. He saw civilized ladies and gentlemen gaze down from the platforms with such loathing and scorn. And, yes, pity. He did see pity. My point is they know right well what is happening here. You did, too. You knew some of it. So why are you going to help now? Why did you not stand at that gate when they turned you in, and yell for Captain Wirz? They would have sent for him. He would have come. You would've been out of here in half a shake of a lamb's tail."

The sounds of the suffering filled the air, feverish groans for water and groans unintelligible. Next door, a man cursed and bellowed, "I was not thrice wounded in battle to be et up of lice!"

"A few weeks ago I sat to dinner with a sentinel posted here," said Reverend Gillette. "There was great torment upon that boy. He said nasty things of Americus, and then he said this: 'Maybe I would change my mind if just *one* of them—' and the rest was unsaid. It haunted me, what was unsaid." Then it seemed as if the preacher spoke to himself. "Just today I had an appointment with the provost marshal to look into affairs here. I had intended to apply for a pass of inspection on the grounds of religious duty. It seems I have obtained that pass. I knew it the minute the door locked behind me. The Millards' dance is a noble cause. But the need here is immediate. Believe me when I say we did not know." His voice dropped. "*I* did not know. Maybe I did not want to know. Maybe I never believed us capable of turning away from this."

A knot grew in Lew's throat. He bit the inside of his cheeks to keep it together. Maybe what killed Brewer was not personal despair, but the despair of knowing he could not help his people. Lew felt worse than powerless when he saw men die that he could not help. On a battlefield, he could at least stop wounds with leaves, or pull someone behind a rock for cover, or just keep pumping the lead and give his boys a chance. There was nothing here to check gangrene, or diarrhea, or starvation, or exposure. There weren't even leaves.

When he could, he said thickly, "Anything you can do for Harris . . ."

"I will do my best, Mr. Gann."

By dawn, Harris had fallen into a high fever. And Artie Van Slett was dead.

———

Lew and Harris had kept Artie in line when his big mouth threatened time and again to get him into trouble. Artie always needed looking after, always half in attendance on any given orders, always asking later what those orders were—to the aggravation of all—and it was Artie who dragged Harris off a battlefield under heavy fire by his trouser cuff. Artie who first emptied his pockets for any need. Three years with this man. It was hard to let him go.

Harder still, now that Harris was insensible of his leaving.

"Close up ranks!" Harris hollered. "Keep your head down! Fire low!"

Lew knelt at Harris's side. "Artie's going, Harris. Maybe you want to say good-bye."

"What's he going for? Haul him back! Plug that hole!"

"Ain't got all day," a stretcher bearer said outside.

"Give him a moment," the preacher said testily.

"We do have all day," pointed out the other stretcher bearer.

Lew crawled over to Artie and searched his pockets for anything to save for his mother, but they were empty.

"He said he had a pocket watch when he came in, but one of the guards took it," said Andy Rogers.

Lew reverently tied a tag to Artie's toe, with his name and regiment written on it. He closed his hand over the foot.

"Double quick, boys! Bring up that flank, form lines!"

"Lew . . . I know how you feel," said Andy. "Letting him go off alone to that burial place. Nothing but a trench. No words said over 'em. But let me tell you this: when Bart died, and I didn't want him to go off alone, Harris says to me, 'Why, Andy—he'll be with other Union boys, and to the last man they'd have said that's good enough for them.' So you see, Lew, Artie won't be alone. He'll be in a hallowed place. They're together, and that makes it so."

Nothing else could have made Lew feel the tiniest bit better. The bitter thought of Artie as just another fence-rail corpse eased some.

Harris shouted at Charley Reed to get in the rear.

"So long, Artie," Lew whispered, and patted Artie's leg. "Harris says so long, too."

"What are you doing here? Get back, you little pig bladder! I'll gut ya head to toe!"

The preacher nodded at the stretcher bearer, who pulled out Artie by his feet.

"Just you and me, now, out of the whole mess," Lew said to Harris. A tear brimmed and spilled. "We're all gone except us. We are blown off the earth."

"This is no place for children! Lew, look to him—get him out of here!"

"Charley's safe, Harris."

Fevered eyes found Lew. "Safe?"

Lew nodded.

Harris sighed deeply, and lay still. "I could do for some water," he whispered.

Lew looked at Andy. "What have we got to trade?"

Andy shook his head. "We got nothing left, 'less we call back Artie's trousers. I reckon he won't need 'em, but . . ."

"Will this belt do?" the preacher said, unbuckling it from his waist. Lew seized it and grabbed Emery's tin cup.

———

Lew reported to his detachment for roll call, a tedious affair lasting over an hour, then fell out and went back to the tent to get the preacher. The fresh water from the nearby well seemed to have done Harris good, and he slept quietly. Andy assured Lew he'd look out for him while he was gone.

They first went to the southeast quadrant where Lew had found Emery, but Emery wasn't there. There was nothing left to do but wait for rations, a few hours away. Lew took him on a tour of "Main Street," the only avenue within the stockade that had some sort of order to it. It stretched from the north gate to the other side of the pen.

Reverend Gillette was amazed how a closer inspection of Andersonville revealed the aspects of true town life. There was a barbershop, a laundry, even a grocer's stand. Some men came in with concealed Union greenbacks, worth far more than Confederate money; the number of greenbacks a man had in this place could mean the difference between life and death.

They passed a man who called out, "Onions and sweet potatoes! Get 'em at a fairer price than Fetchner's! Main Street, west end! Onions and sweet potatoes!"

"How do they get the goods?"

"Some of the guards will arrange trades between them and

townspeople. There's the sutler's stand, which is more of an official getup—if you want to trade a pair of boots for a couple of potatoes. They are thieves."

They passed a place where a crudely lettered plank announced, HAIR CUTS. TWENTY-FIVE CENTS. WILL TRADE.

"I had an idea of men just standing around, hungry and waiting for parole."

"Once you're used to the idea that you're a prisoner, you settle in to survive," Lew said. "But I'll not go near Fetchner's for any price. It's highway robbery for one thing; it's demoralizing for the next. I saw a man starve to death right outside their booth. They have nothing but contempt for the beggars, and though I understand this thinking some, it is hard to watch men die from starvation with food in reach. The beggars are pathetic, to be sure—the whiny, grasping sort you'd just as soon knock over as help. But still. It is hard to watch. A man will get down low here, and your worst fear is you will become as such."

"Blackberries!" a man cried. "Get your blackberries at Fetchner's! Eggs! Marrow bones!"

"First and last time I got something from a sutler's stand was two years ago. I was missing Carrie's home cooking, so I bought a fried pie. It was cold, greasy, and the edges were wrinkled like corrugated tin to resemble a housewife's crust—tasted like tin, too. I am a fruit farmer, and I couldn't identify what that fruit filling was." The preacher chuckled. "Never wasted my money on camp stores again. And here, it's plain folly to go and be tempted unless you have a pocketful of cash. Harris traded his hat at Fetchner's to fill his belly one time, and he has roasted in this life-sucking sun ever since."

They skirted a man squatting in the middle of the street. The man's action elicited calls of protest from some, indifference from others. Lew glanced at the preacher. "Half the time it's involuntary, they just can't help it—most of us have the quickstep; otherwise they just weren't raised right. They get so down low they just don't care. That is another hard thing to see—men giving up on decent order. Giving in."

"No blessed wonder it is so filthy in here," the preacher muttered.

"Anyplace you go, just take up a handful of dirt—you'll find something squirming in it."

"That so-called creek is a place I'd rather forget. Why are there no proper sanitation facilities?"

"You find that answer, Preacher, and you will have unveiled one of Andersonville's great mysteries." He pointed over the top of the stockade to a distant hill. "Look at all the pine trees about. Wish I could get my hands on this place. I'd send out work crews. Half of these men are going mad for lack of anything to do. I'd have 'em build barracks, I'd drain that fetid swamp. I'd get the water running clear again—I'd relocate the cookhouse and the Confederate camp, as all their refuse goes into the creek before it comes here."

The preacher shook his head. "Mr. Gann, I am truly appalled."

It did something to a man to be listened to.

"I wish more of you would come. Some men are so constituted as to attribute any hardship they endure to malicious intent. It is the way they will see things. But if they met folks like you, they'd see you are regular human beings like us. They'd see you as themselves—ordinary, and caught in war."

"Well, Mr. Gann, on that note, I do think I have observed enough. I have enjoyed our conversations. I see no reason to wait for ration time, and my wife must be anxious. I'll stand at the gate and call for General Winder."

"I'd dearly hoped to get you out without a ruckus."

"Oh, it is a ruckus I aim to cause."

"What will you tell him? I don't want trouble for Emery. He did what he did not just for our sakes, but for yours."

"Don't worry about your friend."

For all his disheveled appearance from a sleepless night in the deep, a light stood in the man's eyes, maybe because he was a preacher, maybe because he had the wild edge of a prophet or a reformer. You could never tell with God men. Sometimes that wild light was just good, old-fashioned good.

"I'll come up with something, Mr. Gann. I am, after all, Little Mite Badger."

———

"I'm turning myself in," Emery said.

Dance had gotten permission from Keppel to trade duties for the morning shift so he could work with Emery at the Federal hospital. Today, Emery was assigned wards one through five. When a man died, they were called in with a stretcher so full of holes that they had to lay the body just right so it wouldn't fall through. Emery worked at fixing it now, tearing a pair of faded kersey trousers into strips and weaving the strips into a lattice.

After a quick glance around, Dance said quietly, "What about your plans for a prison break?"

"If I can't get a single Rebel out, how do you think I'll fare with lots of Yanks? I'll turn myself in, confess all, and they can get up a manhunt for the preacher."

"What about your Lew Gann?"

Emery stopped the feverish weaving.

"What would Hickory Shearer say about your oath to get him out?"

"I ain't done with that! Just leave me be. I'll get him out. I gotta sit with things for a while."

"But how will you get him out if you turn yourself in?"

Emery threw down the stretcher and grabbed fistfuls of Dance's jacket.

Dance grabbed him back. "Stop acting as if you're the only one in trouble, you Alabamian martyr!"

"*You* ain't in trouble, you Georgia dandy! It was *my* idea!"

"You were supposed to have him out at rations yesterday," said a calm voice behind them. They let each other go. It was Sergeant Keppel. "Just a little eye-opener, you said. A little stroll. So I looked the other way."

Emery looked at the ground. "Sir, I am prepared to—"

"He's been found?" Dance said over Emery.

"Oh, he's been found. Yes, he's been found." Keppel had an odd look, one Dance had never seen. "A man presented himself at the north gate and demanded to see General Winder. He was half-naked. Looked like some of Mosby's old gang fell upon him."

Dance closed his eyes. Emery groaned, and put his hands on his face.

"So I took him to see General Winder, and there I was treated to the solitary best moment of my entire life. Thank you, boys. I owe you a mighty debt."

Dance opened one eye. Emery looked through his fingers.

"'My name is William Gillette,' says he; 'I am an adjunct officer with the Confederate Civilian Sanitation Commission. I have finished my surprise inspection of your prison.'" Sergeant Keppel broke into a smile, a thing of which Dance never knew him capable. "Then he digs into his pocket and pulls out a foul old wad of corn bread and peas. Smacks it square in the middle of Winder's desk, and says, 'I will not leave until you eat that.'" Then Sergeant Keppel burst out laughing, another unprecedented event. "I will not leave until you eat that!"

THE SENTINELS OF ANDERSONVILLE

Dance couldn't move.

Awestruck, Emery asked, "What did Winder do?"

Keppel wiped his eyes. "He stared down at that pile like it'd eat *him*. I can still see the worms." Helpless laughter erupted. "Oh, I can't start up again. Oh, my sides ache. . . ."

"What happened?"

He did his best to contain himself. "Well, now. Wirz was there, and he hurries over and cleans up the mess while General Winder just stares murder at that preacher. 'You will hear from us,' that half-naked man said, and he storms out of that office while Winder hollers at Wirz to look up the Confederate Civilian Sanitation Commission." Off he went in another round of laughter. "Oh, it hurts. I thought I'd die holding it in." Keppel blotted his eyes with the heels of his hands. "Boys, I am in your debt."

Debt? Dance said quickly, "Say, Sergeant Keppel—do you think we could get a pass for the F.A.P. meeting in Americus tonight?"

"Certainly. We'll manage it. Wish I could go myself. Well, go on now, get back to duty. Drover! Zeeff! Get over here. You gotta hear this. . . ."

They left him laughing.

———

A man stood at the door, hat in hand. "My name is Lucerne. I got some information, Mr. Howard. I got a pass to come give it to you."

Detective Joseph T. Howard hated the room Winder had given him. It was in the back of the Americus depot, and it was little bigger than a wallet. Investigation into covert Yankee activities was an unappreciated patriotic duty appointed small consideration and even smaller remuneration. He lit his cigar and drew upon it several times. He'd be in Richmond, if things weren't so hungry there.

"What information," he said.

178

"'Bout the missin' preacher."

"The missing preacher is found. He was in the prison. It was only a lark."

"Wudden no lark. It was them as call themselves the F.A.P."

Howard stopped mid-draw. He blew a cloud, and set the cigar on a tin plate.

"What have you got to say?"

"Well, I am one of the turnkeys. And that boy from Alabama came to me and—" His eyes narrowed. "I ain't sayin' more. I want a barrel of whiskey and a monthlong furlough. And when I come back, don't want no more shuck-about duty. I want a picket-line postin'. And I want it wrote on paper." He pointed at papers on Howard's desk.

A civil investigation into prison conditions, Gillette had said a few hours ago, when Winder sent Howard to track him down for questioning. He was an adjunct member of a new committee called the Confederate Civilian Sanitation Commission. No, it wasn't government. No, the provost marshal didn't know about it. It fell under civil auspices and fell in with his duties as a minister of the gospel. He quoted the Bible a few times.

Traitors could quote the Bible.

This came on the heels of the Stoneman raid. What if . . .

What if it wasn't a kidnapping at all?

Howard reached for a pencil and paper.

What if they were connected, this and the thwarted Stoneman raid? What if this F.A.P. had scouted out the land for Stoneman and his cavalry? What if the F.A.P. was in the prison for the express purpose to scout out weaknesses for another raid like Stoneman's, and what if this time it was successful?

Maybe the old man wasn't so paranoid.

Of course, *he* didn't connect these dots; that was Howard's job, Howard the unappreciated.

He looked at his pocket watch. The F.A.P. meeting was two hours and change away. Was it time enough to assemble witnesses?

Howard smiled until his lip disappeared. "I believe we can make a few satisfactory arrangements, Mr. Lucerne. And yes, you will have it in writing. Now. Sit down, Mr. Lucerne, pull up a crate. You are one of the turnkeys. . . ."

13

On January 19, 1861, Georgia was the fifth state to secede from the Union. The date was considered a day of independence, and in '62 and '63 Americus had noted the occasion with speeches from local potentates and songs from the Americus Brass Band. This year, the date had passed unmarked. It was an odd thing to come to mind, Violet reflected, as she helped Mother plate the gingersnaps.

"How is Papa?" Violet asked carefully. Mother was in an unpredictable state. She either very much wanted to be asked her mind on things, or not at all. Starting out with Papa was a safe approach.

"He is preparing a speech, though I told him to make sure he had a prison bag prepared as well," she said. She fanned the gingersnaps into a decorative pattern on a serving plate, didn't like the result, and started over. Two more hurried attempts failed to produce satisfaction, and she gave up and pushed the plate to Violet.

"I saw him in his office. I think he was praying," Violet admitted.

"I am *deeply* disappointed in this town," Mother declared, lips trembling, earrings trembling. "To think that your father should be dragged down for *questioning*. I *de*clare, it is irreconcilable to reason."

"Judge Tate stepped in, Mama. Nothing will happen to Papa with Judge Tate around."

"Precisely! If something could happen to your papa—your good, dear, devout, kind, Christian, upstanding papa—what could happen to Judge *Tate*? Clara must think the very same! What is happening to this town?"

"I wish I'd never posted that handbill. I only wanted to help those miserable creatures."

Mother's hysteria instantly quelled. She seized Violet's hand. "Violet, dear, your father and I are desperately proud. Not another thought." She squeezed her hand. "At least Reverend Gillette is safe. That is a comfort. Goodness, what events. A kidnapping that wasn't a kidnapping."

Violet brightened. "Lily said that Mr. Runcorn heard he is forming a commission to look into the conditions at the prison. Does that not hearten?"

But anxiety returned. Mother put a hand to her cheek. "Ravinia Runcorn snubbed me at the post office. Snubbed! Did you ever think the day would come? Mrs. Norton Stiles, an object of scorn. I am *checkered*." She shook her head, dazed. "What will come of this meeting? To think I was nervous about the Knitting Brigade!"

Lily popped her head around the corner. "Dance and Emery are here! Their sergeant gave them a pass!" She disappeared.

"Well, that is some comfort. They are soldiers. If things get ugly, they can do . . . soldier things. Go receive them, Violet. I will deal with these snaps." She laid a decorative sprig of lavender on the plate, and surveyed the result. "*Something* will be pretty today."

———

"Why are you so gloomy?" Dance said.

"Why are you so cheerful?" Violet smoothed her skirts in precise movements. "My father brought in for questioning . . . Ravinia Runcorn, snubbing my mother. Our family is *never* snubbed. Nor do we snub. Except when it is deserved. And even then it is more of an *instructive* look. Purposeful. Meant to inspire corrective behavior."

"Could you demonstrate?" Dance asked.

Violet did her best, snubbing a tree, until she realized he was laughing. She scowled.

Dance and Violet sat in chairs on the edge of the lawn near the drive. They were posted to welcome folks when they came. Emery lay spread-eagled on the ground in front of them, staring at the sky. A look of ineffable peace was upon him. He had acted like a man apart, from the moment she'd first seen him.

"Look at that sky," he said dreamily.

Violet leaned forward on pretense of adjusting her shoe and sniffed. She did not smell whiskey. Well, he was from Alabama. Perhaps his behavior was usual for Alabama. She did not know many out-of-staters.

"Violet, what are you all fuss and feathers about?" Dance asked.

"Dance Pickett, what is wrong with you? How are you both in such a fine fettle? Do you not feel the tension in the air? It is as the Knitting Brigade. We did not know what to expect, and things *did* get ugly. Well—not as much ugly as *uncomfortable*. And certainly *revelatory*. This is altogether different. Multiply yesterday by twenty." She looked at Emery, and her voice lowered. "What of your . . . *plans*, Mr. Jones? *Our* plans. Have you devised any yet?"

"Oh, they're comin' on fine. I'm restin' today. Appreciatin' things. Tomorrow I will put all my faculties in it. Does anyone take time to notice the sky? There it is. There it has been all along. I am astounded."

"Violet, here's the truth," Dance said. "We have a guest speaker coming later this evening. He was supposed to be at the Millard dance, but he has had a *revelatory* experience himself. He insisted on being here, not there, and this is yet another thing to give me hope for this town. He said to us, 'Why should I bother with them? They will not hear. I will go where I will be heard.'"

Violet began to feel better. "Who is he?"

"It is a surprise." Dance took some gingersnaps out of his pocket and flipped one to Emery.

"Oh, just tell me."

"I hope he tells about the corn bread and peas," Emery said.

"If he doesn't, I will. Violet, do not trouble your heart. Things will turn out right. They generally do."

"I hope so." She hesitated. "This is not the first time I have been . . . disillusioned."

"Do tell," said Emery.

"A man came to town with a poor Confederate soldier who had lost both his legs in the war. They were here to raise money for our boys at the Augusta Hospital for Confederate Soldiers. The man was a pitiful sight. Well, we had a benefit and raised a pile of cash and sent them on their way . . . and it turns out there *was* no Augusta Hospital for Confederate Soldiers." She eyed the boys ruefully. "Guess who led the benefit."

Emery and Dance laughed.

Warmth crept high in her cheeks. "It is *not* funny! My sisters and I went to each and every business in Americus for a pledge of support. I was *adamant* that they should participate and show themselves as true Southern patriots by modeling Christian kindness."

Dance howled and slapped his knee.

"Oh, stop! We had a picnic, a dance, *and* an auction. Do you know how much money those good people raised? Over a thousand dollars! One thousand twenty-four dollars and nineteen cents." She pounded her leg with her fist. "Those *despicable* thieves! And *I* gave them the money—with great ceremony! Stop laughing this instant,

Dance Pickett. I couldn't show my face in town for a week. Oh, I'd like to hunt them down. Legs or no legs!"

Dance wiped tears and gave Emery a push with his boot. "Do you see why I adore this girl? I thought this day couldn't get better."

"I do not like amusing you!" Violet sat and fumed, until anxiety made her forget about Dance. "Will anyone trust me enough to come?"

Dance sobered. "Violet, what has it to do with you? It has to do with those prisoners."

"Someone's comin' tonight they *will* trust," Emery said, lips twitching. He still looked as expansive as if he had done the world an enormous favor and was basking in the glory of it.

"I insist you tell me."

"You'll see very soon."

"Say, I wish to know more of your . . . friend," Violet said. "The one in the—you know where. What's he like?"

"Well, if it didn't swell the head of the man sittin' next to you, I'd say he was like him. He's steady. Makes me laugh. Comfortable to be around. Has a philosophical bent."

Dance flipped him a gingersnap. "Every time you say something I like, you'll get another."

"What did you see in him?" Violet asked.

"What did I see in him?" Emery held the cookie, concentrating for the right words, studying the sky. "Give me a minute. This is a quality question."

He was a handsome young man, Violet reflected. Lily had told the family one evening—after she had laid down her romance novel—that Emery was possessed of "unfettered grace." Posey told Lily she was on dangerous ground and instructed her to redirect her affections for her own good.

"I saw things I liked," Emery mused. "I saw things I knew, in that standoff. I recognized him." He smiled and bit the cookie.

"And you plan to get him back to hearth and home," Violet said wistfully. "To his wife and his children, his farm and his dogs."

Emery finished the gingersnap. "Lew read me some of his letters. I got to know his family. I feel—" Emery shifted a little, as if the next part were a little more than he cared to tell.

"You feel what?" Violet prompted, leaning a fraction closer.

Grudgingly, he said, "Protective." Dance flipped him a gingersnap, and he threw it back at him.

Violet smoothed her dress. "Papa is preparing an inaugural speech for the society. Are you boys going to say anything, as founding members? I have a few notes, myself."

"Emery's got something to say," said Dance.

"I got something to say if it needs being said."

"You are fearless," Dance said, and flipped him another gingersnap. This one he ate.

"I intend to sit this one out, however, as one is coming whose sandals I am not fit to unloose. If he said what he did to Winder, what do you imagine he will say to others?" Emery chuckled. "To think, the worst thing I ever did turned out to be the best."

"What *are* you talking about?"

But the answer would have to wait. Lily came hurrying over from behind a tree where she had posted herself to spy a little sooner the ones who came.

"The Bigelows are coming!" she reported. "Hettie Dixon! Constance Greer, even though she *said* she'd be at the Millards'!" Then she said, "Violet, you won't believe it—the *Runcorns* are coming! I've got to tell Mama!" She ran off.

"Oh no," Violet said. She realized she'd clutched Dance's arm, and let go. "They may have come to be indignant. It *is* an indignation meeting . . ."

"Steady now, Violet," said Dance mildly.

Do you see why I adore this girl? he had said. Why did men have to bandy about important words? Why couldn't he say, *Do you see why I admire this girl?* or, *Do you see why I enjoy the company of this girl?*

But all frivolous thought fell away, for marching up the drive with her potential powers of snub at the zenith was Ravinia Runcorn. The three rose and waited to greet her.

She approached . . . she approached . . . she laid glittering eyes on Violet for one cold, piercing instant . . . and swept past without a word.

Violet's welcome died on her tongue. Silas Runcorn, sweating and carrying two picnic chairs, nodded to them with a "How do," and followed his wife.

"Snubbed," said Violet, stupefied.

"Violet, you have enjoyed the center of polite society since birth," Dance said. She looked to see if he was mocking her, but he had something else to say. He took her hand and, before she could blush, kissed it. "I would rather have you here, on the unpleasant outskirts, where things are not safe. This is where you can do something. It suits you."

He released her hand, brushed gingersnap crumbs from his vest, and went off to greet someone.

———

"'All we ask is to be left alone,'" said Dr. Stiles. "I wrestled with several ways to open this meeting. Jeff Davis's words leapt to mind, those as he spoke to our Confederate congress. Didn't those words just blaze through the South, setting fields afire like Samson's foxes? All we ask is to be left alone."

He looked over the crowd. Some stood near the trees; most sat on blankets or chairs. There were a few unfamiliar faces, but most he knew. Some of Polly's family was here—Grandpa Wrassey and her brother, Charles. Some were military, posted in Americus or

Andersonville. There were a few business owners, a few community leaders, a few of his patients. One fellow he knew to be a writer for the *Macon Telegraph*. Unfortunate, that. He had a piece to read from the *Telegraph*, and it took no nerve until he saw the man.

Lily had informed him that forty-seven people were present. He owned to himself that the number was disheartening for a good-sized town with a war-swelled population, even with a dance going on. He wondered if Violet and the boys felt the same. But he determined that from the moment of his first footfall out of the study he would not judge the ones who did not come. It was tangled up in that, all the problems of Andersonville Prison, the judging of other human beings; Norton Stiles, before God, would not be part of it.

"Most of you know me, but for those who don't, I am Dr. Norton Stiles. I am over thirty and have practiced medicine for over seven years." He smiled wryly. "That means I have qualified for exemption from military duty." A mild chuckle rolled across the crowd. "Like many of you, I volunteered my services for the war effort. I serve once a week at the Federal hospital. Let it be known I applied to work at the Confederate hospital in the town of Andersonville. But they had an abundance of doctors there, and my application was rejected. A colleague persuaded me to help at the stockade. Now some of you know Captain Wirz, the commandant of the prison." He paused to allow for the murmur of general disapproval.

"That foul-mouthed old Hessian," one of them muttered.

"Well, I have something in common with Captain Wirz," said Dr. Stiles. "He will not allow his family to go near the prison stockade. He has his reasons, and I had mine. As for myself, I was wrong."

He glanced at Violet.

"I was wrong to keep silent with them, and I was wrong to keep silent with you. Look at us. We are not many, are we? I wish there were more, for I would tell what I have in my heart for this town, and it is not rancor and it is not judgment. It is something closer to love, for I dearly love this town. My wife and I settled here over twenty years ago, when it was just scratching out an existence. How we have grown. The churches, the schools, the businesses. The town square, with our lovely water oaks—I sponsored one of those trees and planted it myself.

"We have known very prosperous times in Americus, and now we have known war. And this war has broken our hearts. I do not believe any of us here has not suffered loss; if not a son, or a husband, or a father, then the sons, husbands, and fathers of those dear to us. No one untouched, and we are bound together in grief. Polly's brother lost a son, and my daughter lost her fiancé." He paused. "And then this war brought something else to the doorstep of Americus. Something deeply alarming."

"We never wanted it!" someone called.

"Did we not refuse to help them clear the land, in protest?" A man stood up. It was Arvin Probity. He looked around. "I am not here to feed Yanks—I'm here to protest it! And I'm missin' a dance to do it!"

"Sit down, Arvin. Let the doc have his say, and then you can have yours." It was Judge Tate, and Arvin sat down.

Dr. Stiles put up a hand. "I objected to the building of that prison right along with you, Arvin. You know I did. No one wanted that kind of danger so close to our families. It seemed to us, then, a grave potential threat and so it is today—even more so, with the prison population at numbers we could not have imagined. Is not this threat with us when we go to sleep at night? Is it not there when we toil by day? Someday Andersonville Prison will be shut down, and we will all rest easy once more. For now I have fears about that place, though I keep them quiet and wrestle with them on my own terms, as does everyone else."

"I reckon I had to teach my wife to shoot," said Jackson Green, a hostler for the hotels. "Any escaped Yankee comes by my place, he'll eat lead for sure."

"I had to learn as well," said Dr. Stiles. "I taught Polly and my two oldest. Did we ever imagine such a day would come?" Then he smiled. "I bought a .38-caliber pepperbox, and my girl Lily says to me, 'Papa, I do not know what a caliber is, let alone if .38 is enough that I should be impressed.'" A few smiles at that, and some looked about to see Lily.

"We defy our fears by ignoring them, in the grand tradition of the South. And we have all seen that General Winder certainly does his job to prevent a prison break. He is determined, and for this I am grateful. But I wonder if our determination to ignore our fears has not swept us into an ignorance we never meant. Something that went too far, perhaps upon the foundation of 'All we ask is to be left alone.'" He fished inside his vest pocket and brought out a newspaper clipping. He glanced at the newspaperman.

"I have a clipping from the *Macon Telegraph*. It is dated May 7." He read: "'Mr. Fiddlerman informed me that the prisoners unanimously expressed themselves much better pleased with Andersonville than anyplace they have been since captured. They are now living bountiful on the very best that southwestern Georgia can afford. Their daily ration consists of one-third pound of good ham or bacon, and one and a half pounds of meal. They also get peas and sometimes fresh and pickled beef. The patients in the hospital, in addition to ham and meal, get rice flour, potatoes, chickens, and eggs.'"

"That's a lie!" It was Dance Pickett, on his feet and red-faced.

"Which part of it, Mr. Pickett?" Dr. Stiles asked. "Incidentally, may I introduce Dance Pickett, a sentinel at Andersonville. You may have heard of his father, James Weld Pickett, from Augusta. He is second cousin to my wife. And no . . . not related to George. You were saying, son?"

"*All* lies!"

Dr. Stiles adjusted his glasses. "Why, Dance, do you mean to say that out of nearly thirty thousand men in that stockade—yes, thirty thousand—that not one of those men would agree with these printed words?"

"Not one!"

Dr. Stiles lifted his eyebrows in surprise at the clipping. He folded it and put it in his pocket.

"They are Yankees! What would you expect?" someone called. "You know they're lyin' if their mouths are open!"

"Howell Cobb toured the place!" said another. "Said all was fine!" His voice lowered. "He said those Yanks are getting as good as they deserve."

Hettie Dixon waved a fan for attention. "Dr. Stiles, give us the facts, please. I do not wish to be hampered by speculation. Are those men starving to death or not?"

"That cannot be!" a woman said angrily. "The Confederate States of America would never allow such a thing—Yankee brutes though they be!"

"Dr. Stiles?" said Hettie.

"Here are the facts, Mrs. Dixon. There is fearful overcrowding, insufficient food, appalling lack of medical supplies and personnel, no decent shelter, no system for sanitation—and on a day with a strong breeze, you all know what I'm talking about. That we can smell a place from ten miles out should make the sanitary conditions plain. Thousands have died thus far, and yes, Mrs. Dixon, the main reason is starvation. It is not disease.

"No, hear me! I know what you've heard. Breakouts of smallpox or this or that to explain the thousands of deaths—it is not true. I am a medical doctor. Most of the diseases in that stockade are either a direct result of unsanitary conditions, or a direct result of diet. And it is a starvation diet, yes—right here in Sumter County. These are the facts, and they are incontrovertible."

The newspaperman stood as he raised his hand. He looked around. "Let it be known that the aforementioned editorial piece, of which I personally was not the author, was published almost three months ago. Since then, the *Macon Telegraph* has changed its position on the conditions of that prison. We are in accord with the newspapers in this area. They have issued appeals for help for those prisoners. I heard of this meeting and I've come down to see what you all are doing about it."

"We don't read the newspapers anymore! Full of routs and retreats, always retreats!"

"Let the gov'ment take care of that pen!" someone called. "Have we not put our trust in them?"

"We cannot look to the government to help these men," said Dr. Stiles. "Our government has failed them. It rests on us to step in and do what we can."

"That's a mighty thin screen, Dr. Stiles," said old Harmsen Jacob, standing at the edge of the group, arms folded. "I see a hint of treason through it."

"Were you not arrested on just such suspicion?" another added.

"He was not arrested! He was questioned!" Polly had kept her peace until now, but this last accusation proved too much for her. "Judge Tate put an end to *that* nonsense immediately!" She nodded at Judge Tate.

"Those Yanks are trespassers, in every way the word can be used!"

"You doubt our government! That *is* treason!"

"Well, now, that is hasty," said Harmsen Jacob. "It is certainly not treason to *doubt* our government, but we are lawbreakers if we take the reins into our own hands. That is where I see this heading."

"Is not the cornerstone of our nation that we have seceded from a government with whom we did not agree?" Dr. Stiles asked. "Did we not then take the reins?"

"Doctor, now that is going too far!"

"Mighty thin," Harmsen agreed.

"Well, then, I have another paper, if you wish to know the mind of some of our *government-appointed* military, regarding Andersonville," said Dr. Stiles. He took a paper from his other vest pocket. "Many of you know Colonel Alexander Persons, he who was formerly in charge of the prison. Some of you know his family from Fort Valley. Colonel Persons protested conditions at the prison early on." He looked over his glasses at the people. "He protested structural and *logistical* things, very important *foundational* aspects of the prison. He took upon himself to address them by personally condemning Andersonville through a legal injunction he brought against it. But he was warned—I will say that again—he was *warned* that he would be subjected to—" he raised the paper and read from it—"'a hurricane of wrath and even personal abuse from the people of the surrounding country if he did not drop his demand for an inquiry and hearing.'"

He looked over his glasses again. "This warning came from the Honorable Richard H. Clark of Albany. Colonel Persons, you remember, was removed from his post and reassigned elsewhere. Now in the confusion of duty assignment at Andersonville, at one point his duties overlapped with those of Captain Wirz; and when he left, Captain Wirz replaced him. A captain replaced a colonel. I will leave you to puzzle that out yourselves."

He folded the paper and replaced it in his pocket, then folded his glasses and tucked them away. "There are many things I cannot answer of Andersonville Prison, and I do not propose to solve the larger problems of its government, for I am not equal to it. I am not a politician, nor even a community leader. My job is simple: to alleviate suffering in whatever ways I can. I wish to give others an opportunity to help because the need is overwhelming, yet within that overwhelming need I do not suggest impossibilities. Though war is upon us, and we have suffered ourselves, we *can* augment what food the government supplies to the prison, enough to make a difference in whether a man lives or dies. Scurvy comes from lack of decent food, and the effects are hellish."

"We are not barbarians! I read in the newspaper that those boys get the same rations our boys get!" someone shouted.

"If that is true, it would stand to reason that scurvy would present itself at the Confederate hospital in the town of Andersonville. Yet my colleague there reports he has not seen *one* case of scurvy."

A man stood up, raising his hand. When Dr. Stiles nodded at him, he took off his hat. "I'm Timothy Bigelow, for those who don't know. I'm an alderman. I've served on the town council for three years. Norton, I want you to know I am in full support of all you say. Back in May when Howell Cobb reported on the conditions, it was around the same time my wife had attended a picnic there; she brought back a report in direct contrast to his. Well, either my wife was wrong or General Cobb was. I let it bother me for a time, probably longer than I should, until I paid a visit to the prison myself."

Bigelow shook his head. "No words. I looked into the hospital, too. No words! I tell you, conditions in those wards are something out of a deep reach of hell. There was no medicine and no medical supplies. Not even a pan to be sick in, and if they were sick on the ground, there it lay. Not even sawdust to cover it up. In most cases, those boys didn't even have beds. They lay in such misery and filth as cannot be described. I said to the man in charge, 'Where are the sick pans? Where are the beds?' He said, 'There is nothing to be had.'

"Now here is where things get awfully difficult. I certainly believe that Americus can do something to help alleviate that suffering. But there is something else we need to consider. A few weeks back, General Johnston was relieved and replaced by Hood. Whether that will be a good thing, as far as stopping Sherman's advance, well, we do not know. As your town councilman, I do know this: even now, we are preparing to receive heavy casualties. Yes, *we* are, right here. Some hospitals are being evacuated as I speak, and before the end of the week they will set up right here in Americus, right in town square. If Atlanta falls—"

"God forbid!"

"Hood forbid!"

Bigelow held up his hands and said, "*If* Atlanta falls, then we need to prepare ourselves—at the very least for receiving casualties, but far more than that, we'll need to prepare a defense. The militia and Home Guard are already making plans."

"Goodness gracious!" Constance Greer gasped.

"Oh, I wish General Lee stood before Sherman! He'd never have made it into Georgia!"

"Him and Grant are still arm wrasslin' in Petersburg."

Bigelow said, "Please—let me finish this point and I am done. Much as I am in deep sympathy with the plight of those at Andersonville, for I have seen with my own eyes what they suffer, this very meeting comes at a precarious time, as does our possible intervention. Should we not prepare to expend what resources we have for what is coming? Our town is soon to be overrun. It may double in population."

"Goodness gracious . . . he has a good point."

"Well, you can see why he's a councilman. That's common sense talkin'."

Hettie Dixon waved her fan. "But men are starving to *death*, daily. It seems to me we should take things a day at a time, as comes recommended by Jesus, for sufficient unto the *day* is the evil thereof;

if a man is starving *today*, ought we not help that man? Ought we not let tomorrow take care of itself?"

"Mrs. Dixon, I am a council member whose business is precisely concerned with that of tomorrow."

"Oh, dear. Another good point."

"Points, points," Hettie said crossly. "All these points, and no one is fed."

"Mr. Bigelow, I am in deep respect of your counsel and wisdom," said Dr. Stiles. "I also think Mrs. Dixon has counsel we cannot ignore. I believe both of you are right, and I believe we can attend to both. We *must* attend to both! Now, I have a strategy in mind. The enormity of the prison is beyond my scope, and I have heard shocking reports of food actually turned away from the gates, for reasons I cannot fathom—filthy bureaucracy comes to mind. Here is what I believe we should do. If we cannot feed the entire prison, let us focus on the sick at the Federal hospital. A steady, nourishing diet and gentle care will help those boys and—I believe with all my heart— save some. We can augment what the government does supply, we can gather supplies such as bandages and lint packing, and I have hope we can even provide better medical treatments. I read of a man in Columbia, a Joseph LeConte, who has produced medicines in his own laboratory for the Confederate army. I propose that we —"

"Dr. Stiles, forgive me, but I wish to know what is your personal motive in this." It was Lloyd Fremont, a hotel owner. "You were taken into custody to be questioned about your own loyalty to the Confederacy; I think it important for us to understand the motive of this F.A.P. society. Is it about feeding starving men, which I can do no matter if that man is a Yankee, or will it apply *too much* gentle care for those soldiers, which may in fact *lead* to Union sympathies, and thus divert from the objective entirely? This is the fear which I believe many of us have." He regarded the crowd, and many nodded. "I wish to be involved in this enterprise if I can feed starving men. But I'll have no part of comingling the purity of that effort with politics, or to bring upon my family any whisper of treason. I despise the very notion of having to defend myself as a citizen of the C. S. of A."

"That is a very fair observation, Lloyd; goes straight to the heart of it," said Dr. Stiles. "I had to give grave consideration to the oath I took as a young physician when asked to volunteer at the Federal hospital. In truth, I was very reluctant. But I had to ask myself, am I a Southerner first, or am I a doctor? Am I a Rebel first, or a human being? I concluded that my personal motive is to go back to my Hippocratic oath: 'I will come for the benefit of the sick according to my ability and judgment. I will keep them from harm and injustice.' Everything changes, Lloyd, at one look into their circumstances. I no longer see a man who wishes me ill—I see a man who needs help."

"That is all very well for you," someone said. "But what of those with no Hippocratic oath?"

———

"Oh, I am so *tired* of this," Violet groused in a whisper to Dance and Emery. "Why can't we get on with practicalities?"

They sat at the edge of the gathering, Dance and Violet in chairs, Emery sitting on the ground next to Dance. As the evening progressed, Emery looked down the drive with greater frequency.

"You started it," Dance said to her. He was glad she did.

"I did not start *this*. I am bored to *death* with these irrelevancies."

"I think it's very interesting. You've got the town at least talking about it."

"They have said nothing to interest *me*." She shook the papers she'd retrieved from the house. "I have Americus broken down by streets. All we need to do is assign one day of the month to every

197

street in the districts and the outlying properties, and we will have certainly made headway in supplementing government allowance."

"What of Captain Wirz?" an elderly man was saying. "I want to hear more about him."

"It thrills me to see it." Violet admired her papers. "I wish to *get* to it!"

Dance put up a hand and whispered, "He's talking of Wirz."

"Captain Wirz is a very vulgar man!" said Constance Greer. "He said something *very* unchristian to Ann Hodgson."

"Well, I *have* heard things about him," said another in a cautionary tone.

"He's a Hessian—what do you expect?" someone called.

Then Dance watched Dr. Stiles closely. For just a second, Dance thought he saw something other than the patience from which Job could take lessons; but whatever that flash was, weariness or frustration, it had passed. Dr. Stiles said with his customary implacable calm, "I am not here to impugn another man's character. I am here to learn what is in ours. This war won't last forever, but what we do here today might."

"But I wish to understand things, Dr. Stiles," said the elderly man. "I am undecided as to what course my wife and I should take until I understand things. Is there no representative of the prison here?" He looked about. "I would like to hear what the administration has to say about these allegations against them."

"Stuff and nonsense!" Violet growled under her breath. "What is there to say? Men are dying from starvation!" Then she called out between cupped hands, "Men are dying from starvation!" She ducked behind Dance.

"Where is the preacher?" Emery whispered to Dance. "He should have shown by now."

"Seems we forever wonder that of him."

"What preacher?" Violet said. "Reverend Gillette?"

"Dr. Stiles, you surprise me," a voice cut clear. It was the woman who had snubbed Violet. Mrs. Runcorn.

"Friends of Andersonville Prison. *Friends.*" She pulled the word along. "Is it any wonder you were brought in for questioning?"

A silence fell across the crowd.

"There was not enough of my boy to send home," she said, standing up. "We tracked down two boys in his regiment who saw Jamie die. The first bullet killed him, straight through his neck. He was gone; he was dead. But that wasn't enough for those Yankees. They came up the slope, overwhelmed our troops, and forced them back. As they retreated, these two boys saw a sight to give them nightmares the rest of their lives. Those Yankees took their vengeance upon my boy."

She took a moment. "I *will* not weep before you, and be made an object of pity." Her eyes glowed, but no tears came. "They made sport of his body, for Jamie was a leader, and had done gloriously that day. They bayoneted him, sticking him repeatedly like demons from hell, but even that wasn't enough. One Yank took powder from a caisson box and threw it over my son. They lighted my boy up. There was nothing left of him. Nothing but ashes. And you would be *friends*—" the word pulled along—"to such as they who would desecrate so precious a form fashioned in the image of God. You all knew my son. Was he not a kind boy, and good?"

The crowd was silent, save for stifled weeping.

"For this and other atrocities brought down upon the South, I say of those men in that prison, if they suffer, they suffer according to the will of God, who is not mocked. It is justice. I will not interfere with the hand of God upon that place. To do so is not only treason upon the South, it is treason upon God."

She sat down.

Emery Jones shot up. He made his way to the front where Dr. Stiles stood, his face ashen. Emery took off his hat. "I've been waitin' for someone to come. He'd say what I have to say much better."

"He'll try and follow *that*?" Dance whispered, feeling sick.

Emery looked directly at Mrs. Runcorn. "I fought in a unit with brave boys such as yours, ma'am. Before my eyes, I lost them, good as yours. One word comes to mind when I think of the men in that prison: *mercy*. Maybe they deserve help and maybe they don't. But I don't know as it's a question of deservin'. I seen a lot of things out of those Yanks the last few years, good and bad. I reckon they seen the same of us, for men are the same on both sides of the line."

Eyes went to Mrs. Runcorn. Her look upon Emery was chillingly impassive.

"I'm posted at the prison, on dead duty. I watch over a squad of Union boys who are detailed to carry out their dead to the dead house. Sometimes I work in the Federal hospital. The condition of those bodies . . . ain't no describin' it. You have to see it to believe it. It is like a theater show in hell. What the doc says is true, all of it. I've seen—" He paused. "I saw a man with scurvy try to eat a piece of corn bread. Some of his teeth and bits of gums were left behind in the bread. He gave up eating it.

"I have carried out bodies gone so bad they break apart when you pick 'em up. I've seen maggots and flies and lice feed upon *living* men, boys so far gone they had not the strength to push 'em away. And thin? Thin as sticks. I do not think this is the hand of God visited upon them, ma'am. I think, in fact, it is the opposite."

Mrs. Runcorn rose.

She had remained impassive throughout his speech. She looked as if she were in a world of her own making, no crowd of people, nothing at all. Wherever that world was, all was dried up there.

She started to leave, then looked at Emery and asked vaguely, "Was mercy shown my boy?"

She looked behind for her husband and began to walk away. Then she stopped, and all eyes followed hers.

Up the drive came Reverend William Gillette, flanked by several men. His hands were bound.

"Is that Reverend Gillette?" Hettie Dixon gasped.

"He shaved his beard," said someone in awe.

"There he is," said one of the men flanking the preacher, pointing at Emery Jones. "That's him."

"Lucerne." Dance jumped to his feet. The turnkey Emery had bribed.

"Is that the man?" Detective Joseph T. Howard demanded of his prisoner. Reverend Gillette looked up and when he saw Emery, looked down again. He nodded.

The detective motioned with his head, and two men went over to Emery with a set of iron manacles.

"What have we got here?" said Judge Tate, rising.

"We've got ourselves a mess, Judge." Howard looked at the preacher. "It seems this man falsely represented his purpose for spending a night in Andersonville Prison. It appears it was not for some sanitation commission, which we have discovered does not exist. This organization, the Friends of Andersonville Prison, may in fact connect to the recent attempt by the Union general George Stoneman to break out prisoners. And that boy over there is one of the ringleaders."

The crowd gasped.

"Why, you *traitor*," someone hissed at Emery.

"Reverend Gillette?" another cried. "It can't be true!"

"I thought this was all straightened out," Judge Tate said.

"There is nothing straight about this," said Howard. "We have one of two very bad possibilities as to what transpired: I have a wit-ness right here who says that boy paid him to look the other way while he turned this preacher into the stockade for the express pur-pose of determining its weaknesses, and so to pass that information along to the Union lines."

"That's a lie!" Dance shouted.

"I'm with Pickett on that part," said Lucerne. "It wudden like that."

"Let's go to the courthouse and talk this out," said Judge Tate.

"I say talk it out right here," said Lloyd Fremont. "We have a right to know what is going on. We have all the right in the world if we have to take immediate action to protect our families."

"All right, then," said Judge Tate. "What is the other bad possibil-ity you spoke of, Mr. Howard?"

"That the whole thing *was* a kidnapping, as originally believed."

"There it is." Lucerne nodded.

"Reverend Gillette, help me clear this up," said Judge Tate. "Were you in fact kidnapped?"

"I read the note on the board myself," said Arvin Probity.

Reverend Gillette sighed. "I've been trying to tell these men it is an awful mistake. I am not a Union conspirator." He looked around. "You all know me! I am not a spy, nor do I even have Union tenden-cies. I am Southern to my marrow, and this is a witch hunt." He looked at Emery and said reluctantly, "Yes, I was kidnapped. But it was because that boy has a friend in the prison who—"

"A *friend*? A *Yankee* friend?" someone called.

"Oh, my goodness!" said another, clapping a hand to her head. "*Friends* of Andersonville Prison!"

"Oh, hear me out," said the preacher, irritated. "That boy turned me loose in there for humanitarian purposes. To take off a blindfold, he said. And yes, I was blind."

"So you *were* kidnapped," said the detective.

"Yes, but—"

"There you have it, Judge Tate."

For a moment, not a word was spoken.

The preacher shook his head. "This is not what truth is for." His voice rose. "Hear me, people. I went into the worst place I've ever been not of my own free will—but I *stayed* because of it! I do not hold that man accountable." He looked at the judge. "I choose not to press any charges whatsoever."

"There, you cannot come to this traitor's aid," said Howard. He looked at the judge. "This boy is a soldier. It means this is out of your hands, for you are a civilian judge."

"But it happened to a civilian," someone pointed out.

"Wait a minute—have we got our laws set in place as *our* laws yet?" someone else said. "Maybe that's a *Union* law."

"By the preacher's own mouth, I say let the boy go," said Timothy Bigelow. "Sounds like he was just trying to do something good."

Judge Tate shook his head. "Gentlemen, I'm afraid it is out of my hands. The detective is right. Jurisdiction is tricky. This may even have to be heard before a supreme court. But first, they must pull together a military tribunal."

"Do we have a supreme court yet? A *Confederate* supreme court?"

"Of course we do," said Judge Tate, annoyed. "All is not willy-nilly. We have our halls of justice, same as they. You make us sound like bandits. Wait one minute," he said to the men leading Reverend Gillette away. "You can at least turn the preacher loose."

"Certainly not," said Howard. "We have not yet got to the bottom of the other bad possibility—that there was in fact a conspiracy. How will this town sleep at night until they know the truth?"

"Another night in the deep. At least there will be decent food and water." Reverend Gillette looked at the crowd. "I had a very different speech planned for tonight. One that I'd hoped would open eyes and set you all to action."

"Action, is it?" said Arvin Probity. "Then tell us—why did you shave your beard? I have heard of such as that, men taking an oath to undermine government, and then they shave their beards to show it. Why . . . even Dr. Stiles shaved his beard . . ."

"Goodness gracious," Constance Greer gasped, curled ringlets swinging. "Well—Dr. Stiles, certainly not. But the reverend *is* a Methodist. I do not know their doctrines. . . ."

"I shaved it, good lady, because it had lice from the stockade," the preacher said wearily. "I did not want to bring them home."

"Oh. I should think not."

The men pulled him into step and led him away.

"But this is scandalous!" a woman protested. "Reverend Gillette! He is a *good* man!"

One man held Emery's arm while the other fastened the iron manacles on his wrists. He seemed too dazed to resist.

"What a great mess you have made, son," said the judge, "whatever your intentions."

They pulled Emery away.

Dr. Stiles hurried over to Judge Tate. "Can you not do something, Harlan?" He watched as the group walked away. "That boy is no kidnapper."

"Norton, I wish it were a matter of kidnapping. But if they prove it to be other, if it is treason . . . the boy will be hanged." He looked at Dr. Stiles. "Then things will not look so good for you either, my old friend." He picked up his picnic chair. "Do you know, some days I hate the law. Wish I had taken up boxing. It is a manly art."

Dance ran to the group of men. "If you're taking him, take me too!"

Emery yanked from their hold. "Oh, be still, Pickett!" The blue eyes were on fire. "It's up to you, Dance. Don't let me down. I'm begging you." The men seized his arms and dragged him away.

"Emery!" Posey cried. She scrambled down from the magnolia tree. "Emery, what are they gonna do to you?" She ran for him, but Dance caught the child and picked her up. "Dance, don't let him go! What are they gonna do?"

Howard, following the group, paused at Dance's side. "It's up to you, is it? *What* is up to you?"

"It's up to me to get him out, of course, for he is unjustly accused." He patted Posey's back. "Don't cry, Posey girl. That is what I mean to do." He glared at the detective and turned away, Posey clinging fiercely and sobbing her heart out.

He felt like crying himself, for he knew exactly what Emery meant.

It was up to Dance to get Lew out.

PART THREE

June 20—
We are sick and faint and all broken down, feverish &c. It is starvation and disease and exposure that is doing it.

June 21—
Some one has much to answer for.

—FROM THE DIARY OF JOHN RANSOM, ANDERSONVILLE SURVIVOR

Sunday 14.
Men that are laying around without shelter are dieing off by scores. The most wicked sights that man ever beheld are witnessed here daily.

Sunday 21.
Joe Herrin is geting badly cripeled up with the scurvy but there is no salvation for him if he has to stay here. His fate is hard to bear.

—FROM THE DIARY OF EUGENE SLY, ANDERSONVILLE SURVIVOR

17th.
How I do wish I was home tonight, how happy I would be, how would Sister feel if she knew how and where I was. God forbid she should know it, till I get out of this.

3rd.

Hot and dry, am very stiff in my neck and arms, so I can scarcely get them to my head. Tis very disagreeable to be in this Bull Pen. Took quite a number out to day.

—FROM THE DIARY OF ALFRED VOORHEES; DIED IN ANDERSONVILLE, AUGUST 13, 1864

Friday, July 22, 1864
Middling Cool and pleasant

Monday, August 15, 1864
The most Beautiful Rain Bow I ever saw just at sun down

—FROM THE DIARY OF CHARLES LEPLEY; DIED IN ANDERSONVILLE, SEPTEMBER 11, 1864

14

HARRIS GILL WAS DYING, and there was nothing Lew could do about it.

Two weeks a prisoner, and Lew was no longer a skipping stone. He could not eat a piece of corn bread, if it happened to come baked that day, without thinking of Carrie's blueberry jam. And then he thought of Carrie, and the children, and green places, and it was no use packing them away. He tried, but it didn't work for long.

A new messmate had taken Artie's place: Martin Kellerman, 10th Connecticut Infantry. He was a man who had had no shelter for two months, a pitiful creature content to lie and sleep all day in the newfound riches of a shield against the sun. Would Lew become as he? Skeletal, vermin-bit, lost? The only time he roused was for the three *r*'s—roll call, rations, and relief—and when Lew recounted battles. He seemed to come forward from a shadow corner of his soul then and listened with interest. When the tale was done, he'd shuffle back to that corner and resume a gray survival once more, something a little more than existence, a little less than endurance.

Lew switched aside the tent flap and crawled out. It was a Hotel Ford policy to delouse oneself upon waking. This morning he picked off fifty-seven of the little demons. He scraped them together, ground the squirming pile under his boot heel with glorious vengeance, and set out.

He took three steps before he had to stop and readjust the packing in the hole in his boot. It was a gummy thatch of burlap bookbinding torn from the spine of a book Andy had found. Andy preserved the pages of the book with devout fanaticism, fearful to lose any sort of entertainment, even if it was written in a foreign language.

"What do you think, Carrie? Bit of a foreign-language book from a foreign-language place stuck in the boot of a Pennsylvania boy in Georgia."

Lew observed his new life situation in a never-ending monologue to Carrie, sure to make others think he'd boarded the train to crazy if his low mutters were overheard. But talking to her made him feel better.

"I'd like a chair, Carrie. My body aches to conform itself to that civilized structure.

"Remember the camp beef I told of, so pickled in brine you couldn't eat it without several soaks? What I wouldn't do for a taste of salt now. Never knew what a real pleasure it was.

"Carrie, you mustn't think the whole South bad. On the way here our train stopped in Forsyth, and there a woman waited to do us a kindness. 'You boys must be hungry,' said she, and passed out fresh biscuits to us prisoners. 'I had boys, too. They were always hungry.'

"Carrie, I didn't know the word *exposure* until this place. I see its effects on a man called Martin, and now I know the word."

It helped Lew to tell her these things, but it did not take from the fact that Harris Gill was dying, and there was nothing he could do about it.

Every day he left the tent early and spent the day rambling. He made a full circuit of the stockade five times a day, and each time he stopped to see how Harris was doing. Sometimes he fetched water, if the crease-faced boy was on duty, and brought it to Harris. Often he stayed long enough to tell Martin about a new battle he had thought of.

He stopped to watch a trade between a guard and a prisoner. The prisoner handed over two brass eagle buttons. The guard held them to the sun, and then handed over sweet potatoes. He thought of the skulker who had killed Charley Reed and Colonel Ford for buttons. He stood long enough for Harris Gill to say in his mind, "Pack 'em away, Lew," and when he came to himself realized the two traders were long gone. He ambled on.

He stopped and listened to a Confederate guard speak from the seat of the rations wagon to an interested group of four new prisoners. "Things is hard for us, too, Billy boys. We ben taken away and our women left to pull in crops. How they gonna do that with all else they got to do? Some of us have cut and run, and you tell me where the shame is. You jes try and stay put when your fam'ly is starvin'."

"I tell you what I'd do," said a prisoner hotly. "I'd cut out right quick. Family first."

The guard nodded. "That's my thinkin'."

"Say, where you from, secesh?"

"Bowlin' Green, down in Florida. You?"

"Kilbourn City, Wisconsin."

"Nice up there?"

"I'll say. Good fishin'."

"What kinda fish you all catch in Billy land?"

Lew moved on, not because the conversation got any more or less interesting; he could just about time the restlessness in his feet. He had set some sort of schedule with his circumvention of the stockade and needed to keep to it. He walked all day, and at night when he lay down, he couldn't sleep until his legs stopped jerking.

In a place teeming with men, usually so thick you could not stretch out your arm without touching someone, the only place he could be alone was in his mind. There, he plucked a dried milkweed pod and broke it open, sifted its silkiness and sent it on the wind. He ate a pint of blackberries as he walked his orchards. He pulled tearful little Helen out of a pricker bush, set her on a stump, and patiently picked the prickers from her hair and dress.

Lew came to the sinks on the southeast side of the stockade.

"Well, Carrie, here is what you do. Take a potful of foulness. Thin it with greasy water. Add men. And there you have Stockade Creek from which we bathe and some, from cruel thirst, drink."

"Demoralizin' hot."

A man stood next to Lew, hands in his pockets. Lew had seen him before on his ambles, for he was an ambling man too.

"It is surely that. Not used to this heat. Where you from?"

"New York—9th Volunteers. I think this place lacks initiative."

Lew laughed.

"Name's Vance Edward," the fellow said, smiling.

"Lew Gann, 12th Pennsylvania."

"Where you mess?"

"Up a ways, middle of the northeast quadrant. Me and three other fellas. One from Connecticut, one from Delaware, and a man from my own regiment. You?"

"Got a fine little put-together up on the northwest side. Two other fellas. What battle you taken in?"

"Kennesaw."

"Spotsylvania. I've seen your limp. You get that at Kennesaw?"

Lew nodded. "It's mending, but slow. How long you been here?"

"Two months, going into three."

"You look pretty good for that," Lew said. "I appreciate any trade secrets. I've been here only two weeks and must have lost ten pounds. The lice are just about making off with my hide."

"Well, you look all right, and if you're careful you'll keep that way. The sand at the northwest corner is the cleanest. I scrub with it every day. I've also accustomed myself to getting by with little water, even clean. There are a lot of little things I can tell you, but the most important is to keep your spirits up. When those go, the body will follow. I've seen it happen to the most disciplined."

"It is a relief to see anyone who does not lose his head," Lew admitted.

Vance observed a man sifting through the brown water. "It's a wonder we live at all."

"What's he looking for?" Lew asked, repelled.

"Roots. We used to get roots from there to dry out and use to cook our rations. The roots are all gone. But he doesn't have anything better to do."

"I'd sure find another place to do nothing better. What are some things you do for your spirits?"

"I keep moving. Like I've seen you done. And I think about my wife and three boys."

"I was told that's the last thing I should do."

Vance shook his head. "That's crazy. 'Whatsoever things are true and honorable' and all that, 'think on these things.' They are that. They give me hope. Hope awakens courage."

"Carrie does keep cropping up. I can't keep her out."

"Keep her in. Well, I better move on. About this time I meet with a fellow and play checkers. I'll see you around, Lew."

"Yeah, see you around, Vance."

He ambled off, and Lew watched him go.

Almost back to Hotel Ford, he stopped at the well. The crease-faced boy was on duty. He untied Emery's tin cup from a belt loop and held it out.

"They're on to me," said the boy. "Make as if to give me something. I'll put it in my pocket."

"I'll give you something real." He pulled out a few folded pages of the foreign book and handed them over.

"What language is this?" the boy said.

"Don't know."

The boy took a moment to examine the pages. He folded them carefully and tucked them down the front band of his trousers. Then he lowered a bucket and brought up fresh water. It was a little muddy, to be sure, but it was far cleaner mud, and of the genuine kind, than over in Stockade Creek. He poured some into the tin cup, waited until Lew drank it, and refilled it.

"Where did you get that scar?" Lew asked.

"Gaines Mill. Thought I'd die. Here I am."

"How old were you then?"

"Fourteen."

"You are sixteen now?"

"Yep."

"If you told Captain Wirz, I bet he'd get you out."

"Would you leave your men?"

"No, I would not. Say, we've wondered—why do you give the water for free?"

"Seems right."

"What's your name, son?"

"Carl Wolfgang."

"Much obliged, Wolf." Lew turned to go.

"Say," Wolf called. "How's the Irish doin'?"

"Not so good."

"He called a reg off me once. I wish for the best."

———

"Fill the line, boy-o! Run to it!"

Martin Kellerman sat in the corner, arms about his thin knobby knees, watching Harris. Andy Rogers was gone.

"How is he?"

It took a moment for Martin to realize that Lew was in the tent, let alone that he had spoken.

"Fine." Then he said, rousing fully, "No. Not so good. Andy's gone to see about a stretcher for the hospital line."

"I don't want him there," Lew said, sitting beside Harris. "Got some water for you, Harris." He helped him drink. Then he dipped the edge of his shirt cuff in what was left in the cup and tried to wipe some pus from Harris's lip.

Harris weakly pushed his hand away. "Get your bonny arse back on the line."

"Will do." He finished wiping away the pus, then scrubbed his shirt cuff against his leg until it felt hot. "How goes the battle?"

"Well, they gave us the wrong caliber bullet. I can throw 'em better than shoot 'em."

"We're out of percussion caps," Lew said. "Might as well throw 'em."

"Oh. All right then." His eyes closed.

"That'll be a better way to go," said Martin, watching Harris, "than out there."

"You planning on dying anytime soon? You've made it this far. Don't give up the ship."

"You never know. Only now I got some pride back. Glad for someone to yell at me to pick off lice."

It was the longest conversation he'd had with Martin. "How long have you been here?"

"Don't remember."

"What battle were you taken in?"

"Don't remember that either. I'm with the 10th Connecticut. That's all I know. I was in a tent with some fellas, once, but they weren't as nice as you boys. Kicked me out when they found someone better. Rebs ain't the only mean ones."

"We won't do that, Martin."

"I know it. Even a wreck like me knows it." Exhausted by the talk, he lay down and was instantly asleep. Martin Kellerman was taller than Lew's five-ten, and maybe weighed a hundred and twenty pounds. His skin looked like frost on scrub grass. Somewhere a woman wondered where her boy was. He is here, Mrs. Kellerman, though you will not know him.

Lew's chest cage held one thing: powerlessness.

"Carrie, I am glad you are not here to see this. I don't know what you would do. Harris Gill and Martin Kellerman are dying, and there is nothing I can do about it."

He crawled out of the tent and started walking.

15

LACK OF EVIDENCE and personal recognizance cleared Reverend William Gillette of all suspicion of treasonous activities. Lack of evidence cleared Corporal Emery Jones of the same, but before kidnapping even made it to the table, the convened assembly at the Americus courthouse, consisting of both military and civil counsel owing to the involved nature of the charges for both men, found Corporal Jones guilty of something else.

A representative for the prosecution cited Article 41 of the Articles of War for the Government of the Army of the Confederate States: "All non-commissioned officers and soldiers who shall be found one mile from the camp without leave, in writing, from their commanding officer, shall suffer such punishment as shall be inflicted upon them by the sentence of a court-martial."

The morning the reverend was kidnapped, Emery Jones had gone to Americus without leave. Americus was ten miles from the military barracks at Andersonville. Corporal Emery Jones of the 22nd Alabama Volunteers, Company C, was court-martialed for desertion.

With Atlanta threatened, affairs of every nature were put in order as quickly as they could be, and the affair of Corporal Jones was settled by the minimal amount of commissioned officers required for a court-martial. Because Corporal Jones had not only deserted but had given cause for suspicion of Union fidelities, the court-martial handed down the full measure of punishment as directed by the General Orders of the War Department regarding deserters: that those convicted were "to be shot to death with musketry, at such time and place as the commanding General may direct."

Shot or hanged.

Corporal Emery Jones, incarcerated in the camp barracks at Andersonville Prison, was sentenced to hang by the neck until dead on Saturday, August 6, 1864. He had four days to live.

The court-martial adjourned, leaving behind a stunned Stiles family, a stricken young sentinel, and a pale Corporal Jones.

———

Sherman harried Atlanta, Americus prepared for invasion, and Dr. Stiles took to his office.

The Home Guard drilled daily with freshly pressed men from all over the county. Overage volunteers from Americus were assigned to guard duty at Macon or at Andersonville. A hospital began to set up wards in a series of buildings on the west side of the public square. Newspapers could not keep up with battles and troop movements. Military personnel hurried about with hateful telegrams and posted some of them on the bulletin board where many citizens took to hanging about.

If Atlanta fell, where would Sherman go next? Would he head east for the other major cities, Augusta and Savannah? Or would he continue south, for Macon and then for Americus?

"He ain't gonna head south. That'll stretch his supply line too thin."

"What of that? They are amply supplied and live bountiful off our land. They gonna blow right through to the tiptoes of Florida. The South is finished."

"Atlanta's the prize, not 'Mericus. Either way, Sherman takes Atlanta, and yes, sir—we are finished."

"We'll see how that John Bell Hood answers."

"He ain't Johnston."

"He ain't. But he's what we got."

"Say, it's a shame about that boy."

"Yes sir, it is."

"Reckon they gotta stick to the cuss end of the law."

"There's gotta be law."

"It is a necessary evil."

"Yes sir, it is."

"I just wish they weren't gonna hang him. Meant well."

———

Posey cried for two days. Then she wiped her nose and said, "Posey Stiles, you shore yourself up. You will do Emery no good."

She sought her father to see what good she could do, and all he said was, "Draw him a picture."

"Draw him a picture," she scorned as she stomped away from his office. "A thumping lot of good that will do."

She brightened a little. Emery was from Alabama. He did not know Sumter County. She could draw a map on the back of the picture in case he escaped. The jailer would not notice if she drew it very lightly. She knew just the pencil for the job, and she ran for the Pressing Needs box.

———

"Well, look at those dark circles. The only word I can use to describe you right now is *wan*. I do not like the word, nor do I like the state you are in. Do I see another victim of Andersonville in front of my eyes?"

Dr. Stiles looked up from the newspaper. Hettie Dixon stood in the doorway of his office, a basket on her arm. She shut the door. "You are not even reading that."

"Polly send for you, did she?" He looked at the paper. "General Winder is fortifying the Andersonville stockade with an outer wall against an imminent Sherman attack. Hadley's editorial says all this conscription of the citizens for horses and mules and slaves amounts to nothing less than taxation."

"Polly told me you had a visitor the other day. A Colonel Chandler."

"He was sent to inspect the prison."

"What did you tell him?"

"Everything. It seems at last the prisoners have a voice."

"They had one in you." When he didn't answer, she said, "Do you think Colonel Chandler will be heard?"

"There, my faith falters. He plans to tell the truth of Andersonville. Such will be put down."

Hettie sat in the consultation chair in front of his desk. She took knitting out of the basket and began to knit.

"Polly hasn't seen you like this since little George. That's the last time she sent for me, regarding yourself."

He put the newspaper on the desk. He took off his glasses, folded them, and put them in his vest pocket. He sat back to look out the window.

Hettie's needles clicked.

"When will you get back to seeing patients, Norton?"

"Oh. Shouldn't be long now."

"When will you get back to the Federal hospital? Today *is* Thursday."

"That is out of my hands. They will not renew my pass. Do you know, I think they liked the *idea* of helping the prisoners? The thought of feeding an enemy has a fine revolutionary pull, for it is a radical kindness. Perhaps we fill up on thoughts of radical kindnesses and find ourselves sated. If on vapors."

"Intentions and actualities seldom meet on the same plane." Hettie's needles clicked. She pulled a length of yarn out of her basket to keep up. "What I wish to know is when we will have the next F.A.P. meeting."

"There are no friends of Andersonville Prison."

"What about Colonel Chandler?"

He didn't answer.

The clicking stilled and Hettie said, "Norton, out of curiosity, what other things were you going to say at that meeting before it was interrupted? I was particularly interested in your plans for the hospital."

"Hettie—please."

"Just tell me one thing you were going to say."

He was still for a moment, then abruptly snatched a sheaf of notes from a corner of his desk and shoved them at her. He resumed perusal of the day outside the window.

She selected one at random, held it out as far as she could, and read aloud: "A Confederate surgeon reports that one in four amputations in a field hospital results in death." She looked at the doctor. "What were you going to say about that?"

Dr. Stiles answered only because he had fallen to a distracted state. "I envied those odds. Nearly every amputation at Andersonville results in death. It is hard enough for a healthy man to stand an amputation, but a man decimated by Andersonville . . . They have one in four who die. We have one in four who live. And that is a good day."

After a moment, Hettie put the note back.

She knitted long enough to turn the heel of the sock and then asked, "Norton, do you know why we must *visit* widows and orphans in their despair instead of merely sending them a note?"

He didn't answer.

"Because everywhere we go we carry the divine spark. We can all do with a little more of the divine spark if it sits down next to us for a spell, can we not?"

"I see nothing divine or sparkly about severing a gangrenous limb from a body shortly to follow. I have no pass, Hettie. I am cut off. There is something comforting when you realize there is nothing more you can do. You have done your best, and it is out of your hands."

"Oh, you should not be comforted a whit, Norton Stiles. Whoever told you it was out of your hands? Has *God* dismissed you from your duty? Hmm. In our most trying times, God has the temerity to ask us to walk a little farther. And that is what he wants you to do, *pass* or no pass. He wants you to get back to it."

"I'm tired."

"You've taken time to be tired and you are done, sir. You've got seven women on the other side of that door walking all over their hearts, they've gotten so low 'cause of your 'tired.'"

"I'm still tired."

Hettie rested her knitting in her lap. "Isn't it a puzzling truth? The very thing that makes us tired is the very thing that refreshes once we get back to it; and we must not get back halfhearted." After a moment, she added gently, "I think you came upon something extraordinary in its evil scope. It would tire anyone."

"Oh, it's not just that. Emery Jones will hang in two days because he wanted to help others. The law is for lawbreakers—he is no lawbreaker, not by the spirit of the law, of which we do not seem to be custodians any longer. There is only the letter of the law, and it kills. And I am tired, tired of it all."

"Norton Avery Stiles, look at me."

He did so.

"I am sixty-four years old. I've got at least a dozen on you. I have come to know that we must accustom ourselves to pain and injustice and things we just don't know what to do about. But we are *fitted* to other things. Made to meet 'em. And those we carry best as we can. Now God has someone else fitted to that boy. He is not yours to carry. Yours is Andersonville. You are fitted to it. Now get back to it."

He didn't know what to say.

Hettie said, exasperated, "Yes, it is as simple as that. Behold, you are sprung from your dark cage. Mercy, but revelations come cheaply enough. Putting feet to 'em—now, that is something else."

He still didn't know what to say.

She said kindly, "Action is a tonic, Norton. It is precisely when a body does not know what to do that the answer is easy—do anything. Preferably something small and kind. When we attend small things, the other part of us works on ways to get back to big things. What has Ellen got in the larder?"

"I'm not hungry."

"Oh, for heaven's sakes. It's not for you." Sounding much like Ellen, she muttered, "How *long* will I be with you? How *long* will I put up with you?"

"Who is it for, then?"

"What time is it?"

He looked at her for a moment, and then consulted his pocket watch. "Quarter past twelve."

"We have time enough to catch the one-fifteen. Do not stop and think, sir, or you will fill up on vapors." She put the knitting into the basket and stood. "Rise up, Norton Stiles. Let us raid the larder and make off with the goods. I will distract Ellen, and you will fill my basket and cover it with knitting. Today we shall visit the Federal hospital and find ourselves a hungry man. I dearly love to feed hungry men."

"Oh, what good will it do, Hettie? The need is too great."

"Oh, for—it will do good for the one we *feed*. Ask him, if you don't believe me! Come, let us away! I may be sixty-four years old, but today I feel fifty."

"I don't have a pass."

"Well, Jesus did not have a *pass*. I can't think of everything. You have a ten-mile train ride to figure that out." She held out the basket.

Doctor Stiles studied it for a good long minute, and finally took it.

"We don't have to *raid* the larder. Ellen would give willingly."

"What fun is that?"

———

"Do you know how many times I had to recite the Articles of War? All hundred and one of them, plus sections? Never thought one should spell my demise. Article 41 is a shorty, too. You'd think a man's death would be more complicated."

Emery was being held at Castle Reed, a small walled stockade just east of the Andersonville depot. It formerly held Union officers until they were transferred in May to a camp near Macon. It now served as a guardhouse as well as a punishment facility for Confederate guards. Emery was allowed two visitors per day, and this was his second— Dance had passed Reverend Gillette on the way in.

Dance sat on the floor against the wall. There was only a cot in the room. Emery sat on the edge of the cot, his knees bouncing up and down. "Do you know how many times I've slipped away from camp without a pass? We'd sneak past the pickets and go on foraging sprees." He chuckled. "Went to a Yankee dance, once, if you believe me. I can dance pretty well and so they forgave my heritage. I hope

you have not come to be glum. Rest yourself content, Mr. Pickett, for
I do not intend to swing. You look like you haven't slept in a week."

"Why do you look like you swallowed sunbeams?"

"You'd rather have me all laid out and squallin'?"

"I'd have you face reality."

"Well, I may have figured a way out of this fix. But I need to sit
with it some." He chuckled. "Sunbeams . . ."

"The preacher looked as shabby as I feel."

"Did you hear me? I may see a way out."

"Is that so?"

"The answer is so plain a blind man can read by it. I have already
given a clue."

"What clue?"

"Oh, you're a smart boy—figure it out."

"You're tunneling out."

"When did I give that clue?"

"You bribed the guards."

"Nope."

"You have dangerous friends. They're coming to bust you out."

"All my dangerous friends are with the 22nd Alabama, beatin'
Sherman." Emery hummed a snatch of "Bonnie Blue Flag" and said,
"Wish I had somethin' for my hands to do. They won't let me finish
weavin' that stretcher. I don't see how rag strips are implements of
bust-out. The preacher brought a Bible, and that was nice, and a picture from Posey Stiles. Look here—she drew me a map for escape on
the back. That's me right there, knifing a guard." He grinned. "That
little girl. We woulda been best friends if we was kids together."

"It has something to do with the reverend."

"Nope."

"Dr. Stiles?"

"Nope. When am I to be hung?"

"Hanged. Eleven o'clock on Saturday morning."

"I need to keep that in mind. It may spur cogitation. Saturday is how many days off?"

"Two. Posey gave you a key along with the map."

"Nope."

"A nail file."

"Listen, Dance, what progress have you made with Lew's case? It weighs on me. No slur on your capabilities, but I am more comfortable with his fate in my hands than yours. You are distractible."

"Progress—what progress? No progress! I can't think past more immediate realities, you Alabamian haystick! So should you! Tell me your idea before I get angry."

"Listen, there is something you can do for me. The preacher brought an onion poultice for Lew's friend, Harris. He took it to both gates but was turned away. Can you—?"

"He gave it to me. I left it outside the door. It stinks. I'll see what I can do. Emery . . . Gillette says you will not give information to get hold of your folks."

"I won't trouble them over something that most likely won't occur."

"Most likely . . ."

"Well, since when do my ideas ever land strictly as I mean them to?"

Dance went to grab him by the neck and shook his fists in Emery's face instead. "Then tell me what it is! You'll have two minds on it."

"I want your mind on helpin' Lew Gann."

"Well, I've never met him. It's not him I—"

"I want your mind on helpin' Lew," Emery repeated patiently. "If you will be a leader in our country one day, and I see congressman shinin' down on you like a portentous light from heaven, then you must puzzle out for yourself what an Alabamian haystick just about has. Mercy, but I have given a whopper clue. Meantime, tell me your plan for Violet Stiles. You better fashion one quick before some other swell comes along."

There Emery sat talking a mile a minute, trying to distract Dance, looking out for Dance—when *he* was the one about to die. And there wasn't a thing Dance could do about it. No more than he could do anything about Andersonville.

Why did he want to be a lawyer, anyway? How did one fight injustice with unjust laws? One of the few people he cared about was about to be murdered by the very law Dance had been raised to revere.

It was a dark flood rising inside, and he had no place to go. He'd rise to the top and the dark flood would catch him. They'd find him dead on the street one day, dry as cotton, never knowing he'd drowned in his own skin.

He did not want this dying man to see his despair—likely no more than Emery wanted Dance to see his.

He brought his mind back to Emery's rattlings.

"... that you two are suited. Wish you'd ken it. What is more, the fact that you did not kiss her on that porch is something from which Hickory Shearer would fashion a month of maxims."

"Well, that is completely irrelevant. Besides—well, Emery, you are better looking than I."

"I know it," Emery said simply. "But I am taken, else I'd twist my heart to a wreath and lay it at her feet."

"Who has taken you?"

"Lew's sister, Laura. She has got some memorable sass. She is Posey Stiles all growed up."

"Isn't Lew from Pennsylvania? When did you meet her?"

"I haven't." Then he confessed, "I hope she is not ugly. Plain can be beautified by sass, but there is not much you can do with ugly. If she is, in fact, pretty, well, that's just a windfall; it's the girl I want."

He thought a minute, and said firmly, "I will situate myself to ugly if I must. I will be kind to her. Love beautifies."

"What has she done to warrant your affections?" Dance asked, truly curious.

"I read some of her letters. And Lew's told me of her. His fondness and admiration are clear. She's his favorite, and he's told me many stories. One story did me in. Fort Sumter had fallen, and—"

The key scraped in the lock and the door swung open. "Time's up, Pickett."

Dance sighed. "I wanted to hear that story." He got up.

"It'll keep. Lew is not an ugly man. Perhaps absent of ugly in a male runs likewise for females of the same blood. I'm ashamed it worries me. I will put it out of my mind."

Dance paused at the door. "Your uncle and aunt have the same last name as you?"

When Emery did not answer, it was then Dance saw a crack in the cavalier surface. He sat still, hands curled around the edge of the cot.

"There is no idea," Dance said quietly.

Emery didn't answer.

"What's your folks' name?"

He shook his head, staring at a spot on the floor.

"Emery, you're not being fair to them. They can be reached through the war department at Huntsville. A telegram will put them on the next train."

"I did no genuine wrong by any stretch of common sense." He picked up Posey's picture and set it back down. "Write 'em a letter later and tell 'em the truth. They don't need to be pulled off the farm and see me hung for something as stupid as no pass. It has no meaning."

"It's Andersonville. Men die for no meaning."

"Wish I was hung for bustin' out Lew."

228

"Hanged . . ."

"Pickett, get moving," said the guard.

"If you told me your idea, maybe I could help."

"Help Lew. He's in there 'cause of me. I kept one oath I shouldn't have and made one I can't keep." He looked up.

When Dance saw his eyes, he knew it was over. There was no scheme there, no fight. Only worry—and not for himself.

"Keep my oath for me, Dance. Then I can die with all my heart."

16

VIOLET STILES WAS READY to climb into mourning black. It felt as if the town of Americus had died. All she had *known* them to be turned out to be merely all she had *thought* them to be.

Dance was right. He had warned her, and she hadn't listened. And what else had he said that day when they were all on the porch and she hadn't listened?

He had been walking away, and she was losing him, and he had that dark and awful look on his face, and then he came back up the stairs two at a time, his face freshened, and full of hope.

What was it that was said to make him come back like that?

Violet watched a dried-herb bundle sway in what little wind the day brought. It had been raining off and on, and the forgotten bundles tied at the iron rail were alternately wet and dry for days on end, and had likely lost their potency.

She had been too stirred up in plans and passion that day to note what had changed his face to that intensive thought and hope. But she did recall that she had not listened to him, and all she remembered now was when that hope receded and became blank and he just went along with all their plans.

With *her* plans.

What had been said? Who said it?

Maybe it would come to her on the way to see Judge Tate. She had a question for him.

———

"Judge Tate, does the president alone have the authority to forgive a death penalty—or could a governor do it?"

Judge Tate saw that the wrong word from him could plunge Violet back into the state from which she had quite recently come, and only someone past pity would do that, for clearly this misery meant the girl was in love with Emery Jones. So he worded his response carefully. While he would not crush hope, neither would he give it falsely.

"A governor certainly has authority to commute a death sentence," he said slowly. "In fact, had Governor Wise commuted the sentence of John Brown, the North would not have a martyr on their hands. But, child, you must understand—this is a very, very difficult time for Governor Joe. Sherman bears down upon us and all of Joe's efforts are for stopping him. I believe there is slim chance you could get an audience with him. I don't believe *I* could."

"Hmm," Violet said thoughtfully. "Maybe J. W. Pickett could."

———

Violet went to the telegraph office—to find it closed. A note on the door said, MACHINE BROKE DOWN. PROCEED TO ALBANY OR ANDERSONVILLE FOR NEAREST OFFICE. She peered through the glass. Two perspiring men worked on the machine while a glowering, cigar-smoking Confederate officer looked on.

Growling, Violet quickly rummaged in her bag. She didn't dare chivvy Silas Runcorn into a free fare. Maybe she had enough for the fare *and* the telegram. She counted out the coins and looked at the posted fees on the office door.

Oh, dear. Enough for a two-word telegram and one fare.

She raised her bag to dash it to the ground, then she caught sight of Papa and Hettie Dixon strolling over to the ticket counter on the train platform.

———

Violet was very glad for Hettie's ideas for the next F.A.P. meeting. After Violet told them about her telegram plans, Hettie's chatter kept her and Papa occupied and left Violet alone with her thoughts.

What had Dance said on the porch that day?

She closed her eyes and put Papa in his chair, herself and Emery at the rail, and a belligerent Dance walking away from her plans. Then came, *Yes, that's it exactly! That's the truth, Violet!* and he was belligerent no more. His face was flushed and vibrant and those brown eyes, those deeply expressive brown eyes—

What was the truth?

To feed these enemies is to forgive them. That, my girl, this town will not do.

Papa's words. Dance came swooping in to confirm those words, and it angered Violet, it seemed as though he was at his pompous university best, then, eager to quell her enthusiasm with his arrogant cynicism and worse, his hateful *instruction*. But it wasn't true, that's not how it went. That face was the truest he'd ever been. And what did he say?

Don't get this town involved! But if you want to help, then—

And Violet had cut him off.

He had seemed cut off ever since.

She hadn't listened to him. She'd just roared on with her plans.

—

Hettie and Papa had business with the Federal hospital. Papa, with a curious blush, said he had a packet of herbs that Dr. Stevenson could use in surgery, as their properties worked like lint to stanch the flow of blood and may indeed have inhibiting agents against infection. More curious still, Hettie told him it was too much detail and that he needed to refine his technique. They walked off laughing softly.

At least Papa was laughing again.

Violet shook her head, mystified, and went to the telegraph office.

She did not have nearly enough money for all she wanted to say. She worked and reworked the message until $1.09 paid for the following:

Dear Cousin Pickett. Innocent man to die 11:00 a.m.
Saturday unless you intervene. Come at once to Americus.
The Stiles Family.

The important parts were covered. They would explain every-thing once he arrived, but she didn't have money to tell him that. She had to argue with the telegrapher that *11:00 a.m.* should count as one word as it had one meaning, and she got her way.

Papa told her to wait until he and Hettie returned for the next train to Americus. He added, "Violet, for the time being, it will not do for us to—Listen, I don't want you to visit Emery or Dance or any prisoners or any places of government or to even *look* as though you would give aid to *anyone*."

"Don't worry, Papa," Violet said, uncharacteristically meek.

"I want you to stay right here after you send that telegram."

"Yes, Papa. Say hello to Dance if you see him. And, Papa . . ."

With all her heart she hoped J. W. Pickett would come and be moved to pity by Emery's case, and then take that pity and convince his intimate acquaintance, Governor Joe Brown, to extend mercy and pound a mighty stamp called COMMUTED on Emery's sentence. If everything went right, that would happen. But nothing went right, these days.

"Tell him we will be here on Saturday morning. He will not have to—" She paused. "He will not be alone."

———

As Violet left the telegraph office, she saw a familiar face. Ann Hodgson saw her at the same time and waved.

Ann sat in the front seat of her farm wagon, James at her feet. Isaiah, the field hand, sat next to her holding the reins. Little James held out his arms to be picked up. Delighted, Violet did so.

"What a handsome little man!" He grasped her bonnet string and shook it. She seized his fist and kissed it.

"Isn't he just?" Ann beamed. "I want to have six more."

How could Ann remain so cheerful and so in Andersonville, despite the abuse she took from General Winder and Captain Wirz? Those *despicable* things they said? Yet there she was, fresh and confident—and back to her original business, said a covered corner of the wagon bed.

"You are fearless, Ann. Look at you. Where are those supplies bound?"

Ann gave a wink. "Not up to the gate, I'll grant you."

Violet looked around and lowered her voice. "It is truly for the prison?"

"It is. I have . . . a *setup*."

"What sort?"

"I cannot say. But whatever donations I receive are smuggled in and freely given." Her smile dimming somewhat, she admitted, "It

THE SENTINELS OF ANDERSONVILLE

is not much. But it is something." She looked Violet over. "I heard your society took a sound drubbing at that meeting, yet still you live. Bully for you. Don't let them get you downhearted, Violet."

"How do you know I've been downhearted?" Violet said, ruefully.

"I was, too. Then I said, 'What of it? Now I know the ways I cannot help; I will find ways I can. And if I can't find them, I will make them.' You can, too, Violet. When is your next F.A.P. meeting?"

"Hettie was just talking of it. . . ."

"Let me know. I'd love to attend—now that the riffraff are sorted out."

"But no one will show."

"I will. And Hettie. And you. Constance Greer will do whatever Hettie does. There. We are four."

Sudden tears came. Little James shook the bonnet string and put it in his mouth, and then offered it to Violet. Ann reached to squeeze Violet's shoulder. "Pull together your determination, my old friend, and do as you set out to do. Do as you *want* to do."

Suddenly, Violet did not want to cry at all. "As I want to do? Ann, those are not Christian things."

Ann pulled back a little, surprised but curious. "How do you mean?"

"I *want* to go up to Captain Wirz and General Winder and whoever else brought such pitiless suffering upon those men, on purpose or *not*, and I want to put my hands around their necks and choke them short of death!"

"Why, Violet Stiles." Ann sized her up anew. "I think we understand each other."

Violet's hands were afire, and she said, "I'll be right back." She handed over little James, seized up her skirts, and ran for the commissary building.

She burst into the dimness and pulled back her bonnet, looking around for Corporal Womack, then ran behind the service counter.

"Miss Stiles?" said Corporal Womack, his head appearing over a stack of meal bags. He set down the bill of lading. "Ah, you are not supposed to be behind that counter as you are a civilian. May I help you?"

"You certainly may! I need pen, paper, tacks, and a hammer!" She stopped rummaging and looked up. "Why . . . I do believe a certain detective may restrain my action once he discovers it. . . ."

"Is that so?" said Corporal Womack, his face hardening. "Why, I've got paper galore, Miss Stiles. You just wait right there. Paper galore." He ran for the back room.

———

AMERICUS, ANDERSONVILLE, OR WHOMSOEVER WILL

Is it possible you think yourself DETAINED from Feeding STARVING Prisoners? Come to the Glorious Outskirts of Society for the SECOND . . .

Friends of Andersonville Prison (F.A.P.) Meeting!

We shall meet AGAIN on the Pleasantly Situated Lawn of the home of Dr. Norton Stiles and Family. We shall meet EVERY TUESDAY NIGHT until KINGDOM COME or until they SHUT DOWN that HELLISH PLACE.

Whichever comes first.

"How many copies you gonna make?" said the corporal.
"As many as I can manage before my father comes back."
"Well, I am a fair hand at lettering. Can I help?"

"Certainly!"

They worked quickly, dipping and blotting and scratching, and after a few moments, Violet said, "Do you think it will make a difference?"

"I don't know, Miss Stiles." He pulled back to survey his work. "I just wish those boys could see it."

17

"WELCOME TO ANDERSONVILLE," he'd once heard an inmate greet newcomers, "the place where God has died."

Dance Pickett slouched at the rail, chin on his fist. *Americus, Americus.* He'd let himself believe they'd rise up and show him that God had not died.

Losing hope in Americus meant losing hope that he might one day win Violet Stiles. He didn't know how that was true, unless this ball of despair just bled all over everything else. That F.A.P. meeting made everything black, Emery's situation made it blacker, and all conspired to make Violet unobtainable. For he knew all had to be right before he could have her, and it would never be.

A new blackness occurred to him: not to obtain Violet was not to obtain the Stiles household. This war would end, and he'd have to face a Stiles-less life.

Mrs. Stiles strove to teach her daughters all the elements that promised a completed Southern lady—graciousness, kindness, forbearance, impeccable manners, perfect discretion, and never appearing in public

239

in a disheveled state. These were the things she thought she herself possessed in spades. Dance was glad she did not, for the result was an independent group of girls with a mildly rumpled upbringing and far less tendency to fashionable outbursts, such as the current trend in fainting. Lily once reported that she had tried fainting at a party and did not like it; she felt ridiculous, and besides: "What's the fun of fainting if you *miss* anything? Anything worth a faint is far more worth *not* fainting."

Mrs. Stiles believed she was producing daughters who were beyond reproach, admired, and perfectly in step with the times. In fact, they were admired precisely because they were a half step out of time with the conventional dance of graces. There was something old-fashioned about the Stiles girls, so old-fashioned it was original. The sisters of his college friends were as interesting as a gluey pot of overcooked okra compared to Violet Stiles. And she'd never have him because next to Emery Jones, for his handsomeness and his F.A.P. passion, Dance was the okra.

Americus and Emery and Violet were depressive-enough subjects, but then along came Lew Gann, weighing on Dance like high tide on a beach.

Dance watched a man totter carefully along the deadline. He was little more than a walking bag of bones. He put a hand to the rail to steady himself, then pulled it away and looked up fearfully. He must dwell in a different part of the stockade. No one was shot here. Dance had once fired a warning, but only because Wirz was nearby.

"Pickett, you up to somethin' again?" said Burr. "'Cause I am nervous."

"I am never up to something. I watch and I wait. For what, I do not know."

"How's that boy doin'?" Burr asked.

"He passed an onerous thing to my keeping."

"What is that thing?"

240

"An oath."

"Oaths are surely that."

Dance watched the man totter past.

"Say, Burr—do you think Old Abe would do me a favor? I need to find a man. That poultice is for him."

Burr gave a little whistle and got Old Abe's attention. He shuffled slowly up to the deadline.

"Looks like he's getting sick."

"He is."

"Sorry to hear it."

"What you want, Mister Johnny Old Reb?" Old Abe called up. "You got something good for me?"

"Oh, I'll give you a chance to *do* good, you old ragbag." He swept a hand to Dance. "Behold the man."

"I'm trying to find someone," Dance said down to him. "I do not know where he messes and cannot get a look at detachment rosters."

"Well, that don't matter much. We don't stick much to detachments," said Old Abe. "We fall out where we will after roll call. What's his name?"

Dance went to say Harris Gill, but instead said, "Lew Gann."

"What battle was he took in? Sometimes you find men quicker that way."

"Kennesaw Mountain."

"I'll ask around."

"If you find him, ask him to come see me. I've got something for him."

"I'll do that."

"I'm grateful."

"Aw, it gives me something to do." Old Abe limped off into the crowd.

Lew was with Harris Gill. Lew would come and get the poultice for Gill, and Dance would get a chance to size up the one who had captured the respect of a man whose respect was worth having.

———

"Fine thing happened on Kennesaw, Lew," Harris Gill whispered. "Don't know if I told it."

"I've heard it," Lew said. "Ran into some other Kennesaw boys and they told me. That's some story. I hope it is properly put on paper one day, for it is worthy."

"What is the story?" Martin asked, and Lew told it.

During battle, a thicket that had sheltered wounded Union boys caught fire. There the helpless men lay, flames nearly upon them. Seeing the situation and risking a hail of enemy bullets, a Confederate colonel leapt to an outcrop and waved his handkerchief like a banner. He cried out to his foe, "Get your men away! We won't fire a gun until you do! Cease fire, boys!" he yelled to his own. "Cease fire!" An instant cease-fire ensued, both sides, and the Federals were dragged to safety. In the last moment of the brief truce, a Union major ran to the Confederate line and presented the colonel with his own pistols in gratitude. He ran back, and battle resumed.

"Thought I'd watch you die," Harris said hoarsely, fevered eyes upon Lew. "Along comes that Reb just a-blazin'. Where is that Reb, Lew? I want to buy him a drink."

"I don't know." Lew could not look at those eyes long. They were disturbing. He took off his boot and pondered the hole. He'd lost the packing today. "Haven't seen him in a while. He was likely reassigned. Maybe sent to the front. Wish I'd had a chance to say good-bye."

"You see things like that, boy-o . . . and you see the world new," Harris whispered. He plucked restlessly at his shirt. He murmured something indistinct, and then was still.

Lew held the boot tight. If he could just find some packing for this hole, if he could just find some packing, if he could just find some packing . . .

———

While Dance and Burr waited for Old Abe, Dance tried to get where Emery had in his thinking.

"That country swab had an idea that might spare his life, but he won't tell me on account of the oath. He won't have me in trouble for helping *him*, no sir, but he doesn't mind if I get in trouble for helping a Yank. I find it selfish."

"Hmm. Well. It is a pickle, I will own."

"I can't get to Emery's idea."

"Will something in that scrip o' yours push you along?"

"The only thing that comes to mind is a quote by Algernon Sydney. 'That which is not just, is not Law; and that which is not Law, ought not to be obeyed.'"

"Oooh. Say that again."

Dance did.

Burr whistled. "Them are sturdy words, and fearsome."

"This whole county should tremble."

Someone was coming up the ladder.

"Dr. Stiles," Dance said, surprised.

"You're Doc Stiles?" Burr said. "Well, I don't know what to say."

Dr. Stiles touched his hat and nodded. "Gentlemen. I was in the neighborhood with Mrs. Dixon. We tried to see Emery but they wouldn't let us." He looked a little nervous. "I've never seen into the stockade before."

Burr stepped aside, and he went to the rail, grasping it once there.

"Oh, mercy," the doctor breathed.

"Take your time, Doc. It is a load." Burr surveyed his domain. "They are devils, but they are poor devils."

"Burr—is that Old Abe?" Dance asked.

"It is."

"Looks like he's had a day of it," Dance said.

"It is that scurvy."

Dance retrieved the onion poultice from the corner of the platform. He showed Dr. Stiles. "Reverend Gillette brought this for Lew Gann's friend. Onion poultice, for infection."

"That'll help some," the doctor said, but he was distracted; his eyes went back to the astounding sight of thick thousands of thin, shabby men.

Dance watched Old Abe's approach. No one accompanied him.

"Hail the perch!" Old Abe limped to the deadline. "Well, I found your man, but he did not have interest to come. His friend just died. And I am tired, so I will go and lay me down." He turned away.

"Wait—come back here," Dr. Stiles called. He took the onion poultice from Dance and tossed it. "Break it open and eat it. It'll do you good."

"Hey!" shouted the tower guard on the north side of the holding pen. "What you throwin' down there?" He unshouldered his rifle.

Dr. Stiles's hands came up. "Just an onion poultice. For scurvy. I'm a doctor."

"That's against regulations! Burr, what're you thinkin'?"

"He didn't know," Dr. Stiles said quickly. "I'll go through Captain Wirz next time."

"We get in trouble for such foolishness! You ask Burr how long they stuck him in Castle Reed for throwin' down a loaf of bread."

"Well, that wasn't bread," Old Abe objected. "That was a peach something or other. It was sweet. Not like bread." He lifted the bundle and said, "I'm obliged." He limped away.

"Onions are an antiscorbutic," Dr. Stiles said.

"That's good thinkin', Doc."

"He is not past help."

"What helps best?"

"Well, from what you can get around here, green corn. Lemons, peaches. Any fruit or vegetable will do." Then he said, "Say . . . my neighbor has a lemon tree. Those lemons get very large, with a thick skin. I do not know their variety. He told me once. I will ask for some."

"Just don't say it's for the prisoners," Dance said. "Say it's for anyone else. They'll punish you for even thinking it. God forbid from heaven we should give these men a lemon."

Dr. Stiles looked at him.

"Oh, I'll say what I want about Americus," Dance said, pushing away from the rail, his heart suddenly racing. "But you know what? I don't have to." He threw an arm to the stockade. "Here it is! This'll tell the story of Americus! I'll say plainly, Dr. Stiles, I am sick and tired of you defending them, and when I see you that's all I see, just one big excuse for Americus. Nothing got done at that meeting, did it? Just talk and talk. Nothing ever gets done!"

Dr. Stiles stared out on the immense snarl of humanity. "It's true. Men die from attrition, and I can't stop it. But maybe I can bring someone a lemon."

"Oh, that's a fine ditty. There's a brand-new maxim. Let's teach it at our universities and churches. 'Bring someone a lemon today!' That'll turn the tides, Dr. Stiles. Ain't it just Jesus." He shouted into the stockade, "Take up your pallets and walk, you Yanks, for this man will bring you a lemon!"

"What's going on over there?" called the guard in the closest tower.

"Ease up, Pickett," Burr said.

A man near the deadline looked up and shook his head. "Always knew you Rebs were crazy."

"You said Americus might not remember who they are. Well, they sure didn't, did they?"

Dr. Stiles took a last look over the acres of men, as if committing the sight to memory. He touched his hat to Burr, and started for the ladder.

"I hate Americus," Dance spit.

"I am Americus."

"Then I hate you too!"

Dr. Stiles stopped without looking back. His shoulders slumped a little. "Dance, you are not eaten up because of what others will not do, but because of what you won't. You knew the answer to this place long before Violet did."

"What is the answer to this place?" Dance shouted, his voice breaking.

The doctor turned. "It has nothing to do with a people rising up, but a person. One person, just one. I blame Americus no longer, and no longer will I try to rally them—but I *will* rally myself. If it's a lemon, if it's just a lemon—Dance, if it's *just a lemon*—if a lemon is all I can do, then I will do it!"

Men in the stockade near the north gate paused to look and see what was happening in the sentinel's tower.

Dr. Stiles went to touch Dance's shoulder, but didn't. "Oh, son. What are they not doing that you wish you would?" He looked once more to the stockade. "No. Americus does not remember who they are. But I'm remembering who I am. You can too."

He went to the ladder and climbed down.

Dance went to the rail and held fast. He put his head down.

He was just one man trying to hold it all together, trying to keep the dark flood down. He shook, and wondered that the rail did not burst to powder in his grip. He wanted to tear down the world, and that would be the easy part. But he had to tear down himself.

"You keep on goin', Pickett," Burr said softly. "You're doin' fine, son."

———

Hours passed. The sun headed west, and Dance and Burr said not a word to each other.

The usual ennui came once more, and Dance sank to a slouch at the rail. It was easy to see when an officer came by, and he'd save the straightening for then.

Two more hours and his watch would end for the day. And maybe Emery Jones couldn't be saved, and maybe all of these prisoners couldn't be saved, but he knew a way to save Lew Gann. He had known all along.

Some prisoners had tunneled out, but Turner's dogs tracked them down and brought most of them back. A few got out by bribing turn-keys, but not many, and those turnkeys had been found out. Some tried to play dead and were brought out on stretchers; Wirz was on to these, and now each body brought out had to be ruled dead by a physician. A few had escaped from the hospital, but they were easily tracked, as most were too weak to get far.

Dance knew a way to save a prisoner that was so easy . . . a blind man could read by it.

He pushed from the rail.

Mercy, but I have given a whopper clue. A blind man could read by it.

Dance had only been there a moment or two. What clue?

Back through it, Dance, back it up until—

And there it was, and calm came with it.

"Well. He did give a whopper clue."

Maybe Emery Jones *could* be saved.

"You get to it, Pickett?"

"Maybe." He felt a little better. In fact, as pieces began to fly together and form a solitary notion, and when Dance prodded that notion and found it solid, he felt much better—and brightened prospects for both Lew *and* Emery brightened the prospects with Violet.

He went back to the rail. "How'd you win your wife, Burr?"

"She won me."

"How'd she do that?"

"She was herself, and I liked it."

"It didn't have much to do with you winning her?"

"What do I got in me that she'd want? I liked what I saw in that girl, and determined her as mine."

"Well, how did you go about it?"

"Went up to her one day and said I'd marry her and no other. Then I went off to bide my time."

"How long did you bide?"

"Two years," he admitted. "She didn't like what I said. But she come around."

"It was worth it?"

"Twenty-six years of worth it."

"Burr, will you do something for me?"

"I will."

Dance went to his scrip in the corner. He took out a pencil and piece of paper and began to write as fast as he could.

Violet, I want you to marry me. Here is how you won me: When you came to the prison, you fought to reach that dying man. Doing so, you reached me. You were yourself. You were who I hoped you were all along. So I will marry you or I will marry no one, but I must do something first. I do not know how long it will take. Wait for me, because I am yours, and you, Violet Wrassey Stiles, are mine.

                                                          Dance Weld Pickett

He folded the note and slipped it into the leather scrip, making sure it was the top paper. He fastened the leather string and handed the scrip to Burr.

"I can't do two things at once. But I think my father will come and see about one of them. He is a retired lawyer and loves to meddle. Especially if it has to do with law."

"I am nervous again."

"Get this to Violet Stiles. And get me Old Abe. Have him at the gate in a quarter hour—wait!" Dance snatched back the scrip and hurriedly opened it. He found an envelope. He took a piece of paper, folded it, and slipped it into the envelope. He tucked in the envelope flap, wrote a name on the front, hesitated, wrote more, and put the envelope in his pocket. He retied the scrip and gave it back to Burr. "There. Old Abe at the gate, a quarter hour."

"I am more nervous than I ever been!"

"Say hello to my father for me. He'll arrive sometime tomorrow. This time, he will come." He ran for the ladder. He ran back to Burr and shook his hand heartily, and ran for the ladder once more.

Burr looked at the leather scrip and wished with all his heart he could read. But it did not take a reader to smoke out how Pickett planned to help the one called Lew, not standing at this post all this time and seeing all from the same place.

An ache pierced his heart, and he looked over the stockade.

———

They wouldn't let Dance see Emery Jones, as he'd had his quota of visitors for the day.

"And no, you can't see the Articles of War 'cause they are for punishment only and not for reading any old time someone pleases, as this ain't a library. And furthermore what are you doing off your post, Dance Pickett? Just because your daddy is some kind of to-do, that don't give you the right to—"

"Oh, have it your way," Dance groused at the guard. He stepped back and shouted, "Emery!"

"Dance?" came a faint voice from within. "That you?"

"It's the Articles, isn't it?"

"Figure it out, did you? That's my boy."

"Enough of that!" said the guard.

"Not quite. This peawit won't let me read them. Which one?"

"I was thinkin' of Article 22. But I don't know if there's enough in it."

"Article 22. Listen, one more thing: The oath is fulfilled. You hear me? It is done, Emery. All is well."

No answer.

"You hear me?"

"I heard."

"You get on, Pickett, or you're gonna join him! Try me!"

"See you later, Alabama."

Emery did not answer, and that was all right.

Emery had to know that Lew was taken care of before Saturday morning. But maybe Father would come and meddle. He might not come to the aid of Yanks, but he might for a Confederate soldier, especially if the law could ferret out his innocence. If something in Article 22 could do so, Father would find it.

He had to word it perfectly.

He ran to the telegraph office in the Andersonville depot, sent a message, and raced back to the stockade.

———

Late that afternoon, J. W. Pickett of 14 Glastonbury Street in Augusta received two telegrams. Both times he feared it was about his oldest son, Beau, and both times it wasn't. The first was a cryptic missive from the Stiles family. The second was from Dance.

Dear Father. Come at once, and bring a set of the Articles of War. Study Article 22 and see to Emery Jones in Castle Reed. He is unjustly sentenced to death, Saturday 11 a.m. Law can save him. I'd do it myself but I have been called away. Gratefully, Dance.

Gratefully? Since when had Dance been grateful?

"Is it Beau, sir? Is it Dance?" said a worried Mammy Wallace, their old nurse. "Is all well?"

J. W. Pickett roused himself. "All is very well indeed. He is grateful! A sure sign he is growing up, thank God. But don't put off your prayer shawl just yet, for our Dance is sent to the front. I am glad for his chance to prove his mettle and pray he escapes Federal wrath—but oh, this gladdens me more!" He shook the telegram. "Two happy things herein, Mammy Wallace! 'Law can save him,' says he—he'd *do it himself* if he could! Oh, it joys me to my toes!" He did a tiny shuffle dance in place.

"What is the next happy thing?" said she.

"Recalled to life!" roared J. W. Pickett. "Was Sydney Carton the hero of *A Tale of Two Cities*? I think not! It was the old lawyer, Mammy Wallace, the old lawyer!" And off he went to pack his bag.

———

Dance followed Old Abe along the deadline, heading north, and didn't dare look up to see if Burr was watching.

It was an easy thing to get the turnkey to open the pass-through door in the gate. Dance simply showed him the envelope and said, "General Winder wants me to get a signature. It may take some time."

"My watch ends in an hour," said the turnkey.

"If I'm not back by then, tell your relief I'm coming out. Name's Dance Pickett."

"I know who you are."

Yes . . . but his relief didn't.

A new turnkey on watch rotation had replaced Lucerne, he who betrayed Emery for a barrel of whiskey and a furlough. The new man did not know the face of Dance Weld Pickett.

He felt curiously light as he followed Old Abe.

The people of Americus were terrified these men would rise in cutthroat revolt; yet here Dance dared to go and fetch a "signature" without an armed escort. He wasn't even questioned by the turnkey. Mosby's gang, the only real trouble in the pen, had been put down last month, and the new Regulators did a fairly even job at keeping peace. When it all boiled down, these were just men; some were bad, but most were good—like any place in Georgia. He was safe enough in the company of this lame man.

A tumult of thought billowed within, pierced through with sharp exhilaration, and he wished for paper and pen. The pen would turn billowed thoughts to shapes, and give them habitation. Then he'd lay them to rest in that sanctuary of hope until the day came when it was safe to bring them out.

One thought floated free in the tumult, shaped and waiting for ink: I have seen what this place has done to men, and I admit I am afraid it will come to me, too, but better this fear than the other, that God has died. I saw him today in a man who spoke of lemons.

In his mind, he wiped the pen and stoppered the ink; he dried the page and slipped it into the scrip. He gave the scrip to Violet and kissed her good-bye.

Dance Weld Pickett, adored son of James Weld Pickett, the ardent secessionist, the confidant of Governor Joe Brown, and the hater of all things North, was about to become a blue-belly Yank.

PART FOUR

Once inside . . . men exclaimed: "Is this hell?" Verily, the great mass of gaunt, unnatural-looking beings, soot-begrimed, and clad in filthy tatters, that we saw stalking about inside this pen looked, indeed, as if they might belong to a world of lost spirits.

—PRIVATE WILLIAM B. SMITH, 14TH ILLINOIS VOLUNTEER INFANTRY

Tuesday, July 19, 1864
Men, strong in mentality, heart and hope were in a few short months . . . reduced to imbeciles and maniacs. . . . the slowest torture to him who still had a clear brain.

—FROM THE DIARY OF CORPORAL CHARLES HOPKINS, 1ST NEW JERSEY INFANTRY

18

"YOU GOT ANY MORE STORIES?"

Lew lay on his side, his back to them. "No, Martin. No more."

All he had were lost friends . . . and no place to lament them.

"Leave him be a bit, Martin," Andy murmured. "He'll be all right."

"I thought it might help if he talked," said Martin. "We all pull our weight here at Hotel Ford. We look after each other."

"Yes, we do," said Andy.

Martin lay down and fell instantly asleep.

Smoke gave battles a sense of unreality. In some battles, you waited for the smoke to clear to get off a shot, wondering the whole time if it had cleared sooner for the enemy.

Lew would take that smoke over this. He'd take the unbearable sense of waiting, almost shot; he'd take turned-up earth and wrecked caissons and blown-up horses to lying down and taking this. They could not fight here. It was all mental living. All figuring out how to make a handful of food last a day. Figuring out water. Figuring out how to doctor someone with nothing, and you weren't a doctor to begin with.

They could not kill what tried to kill them. They could not even throw a punch, and the powerlessness was unmanning. They had to take all that was poured upon them because they were soldiers and that's what soldiers did and they died by the thousands doing so.

"We can kill lice," Andy said. "There's always lice, the dear little vermin . . ."

Lew came away from his thoughts.

"There is a twofold reward in it," Andy said, as if asked. "We fight back, and we keep clean."

Well, it was true.

Lew wiped his face. "How do you know just what I need said?" He rolled over to look at Andy.

"Because that's how I felt when Bart died. I went on a wild-man lice-killing spree. Killed 143 off myself. Consigned them to a minia-ture abyss, wherever bad vermin go. It was a personal record, and it did me good."

"What's the most you've heard of?"

"I heard of a man on the south side who killed above a thousand off himself. But you know rumors. Could have started out half that." Then he said, "I don't know if my folks know about Bart."

"Have you written to them?"

"Can't get paper for it. I don't know how things are reported here, officially. I hope they have a record of us. That's a little fear I have. We'll just get swallowed up. No one will know."

"There is an official record, and I know the boy who keeps it," came a soft voice at the tent flap. The flap rose, and a face peered in. "His name is Dorence Atwater. But my name is Lew Gann."

"That's my name," Lew said, feeling foolish.

"Not anymore. Yours is Dance Pickett." He put out a hand. "Nice to meet you. I am here courtesy of a mutual friend."

Lew sat up. "What has he gone and done now?"

"Clearly you know him. Well, he is in trouble, some. I hope my father will get him out." He crawled inside. "It took a while to get here, so we need to hurry. Burr is on duty another hour, and you must get to him before he leaves. We have to switch clothes." He took off his hat and began to unbutton his shirt. "There is a new turnkey on duty tonight. He does not know my face. Give him your name, which is Dance Pickett, hold up this envelope, and tell him you got the signature for General Winder. He'll let you through."

Lew stared.

"Do I have to repeat myself?"

Lew nodded as he pulled off his boots.

—

Someone was coming up the ladder.

Pickett's hat came into view, but it was not Pickett's face beneath it.

"You must be Lew," Burr said.

"A terrified Lew."

"I heard you below. You did all right."

"Good. I was nervous."

"I am that, around Pickett. Well, what'd he tell you?"

"He said he was sorry, but he had no plan past getting me to you. He said maybe go see Ellen, a servant at the home of Dr. Stiles. Said her church stands by to help."

"Yep. The coloreds round here got a system set up for escaped prisoners. 'Course, I don't know anything about that. One thing at a time, and first we gotta land you safe to my place. This is a pickle."

Lew started to apologize, but Burr waved it off. "I don't mind pickles. But I got to think. I got to get you out as Dance Pickett. There is all manner of comin' and goin' at watch change. Dusk will aid us, but still, it will be a tricky time. Come stand by me and look out, like you seen us do, and I will think."

"Where is Emery Jones?"

"That is a separate pickle," Burr said softly, knowing what he did about good, bright boys. He'd lost his own early on, and today he'd lost another.

"One pickle at a time," he said, and produced a smile. "Now, I saw you walk up to the gate, but Dance don't have a limp. Hope you can manage to walk like a spoiled-rotten dandy for a spell."

———

"That is not Lew. He is wearing Lew's clothing, but he is not Lew."

Andy roused from sleep. "What's the matter, Martin? Stop that! What are you doing?"

"Knockin' some sense into my head, like they tried to at Mosby's camp. He is wearing Lew's clothes, but he's not Lew. I feel tricked."

"Martin, stop it—it's okay, all is well. Lew got out last night. Isn't that fine?"

"Where did he go?"

"Outside. He's gonna make it back to Sherman and give the Rebs a shellackin'."

"What is outside this place again?"

"Well . . . same as inside. War."

"I want to go where Lew is. We take care of our own."

"We will, someday. But for now, we are going to make pretend that *this* man is Lew. We are even going to *call* him Lew."

Martin shook his head. "I don't like that."

"Nevertheless, it is what we must do." Then, "Lew *told* us to."

"He did?"

"Yep."

Martin rubbed his palm on his forehead. "Well . . . all right. I don't understand it, but all right."

"You'll understand someday. I see you getting better every day,

Martin, you know that? Now go outside and pick off lice. Don't stop until you get to a hundred."

"I can't count that high. I used to."

"Get some stones. Remember what Lew said? Each time you count to ten, set aside a stone. When you see ten stones, you will have counted to a hundred."

"Andy, can a man eat lice?"

"No!"

"But I've seen—"

"No! We'll never get down so low. Not here in Hotel Ford."

Martin nodded. "All right, Andy. Not here in Hotel Ford."

"Go pick 'em off and kill 'em."

Martin crawled out. Andy nudged Dance. "Hey."

"I'm awake." He sat up and started scratching. "Not sure I slept."

"You didn't say much after Lew left."

"I wasn't much inclined."

"My name is Andy Rogers." He gave a brief history of Hotel Ford and its lodgers. "What worries me is Martin. He's on the simple side, if you haven't noticed. Best we could tell, he ran with Mosby's gang early on. We think he went mad, and they kicked him out. Or they kicked him out, and he went mad. Lew took him in when Artie died. Our policy is four men in here at all times, because it is not in our conscience to take up all this space for less. But this time we'll wait for a fourth until you leave."

Dance glanced around ruefully. All this space. It was hardly five feet square. Not much bigger than a sentinel platform.

"When do you plan to get out of here?" said Andy.

"Same as you."

"I don't follow. I'm waiting for exchange or for the war to end."

Dance shrugged and nodded.

"You came in here with no plan to get out?" Andy said, incredulous.

"If I get out now, I'll be court-martialed for treason. But if the North wins like all signs say, then they'll sort me out with the rest, and I will eventually get out of this with no lasting consequences."

"Well—you got anyone on the outside to keep you living? You won't last long on what they feed us."

"I hope a guard at the north gate will slip me something now and then."

"I see you have not thought this through."

Uneasily, Dance said, "What do you mean?"

"You can't go to the north gate. You can't go anywhere. You are known. Anyone who sees you living among us will think you came as a spy. They'll think you're here to report tunneling or other nefarious activities to Wirz."

"How am I known?"

"How are you—? You've been on the north gate since I came! Sometimes other spots, but mostly there. You can change your clothes, but you can't change your face."

"So you have seen me . . . and I have not seen you." Dance chuckled bitterly. "I am Americus."

"I imagine we are a lot to look at. It would be interesting to see us from high up." He motioned outside with his head. "Listen, Martin could be a problem. I can keep you secret. We'll keep you in here as sick, and you can move about at night. I'll fetch your rations during the day for roll call, and my sergeant won't question it right away. We'll get by a few days that way, until we figure something else out. But Martin worries me."

"If I *am* discovered . . . will they do anything to you?"

"I don't care to think that far." He studied Dance. "Why did you do it?"

Dance scratched beneath his collar, then sent a squint of disgust down his shirtfront. "I don't know." He let his shirt go. "It makes sense if I don't have to say it."

"I'll say this: I like Lew. You picked a good man to do a good turn."

"I didn't do it for him. That I do know."

——

Martin did not find the ten stones where he had left them. Likely they had been stolen. He picked his way along, collecting new ones. Soon he found himself in a place he did not want to be, and that was near Mosby's old gang. Most of the bad ones were dead, as they strung up six of 'em. But some weren't strung.

He about-faced to scurry along for Hotel Ford.

"Say, there! Wait up, old Martin!" It was Elliott.

"You are looking fine these days." It was Stern.

"Lew got me new clothes. I need to get back to Hotel Ford."

"What else did Lew get you?"

"Nothin'." He tried to sidestep, but Elliott moved with him.

"You sure about that? You got new clothes, you put on weight— no one does that here. This Lew must have something he can contribute to the Fund."

"What fund?"

"My fund."

"Well, Lew's not here anymore," Martin said, and it felt fine to say.

"Where'd he go?"

"He's gone to give the Rebs a shellackin'. We got a new man. He wears Lew's clothes, but he ain't Lew. But Lew wants us to *call* him Lew."

Elliott and Stern exchanged puzzled looks. Elliott shrugged.

"I reckon this man can contribute to the Fund on Lew's behalf."

Martin said unhappily, "Maybe."

"Why don't you take us to Hotel Ford and we'll see. If he doesn't have anything, he doesn't have anything. Right? We won't hurt him."

"You won't? 'Cause we take care of our own, there."

"We ain't like Mosby was," said Stern.

"You didn't see *us* hang, did you?"

"Well . . . okay. But make sure you call him Lew."

———

"What do you think, Elliott?"

They didn't get much of a look. But it was enough to prod a sleeping fire in their bellies. Andersonville was all about survival, but now and again came a chance to remember they were soldiers first, and not mere survivors.

"He's from the north gate, all right."

"What are we gonna do?"

"That smug Reb thinks he'll just come in and roust out tunnels for Wirz like he's some kind of Southern Stoneman on a raid. Like Wirz is his Sherman."

"We gotta stop him."

"He ain't Stoneman," Elliott seethed. "Ain't fit to wear *them* boots."

"You ever see so bold?"

"It's bold of Wirz. He'll just stash his man in a tent, let him run like a hound in our midst . . ."

"Well, he's done it before. What are we gonna do?"

Elliott halted. He put up his hand. He looked at Stern.

"Let's get up a council. Mosby ain't here anymore, and he never was too smart. When he was hung, a lot of old bad things were hung with him. I want to do things proper." He felt a fevered rush of nobility and put aside as trifling what had drawn him to Hotel Ford in the first place. "I want to do our duty as Union men."

Stern nodded. "That sounds right. For the boys who perished tryin' to get to us."

"And for Stoneman."

19

J. W. PICKETT had the matter in hand, but he had one thing against him, or rather, Emery Jones did—the presiding brigadier general did not like J. W. Pickett. He had tussled with the old man in a court-room once before, in civilian days and in a place far away; he found Pickett's manner insufferable then and found it intolerable now.

Most intolerable of all was to preside over this frittering affair while Sherman bore down on Atlanta, the hub of the South, the centerpiece clockwork of the Southern rails—telegraph wires crackled with news, and yet here he languished, listening in pain to J. W. Pickett.

Pickett was old, but he had not lost his fondness for superfluity.

"I rode all night to get here, for duty bade. I spent all morning in a dirty cell with Corporal Emery Jones, for duty bade. And I am deeply shocked that the men in this tribunal did not once think of Article 22, when duty bade. Why should it take an old country law-yer, past his prime and turned out to comforting pastures, to find therein—reclamation?" The word echoed.

265

The brigadier general rolled his eyes, covering for it by rubbing his eyebrows. He'd seen a copy of the telegram himself. It wasn't J. W. Pickett who had thought of Article 22. He glanced around the courtroom; the boy who had wasn't here. He was likely on duty.

"For this boy has been reclaimed!" Pickett drove a finger to the ceiling.

"Mr. Pickett, proceed to your point lest Sherman get to it before you." A titter rippled through the courtroom.

J. W. Pickett put on his spectacles. He took two papers from the table, one for each hand, and read the paper in his right hand.

"A summation of Article 22 states thus: 'No noncommissioned officer or soldier shall enlist himself in any other regiment, troop, or company, without a *regular discharge*—" he looked over his glasses—"from the regiment, troop, or company in which he last served. . . . And in case any officer shall *knowingly receive*—" he looked over his glasses again—"and entertain such noncommissioned officer or soldier, or shall not . . . *give notice thereof* to the corps in which he last served, the said officer shall, by a court-martial, be cashiered.'"

He raised the paper in his left hand and waved it.

"This order for Corporal Emery Jones, signed by Captain Russell Graves of the 22nd Alabama Volunteers, states he is to report back *immediately* to his regiment once he delivers his prisoner to Andersonville. Instead—Corporal Jones was detained. He should be standing in front of Atlanta as we speak, right beside my own son, defending this country from the gathering horde. Instead—this boy was unlawfully held back from his regiment and *swept* into that of another, conscripted if you will, not of his own accord, not of his doing, in *direct violation* of signed regimental orders—" he shook the paper—"with no notice given to the corps in which he last served." He smiled a little and allowed the words to hang, admired. He consulted again the paper in his right hand.

"Now this boy is on trial for his *life* because he went to Americus without a pass. I will say again—a pass. His *life*, for a pass. A little piece of paper in his pocket. I understand the need for military order—I have two sons in the Confederate States Army. But this sentence of yours—" he looked at the council—"seems vindictive to the extreme, as we all know this boy merely wanted to do a good turn . . . so says Reverend William Gillette over there."

"How it *seems*, vindictive or otherwise, is irrelevant," said the presiding brigadier general.

"Just so! We shall then abide by Law, for therein we find comfort in its plumb line. Article 22 was violated before this boy had a *chance* to trot into town without that little pass—an item, by the by, which a Sergeant Keppel from Andersonville Prison said he'd have been more than happy to issue, had Corporal Jones asked. 'Will a piece of paper save his life?' said he. And he snatches a paper and writes out a pass and gives it to me with no small coloration of what he thought of the sentence handed down here days ago."

"What the sergeant thought—"

"Yes, yes—irrelevant! Just so! We are perfectly agreed. I will tell you what *is* relevant." He raised the Articles of War. "Emery Jones would not have *been* in Americus had the Law been obeyed. Article 22 states that *Emery Jones* was not in the wrong for being conscripted to duty at Andersonville—on the contrary; considering the chain of command, this immediate cashiering by court-martial of the officer involved in *violating* this law pertains to . . . well, you." His eyes fastened on the face of the brigadier general.

A rustle sounded in the courtroom, from council and from audience.

"A court-martial for *you*?" exclaimed J. W. Pickett, fists on his hips. "Why, it is absurd!" He let the words hang. "As absurd as holding this boy back from his duty in Atlanta one minute longer."

The brigadier general infinitesimally shook his head. If he had time, he'd blast that article so full of scatter shot—with some for J. W. Pickett, too—that it wouldn't stop leaking for a century.

He had not the time nor the desire to mount a rebuttal. He looked at the manacled Corporal Emery Jones, staring at J. W. Pickett in something like dumbstruck hope, and just didn't care what happened to the boy. He followed the boy's gaze to J. W. Pickett.

He called for a recess, and the other four followed him into consultation in a back hallway of the Americus courthouse. He made a suggestion, and they concurred quickly—too quickly, and had to wait for an appropriate time before returning to the courtroom.

"With regard to the new evidence brought before this court, the sentence of death by hanging for Corporal Emery Jones is overturned," said the presiding brigadier general, and he allowed for reaction in the courtroom, particularly from the family of Dr. Stiles. "The court fully recognizes and upholds Article 22, and had Corporal Jones produced his orders early on, we all might have been spared a lamentable squanderation of much-needed time." He raised a hand. "However . . ."

The room quieted.

"The court does not like what this man represents—an unmanly softness for the enemy, when softness does not win wars. Mr. Jones, you declared in front of several witnesses that the Yankee you delivered to that pen was a *friend*. Do you like the Yankees so much? Then go to them. You are forthwith dishonorably discharged from the Army of the Confederate States on the grounds of suspicious liaison with the enemy. You are forthwith exiled from the Confederate States of America, and should you ever set foot on Southern soil again, you will be executed.

"Major, make arrangements to have him escorted at once to Mobile Bay. If that is the last Confederate port open in the South, that is good enough for me—I'll have you out on the next ship if it is a broken-down packet sloop or a slumgullion blockade runner bound for heathen lands. Atlanta is besieged, yet I am forced to put out brush fires." He pounded the gavel. "This court-martial is adjourned! You all get back to your duties. Sherman comes."

He lingered long enough to catch the falter on the pompous old face of J. W. Pickett. When Pickett looked his way, he said, "Was that vindictive?" and left the courtroom somewhat compensated.

———

There was scarcely time to say good-bye. The provost marshal allowed Emery ten minutes with those in the courtroom before they took him to the Americus depot. From there, he was under custody of the provost marshal until Andersonville, where arrangements were being made to escort him without pause to Mobile Bay.

Left in the room after the others filed out were the Stiles family, Reverend Gillette, Hettie Dixon, a grizzled guard from the stockade, and J. W. Pickett.

Mrs. Stiles set Posey free and she skipped down the aisle to him, hands in the air, dress flouncing. Rosie and Daisy ran behind her, jumping and laughing. Posey threw her arms around his middle.

"Hello, Traitor Christian!" said Emery.

"You shall not die, Emery Jones!" She looked up at him. "Where is Mobile Bay?"

"Why, it's in my home state. I reckon they'll give me a fine send-off. Brass band, dancing, fried chicken."

She rattled the manacles on his wrists. "Why don't they take these hateful things off?"

"I don't mind so much." He winked. "I reckon if I am trussed up, they'll feel safe around me. Say, I need to thank you for that map. Sure woulda come in handy if I had a chance to whack that guard."

"No chance?" she asked, and tried out under her breath the word *whack*.

"They had me occupied in daily tortures. Their favorite was the rack—if you haven't noticed I am two inches taller. Yet whatsoever multifarious cruelties they applied unto me, they had nothin' on that mule. He prepared me for the worst. I thought I was eating cake. I ever tell you that mule's name?"

"No."

"General Winder. Ain't *that* a scary coincidence."

"We had hoped for the best, Mr. Jones," said Reverend Gillette, with disappointment he couldn't hide, "and we got it—" a respectful nod at J. W. Pickett—"but this . . . we did not expect. I am deeply sorry for it."

"Well, Preacher, coming from the man who has most occasion to have aught against me, I am truly affected."

"Oh, Emery," Violet said, and squeezed his arm. She *wanted* to throw her arms around him and wail her heart out, for the South was about to lose one of its shiningest men; but she didn't want to give anyone the wrong impression. Of course, if it weren't for . . . *the other*, why then, she would be happy to give such an impression, for Emery was a quality man. But with . . . *him* around . . . why, Emery felt like a brother.

"Where is Dance?" She glanced around. "Is he on guard?"

"My son is called to the front," said J. W. Pickett, drawing himself tall. "He is now engaged in *real* soldierly duties."

"Dance?" said Dr. Stiles. "I thought you had meant Beau."

"I received a telegram from him yesterday."

"Dance, called to the front?" Mrs. Stiles said, her hand going to her throat. "Why didn't he tell us?"

Lily slipped her hand into Violet's.

"Called to the front, Cousin," J. W. Pickett affirmed. "I only wish I could've told him how proud it made me."

"Your son has been at the front since his posting at Andersonville."

All looked at Papa. His eyes had a sudden perilous light. His hands lay flat against his sides where they would do no harm. Violet knew that pose—she did it all the time. She looked at him in awe.

"Have you *once* told him how proud you were?" he asked Dance's father.

"Why, I—"

"Emery!" Posey said. "What's wrong? Is the front bad?"

Emery had gone pale and did not seem to hear Posey. Then he looked at Violet as if to ask a question or convey a very important message, but Violet had no idea what that message was—her head was all a muddle.

"We shall pray a hedge of protection," Hettie Dixon told Violet, placing her hand on Violet's arm.

"Oh no! That means the front is bad!" Posey said. "Why's he gone there?"

"I'm not sure he has," said Emery.

"Time's up, Jones," said the provost marshal.

"What do you mean by that?" Violet said to Emery.

"Why, he told me himself where he went," said J. W.

"Emery, what do you mean?" said Violet.

"What did he say?" Emery asked J. W.

"Why—" Mr. Pickett thought for a moment. "'Called away,' I believe. It is the same thing. Where else would he be, with Sherman coming?"

"Come along, Jones," said the provost marshal.

Daisy looked up at her father. "Papa, what does *exiled* mean?"

"It means Emery's going away a bit, but he'll be back someday," said Dr. Stiles. "Especially if the North wins."

"Then I hope they win!" Rosie declared, then clapped her hands over her mouth.

"God protect you, son," said Reverend Gillette, and extended his hand in blessing and farewell.

———

They took Emery away, and Posey ran off to cry. Rosie and Daisy decided she should not go it alone and followed. Mrs. Stiles asked everyone over for tea, and all left the courtroom with heavy hearts. Except for J. W. Pickett. He led the procession to the Stiles house and took up with Hettie Dixon on a subject Violet could not hear.

She trailed behind the group, walking hand-in-hand with Lily, who had placed herself at Violet's side to shield her from the world.

"I don't know what to feel about Emery," Lily said. "It is one thing that he shall not die, it is another that perhaps we shall never see him again. How these men have blown through our lives . . . Violet, we will do as Hettie says. We will pray for Dance, more than we ever prayed for Ben. I don't think we prayed as much as we could have. You don't pray as much when you think you're going to win."

"What did Emery mean?" Violet wondered. "Did you see his face?"

"I don't have the heart to tell Posey I *think* I am in love with him."

"I'll tell you the one to be in love with: Corporal Womack from the commissary building in Andersonville."

"Really? What do you mean?"

"Say . . . Miss Stiles?"

The girls stopped and turned.

The grizzled guard they had seen in the courthouse pulled off his hat. "I reckon I have something for you." He unslung a leather scrip from his shoulder and gave it to Violet.

"Why . . . this belongs to Dance," she said.

"He told me to give it to you before he left."

"Why didn't he take it with him? He's never without it."

"I reckon there's something important in there he wants you to read."

She looked at the scrip. "Emery doesn't think he was called to the front."

The guard did not answer. He only gazed at the leather scrip as if he looked at something in the distance, and that distant thing was bleak. Then he held his thumb out toward the depot. "I gotta catch the train. My sergeant'll have a fit if I ain't back on time. I got leave only for the hearin'."

"Thank you, Mr. . . . ?"

"Ain't no mister about it. You can call me Burr."

"*You're* Burr?"

He pointed with his hat at the pouch. "Look to them words, Miss Stiles. Them are fine words." He put his hat on, tugged it down tight, and left at a trot for the depot.

—

Burr sat a few rows behind Emery on the train and saw there would be no chance for private words with the boy. So he worked it over good in his head, and then got up and took the seat behind him. The provost marshal looked over his shoulder and whisked a mildly stern look at him. Burr pointed at Emery.

"I got some parting words of consolation for the boy, as I ain't ever gonna see him again."

The provost marshal shrugged and looked out the window.

"Well, boy, it's the North for you, eh?"

"I reckon so."

"Maybe it ain't so bad, so you take heart. I got two cousins. One

273

is a Yank, and one is like you. My cousin who is a Yank came down for some time, but now he's gone back home. He's much happier."

It came to him slowly, but when it did some of the misery cleared from the boy's face, and Burr gave a tiny encouraging nod.

"Well, I do have some Northern ancestors," the boy said. "Perhaps I will find a welcome." He halfway glanced at the provost marshal. "What of your other cousin?"

"Well," said Burr—and his breath caught. "He's gone away."

Emery looked like he wanted a lot more than that, but Burr could say no more. He gripped Emery's shoulder, and went back to his seat.

Burr was glad he caught on about Lew. He wasn't a fair hand at words like Dance.

This morning his wife had found a note on the table. Lew said he didn't want to bring trouble on this house, so he had slipped away in the night. He said he'd try and connect with field slaves who could get him through to Sherman. He thanked Burr and his wife, apologized for helping himself to some peaches and bread, and asked them to burn the note.

Burr looked out the window and wished Lew well, and put the same, and more, to Dance.

20

Why would Dance part with his leather scrip?

Violet had slipped upstairs and put it in the room she shared with Lily, lest J. W. Pickett ask questions. She couldn't wait to get to it. This teatime felt like a funeral wake, and she was in no mood for somberness. Emery was saved, it was time to move on—what was exile compared to death?

The scrip was a sanctuary, he'd once called it, a place to put sacred things. She asked him what, and he told her poems, and quotes, and things he didn't want to forget. She didn't dare ask, then, if he would show her some of those things. She thought he might, someday, but not like this.

Would she find what she already knew of him? She'd find creeds and manifestos, surely, as manifesto was likely the better part of Dance—but what of other things like colors and beauty? Deeply feeling things? She knew it of him, but wanted to see it on paper, this collection of Dance.

What was he like at college? What was his life before Andersonville?

What was his growing up? It was all a blurred brown place to her, a nothingness that needed to be filled in.

"I will say, the stench is awful," J. W. Pickett was saying. "He did not exaggerate that."

"He asked you to come, and you would not?" Dr. Stiles said, and now Violet's attention was sure. Something about Cousin Pickett must pique Papa.

"It is a particular determination of mine that my boys should press through difficult things on their own."

"Yes," said Hettie Dixon, taking a sip of her tea. "And sometimes they need their father."

"Four times he wrote!" J. W. held forth in his rich courtroom voice. "Four times I said, 'Dance, did I not raise you to press through impossibilities to solutions? Use your noggin, boy! What have *you* done to change those conditions?' Well, the next time he wrote I could see he was reborn—'Study Article 22,' says he. 'I'd do it myself but I have been called away.' I'd do it myself! Oh, what it does to a father to see his toil come to fruition."

"Every now and then, perhaps once in a lifetime, one comes across something uniquely evil in its scope," said Dr. Stiles, and Violet lowered her teacup. "Your boy . . . this town . . . myself . . . Reverend Gillette, and my beloved daughter . . . we came across something so evil no platitude can serve it. There is no pressing through. There is no answer. We need each other to confront it, and he needed you. Part of a father's job is to know when that is."

Violet set down her teacup and stole upstairs.

——

Her hands were afire for Dance's leather scrip. Something in Papa's words did it. Why it should compel her to the scrip, she did not—

The bedroom door was ajar.

The scrip lay opened on the bed, pages strewn all over. Reading one page quite intently was Posey.

Posey glanced up, and jumped. She put the paper behind her back.

Violet shut the door, and turned fire-hot but harnessed fury on Posey. The parlor was directly below—they must not hear Posey's death throes, for Violet was going to kill her.

"Posey Eden *Stiles*!" She was so angry she could barely get anything out. "You little—That is *mine*!" She went to the bed and began to snatch up the papers.

"It is not! It's Dance's! These are his sacred papers!"

"Keep your voice down!" she hissed.

"I thought we'd find out where they sent him," Posey whispered back.

"What have you got behind your back? Give it to me!"

"I think you're going to like this."

She brought out a lettered page. It was the *Americus, Americus* handbill.

"You know what this means," Posey said. "You are sacred to him."

Violet took the bill. "Why, I thought he . . ." She sank to the bed. "What else is here?"

"Things I can't understand. Like this." She selected a paper in the pile, and gave it to Violet.

That which I have feared the most has come upon me, for I am like them, and they are like me.

"What's he mean? Or how about this one."

The poet's eye, in a fine frenzy rolling, doth glance from heaven to earth, from earth to heaven . . .

"I think it's Shakespeare."

"This one is a doozy."

"Mother does not like that word," Violet said, taking the sheet.

"Who is Dante?"

277

Thy soul is by vile fear assail'd, which oft
So overcasts a man, that he recoils
From noblest resolution, like a beast
At some false semblance in the twilight gloom.

Speed now,
And by thy eloquent persuasive tongue,
And by all means for his deliverance meet,
Assist him.

"Oh, Dance," Violet whispered.

Spread on the bed was a lifetime of collected pages and bits. There were a few small daguerreotypes of young men in proud poses, likely his classmates. Some letters, some clippings from newspapers. Blank paper and envelopes, two pencils, a secure little pouch with a pen, wiper, and bottle of ink inside. Mostly it was pages and pages of written things, some quite yellow, some new. There was likely some organization to it before Posey got her hands on it.

"Some of it is plain boring. Here is some claptrap from someone named John Donne. I can spell better than him."

Violet took the page.

No man is an iland, intire of it selfe; every man is a peece
Of the continent, a part of the maine; if a clod bee washed away
By the sea, Europe is the lesse, as well as if a promontorie were,
As well as if a mannor of thy friends or of thine owne were; any
Man's death diminishes me, because I am involved in mankinde;
And therefore never send to know for whom the bell tolls; it tolls
For thee.

TRACY GROOT

"I don't think this will tell us where he is," Posey said of all the papers.

Violet had an instinct for the contrary. She pressed the page to her heart.

"Do you know where the front is?"

It was a moment before Violet could answer.

"Atlanta's the front right now. Just before it."

"The *front* is in *front* of Atlanta. What's this?"

Violet looked it over. "A class schedule, I think, for university."

"This?"

It was well worn. She read through it, and smiled. "Well, Dance Pickett. It's a rejection from the U. S. Patent Office. Dated 1852. He invented some sort of hand-mixing tool, but apparently someone else did so first. He was only—" she calculated—"eleven years old. Look here—he was commended for his ingenuity at such a young age."

"Why would he give up these treasures?" Posey said.

"I suppose to put them in safekeeping until he returns. Soldiers lose things, I expect." She began to gather the pages and set them to order. "Posey, I'm not angry anymore. You meant well."

"I *always* mean well. I am misunderstood."

Violet unfolded a sheet of paper.

Posey sighed. "Well, I'm gonna go see if Cousin Pickett ate all the cinnamon cakes."

Violet did not answer. She kept reading.

———

Posey slipped out and made sure to close the door. She certainly didn't want Cousin Pickett to see Dance's scrip, as he was sleeping in *her* room now, confound him, and had to walk past Violet's to get there.

"Always the youngest who gets ousted," she complained as she

279

tramped down the stairs. She stopped at the window on the landing, for something outside caught her eye. Two kids standing on the lawn. One was Tessie Robinson.

Posey hurried down the stairs. She must get to the cinnamon cakes before Ellen gave them away.

———

Violet paused at the bottom stair. She knew she was never to appear in public in such a state. But there was nothing for it.

She squared herself and went to the parlor. The men rose as she entered.

"He did not go to the front." Violet held up the leather scrip.

"Why, Violet," Mother said, rising from the sofa. "What is wrong? Darling, you are disheveled."

"Never mind that. Dance has proposed. I have accepted."

"He *proposed*?" Lily shrieked.

"Darling, when did he propose?" Mother asked. "Oh, this is lovely. Questionable timing, but lovely."

"He proposed here." She held up the scrip.

"Why . . . that belongs to Dance," said J. W. Pickett.

Violet looked at her father. She felt like she was falling. "He's gone into the prison, Papa."

"Why . . . that was unwise," Reverend Gillette said. "They might think he's a spy. They thought *I* was a spy."

"Dance, gone into the prison? Whatever do you mean?" said J. W. "Why should he do such a thing?"

"He had to," Violet said.

"I know why," said Reverend Gillette, and for a moment it looked as though the preacher were the father, a fiercely proud one. "Emery Jones had plans to rescue his friend. Maybe Dance took part in that."

"He took part in *what?*" said J. W.

"Are you sure he went in?" Papa said, glancing at the scrip.

"Yes, Papa, I am sure. We can ask the one who gave me this. His name is Burr. And while we are there, we shall have Burr summon Dance and we shall tell him I've accepted his proposal and he must come home immediately, whatever his reasons for going in." She went to the hat rack for her bonnet.

"Violet."

She halted two steps from the hat rack. She tried very hard to remain calm.

"By the time we get there, it will be evening," Papa said. "Burr will likely be off duty."

"He must not—I do *not* like the idea of Dance spending *one* night—"

"He'll be all right," Reverend Gillette assured.

She turned to him. "But you said—"

"Hotel Ford will look out for him, like it did me. Norton, I do recommend we take the first train tomorrow. Perhaps we can borrow a brougham. But he will be fine, Violet. A night in the deep did me no harm. What is more . . . we can give Dance a little time to do what he set out to do."

"Hotel . . . ?" J. W. Pickett shook his head in confusion, then demanded, "And who is Burr? And how can you all assume Dance is there and not at the front? This is preposterous. You imply that my son is a lawbreaker."

"Andersonville Prison has broken every law," said Reverend Gillette. "Whatever your son is up to, it is to *right* something."

"Violet, did Dance *say* he was going in?" said Papa.

"Everything *in* here says it." She clutched the scrip to her stomach. "This is the man I will marry. I will marry him or I will marry no one."

Ellen hollered from the kitchen, "Praise de Lawd! Fo' mo' to go. Den I can look Jesus straight in de eye."

"Well," Papa said—and it seemed for the first time in a very long time, he was himself again—"tomorrow, then. First train. We will fetch him home."

"You will find he is not there," J. W. Pickett said crossly, but far less certainly.

"Perhaps so," said Papa. "But I think he is."

"Papa," Violet whispered, for she could not trust her voice, "he is who I hoped he was all along." I am yours, and you, Dance Weld Pickett, are mine.

Mother sank to the sofa, weeping. Lily joined her, weeping and laughing, and soon Mother laughed, too.

21

"THEY SAY YOU ARE A TRAITOR."

"I am called that. Though I prefer Traitor Christian. You can call me T. C. for short."

"You are the only traitor we know," said the boy.

The two children, eating cinnamon cakes as they went, led Posey Stiles through fields and woods and more fields to an old cave dug in the back of a hill, not far from the river. The hill, it was said, was part of the grounds of the Creek Indians who had once inhabited Americus. No one knew if the cave was of Creek or white settler origin. People played there as children and forgot about it when they got old.

The two children pulled away brambles and branches and stepped aside for Posey to see.

Posey peered into the darkness.

"We didn't know who to go to, except a traitor."

When Posey saw what she was meant to see, she gave a little wave and received a wave in return. She didn't know that face, but she knew those clothes. She drew back.

283

"You did right," she said. She put her hands on her hips and scowled thoughtfully in unconscious imitation of her mother.

"What do we do?" said Ambrose Fremont, a boy a little older than Posey. It made Posey feel important to be consulted by an older child, and a boy, to boot.

"What do we do?" Tessie echoed, scowling in imitation of Posey.

"I must think on it. It is not easy being a traitor." She thought hard, as if planning a move at checkers. She could jump this way or she could jump that; it was very important to choose *one* move, and it had to be the best one.

"I want to be a traitor," Tessie said enviously. "Mama won't let me."

"Just another thing to be borne, in this old war," Posey said kindly. She looked at Ambrose. No one knew exactly where Fremont loyalties lay. Whatever Posey decided to do, she had to know. "You for us or against us?"

Ambrose looked from Posey to Tessie, and then to the cave.

He drew himself tall. "I am for, though they slay me."

Posey smiled and thought maybe she'd let him come courting one day.

"That suits me down to the ground. Tessie, you shore yourself up; you have played an important part. We must fetch Ellen, and that right quick."

———

Posey leaned on the chopping block. She put her nose down to it. It smelled of onions and turnips.

Posey had not seen Ellen this cheerful in some time. Ordinarily she'd take advantage of it and wheedle cakes or biscuits or pudding out of her. But the time called for steady thinking.

"Why you need me to come?" Ellen asked crossly. "I ain't got time." She clattered a lid onto a cook pot and snatched a spoon, humming.

"Never in my life have I needed you more than now."

Ellen slowly turned. Hands went to hips. Black eyes fastened on Posey's. It was time to run when there was more white than black, but so far, Posey did not have to run.

"Posey Eden." A squinty eye trembled. "What you up to?"

Posey drew a deep breath, and said bravely, "Traitor deeds. You best summon your courage." She took Ellen's hand and they left the kitchen.

22

"HALF PAST ONE, and all is well!" a sentinel called in the dark. Dance listened to the call make its way down the wall.

In less than twelve hours, Emery had an appointment with the scaffold. Had Father come? Did he find anything in the Articles? Dance wished he could drop by the north gate and ask Burr. But he was cut off from the doings outside and had to get used to it.

Why did he do it? Andy's question had stayed with him all day long. It spoke loudest when Andy came back from collecting rations and gave Dance a handful of meal; it was a no-bake day for this side of the pen. Today the other side got theirs baked.

Dance sifted through the cornmeal. No wonder the men were sick. Aside from what was *in* this meal, some had no way to cook it. No fire, no cooking pot, many times not even a tin cup—some carried their ration from the wagon in a knotted shirtsleeve. He'd seen it all from the top of the stockade wall. He'd seen men so hungry they didn't even mix it with water first, just ate it dry out of cupped hands.

Why did he do it? It seemed very important to find that out. His gut knew, but if he knew it upstairs as well as downstairs, it would strengthen him for whatever lay ahead. Truth makes free. It was something preached at both Methodist and Episcopalian churches. It was something he believed.

Dance gazed through a hole in the tent. He could see a star through it if he leaned enough. This little star through a ragged tunnel hole—he began to understand how isolated these men felt from the rest of the world; it was one thing to watch it, it was another to sit in it.

Coming in didn't mean anything to these men, because now he couldn't help them at all, he was as helpless as they.

Then the answer sprang free, and it was a question, too.

What are they not doing that you wish you would?

Dr. Stiles had scooped him out with a shovel, left him raw and empty.

"Come on out, Johnny Reb," whispered a voice outside. "We know who you are."

"Wait." Dance sat up. "Andy—I kept waiting for *them* to do something. But I was waiting for *me*."

The tent flap rose. "Come on out." He wasn't whispering anymore.

"Oh, hold your horse," Dance said. He shook Andy awake.

"What?" Andy said, rubbing his face.

"I wanted Americus to help these men."

"What's going on over there?" said someone down the way.

"Pipe down, it's none of your business," said the man. "Come out right now, secesh."

"I said hold your horse—I'm saying good-bye." He turned back to Andy. "But Americus didn't. The 'didn't' bled on me, and here's the thing: I let it."

Andy sat up. "What the sam hill is going on?" He looked at the raised tent flap, and saw the shadows outside.

"I couldn't watch you boys, so I watched Burr. He never went along with it. He stayed himself. Well, this is a relief. I know it in the attic, as Emery would say." He clapped Andy's arm. "So long, Andy. I hope you survive." He crawled out of the tent.

Three men waited in the darkness. He got to his feet. "I can put up a caterwauling fight and bring down all kinds of attention on you and me, but I'll not do it if you promise me something."

"Wait! Where are you going?" Andy said.

"What's that?" the tall one asked Dance.

"On my Christian mother's grave, the boys in that tent had nothing to do with me coming in."

"All right. That's good enough for me." He took Dance's arm.

"Wait!" He yanked free, and dropped to his knees. He put his head under the flap. "A chief diversion for me and my friends is to point out hypocrisy. It is a pleasurable vice. But I held Americus to something I wasn't doing. And now that I'm doing something, I don't hold them anymore. Isn't that interesting?"

Hands grabbed his legs and dragged him out.

"Let him go!" Andy shouted. "He's done nothing wrong!"

"There goes the new Lew." Martin sat up. "Where's he going?"

"What's going on down there?" called a sentinel from a tower.

Andy lunged for the opening, but fell over Martin and took the tent down with him. By the time he divested himself of both, the dark figures and Dance were gone.

23

THE TRAIN SCHEDULE did not suit. Only troop trains were going through, bound for Macon and then for the front. Violet did not care if they rode a troop train or not. She argued with the man in charge, whose title she did not know, and said it was going past Andersonville on the way to Macon *anyway*, surely it could slow down to drop them off. It was not allowed. Civilians had no part, said he, in the drama about to play out.

The party of four—Violet, Dr. Stiles, J. W. Pickett, and Reverend Gillette—went to the hotel hostler in the back of one of the inns, and rented a two-horse carriage. It was an hour to Andersonville by carriage, and only if the horses were swift.

Violet clutched the scrip in her lap. It was Saturday morning, the day Emery was to be executed. Now he was on a train bound for exile and she was in a carriage bound for Andersonville and that left only Dance from this F.A.P. triumvirate. *I must do something first,* he said.

Then do it, Dance. Do it quickly, and come back to me.

———

Elliott was perspiring. He did not want to show himself weak, but couldn't help the sweat. He knew what he had to do, but that didn't make the doing easy.

It was easier to be like Mosby, just a grubbing brute. This took thinking. This went to the heart of things. This was a matter of country, and it rose above mere survival—this was *principle*, but he didn't like what principle demanded. They had to give Wirz a message, a strong one, so he'd quit sending in spies.

They had kept the north gate guard in the little pine-bough lodge most of the day. The Reb lay on his side in the center of the group. He was bound hand and foot, his mouth stuffed with scraps of cloth and carefully wrapped with the same so no one would hear him.

He said he wasn't here to find tunnels, but no one believed him. Why else would he be here?

"You want me to—?" said a sympathetic Stern, and Elliott said, "No!"

Perspiring, he picked up a strip of cloth and began to wrap his knuckles.

———

Papa asked Reverend Gillette to stay with Violet in Andersonville while he and J. W. went to see Burr. It told of Violet's otherworldly preoccupation that she accepted this without fuss and went to sit on a bench outside the train depot.

"It takes a brave man to open the eyes of another," said Reverend Gillette after they had sat for a time.

"It takes a brave man to open his own," Violet said, glancing at him. "He said you have only a small measure of hypocrisy. That is high praise from Dance."

Reverend Gillette chuckled. "Well, I think you've found your match, Violet Stiles. No one else could manage you."

"I do not intend to be *managed*."

"I think you'll find we manage each other. That is the best marriage."

Violet rubbed a water stain on the scrip. "It is very bad in there, isn't it?"

Reverend Gillette made a move toward his face, and stopped. Ruefully, he said, "I keep forgetting my beard is gone. It helped me answer things." He sighed. "It is bad, Violet. And it is vast."

"How will they find him?"

"The question is, will he be found? I do not know what is in his mind. I'd like to know what that guard knows."

———

Burr leaned on the rail. From the rising of the sun to the going down of the same, Burr had stood this watch every day with Pickett for many months. It was lonesome without him. Half the time he had his head in the pines, the other half he said things to make a man whistle.

Someone was coming up the ladder.

"Why, Doc Stiles. I just seen you yesterday."

"Hello, Burr." He took a lemon out of his pocket and gave it to him. "This is for your friend."

"Well, I'm obliged."

"Burr—Violet read Dance's papers."

Burr looked at the lemon. He ran his thumbnail along the skin of the lemon, and lifted it to his nose. "That's a smell of heaven around here."

"Where is Dance?"

"Well, I ain't gonna say. If he turns up and they know where he's been, it's the same for him as that Jones boy. Only he ain't gettin' out of it, as in their eyes he'd have done far worse."

"We know he's gone in. We want to get him out, before there's trouble."

Burr studied the lemon. "There's already trouble."

"How do you know?" said Dr. Stiles, fear springing up.

"I asked Old Abe to check on him today. He's not there. They got to him."

Dr. Stiles grabbed his arm. "Who got to him?"

"They, they!" Burr's lips trembled. "They who believe he means harm. There's no fetchin' him now. He's gone."

Dr. Stiles released him. "What do I do?" He looked out on the mass of men. "What do I tell my girl?"

Burr raised brimming eyes. "You tell her he did well."

"What do I tell his father? He's right below."

Burr drew his arm across his face. "Why don't he come up?"

"He doesn't want to."

Burr froze. He handed the lemon to the doctor. He unshouldered his musket and went to the ladder. The musket went to his eye, and he drew a bead on J. W. Pickett.

"You get up here," Burr called down.

The old man looked up.

"Oh, it ain't a fancy rig the regular army gets. But it'll blow a hole in a man. Get movin'."

"Burr, don't—he's just afraid."

"Fancy-pants what never put themselves in the way of mizry will find naught but mizry themselves. Start climbin', you old rooster."

The old man started climbing. He got to the top, and Burr backed away, gun trained on him.

"You want to get hold of where your boy is?" He motioned with the rifle. "Take a look. He went to them, 'cause you would not."

J. W. Pickett hesitated, then firmed himself and came forward.

Burr and the doctor watched him for several moments as he took in the sight. He could not seem to move. Then he staggered and fumbled for the rail. The doctor seized his elbow.

He pulled away and lurched again for the rail. He cried out over the pen, "Dance! Dance!"

Men in the stockade looked up and shook their heads. "Crazy stinkin' Rebs."

"And always that tower."

"Dance!" the old man cried piteously.

"How can we dance?" one shouted back. "Ain't no music."

———

"Here they come," said Reverend Gillette.

Violet jumped up—but Dance wasn't with them.

Papa was supporting J. W. Pickett.

Reverend Gillette hurried over. "Is he all right?"

"He's taken a turn. Let's get some water. Easy does it, Cousin."

They helped him to a bench and Reverend Gillette went for water.

"Papa . . . where is he?"

"I don't know, Violet girl."

"Well, your face says something else," she snapped. She looked at the lost old man on the bench. "So does his."

"Violet . . ."

"Do not touch me."

"Come here, my darling. No—Violet, where are you going?"

"I'm going to fetch him." She started for the stockade and broke into a run, dropping the leather scrip.

He ran to catch her. He pulled her into his arms and held tight.

"Is he lost to me, Papa?" she cried.

"I don't know," he whispered, and held her close. "I don't know."

A sob broke loose, but it could not unravel now. She pushed away and when Papa tried to follow, she held up a hand.

"I must know my course." She paced back and forth, hand on her head, and then said, "I will not believe anything bad until my eyes tell me different. Until my *eyes* tell me different. Is that clear, Papa? That is my course. What is *our* course?"

"We can't take it to Wirz or Winder. He left his post—he's already in trouble. If they find out, it will be far worse than being absent without leave. Burr will watch. We will wait."

"Then we will wait. We will wait. That is our course."

She walked back toward the depot, snatching up the scrip on the way.

24

THE RISING SUN FELL SOFT on a patch of Yankee blue lying in front of the gate. Yellow rays slowly illumined the still, dark heap, and the guard on tower watch leaned to look. He'd had a feeling it was a man, but he waited for sunrise to be sure.

The golden aura made it plain.

The guard sighed. Well, Burr came on watch in a few minutes. Let him take care of it. He just wanted to get home to his wife and breakfast and a few hours of respite from this godforsaken place. He'd pretend he did not see, as was Andersonville custom. His partner was sleeping; he'd keep him distracted when he awoke and so cause no undue fuss.

———

"I'm gonna get me a Yank!" piped the runt, as he waited with Burr for the other two guards to come down. One came down frowsy and sullen, a slovenly man who looked like he just woke up. Fine sentry, that one.

"How old are you, brat?" Burr said. "Nine? Ten?"

"Twelve!" the nipper said indignantly. "Enough to tag me a Yank!"

Burr snatched him by the collar and held him eye-height. "You fire that musket one time and I'll pitch you into that pen. Are we of an understanding?"

"Yup!" he squeaked.

"Gimme your bullets."

The boy fumbled in his bulging pockets and produced enough bullets to lay down a herd of pigs. Burr waited until he'd handed over the last one, then tossed them into the water trough.

The other guard came down and smacked Burr on the back. "Got a present for ya, sitting out front."

"Well, I got one for you." He gave the boy a little shove.

"Wife's makin' biscuits and gravy and I ain't sharin'." He looked at the boy. "Say your prayers, son—that there is Burr, more to be feared than a pack of screamin' Yanks."

"Is the present dead?" Burr called as the guard left.

"Yep."

"Then call me down a stretcher."

"I ain't on duty no more!" He laughed and gave a salute.

Burr grimaced, and then turned a stare on the boy. "Well, get on up there." The boy, white-faced, clambered up the ladder.

Burr smiled a little and had his foot on the bottom rung when the turnkey at the pass-through door said, "Burr—come over here."

There was something in his voice. Burr walked over.

"I ain't sure, but . . ." He opened the pass-through and motioned with his head. Burr glanced at the turnkey, and then stepped through.

The heap of Yankee blue was maybe ten paces off—and Burr stopped halfway there.

"Oh, no," Burr said in a very small voice.

———

Drover found a piece of paper as they gently eased Pickett's body onto the stretcher.

THIS IS WHAT WE THINK OF YOUR PLAN, WIRZ.

"What plan?" Drover shouted to grim-faced Yankees on the outskirts who watched with folded arms. He tore the paper up and threw it at them. "What plan, you fools?"

For whatever reason Pickett went in, it wasn't for Wirz. Dance hated Wirz.

Drover looked down at Pickett's ruined body, clad in Yankee blue, and knew Pickett had done someone good. He looked again to the Yanks, all the fight gone out, said, "What plan, you pitiful fools . . ." He didn't dare look at Burr or he'd come all apart. Burr had gone over the deadline and sat against the stockade wall, watching the sun come up on the spiked rim of the palisade. A thin Yank drawn up with scurvy sat across from him at the deadline.

"You just say the militia don't lose men too," Drover said to no one. "You just say we don't know war. Come on, Zeeff," he said, dashing at his eyes. "Let's get him to his daddy, for I know he is in town."

But Zeeff wasn't listening. Not to Drover. He'd crouched low to Pickett's body, and then suddenly went to his knees and laid his ear on his chest.

Drover's own heart missed a beat.

Zeeff looked up at Drover, and then over at Burr. "Burr!"

———

The guards at Andersonville knew better than to take Dance to the Federal hospital on the grounds or to the Hospital for Confederate

Soldiers in Andersonville; if there was any chance at all of saving his life, he'd forfeit it later if they did. So they took him to the pine-bough dead house outside the south gate—right under the nose of Wirz, on the hill at the Star Fort. They laid him in a corner, and stacked corpses on either side. They stopped what bleeding they could, though there wasn't much of that, and put Zeeff on dead house duty. Then Drover went to fetch the only doctor who would come.

Drover took the magnificent, spirited Maxwell horse from the corral behind Captain Wirz's office, and rode it into flying bits of foam for Americus.

25

It did not seem to Mrs. Stiles that Posey was particularly sick. In fact, as it was Sunday and they were readying for church, she was sure she wasn't. But when Ellen, whose judgment was unerring and absolute, pronounced Posey as poorly, that was that. While Ellen prepared restorative tea for Posey, the rest of the family, with Violet quite remote and poor Cousin Pickett quite silent—which Mrs. Stiles had never once witnessed—set off for the Methodist church.

Ellen and Posey watched them go from behind a lacy curtain.

—

Lew's night in the cave was heaven compared to Andersonville. It smelled of rich, clean earth. Nothing would smell bad again after Andersonville, but for a fruit farmer to spend a night cradled in good clean earth with the sound of the river nearby was as close to home as Lew had come since he'd been away, and the fact that it was here, *here*, so few miles from that hellhole prison, was something fit for philosophical study.

The child came late in the morning with a tall, thin, elderly black woman.

"Well, how did you stand your night?" the child asked.

"I stood it grand. This is a pleasant place, and it reminds me of home."

"I am glad to hear it. You may be the first of many. I wish there was wood you could carve to say you slept here."

"Will I ever know your name?" Lew said. "It is something I would keep in my pocket all the rest of my days."

She beamed. "That is lovely to say, and I will treasure it. But it's best we don't swap real names, for I plan to make a habit of this. You can call me Traitor Christian. What can I call you?"

"Little Mite Badger."

"Well, Little Mite Badger, who isn't so little, here is a poke filled with food, and here is Ell—" She looked up at the black woman. "What shall we call you?"

"Sojourner Truth."

"Sojourner will take you to Elder—what shall we call him?"

The woman thought it over. "George."

"Why, that is kind." To Lew she said, "George was the brother I never met. Now, Little Mite Badger, Elder *George* will take you to someone I do not know, and so on, and so on, and thus we will get you on up to the dreaded Sherman."

"I am deeply grateful, Traitor Christian. Do you know I have a girl your age? She is just as fair and bright. I will speak of you to her one day."

The little traitor smiled. "You tell her I said how do."

———

Posey had just time to dive under the sick shawl on the parlor sofa before the front door banged open. But she did not have to fake sick, and almost regretted it—she could truly "put on the pale" as Mama called it, and considered it a skill—but it was only Rosie and Daisy, and they burst into the parlor, both talking at once.

"What do you think?" Rosie shouted.

Posey threw off the shawl. "I hardly know. Say it quick."

"Papa was called out of service!" Daisy said.

"Whatever for?"

"We don't know," began Daisy.

"But we *surmise*," continued Rosie.

"That it is *not* a medical emergency, as it was not just—"

"*Papa* who was called out, but—"

"Cousin Pickett!"

"So *that* means—" said Rosie.

"Dance is found," Posey breathed. "Where is Violet?"

"She ran out with them."

"Where did they go?"

"We don't know," Rosie said, disgusted, dropping to the sofa. "Mama promised death if we followed."

"That is anticlimactic!" Posey shouted, pounding her knee with a fist. "Blame it all to—" She stopped as Mother walked into the parlor. Then the porch door banged, and Posey saw Violet run upstairs, Lily on her heels.

Posey discreetly reached for the sick shawl.

"Well. You certainly seem better," Mother said dryly.

"What is Violet doing here?" Posey said. "Why does she not run to her love?"

"Papa wouldn't let her," said Mother.

"When does Papa stop her?"

"He put his foot down."

Posey raised an eyebrow.

"Girls," Mother said to Rosie and Daisy, "change out of your

Sunday dresses. We must clear out the Trades Pile and make up a place in Papa's office. If all goes well, and let us pray it does, we may be receiving Dance."

"It *is* a medical emergency?" Rosie said, alarmed.

Mama came close and knelt. "The guard from Andersonville says Dance is in a very bad way."

Posey sat up. "What happened?"

"It seems he was set upon."

"Set upon!" the girls cried.

"You must prepare yourselves—he is in a dreadful state, near death. It seems he has already . . . he has lost vision in one eye." She forced a tremulous smile. "But you know what a fine doctor your papa is."

"The best!" Rosie declared, rubbing her eyes with her fists.

"He'll see him through!" said Daisy. "We all will!"

"So we shall. Rosie, get out the cot and make sure there is no mildew. Scrub it clean if there is, and fetch some bedding. Daisy, put all the trades things in the larder. Ellen and I will prepare Papa's things. Hettie is on her way."

Judging by Mama's calm and clear state, things must be very bad indeed, as she was only this clear when they were. Oh, how Posey liked it better when Mama was frazzled.

As soon as the others left the parlor, Posey slipped upstairs to Violet.

Violet lay on her stomach on the bed, very still. Lily sat beside her, and she had been crying.

Violet was only this still when things were very bad.

Posey came inside, and closed the door. She sat on the floor next to the bed and settled in to wait like women did.

———

Word passed to Sergeant Keppel of a certain body in the dead house. All his days he'd remember the look on General Winder's face when that preacher had slammed a handful of foul prison fodder square in the middle of his desk. It brightened the sergeant's soul every time he called it to mind, and for this he owed Dance Pickett. Yes, the boy had gone AWOL, and yes, Wirz was mad—madder than usual—because with Sherman's advance, several guards had already deserted for the cowards they were. They were sure he was headed to Andersonville to tread the grapes of retribution, because they had too little common sense to realize Atlanta was the prize.

Keppel frowned. They had put Dance in the dead house, but no one could fetch him from there. Wirz had a clear view of the place. He'd pick up on anything unusual, and a doc visiting the dead house was unusual. Especially that doc. Wirz had been feeling poorly lately, but Keppel did not count on this as favorable. He had to intercept any rescue party before they made for the dead house.

There was only one way to get Pickett out, and that meant grim things for the boy. Keppel hoped he stayed half-dead for the time being. The very thought of Pickett waking up in that company put him in a sweat, and he quickly called to mind Winder Stares at Prison Food. He added the preacher's *I will not leave until you eat that*. A smile soon twitched, and he was able to turn his thoughts to practicalities.

Men were dropping so fast, death hastened by the roasting sun, that Wirz had ordered the burial trench to be lengthened. He'd ordered it a week ago, but this was Andersonville—things didn't get done when ordered. Spare shovels for a large detail of men had to be first requisitioned, and then found, and they weren't, as the locals refused any loans. They were ordered from Albany and until they came in, the large detail of men scheduled for dead duty would wait; today there were two, and Keppel swapped those two out for Drover and Zeeff.

He told his corporal he had to check on the shipment of shovels and left Castle Reed for the commissary building.

The commissary building was directly across from the train depot. Whether they had taken a train or the road from Americus, they had to cross here to get to the stockade. Here, Keppel had to intercept anyone bound for Dance at the dead house. He sat on a barrel just inside the door with some old bills of lading he'd borrowed from the corporal.

———

They took the same rig they had rented only yesterday, leaving a note for the hostler since he was in church, and followed the man called Drover. The train was faster, but they didn't bother to check the schedule; they needed a conveyance for Dance, and they would need to keep him concealed.

"He thinks he has lost an eye, does he?" said J. W. Pickett. "Well, he is no doctor. We shall be the judges of that."

Dr. Stiles noted the *we* but did not comment. It was good to see the elderly man lively once more.

"We Picketts have the natural-bred constitution of the mountain man, as our ancestors hail from the Carolina Smokies. Dance was sick but once in his life. Pneumonia. But he pressed through."

"We need to think of how to get him off the compound without notice," Dr. Stiles said.

"Why should that be a difficulty? He is my son. He has done nothing wrong."

Dr. Stiles did not bother with a response. Cousin may yet be sharp in a courtroom, but when it came to his children his thinking went a little dull. He let the old man talk while he mentally tended to damages he had not yet assessed and considered ways to save an eye he had not yet examined; but first, they had to figure out how to carry off a body from a place where all they did was watch, and watch, and watch.

———

Keppel left the papers on the barrel and came alongside the three men. One was the doctor, one was J. W. Pickett, and one was Drover. Drover was arguing with Pickett.

"Sirs, let us turn in here for a spell," said Keppel in a tone not to be overheard, indicating the commissary building. "Let us consider our ways."

"That's what I keep telling him," said Drover between his teeth. "He wants to bring *Wirz* into it!"

"What have we to hide?" Pickett insisted. "Let us simply go to the captain and talk this out. I do not understand why Dance went into that place to begin with. While it is true he is given to hyperbole, I am sure—"

"Shut your mouth and get in there," said Keppel, and Pickett's mouth snapped closed.

Keppel ushered them to the far corner of the building near barrels of sorghum and sacks of rice and, once he was sure they could not be overheard, began to lay out his plan. "Now. Drover and Zeeff will—"

"Where exactly *is* Dance?" said J. W. Pickett. "Your man will not tell me. He said they hid him, but—"

"Your son is concealed among the corpses in the dead house."

That silenced him.

"I've not seen him, but those who have say he is unconscious and that's a mercy." He glanced at Drover. "I've swapped you and Zeeff for dead house duty." He looked at the other two. "Drover and Zeeff will load up the wagon as usual and get him to the Yankee burial ground about a quarter mile north of the stockade. We must stick with the usual times they load the wagon to not invite notice. It is hard, but we must."

"What's the usual time?" said Dr. Stiles.

"Two loads go over before ration time. They need the wagon for rations right after. To save time—"

"The *same* wagon used for dead bodies, used to bring in *food*?" said J. W. Pickett.

"Yes, but—"

"Dance said it's not even washed out. I . . . didn't believe him. Of course—who would?"

"Is he with hospital or stockade bodies?" said Dr. Stiles. At Keppel's impatient shrug, he said, "Hospital bodies are more gangrenous. I am deeply concerned about infection."

"Gangrene!" exclaimed Pickett.

Keppel clapped his hands once. "Listen!" He lowered his voice. "Whichever bodies he is with, he'll go out in the second load. I want to get him out of there as soon as can be done, so I told Zeeff to go ahead and lay out the first load of corpses in the trench but wait to cover them with dirt later. That bought a half an hour, and that's all I dare. Then Drover and Zeeff will come back for the second load as usual, this time putting Dance with them, and then head for the burial trench. Now listen sharp: just past the trench is the main road, and that's where you'll wait for them to bring out your boy. But here's the thorny part: Winder has a picket line standing watch not far from there, a bit further east. Stop your carriage *just* at the bend, and you'll avoid them—there will be a bare space in the pines on the right. That's where our Confederate boys are laid to rest. Well, you all best get going. Good luck. I wish him the best."

Dr. Stiles and J. W. Pickett started off, then Pickett stopped and turned to say, a little distracted, "Thank you." He hurried to catch up with the doc. Keppel and Drover followed behind to the entrance of the commissary and watched them go.

"You think Dance will make it?" Keppel asked.

Drover watched the old man. "He don't believe how bad things are."

"Well, you and Zeeff be careful. I'm tired of losing—hey!"

Drover caught up with J. W. Pickett and made him stop. He pulled off his hat. "Things are grim, sir, and I wish you'd believe it. He's stood much. If he does not stand more . . . well, I want to say . . . what a fine boy, sir."

He clapped on his hat and trotted back to Keppel. "Sometimes, Sergeant, I just wish I wasn't born."

"Well . . . that may cheer you some." Keppel pointed at the handbill tacked to the load-bearing post. "Did you see that?"

Drover went over and read it. "There they go again." His face softened. "Didn't they learn?"

"Some don't."

"Well, I'm gonna borrow this." He took it down, carefully folded it, and put it in his pocket. "If he comes to, he still has one good eye."

———

Dr. Stiles waited, reins in hand, peering ahead. J. W. did not feel like waiting in the carriage. He could not see through the pines in the bend. He couldn't see how far away the picket line was, but if he listened close he could hear the men.

He got down and looked through the thinned pines to the Confederate soldiers' burial ground. A little farther up the road was where they would bring out Dance from the Union burial trench. He went up the road as far as he dared, until he heard voices at the picket line, then slipped into the pines.

He picked his way over a carpet of needles, through pines and spiderwebs and brambles, and came out to an open place.

A mound of earth rose before him. He walked toward it and went around one side. A shovel was stuck in the mound. Then J. W. Pickett stopped short.

In a shallow trench stretched a row of corpses.

He became aware of the sound of buzzing flies, of wind in the pines, and somewhere, a bird. It was quiet here, away from the stockade, just an old living man among many young dead ones.

A distant train whistle blew.

It was a very long trench. Bodies, close-packed, filled it. The end of it was covered with dirt. Another long, covered trench lay nearby. And another. And another. Thousands of bodies lay all about J. W. Pickett in long, shallow mass graves.

Those before him lay uncovered, these boys who had walked the pen his own boy oversaw—Dance, a sentinel of Andersonville; Dance, whose eyes knew them living, who now lay like a corpse among them—these boys, these young men dead from starvation, these wrecked, ruined men.

His son had called for help, asked his father to face with him a thing he could not face alone. And J. W. Pickett had refused to come.

He walked to the edge of the trench and knelt beside it. Dead men tell no tales? These did. He laid his hand on a head. The hair was matted. A few wisps moved in the breeze. The shrunken face, skin stretched tightly over the skull, had the beginnings of an adolescent beard. "Beautiful boy," he whispered, "how sorry I am."

He did not have a clear picture of Dance in the dead house until now.

Did his own beautiful boy lie among corpses like these?

The old man stepped down into the trench to do the same, and so await the fate of his son.

26

DR. STILES looked at the place he had last seen Cousin Pickett, where he had slipped into the pines. Shouldn't they be here by now? Several people had passed, sending curious glances to the stopped carriage; some asked if they could be of assistance, and Dr. Stiles had smiled ruefully and said his cousin was suddenly sick, motioning to the pines.

An occasional whoop and holler from the picket line ahead broke the silence. Now a song started up, not much in tune or in time. The boys sounded as though they had a barrel to share.

What if there was a watch change? What if one of them came this way? And what if it happened when Dance arrived?

———

The old man rose from the dead.

He climbed out of the trench at the sound of the approaching wagon and waited for it to pull up.

Drover climbed down and came to meet him. When he drew close, he shoved his hands in his pockets. "I'll say it straight, sir, I ain't sure he lives. He had a fit not a minute ago, and now he's awful—well, where's the doc?"

J. W. gazed at the wagon bed. "Is my boy in there?"

Drover hung his head. Pickett put out his hand and started for the wagon.

Stacked on top of each other like so much cordwood, beautiful boys.

His beautiful boy lay atop the pile of corpses. How still he lay.

His mouth was open. His face was swollen and bruised. A cloth covered one eye.

"Is this my beautiful boy?" He took his hand and held it to his cheek.

Dr. Stiles touched his shoulder. "Come on, fellas, let's get him down."

Drover and the other man took Dance down as carefully as they could and laid him apart from the wagon. They backed away as J. W. and the doctor went to his side.

The other guard muttered, "Drover, if he—Well, if he—we can't take him back. We can take him to the Confederate site."

"No," said J. W., turning to them. "You'll bury him here." He rose and looked at the open trench. "You'll bury my boy with these."

"There will be no burying yet," said Dr. Stiles, from where he knelt beside Dance. He took something out of Dance's mouth and held up a small wad of bloody cloth. "Here is your fit. He was coughing it up." He rested his hand on Dance's head, ruffling his hair with his thumb. "Let's get him home."

———

They gently loaded Dance onto the floorboard of the carriage. He was unconscious, deeply so, and Dr. Stiles hoped he'd suffer no lasting neural harm. He did not yet tell J. W. that his son would lose his left eye, and he did not yet know what other injuries he had sustained—a cursory examination promised more than mere broken ribs—but he was alive, and his heartbeat was strong. His good eye showed reaction to light.

In truth, it seemed as though Dance was not as bad as he might have been. As though the beating had been stopped short. Why didn't they finish him? Why didn't they keep it up until they knew he was dead?

His physician side went on ahead and staged the removal of the bad eye. He had never performed an enucleation; he would ask for assistance from Dr. McCabe. He was sure to get it, as Dr. McCabe's professional concerns overrode any others.

But his father side said never mind all that—Dance lives, and now so will your girl, so think on practical things later and let your soul rest a bit in joy.

Drover said quickly, "Someone comes. I best get scarce. Send word when you can." He vanished into the pines.

"Cousin, you best come sit up by me, for it will look strange if you don't. On the road to Americus, you can join him."

"Drive carefully, Norton."

"I will."

He turned the carriage around to gain the other side of the road before they met whoever was coming from Andersonville. Dance could not be seen unless another rig was directly next to them and someone happened to look straight down into the cart; but no chance must be taken, and Dr. Stiles would keep as much distance as possible. He stayed as close as he dared to the edge of the road without risking a wheel catching the rim of the ditch.

Two dray horses came into view around the bend, and Dr. Stiles's heart stood still.

On the front seat of the dray sledge was General Winder.

An armed guard sat beside him with the reins, and four armed soldiers stood in the sledge, hanging on to the sides.

"Hold up!" General Winder called. "Who goes there?"

Dr. Stiles drew up, and in the wash of fear, indignation sprang.

"Who goes there?" he repeated. "Why it is I, General Winder, Dr. Norton Stiles from Americus. Do you intend that I should produce a passport to that effect? As you did for those in Richmond?"

"Who is the man next to you?" General Winder leaned and squinted, and when he saw who it was, sat back. A rather pleased contempt came to his face. "What a pair. Sherman comes, and Wirz says your son has cut and run. It is not so hard to believe—the last to join the Cause are first to forsake it. I confess I never dreamed to see a son of the great J. W. Pickett a member of the *militia*. And now Howell Cobb's singlemost prize has deserted. Well, let me tell you something—if we find him, things will not go well for him. I guarantee that. You and your Articles. I will *clothe* your boy in Article 41. I will make it his shroud."

"I have seen what you have done," J. W. Pickett said. "They are just boys. Like ours."

"They are Yankees." The contempt condensed to hatred. "I thought you were a good Southerner."

"I am not. But my son is."

"I have spoken with Colonel Chandler," said Dr. Stiles. "You are in his report. He plans to recommend your removal. Oh yes—I've seen his notes. He calls for another to take your place, one who shall employ good judgment, and energy, and feelings of humanity for that prison. One who does not pride himself on never entering that stockade. One who would have got something *done* had he put forth even *minimum* effort to ease such suffering!"

"Chandler?" Winder seized upon the name with relish. He leaned forward. "Oh, I will tell you of Chandler. He came down here with

314

trumpets ablaze, predisposed from rumor to champion the 'plight' of the Yank, determining beforehand to give an unfavorable report of all he saw or heard, desiring to show himself in a most compassionate light, throwing about his holy indignations. Well, you don't know anything. I am sure he did not tell you that he *himself* is a Yank, you ignorant fool! Oh, yes—to join our ranks he resigned his *Union* commission, only to be taken prisoner by the same! Search it out if you don't believe me. He was exchanged for a nephew of Andrew Johnson. There—your distinguished, your *tarnished* hero." He receded, the baleful gaze exultant.

"Are we not all tarnished?" said J. W. Pickett.

"How you ever evade . . . ," Dr. Stiles said in wonder, as if discovering something for the first time. "What of Chandler?" He stood in the carriage and held his hand out toward the stockade. "There it stands! There is your generalship! All the things you could do to help—you not only do not do them, you *prevent* others from doing them! Can you not see how wrong it is? Can you not see it is entirely evil?"

"Walk on," Winder said to his driver. The driver clucked and flicked the reins.

"Look into that stockade! Look into those graves! Do not look away from them, sir!" Dr. Stiles dropped to the seat. "And if you do, we will not. For we do not answer to you, but to God. The men who survive will tell the truth one day. They will tell of what people did to help them, and of what they did not."

"Hold up, General Winder!" It was Drover. He came from the pines and went to the cart, waving a piece of paper. "I thought you might like to see this."

Winder snatched the paper, recognized it, crumpled and threw it in Drover's face. The driver snapped the reins and the cart lurched forward. Some of the guards toppled. Grinning, Drover watched them go.

"What is that?" Dr. Stiles asked.

"Well, you oughta know." Drover retrieved the paper, smoothed it out, and handed it to Dr. Stiles. He and J. W. Pickett read it together.

AMERICUS, ANDERSONVILLE, OR WHOMSOEVER WILL

Is it possible you think yourself DETAINED from Feeding STARVING Prisoners? . . .

They finished reading, and Dr. Stiles held it for a moment. It seemed to give off its own light, here in this place.

"Kingdom come, she says," Dr. Stiles murmured. He folded the paper and tucked it carefully inside his vest. "Cousin, let's get your boy home to my girl."

PART FIVE

He who sits upon the throne of the universe knows full well the best methods of action, the wisest discipline for the times, and is surely pledged to make Right triumphant in the end. Peace was the watchword at the beginning of His reign, and it shall be the crowning glory of the same at the last. Then let the fearful and anxious hear a voice from heaven saying unto them—

"Dismiss thy fears,—the ark is mine."

Let them also hear the words,—*Sacrifices are never lost.*

—*Life and Death in Rebel Prisons* BY ROBERT H. KELLOGG,
16TH CONNECTICUT VOLUNTEERS, ANDERSONVILLE SURVIVOR

27

OCTOBER 1864

Burr saw Old Abe, and gave a little whistle. He looked both ways and let go the lemon. It took a good bounce in the dead zone and rolled for Old Abe.

Old Abe nodded. "You give that doctor a handshake and say it comes from me." He limped off, saying over his shoulder, "And keep one for yourself, you flamin' dog secesh."

"That ain't allowed," piped the nipper.

Burr flicked his head. "Shut up or you'll go sailin'. They'll get out forks and knives and say, 'Supper time!' You know what their favorite meal is?"

"What?"

"Rebel Child. They like 'em nice and tender."

Presently, a young Yank came to the deadline. He looked expectantly up at the tower. Burr was about to yell him away, when the piping nipper produced a sweet potato from his pocket. He carefully looked both ways, then tossed it to him. The Yank boy nodded, looked both ways, and sauntered off.

Burr looked down at the boy, who worked up a wad of spit and let fly. He put his chin on the rail and grinned. Burr flicked his head.

The two sentinels settled in to resume their watch of Andersonville.

28

The War of Northern Aggression shuddered to a close. Eleventh-hour measures, reached for simply because no one knew how to quit, would not save the South now. Appomattox, the end of the Southern Cause, was only days away.

The Friends of Andersonville Prison, small though their efforts were in comparison to the great need, continued to do what they could in collecting food and medical supplies; and until General Winder left the prison in the fall of 1864, these had to be given in secret.

On the last day of March 1865, two founding members of the F.A.P. were married on the pleasantly situated lawn at the east end of Lamar Street in Americus.

It was a very lovely and very small ceremony, as Americus had not yet forgiven Dr. Stiles and his family for helping the Yanks. But they would, one day.

Reverend Gillette and his wife sat at a table with Dr. Stiles and his family, along with J. W. Pickett and Hettie Dixon.

"Do you know how many weddings I have officiated?" said Reverend Gillette to a passing Ellen. "This is the best wedding cake I have ever had. I have sneaky plans for a second piece."

"Oh, I got my eyes on you."

Dance, handsome in his dashing eye patch and wedding broadcloth, noticed a particularly daydreamy Posey. He wiped his mouth with his napkin. "What are you thinking, Posey girl?"

"Brother, I am fondly remembering a man who'd have my name in his pocket all the days of his life if he could. He has a girl my age, fair and bright. And for all my days I will only know him as Little Mite Badger."

A cake-filled fork froze en route to the open mouth of Reverend Gillette.

———

APRIL 1865
HANOVER JUNCTION, PENNSYLVANIA

The train came into the station, and Lew reached for his knapsack.

The war was over and he'd made it through. But Lincoln was dead. Harris was dead. His whole mess was gone. He packed them away and stood for no grief yet, but felt great emptiness where they used to abide.

They would come to him in the fruit fields, one day. Harris with his artful profanities, Charley Reed with his drum.

What of Emery Jones? Would Emery come with them? All Lew had known of this war was loss. Bullets took most, Andersonville took the rest. He packed Emery away, not as he last saw him, but coming out of a thicket at a crouch, moving smooth, blasting a skulker Reb.

Lew had mustered out in Baltimore, and the Soldier's Center

arranged a series of telegrams. A work hand would meet him in Hanover Junction, and from there it was an hour by wagon to home where the whole clan waited to welcome him. Mother and Father. His sister, Laura, and her new husband. His brother, Frank, who'd mustered out two weeks earlier. Uncles and aunts, cousins and neighbors. His children. And Carrie.

He'd had only one furlough in four years and hadn't seen Carrie and the children in two. Would they know him?

He smiled, and his stomach fluttered. Well, the children would get used to him. And Carrie would know him invisible.

The train came to a standstill, and Lew stepped down from the car. He looked for the work hand sent to meet him and had taken no more than a step or two when he stopped.

Leaning against a post in a jaunty pose was Emery Jones.

Emery grinned. "Hello there, thunderstruck."

Lew could not move.

"Say something."

"Well, I am trying to tell my eyes what they see," Lew said slowly. "They don't believe me."

"Lewis Archibald Gann, by the way."

"I don't recall telling you my middle name. I do not like it."

"Lewis Archibald Gann—the second. She named Little Mite after you."

It was too darned much. A real live Emery and a named child. He put his face in his sleeve.

"Why'd she do that?" he said, muffled.

"You just thank the good Lord he takes after her and not you. What *I'd* like to know is how you could forget a piece of information like that. Mercy, I'd remember if my son were named after me. We do hope for a boy, but if it's a girl, she is certain to be as beautiful as Laura. We can't go wrong."

Lew came away from his sleeve.

"Yep—just found out yesterday. You're gonna be an uncle. You are stuck with me in perpetuity—Brother." Then Emery straightened and his broad grin left. "Hold on, now, take it slow and easy—yes, I married Laura, and you do not have to look like Armageddon."

"Well, Emery, it is much. I am trying to accustom. Did her intended die in battle?"

"Nope. Once I saw her I went and killed him myself."

Emery took Lew's knapsack. He slung it over his shoulder, and they fell into step.

"I thought you only killed men with bad grammar."

"I also kill fiancés."

"What happened to you, Emery Jones?"

"It is a fine story," he admitted.

The same morning that Corporal Emery Jones was acquitted and exiled, Union admiral David Farragut attacked Mobile Bay. By the time Corporal Jones reached Fort Morgan, that venerable citadel at the mouth of Mobile Bay had been under siege for a week. Jones and his escort rushed to join the embattled garrison and give what aid they could.

Union forces closed in with siege mortars upon the fort, and the Confederates abandoned two batteries on the outer defenses. When ordered to spike the guns on retreat, one battery crew took a direct mortar hit. Emery Jones never made it out on a slumgullion blockader to heathen lands.

"I did enjoy that battle, though I was blown up some." He pulled up his shirt. "Look at that. If you look at it from my vantage, it is a map of Sumter County. A special little girl drew one for me once." He dropped the shirt. "Well, after the mapmakers put me together they made an earnest matter of my exile, and I was sent over as a traitor to the Cause under white flag at Fort Morgan—just after, as a matter of irony, I was awarded a medal for the action at the battery.

"You may surmise that the Union had not much cause for used goods such as I, so they kept me safe under lock and key until they took stock of my talents. I made the rounds of some of your—I mean, *our*, as I am now a blue belly—prisons, a few of which, I am sad to report, gave Andersonville a run for the money: particularly Camp Douglas in Chicago, from which I do not have a solitary decent memory. However, I ended my prison days at Fort McHenry in Baltimore, and I did like it there, for there I took up correspondence with Laura. She came and visited with your folks, as they wanted more details on you; I learned later they came to size me up 'cause *you* gave details of *me* in your letters. Well, I don't know what lies you told, but I am in your debt. We were married in January. I asked 'em to keep it mum in their letters to you. I knew you'd not believe it lest you seen it. You know what, Lew? It is sure nice to talk to you again. We will philosophize and grow fruit trees until we are aged. Well, Carrie and Laura are sure gettin' up some kind of feast. Place looks like a county fair. You'd think someone special's comin' home."

"My sister's name, coming out of your mouth . . ."

"You gonna miss anything from your Southern sojourn?"

"Not much," and he waited through an aching threat of unpacking as Harris Gill's face came up, and Andy and Martin from Hotel Ford, and the sight of those fence rails loaded into a wagon.

One day when he could bear it, he'd let them out. And one day when he could bear it, he'd travel south and visit Andersonville Prison. He'd do something special there—he'd fashion a monument or plant a tree for Harris and the men of the 12th Pennsylvania. He'd make sure their suffering meant something. It did to him.

For now, for now, pack Andersonville away.

"I'll miss only one thing for now, and more when I am able. I'll miss a little girl called Traitor Christian. She helped me on my way."

"Say that name again."

"Traitor Christian."

Emery put his hands in his pockets, and smiled.

Afterword

TODAY ANDERSONVILLE PRISON in Sumter County, Georgia, is a historic site maintained by the National Park Service. All twenty-six acres of the original stockade have been preserved. Visitors to the site can walk the grounds, "heart-drawn," as Joshua Chamberlain once said at the dedication of another battlefield, "to see where and by whom great things were suffered."

In September 1864, against Sherman's advance, the prison began to transfer detachments of men to other prisons in South Carolina and coastal Georgia, until the population decreased from over 33,000 men in August 1864 to approximately 5,000 by January 1865. This figure held steady until the war's end. Andersonville Prison was finally liberated in May 1865.

Captain Henry Wirz was executed for war crimes on November 10, 1865. Speculation rages to this day as to whether Wirz deserved to take the fall for Andersonville. General John Winder died of a heart attack in February of that year before any charges could be brought against him. Southerner Mary Boykin Chesnut, a Civil

War diarist, wrote at the time: "Well, Winder is safe from the wrath to come. General Lovell said that if the Yankees had ever caught Winder, it would have gone hard with him."

Mass atrocity compels us to look as closely for social activists to lionize as for villains to demonize. The truth is, Andersonville Prison had as few documented heroes as it had villains. When I looked for humanitarian effort to shine blazing through speeches and diatribes from podiums and pulpits, denouncing prison conditions and rallying citizens to concerted action, I didn't find that blazing light. But I did find that a different sort of light shone forth in this place of dark suffering.

It shone not from podiums or pulpits, but from individual efforts of people like Anna Hodges and Dr. John C. Bates; Lt. Col. Alexander Persons and Col. Daniel Chandler; Father Peter Whelan and Dr. Bedford J. Head; Reverend Davies, Father Hamilton, Abigail Spencer, and any number of unnamed slaves. These were the friends, the sentinels, of Andersonville Prison. Descendants of Andersonville survivors walk the earth today as a result of the unsung, individual efforts of many such people.

Andersonville Prison is not a story of the public social activist. It is a story of the individual social activist. Dr. Martin Luther King Jr. said, of the parable of the Good Samaritan, that "the first question that the priest asked . . . was, 'If I stop to help this man, what will happen to me?' But then the Good Samaritan came by, and he reversed the question: 'If I do not stop to help this man, what will happen to him?'"

A day is coming, and may be here, when we will no longer look to the social activist to lead us. A day is coming, and may be here, when we will look for small things to do tirelessly within our own sphere, small things that could make life-changing differences for the people all around us. Not as much "what would Jesus do?" . . . but rather, what *will* I do?

When the opportunity to help arises, if it's a lemon, if it's just a lemon, if that is all we can do—let us do it. In that moment, we make mankind our business.

———

Many good books are available if you'd like to learn more about Andersonville Prison, including *Life and Death in Rebel Prisons* by Robert H. Kellogg, *History of Andersonville Prison* by Ovid Futch, *John Ransom's Andersonville Diary* by John Ransom, and the Pulitzer Prize–winning novel *Andersonville* by MacKinlay Kantor. Film buffs, check out the Emmy-winning film *Andersonville* directed by John Frankenheimer and *The Andersonville Trial* directed by George C. Scott.

For more facts on Andersonville Prison and for information about visiting the site, go to www.nps.gov.

Turn the page for an excerpt of Tracy Groot's Christy Award–winning WWII novel

THE SUN CAME warm through the plexishield. The shield squeaked as Tom wiped a patch of condensation. He was no good with words, and he didn't have to be. Plenty of aviators said it for him. One talked of slipping the surly bonds of earth, and of sun-split clouds. Another spoke of rarefied splendor. "Untrespassed sanctity" was a favorite, and those were the words he'd use to tell the folks.

Untrespassed sanctity, he'd say of the English Channel, and of the gut-thrum of his aircraft, of the daily sorties to France, and his placement in the V. It never got old. It was untrespassed. Maybe not invincible, but so far, on his watch, untrespassed.

I know that I shall meet my fate somewhere among the clouds above; those that I fight I do not hate, those that I—

"Angel flight, this is lead." Captain Fitz finally broke radio silence. "Rolling in."

The five Thunderbolts approached the target area, flying in lovely V formation. Tom would ransack his vocabulary for a different word than *lovely* if talking with the guys, but the new guy from Molesworth stayed on his wing pretty as pie. Someday he'd like to hear a liberated

Frenchman say, *There I was, getting beat up by a Nazi; we look up and see this lovely V . . .*

"One and two, take targets on the right. Three and four—"

"Captain! We got movement—"

Antiair flak slammed her belly, blew a hole in the front of the cowling. Tom barely knew he was hit before oil pressure plummeted. "Mayday—this is Angel three. I'm hit! I'm hit."

"Angel three, can you make it back?"

"Pressure gauge says no, flight lead. I'm going in."

"Copy. We'll cap the area." Then, "Good luck, Tom."

"Good luck, Cab," another echoed.

"Guts and glory, Cabby," called another.

Bullets stitched the plane as he peeled off the target. Smoke filled the cockpit, burnt oil singed his nostrils. She was flagging the second she was hit, but he gripped the stick and pulled back to get as much height as he could before bailing.

He tried for a look at the ground but couldn't see through the smoke. Where was he? Too charmed by rarefied splendor and the alignment of his wingman to—

"Normandy," Tom coughed. Northeastern Normandy.

Flak exploded and pinged, black patches pockmarked the sky, and as Tom gained altitude, he heard a conversation in the debrief room.

Then Cabby got hit, and that was it, the whole ground opened up on us. You capped the area . . .

Stayed as long as we could, sir, but it was too hot.

Where was he in Normandy? Caen? Cabourg? Maybe he could—

But the old girl jerked, leveled, and he had no hope of circling back to bail in the sea.

Why do you call him Cabby?

He looks like he jumped outta the womb hollering, "Heil Hitler," but didn't like us calling him Kraut. So we called him Cabbage.

We called him Cabbage.

I ain't dead yet, fellas. I am, however, about to reacquaint myself with the surly bonds of earth.

He waved off smoke, snatched the picture of his little brother, and shoved it down his collar. He jettisoned the cowling, and the plexi-shield broke from the plane in a *whumpf*, popping his ears, sucking his breath.

There were two ways to bail from a P-47 Thunderbolt. Tilt the plane and let it drop you out, or, in what Tom felt was a more stylish way to go, just stand up, rise into the slipstream, let it carry you away . . .

———

Listen, Yank. You get hit, you go down, here's what you do: get to Paris, get to the American Hospital. Look up a doc there, a Yank by the name of Jackson. He's with the Resistance. You tell him Blakeney says thanks. He may not remember me. He's helped a lot of blokes. You tell him thanks for me.

"He looks like a *boche*."

"I saw him go down. I heard him speak. He's no *boche*. He flew one of the new planes. You should have seen them. Beautiful."

"What did he say?"

"Not much. Before he came to, something about a flight of angels and a fellow named Jackson in Paris. Now look at him. He's not going to say anything."

"That's what worries me. We have to find out if he's German."

"I'm telling you, he's no German. He sounds like the man from Ohio."

Tom watched the two Frenchmen watching him and tried hard to pick out words. His mother's friend had given him a little French phrase book from the Great War, when she had served as a nurse with the Red Cross. From sheer boredom between flights, he'd sometimes taken it out. It was in his escape and evasion pack, no longer strapped to his back. Either he lost it in the jump, or the French guys took it.

He was in a dark woodshed with a low ceiling. He remembered fumbling for the chute cord the second he left the plane, waiting until he was clear to yank it. He remembered terror at the descent; he'd parachuted many times, none with fear of enemy fire. He'd never felt so vulnerable in his life, not even after jammed gear and a belly landing—Captain Fitz rushed up with a pint of Jack Daniel's after that one. But the float down into enemy-held land, the air thick with bullets, the ground exploding, that was one for the books. He heard himself telling it to the guys, heard Fitz's laugh and Oswald's quick "Yeah, yeah, yeah, and den what happened?"

I don't know yet, Oz.

He suddenly felt for the photo. The Frenchmen leaped back, and one pulled Tom's own .45 on him. Tom held up his hands and pointed to his shirtfront.

"Picture. Photograph." He added, "Uh . . . *frère*. Picture of *ma frère*."

"*Mon frère*," one of them corrected.

Keeping one hand up, he slowly unzipped his flight jacket, unfastened a few shirt buttons, and looked inside. It was stuck in his underwear waistband. He glanced at the men, slowly reached inside, and pulled it out. He held it up for the men to see. "*Mon frère*," he said. "*Mon petit frère*. He's thirteen."

"*Oui.*" The one with the gun nodded, and slipped it back into his pocket.

He looked at the picture. Mother had sent it with the last package. Ronnie wasn't little anymore. The kid was growing up. Still, same old grin, same cowlick, same rascal shine in his eyes. He ignored the rush of pain and affection at seeing the familiar face in this strange place.

"Can't get a word in edgewise even now," Tom muttered. He held it up to the men. "Kid can talk the hind leg off a donkey." He rubbed the face with his thumb, and slipped it into a zippered pocket in his flight jacket.

"Who is Jackson?" the man with the gun said in English.

Tom's heart nearly stopped; had he said it out loud? He'd banged his head good when he came down in a tight place between two buildings. He remembered a gray tiled roof coming on fast; he remembered sharp pain, sliding to the ground, then nausea, vomiting. Then he went into some sort of daze, vaguely recollected being bundled into the back of a horse cart. They covered him up with firewood, and the dark invited him to blank out. He came to in this place. First thing he did was to feel for the gun now in the possession of the French guy.

What else did he say when he was out? He cursed himself. *Don't go to sleep, Cabby; they'll get everything out of you.*

The one without the gun had a sullen, suspicious expression. He paced back and forth, shoulders and arms stiff for a fight, eyes never leaving Tom. The one with the gun had the offhand confidence of being the one with the gun. Both were in their twenties, both were spare built and thin, both had the work-hardened look of factory or farm workers. Who were they? Resisters? The Maquis—French guerrilla fighters? The Brits trusted these collection crews more than the Americans did, maybe because England and France had had little choice but to trust each other. And what choice did he have?

Should he tell them about Jackson? Every instinct said no.

Jackson was a fellow from Maine, a doctor at the American Hospital of Paris. He had a reputation with the British Royal Air Force as a man to trust behind enemy lines. Tom had heard of him more than once from downed airmen given up as MIA. He once witnessed a homecoming at Ringwood, an RAF pilot missing for four months. Once the initial euphoria of his return settled, the guy, Captain Blakeney, had all the men toast Dr. Jackson, "the patron saint of downed airmen."

What if his captors were collaborators? What if they were French Milice? *One peep about Jackson, and Jackson's a marked man.* How much had he said already? The thought sickened him.

Where was Paris? How would he get there? It hurt to even move his head. He'd assess damage later. He needed a plan, and he always favored three-part plans. *Not a word on Jackson. Get to Paris. Don't vomit.*

"Thees Jackson . . . ," the gunless Frenchman asked. "Ees een Paree?"

"Thomas William Jaeger. First lieutenant, United States Army Air Forces. One four oh nine six—"

"This is no interrogation, my friend. We are the good guys." The Frenchman with the gun strolled forward a few paces and sat on his haunches. He pushed his hat up with the tip of the gun. His brown eyes were lively and measuring; his thin face, amused, or rather, ready to be amused. He had the sort of face that invited entertainment of any sort. His English was far better than the other's. "But we do not know if you are a good guy. Tell us why we do not kill you for a spy?"

"Tell me why I should trust you," Tom said. "I hear you guys sell out your neighbors. Lot of Jews gone missing, too."

The man wagged his finger. "The question of trust lies with us alone." He gestured toward his face. "Attend this handsome face. Tell me if you see a German. Then I will get you a mirror, and you will wonder why we have not killed you yet. Hmm?"

"Lots of Americans look like Germans," Tom scorned. "Some *are* German. I'm Dutch. I was born in the Netherlands. We immigrated to the States when I was nine. I'm from Michigan. Jenison."

"You are very tall. Very blond. Very square-headed. Pretty blue eyes, too. I am aroused." The man behind him laughed.

"Yeah? Come to Jenison. You'll be plenty aroused. And you're puny."

"I do not know *puny*."

"Petite." He couldn't keep the sneer out. Payback for *square-headed*.

The Frenchman shrugged. "I do not get enough meat. I would be your size, with meat." The other man laughed again. "Perhaps from a great height I am puny. You have legs like trees. Trust me, I had to fit them into the cart. Listen, Monsieur Jenison. I am, hmm—" he gave a considering little shrug—"sixty percent you are not a spy. But we have been fooled before. Some of my friends have died because we were quick to believe a pretty face."

"Where did you live in Holland?" came a voice from the shadows.

A third man emerged from the corner of the shed, and he looked nothing like the other two. This older gentleman was dressed like a lawyer. He wore a fedora. The collar of his gray overcoat was turned up, and he wore a red scarf. He clasped black-gloved hands in front. He had no wariness about him like the others. He looked as if he were deciding which newspaper to buy.

"Andijk. A small city in the northern province."

"Where was your mother born?"

"Apeldoorn."

"Your father?"

"Andijk. Shouldn't you ask me who won the World Series? Or what's the capital of North Dakota? Not that I remember."

The man reached into a pocket and took out a piece of paper and a pencil. He wrote something and held the paper out to Tom. "Tell me—what is this word?"

Tom took the paper. He angled it to catch light from the door. "Scheveningen. My aunt lived near there, in Rotterdam. They bombed it off the map. She and my uncle died in the attack, with my two cousins."

The man took the paper back. "I am very sorry for your family. *C'est la guerre . . .* to the misfortune of the world." He turned to the one with the gun. "No German can pronounce that word." The gentleman touched his hat, then left.

"We are not the only ones who saw you go down, Monsieur Jenison. But we got to you first. The man who lives in the house you fell on took a beating because he could not tell the Germans where you were. Do you think you can trust us? Hmm? Because thanks to the monsieur, we now trust you."

"I'd trust you more with my gun back," Tom said.

The man grinned. He had a look Tom liked, that of an amiable scoundrel. He knew plenty of his sort; you'd trust him in a fight but not with your sister. The man rose and pulled out the gun, and handed it butt first to Tom. "You can call me Rafael." He looked over his shoulder at the other guy and gave a little whistle between his teeth. "Give him his pack." To Tom, he said, "Regrettably you will not find your cigarettes. I suggest they were lost in the jump."

"Lucky I don't smoke."

———

The man with the red scarf, known in Cabourg as François Rousseau, walked rapidly to work. He exchanged pleasantries with his bronchial secretary, suggested mint tea, and slipped into his office. He took off his coat and hung it on the coat tree. He left the scarf on; it was cold in the office, but he did not light the coal in the brazier. What coal the company allotment allowed, he brought home in newspaper to Marie and the children. Thank God spring was coming soon.

He rubbed his gloved hands together and settled down to the papers on his desk. But he could not settle his mind. He finally pushed aside the latest numbers of Rommel's new cement quotas and let his mind take him where it would.

Twice he reached for the telephone, twice he pulled back. He had to work it out in his head, every detail, before he called his brother, Michel. He tapped his lips with gloved fingers. Hadn't they improvised for nearly four years? If there was one thing they'd learned under enemy occupation, it was resourcefulness.

It was a fool's scheme, he knew, but Michel was feeling so very low. The idea could have enough in it to beguile him from the latest blow. And it was an *interesting* scheme. That face? That height?

He thought it through, beginning to end, and picked up the phone. Sometimes, answers to problems literally dropped from the sky. There was only one thing a cunning Frenchman should do with a Yank who looked exactly like a proud German officer. Make him one.

Acknowledgments

ac•knowl•edge

Verb

1. Accept or admit the existence or truth of.
2. Recognize the fact or importance or quality of.

I hate writing acknowledgments. For one thing, I may forget the name of someone to whom I owe a limb. Mostly, acknowledgments will never fully convey what I mean. When I say thanks to Tyndale, it doesn't express my appreciation for Kathy Olson's finesse or Ron Kaufmann's ability to portray what I feel. When I mention Eric Leonard and Chris Barr, it doesn't adequately express my admiration for what they do or what their own sentinelhood has meant to me. I can't show you the cruddy first draft Alison Hodgson and Don Pearson talked me out of, and I can't show you the cliff the Guild talked me down from.

I hate acknowledgments. They are feeble and inadequate. But they are all I have, so believe me when I say that this book could not have been written without help from the following, to whom I owe a big fat debt of gratitude: Alison Hodgson, Don Pearson, Chris Marsh, Becca Groot, Meredith Smith, Kathy Helmers, the unflappable Fifth Column, my beloved Guild, and the talented tribe at Tyndale, with whom it was an honor to work once more. You guys are quality down to the ground.

I wish especially to acknowledge the gracious and invaluable help from the staff at the Andersonville National Historic Site, and in particular, Eric Leonard and Christopher Barr. They answered questions I couldn't figure out on my own, most of them very odd, and went out of their way to track down answers. Their contribution to this book cannot be measured. That said, if anyone versant in Andersonville history notes errors of any kind or inferences of any nature, those errors and inferences belong solely to me and not to anyone else.

Finally, thanks to my wonderful family for the Research Trip of Summer '12; to my wonderful dad, who took a trip to Andersonville just because I was studying it; and to my wonderful mother, whose belief in me borders on the insane.

PS—If you mess with me, she will find you.

About the Author

Tracy Groot is the author of *The Brother's Keeper* and *Stones of My Accusers*, which both received starred *Booklist* reviews, and *Madman*, a Christy Award–winning novel that also received a starred *Publishers Weekly* review. Her most recent novel, *Flame of Resistance*, is a 2013 Christy Award winner. Luckily, she and her husband own a coffee shop in Holland, Michigan, where a caffeine junkie can find acceptability and safe haven.

For more information about Tracy and her books, visit www.tracygroot.com.

Discussion Questions

1. At the beginning of the book, Violet Stiles is blissfully ignorant of the atrocities taking place just a short distance from her home. Have you ever discovered something unpleasant or inappropriate happening just outside your circle of awareness? How did you learn about it? What was your response? Do you think we have a responsibility to educate ourselves about things going on around us? Why or why not?

2. Emery Jones and Lew Gann, political enemies, find common ground and become unlikely friends. Have you ever found yourself drawn unexpectedly to someone from a different religious, political, or ideological background? How might such a friendship change a person? How does it change Emery?

3. Dance Pickett has a front-row seat to what's happening at Andersonville. How does it affect him? In what ways can you relate to Dance's attitude? What is it that changes his attitude from resignation to determination?

4. Dr. Stiles is able to do more than most to alleviate the suffering of the prisoners. Yet even he runs into obstacles that seem insurmountable. When have you run into obstacles trying to do something good? What was your response? How can we know whether obstacles are God's way of telling us to move in a different direction or whether they are the enemy's attempts to block us from doing the right thing? What is it that helps Dr. Stiles answer this question for himself?

5. Until Reverend Gillette enters Andersonville and experiences the atrocities firsthand, he is hesitant to ask the people of Americus to help these dying prisoners of war. Have you ever felt compelled to lead your family, friends, or other group in an unpopular direction? What was it that made you feel strongly about the issue, whatever it was? Why, in your opinion, might God sometimes ask us to speak out—or lead out—against the crowd?

6. Violet's mother, Polly, is primarily focused on domestic challenges: raising her daughters, feeding her family during a difficult time, and participating in her community. Do you think her focus is appropriate? What value is there in ministering primarily to one's family, despite the larger societal concerns that may be going on? At what point in the story do Polly's concerns grow beyond her home and family, and what prompts that?

7. Dance's scrip is a sacred place for him, a place where he keeps reminders of what is truly important. How do you think the writings in the scrip help him make sense of the world? Do you have a journal, a box, a folder, or something else like this? What kinds of things do you record? If you've never done this, is it something you think you'd like to start?

8. Different characters in the story struggle with the fact that the needs they see at Andersonville are so overwhelming, they can't figure out where to start in making a difference. Discuss how various characters come to terms with this challenge. What are some of the small things they do? What needs do you see around you that seem too big to address? What is one small way you could start to make a difference, even if you think it won't matter? Will you do it this week?

9. The townspeople of Americus believe the prisoners of war in Andersonville deserve no compassion; these prisoners represent the men who killed their sons, fathers, neighbors, and friends. Think of a situation in which you struggled to "love your enemy." How did you deal with it? How would you counsel the citizens of Americus during this time of war?

10. To better appreciate the feelings of Americus toward Andersonville, imagine a prison housing thousands of convicted terrorists only ten miles from your home. Now imagine that you are confronted with the truth that the prisoners are being treated in an inhumane manner and are dying of starvation, lack of sanitation, and communicable diseases for which remedies could easily be provided. Would you defy social stigma—and the law—to help them? Would you feed these enemies? How would you feel about those who wanted to help them? How would your reaction differ if you had personally lost a loved one in the recent wars on terror?

11. A recurring theme in this book is the Bible's teaching that when civil or military authorities are wrong, Christians have a duty to follow their conscience and obey God. History records well-known leaders of civil disobedience, such as Mahatma

Gandhi and Martin Luther King Jr. Do you think such efforts are effective? What are the dangers and drawbacks? What are the potential benefits, both to those disobeying authority and to society?

12. Which character in the novel was your favorite, and why? Which character surprised you the most, good or bad? What do you imagine Posey Stiles would be doing ten years after the story's conclusion?

TYNDALE HOUSE PUBLISHERS IS CRAZY4FICTION!

Fiction that entertains and inspires

Get to know us! Become a member of the Crazy4Fiction community. Whether you read our blog, like us on Facebook, follow us on Twitter, or receive our e-newsletter, you're sure to get the latest news on the best in Christian fiction. You might even win something along the way!

JOIN IN THE FUN TODAY.

 www.crazy4fiction.com

 Crazy4Fiction

 @Crazy4Fiction